Mary Fleming

SOMEONE ELSE

Rupicapra & Co, Berlin

Cover design: Nathaële Vogel, Andrea Eisler
Logo design: Lamp by Julien Deveaux from the thenounproject.com

ISBN: 978-0-9960290-1-8

to David

Toute existence personnelle repose sur un secret.

—Anton Tchékhov, La Dame au petit chien

I
The Arènes de Lutèce

Elizabeth Teller shut the book on her lap and tilted her face towards the midweek morning sun. It was the first warm day of April and as the light filtered bright orange through her closed lids, she slipped into an irresistibly pleasant, almost narcotic, state of semi-consciousness.

"Maman, look," and an insistent tug on the arm pulled her back from the brink of sleep.

"Where did you find that?" A snail's translucent, spineless body stretched from its shell. The antennae probed the empty air.

"In the grass, over there," said Ariane. "I was afraid he'd fall down." Elizabeth squinted and looked towards the sloped lawns of the Arènes de Lutèce.

"Look how he sticks to your wrist. He won't fall."

"I want to bring him home," Ariane persisted.

Elizabeth imagined the snail dead and dried up, an empty shell stuck to the side of a box. "Don't you think he's happier in the grass?"

Ariane frowned.

"He'd be awfully lonely with us," Elizabeth said, wrapping an arm around her daughter's waist.

"Maybe he doesn't have any friends out here either," Ariane said, her nose pinching stubbornly.

"A lot more friends than he'd have at our house," she laughed.

In the pit of the arena Ariane's brother Gabriel was playing football. As Elizabeth watched him run after the ball that had gone too far, she saw someone walk in from the back entrance.

The smile vanished from her face and she froze as solidly as the stone she was sitting on. Unable to move or to think, she watched the man eat a croissant and observe the boys' game. After popping the last bite in his mouth, he crumpled the paper into a ball and looked right up at her. Seeing no stairs that might lead up to where she was sitting, he walked back out of the arena. Elizabeth grabbed the seat with both hands. *He's finally come. He's finally come to get me—*

"What a surprise."

"Oh!" She jumped to her feet as if prodded with a hot poker. He was standing right next to her.

"What are you doing here in these ruins, of all places?"

"Well I live here. Here in Paris, I mean," she laughed nervously. "So the question is what are you doing here, of all places?"

He pulled out a map of the city from the pocket of his shirt. "Being a tourist. I'm staying in a hotel, right there." And he pointed to the back of one of the buildings that gave on to the old Roman arena. "This your daughter?"

Ariane, the snail having now inched its way up her bare arm, was looking from one to the other of them.

"Yes, Ariane, this is Mr Ross." Just saying the name made her dizzy.

"Troy," he said, sticking out his hand.

Ariane removed the snail from her right arm and shook the hand tentatively, as she was used to being kissed by adults, whether she knew them or not.

"What'cha got there?" he said.

Ariane looked at her mother. She couldn't remember the word in English.

"A snail," said Elizabeth, who, with her spinning head, was barely able to remember the word herself.

"A snail," Ariane repeated, now half embarrassed, half dismissive of a question with such an obvious answer.

Gabby arrived panting, his face bright red from exertion.

"I'm thirsty," he said to his mother in French. Elizabeth's hand trembled as she pulled a plastic bottle of water from her bag.

"How long are you here for?" she asked, trying to keep the quaver out of her voice.

"It's my first and probably only trip to Europe," he shrugged. "I've got an open return." He looked at her with those dark brown, broad-set eyes.

"Where do you live now?" she asked, looking down.

"Vermont. I run a tree business. And you? Been living here long?"

"Almost twenty-five years."

"Meaning since just after I last saw you," he said.

"Yes," she said, clearing her throat. "That's right."

"Two kids, I see."

"Actually four," she said. "These two are twins. They have two older brothers. Teenagers."

"Got your hands full," he said with that tight smile she remembered too, the smile that looked as if once upon a time someone had tried to beat it out of him. It was remarkable, how little he had changed. His hair was still honey blond, his skin smooth, almost hairless, with a permanently tanned look to it. And he was still muscular and trim—not a large man, but well-built.

"Yes, I guess I have." Ariane was chasing Gabby with the snail, and he was yelling at her to stop. Then he swatted her hand and the snail went flying with such force that its shell shattered against the stone bench. She began to cry. Elizabeth said: "I'm afraid I have to get these two home for lunch." She paused. "I should give you my phone number."

"That would be great."

"Here you go," she said, struggling to scribble the number legibly on the back of an old receipt. "Give me a call. If you get a chance. Before you leave."

"Will do."

"Let's go," Elizabeth said to Ariane, who was still in tears, and to Gabby, who was brooding and almost as unhappy about the snail as his sister. As she turned and walked away, her legs felt like jelly. She could barely see where she was going.

***

Her hand was still unsteady that evening as she leaned forward towards the bathroom mirror and put on eyeliner. When the phone rang, the eye pencil skidded across her temple. *Him again? A lawyer? The police?* And she ran to answer.

"Hello, Lizzie."

"Molly. Hi." She collapsed into the wall.

"Just thought I'd try and firm up plans for this summer. You'll be arriving on the third, right?"

"Is that the date? I can't remember." Her head was all muddled. "Whatever you told me. Though I should tell you Lucas might have a complication. He's in a competition to design a new exhibition centre in Rouen."

"In where?"

"Roo-on," she said. "It's a city in Normandy. Joan of Arc?"

"What about Joan of Arc?"

"She died in Rouen."

"OK."

"Anyway, Lucas may have to come late."

"Well I just wanted to make sure you were set. Mum's all worried something will go wrong."

"I've got the tickets reserved for whatever you told me the dates were. The information's at the office," Elizabeth said, looking at her watch.

"Do you think it will have changed, since we were there?"

"Nantucket? I don't know. Maybe. Probably. It's been about thirty years," Elizabeth said with a laugh. The few summer holidays the Lyall family had spent on the island ran a-blur in her mind. "I have to confess I haven't really thought about it."

"Well, we'll see soon enough. Everything all right over there?"

"Just great. And you?"

"I've had three football matches—sorry—soccer games—and one lacrosse in the last week. This New Jersey life is killing me. Long live England and boarding school."

"Right. Well. Listen—I've got to run. We're going out."

"Glad I got you then. Love to all."

"You too."

As Elizabeth walked back down the corridor, music blared from Olivier's room, while a suspicious silence emanated from Gabby and Ariane's door, but she didn't stop to investigate. Back in the bathroom, she vigorously rubbed the skidded eyeliner, hoping she hadn't been too abrupt with her sister. Usually she found Molly's suburban juggling act and scant knowledge of history and geography amusing, even endearing; she was in fact looking forward to seeing her larger family in Nantucket that summer.

She gave her thick dark hair one last tug of the hairbrush and looked in the mirror at her middle-aging face, at its rather sharp nose and chin and cheekbones, and the blue eyes that were almost too blue. *What the hell am I going to do?* She turned quickly from the mirror.

It was no longer silent in the twins' room.

"You didn't have to smash it," cried Ariane. "I wanted to keep it as a pet."

"You didn't have to chase me with it," shouted Gabby.

"Whoa, whoa, whoa," Elizabeth said. "That's enough. As I told you, Ariane, snails are meant to live outside, where it's cool and damp. Where there's lots for them to eat. It would have been cruel to keep it here indoors."

"But he killed it," Ariane whined, the tears welling up in her eyes.

"It was an accident," Elizabeth continued calmly. "An accident that would not have happened if you hadn't been taunting your brother."

"See?" said Gabby. "It's all your fault."

"It is not." Ariane began to cry.

Elizabeth sat down on the edge of Gabby's bed and took one child in each arm. "It's both of your faults. And you both need to forget about that snail so you can finish up your homework." They did not look appeased, though they remained silent. "Come on now." When she gave them each a poke, they squirmed but refused to laugh. "It was an unfortunate incident but now it's over and you must put the whole thing behind you. Okay?" They nodded resentfully. "Good night," she said, kissing each on the forehead. She left quietly, afraid the slightest noise would break the fragile truce.

"Olivier," she called through his door. When he didn't answer, she rapped on the wood.

"Yea!" he screamed over the music, then turned it down.

"Make sure the twins are in bed by nine. Good night."

Elizabeth then walked back down the corridor and through the sitting room to the door that connected the apartment to Lucas's office. She looked at the handle and another surge of panic swept through her. *He'll know, he'll know everything, just by looking at me.* Taking a deep breath, she opened the door tentatively. In the twilight, the room gave off an eerie luminescence, as the dying natural light mixed with the artificial glow of the computer screen. Lucas was hunched over his work table, elbows spread wide, face down low over his drawing.

"It's time," Elizabeth said quietly, remaining in the doorway.

Lucas unfurled his long, narrow back and looked up almost peevishly at her, as if he weren't quite sure who was disturbing him and why. Then he smiled, and removed his rimless glasses.

"Is it eight already?" He rubbed his eyes. "I thought it was earlier." He looked at her with his pale-skinned, bony face and his green eyes, which always looked disturbingly small without the glasses. She knew that to his unaided eyes she would appear as a formless blur but her heart was still thumping in her ears.

"It's past eight," she said, not moving from the doorway, hoping her voice didn't betray her. She tried to sound teasing:

"So unless you want to get there late, like everyone else."

"You know very well I don't mind being the first to arrive. Especially since we have to leave by midnight..." Lucas trailed off as he put his glasses back on and swivelled his chair towards the computer. "I've really got a lot of work."

"You've always got a lot of work," she mocked gently. "And we always have to leave by midnight."

"Just because none of our friends ever gets to a dinner party a minute before nine, and usually considerably later, doesn't mean we have to follow their lead." He turned back towards her as the computer screen went black. "I feel no need to participate in what amounts to a childish competition to arrive last. To show that as a working person with a stressful, busy life, the later my arrival, the busier and more important I must be."

"I know, I know," she smiled at his mild but determined independent streak. "You feel no need to prove anything to anyone. So we'll continue to arrive at eight-forty-five and leave by midnight, whether or not the party is starting up or winding down. Right?"

"Right," he said, standing up. "But first come here and look at my model for the Rouen project." He sounded as excited as a child with a new toy. "What do you think? My assistant and I just finished it today."

Elizabeth nodded. "It looks fantastic," she said looking down at the clean white lines, everything perfectly executed in miniature, from the pedestrians to the trees to the Seine running by. "Really. I'd say it's your strongest statement yet."

"I hope so." He put his arm over her shoulders. "I really do feel I'm launching in a new direction here. I've made the roof soar up at an angle, to give the feeling of the building opening up, reaching out to the river..." *Shouldn't I just collapse right here and now and tell him what I should have told him years ago? But I can't I can't I'm too afraid of his reaction. He thinks I am good but I'm not I'm not at all what he thinks I am not what I am—*

"Elizabeth?"

"Sorry. Yes."

"My motorcycle's still at the shop. Will you get the car? I must say good-night to the children. Is Tristan up in his room?"

"He is." In her pre-occupied state, she had forgotten to climb the back stairs to the *chambre de bonne* where their oldest child was living this year. "Say good night for me."

She went out the front door and descended the spiral staircase of their building. *Cinderella running down the palace steps. It's almost midnight. I will soon be found out, fingered as the fraud that I am and Lucas—if he really does find out, what will he say? What will he do?*

She hurried the last flight and once outside, took a deep breath of the early spring air and put her hands to her head, forcing her thoughts to the evening ahead. The dinner party. With their friends. She would try to engineer a seat next to their host, the book critic Thomas de Croisy, try and convince Thomas to review the book she was currently promoting. The book she was having an unusually difficult time getting the press to nibble at.

Elizabeth opened the door of their Renault Grand Espace. Because parking, especially for their extra-large van, was so impossible, they usually took Lucas's motorcycle in the evening. Though she always wished he'd drive a bit faster, she enjoyed sitting behind him, while he negotiated the Paris traffic. But tonight she was thankful the bike was in the shop—she couldn't even bear his arm over her shoulder, much less the idea of having to lean into his back. Because if they were body to body, wouldn't he instinctively know everything?

She shuddered at the thought but still pulled out of the parking place with a tug of regret. Having circled many times to find it, she knew that later she would have to go round and round again before finding another spot.

***

With an audible grunt of almost physical pain, Elizabeth closed her eyes and put her hands over her face. Thomas had called the book "*sympa*" and just the thought of it made her insides go weak. No more damning a word could fall from a French intellectual's lips. *Sympa*, derisively short for *sympathique*, was what you called the friend, just before launching into a delicate attack of his insurmountable limitations. *Sympa* was a dinner party where the food was as insipid as the company. *Sympa* meant that the book was unquestioningly, inevitably, doomed.

Elizabeth was sitting at her desk in their bedroom the following Saturday. She had been doing her admin, and when she picked up the electricity bill to put it in the pile of bills that Lucas paid, there was the book that Thomas had dismissed. She stood up and walked to the window. It had been raining all morning and for several minutes she just watched the rain attack the panes.

Turning abruptly, Elizabeth returned to the desk, snatched up the book and shoved it into a desk drawer *just as I did with that plastic lighter, I buried it deep in my drawer, hoping that out of sight would mean out of mind. Hoping I could bury the whole night and everything I'd done and not done with it.*

This thought sent her marching purposefully to the kitchen, where she began making lunch. If she could just keep her hands busy, her mind focused on the present, on work, on her family's needs. Because these last few days, since her encounter in the Arènes de Lutèce to be precise, idle moments had quickly become crowded with thoughts and memories she did not want to be there. She began vigorously sawing off pieces of baguette. *The lighter was purple. Purple plastic. It had that boy's fraternity insignia stamped on it. If only I hadn't taken that lighter. Then no matter how strong the smell how nauseous it was making me feel I couldn't have done anything about it. But I did take the lighter and whoosh—*

She gasped out loud, took a step back, knife still in hand.

Looking down at the bread, she saw that she'd cut it all up, even what she'd intended to save for the children's supper. Turning quickly out of the kitchen, she called her family to lunch as if crying for help.

And indeed, the family helped. During lunch Lucas related the latest episode in the ongoing saga of his encounters with Monsieur et Madame Dujoyau, *arrivistes* clients whose pretensions and demands seemed to know no bounds. The stories always got them laughing to the point of tears and today the collective amusement worked on her like soothing ointment. The rain had now let up and as she got ready to take the twins to the Arènes de Lutèce, Lucas offered to go with her, on the way to his errands. Elizabeth welcomed this offer until—*What if he's there again? Stop it. It's been three days and he hasn't phoned. Maybe he's already gone home. Maybe it was just a coincidence. I must try and forget about him. About then.*

And as they walked along the street, skipping from subject to subject—some friends who were buying an apartment beyond their means, a politician they knew who was under indictment for money laundering—Elizabeth's worrying receded. Once they got to the arena, the twins, complaining that it was too wet and none of their friends were there, hung about their parents like raindrops.

"Tell me how your work's going," Lucas said, crossing his arms and bending his narrow, oval head towards her. "I've been so wrapped up in this Rouen business I haven't been very attentive. I'm sorry."

"That's okay," Elizabeth said, as Ariane grabbed her jacket from behind, used her body as a shield against Gabby, who was trying to poke her. "But it is strange around the office these days. With the new management, there are so many subtle changes in the way things are done, in the general atmosphere."

"Like what?" asked Lucas, who had never worked in an office with lots of people and did not quite get the politics. Gabby was now lunging out from behind him to get at his sister.

"I don't know—it's hard to describe—would you children stop it." Ariane and Gabby stopped baiting one another but maintained their protective positions behind their parents. Elizabeth continued: "I guess you'd say that there's a new air of insecurity, suspicion, around the place. Everyone's a bit on edge."

"Here comes that man again, Maman," Ariane half whispered from behind, tugging at Elizabeth's jacket.

"What man?" asked Lucas.

"Hello," Troy said as he walked up beside them and stuck out his hand to Lucas. "Troy Ross."

"Lucas Teller. Hello." Lucas had spent a couple summers in England as a boy and then had studied at Columbia on a Fulbright scholarship for a year. He spoke English well. He raised his eyebrows at Elizabeth.

"I guess I forgot to tell you," she said, clearing her throat. "I ran into Troy here the other day. We were at college together."

"My hotel's right there," Troy pointed again at the buildings backing on to the arena. "I must come to this ruin at least once a day. The place just amazes me."

"Except for the obelisk at the place de la Concorde which Napoléon brought back from Egypt," Lucas said, "this Roman arena is the oldest monument in Paris."

"Funny how it sort of fits right in here today," said Troy. "That's what brings me back—the surprise of it."

"It was buried for a long time," said Lucas.

"Under what?" asked Troy, with a doubting, almost derisive laugh that Elizabeth remembered could sometimes sound infectious, sometimes menacing.

"Once the Romans left *Lutèce*, the arena was abandoned. Later many of the big stone seats were taken out to reinforce the barricade around the Ile-de-la-Cité, on the Seine, against the *Barbares*—" he paused and looked at Elizabeth. "How do you say that in English?" he asked her in French.

"Barbarians," she said, shifting uncomfortably, wondering how long this tortuous encounter might last and where it might lead.

"Barbarians, of course," he shook his head at stumbling over such a simple translation. "Eventually the place got completely buried and it wasn't discovered again until the mid-nineteenth century, when they started digging the way for the rue Monge, where you are staying."

The three of them looked around at the Roman remains in silence. Elizabeth rubbed her arms; the blood seemed to have stopped circulating entirely. Her ability to speak felt equally blocked. Lucas finally said: "The amphitheatre was unusual because the Romans used it for many forms of entertainment— theatre but also human and animal combat."

"Interesting," said Troy.

More silence.

"How long are you staying?" Lucas finally asked.

"Undetermined."

More silence. Lucas sent a perplexed look at Elizabeth, who looked back at him blankly. He blurted out: "Maybe you could come to supper some time."

"That's really nice of you," said Troy, looking straight and stonily at Elizabeth.

"Sometime next week would be all right, wouldn't it, Elizabeth?" Lucas looked again at his mute wife.

"Um. Yes," Elizabeth finally managed. Now they were both looking at her, and she felt as if their eyes were pushing her into a corner. "Let's see. How about Wednesday?"

"I'm not exactly booked up," Troy said, with his tight smile. This time Elizabeth caught a glimpse of his teeth and she remembered that they were crooked, that the restrained smile was also an attempt to hide them.

Lucas turned to Elizabeth and said in French: "I need to pick up that book I ordered." Then he added in English to Troy: "See you on Wednesday. Remind me to show you some of my books on historic monuments in Paris."

"Nice guy," Troy said as he watched Lucas walk away.

"I hope he didn't bore you," she said too quickly. "He's an architect and once he starts talking architecture…" she trailed off, not somehow wanting to complete the thought. The look on Troy's face was too eager.

"I have to say," he said, "so far, the Parisians don't seem as unfriendly as I'd expected. As you hear about."

"You've been lucky," said Elizabeth with an uncomfortable hiccough of a laugh. "They can be pretty awful."

"Like anywhere," he shrugged.

"Right." Again they looked out at the wet arena; Elizabeth had to make a conscious effort to swallow. "Well, I need to get back too."

"What about your address? For the dinner?"

"Ah yes. Of course," she said and, like the time before, fumbled in her bag with trembling hands. This time she produced a visiting card.

"Look at that," said Troy, running his finger over the embossed letters.

"It's nothing special. Everyone has them over here," she said dismissively, though she was now looking at the little white card in his hands with regret, as if it were a cherished possession that in a moment of excess generosity, she had given away and that she now wanted back. "So. We'll see you on Wednesday? At about eight?"

"Okay. See you then." And he held up the card as if indeed it were something he'd won.

Elizabeth took one twin in each hand to help steady her step and she walked out of the arena. *How could I have been so stupid as to imagine for even one second the first meeting was a coincidence? Because I've blocked it all out, pushed it deep down, slammed on the lid, not thought about him, about what happened, and now here we go.*

Back at the apartment, Gabby and Ariane were still baiting each other. Elizabeth said: "Stop it or I'll…"

"You'll what?" asked her sassy daughter.

"I'll put you to bed right after supper."

"You said you were going out tonight," Ariane continued. "You said we could watch a video."

Elizabeth, who could not resist smiling at her daughter's persistence, crossed her arms and tried to sound stern: "Well, I can change my mind, can't I? Especially given the state of your bedroom. If it's not tidied up in fifteen minutes, I will take the video cable and the television plug with me and you won't be able to watch a thing. How does that sound?" The two scampered off with cinematic screams of fear to the room that they'd ransacked during the rainy morning.

She went into the kitchen and began emptying the dishwasher. Their Siamese cat purred and rubbed up against her legs, almost making her trip. "Stop it, Suey," she said irritably. "It's not time to eat yet." The cat sprang up on the counter. *You were lithe as a cat, climbing flagpoles and buildings and that's how the trouble started. That's why the dean of students was after you, he as much as told me so that day in his office that day I lied that day I did not stand up for you. Did not stand by you.*

Later, sitting on her *chaise longue*, she had an inspiration: invite other people to the dinner with Troy. That would be the best way to preclude any awkward turns in the conversation.

This worry settled, she attempted to redirect her attention to the book that she needed to finish by the end of the weekend. But thinking of books, reading, work, made *sympa* ring again in her ears. Though this new book, British rather than American, was not *sympa,* Elizabeth still couldn't be sure it would appeal to the French market. The main character was overweight and repulsed by all things sensual. At first she thought being so un-French would make it work; now she wasn't sure and the nagging worry that she might lose her touch loomed.

Elizabeth had always viewed landing this job as a stroke of undeserved luck. Lucas' Uncle Antoine, for months without a reader, had been desperate and had hired her despite an unremarkable bachelor's degree in literature from a small

American liberal arts college that no one in France had ever heard of and despite a complete lack of experience (her job at the time being temporary archivist at a newspaper, in itself a promotion from her former post of replacement secretary). The job was only supposed to last the time of a pregnancy and a maternity leave but had become permanent when she'd proved to have such a good nose for fiction. The worry, however, that her luck might run out had continued to lurk in the back of her mind.

And as she'd indicated to Lucas earlier, things had changed at work. A large media group had recently bought the publishing house and it was applying a previously unknown financial pressure. They were all wriggling under it. For the last year there had also been Lucille. Lucille Darmon, in her late twenties, had irreproachable bi-cultural credentials. Her father was American and her mother French. She'd grown up in Paris and attended a bilingual school, before going to an Ivy League university, where she had been a star on the varsity squash team. Her self-confidence was boundless, as was her ambition. Or such was Elizabeth's view. She believed that Lucille worked secretively and sidled up shamelessly to editors with the express purpose of undermining her. Just last week, at the editorial meeting, Lucille had convinced the group that a novel she'd loved was "*complètement ringard*"—completely tedious and old-hat—and it was said in such a way as to imply that the description fitted Elizabeth, at age forty-five, perfectly too.

***

That evening she and Lucas went to the cinema with his sister Alix and her husband Roland. Alix was an art critic and Roland a high-ranking civil servant who, in his spare time, published a novel a year. They met at a cinema near Saint Michel that was running a Bergman festival. They had already seen *Wild Strawberries* and *Scenes from a Marriage* together; this evening

Persona was showing.

"That was weird," Alix said afterwards, as they sat down at a cramped table in a Russian restaurant that Roland knew near the cinema.

"Persona," he said, leaning back in his chair and folding his hands. "Mask in Latin. That's what it was, at first. A mask made of clay or bark that actors wore to define their role, their part in the play."

"I think the two actresses were Bergman's old and new lovers," said Lucas, ignoring, as he often did, his brother-in-law's irrepressible flow of unsolicited trivia.

"Did you relate to the one called Elizabeth, Elizabeth?" asked Roland with a smile on his round face.

She smiled but said nothing. Her mouth was dry and her limbs, minus the throbbing left hand that she kept under the table, felt limp. The film had completely undone her.

"Better to be the new, rather than the old lover of the director, I suppose," said Alix.

"Better the actress than the nurse," Roland said.

"What was that horrible newsreel on television near the beginning, when the actress was in hospital?" asked Alix, with a shudder. "Where the man lit himself on fire right in the middle of the street."

Elizabeth downed the shot of vodka that had been placed before her.

"It was in Vietnam, at the beginning of the war," said Lucas. "Self-immolation was an act of protest by certain Buddhist monks. Isn't that right, Elizabeth?"

"I'm not sure," she hedged. "I was just a girl then too."

"But you're our resident American," said Roland.

"Only half."

"Is it your father or your mother who's American?" asked Alix. "I can never remember."

"My mother. My father's English." Then, to distance herself even further from the American who knew all about self-immolating monks, she added: "I grew up mostly in London."

"An international childhood," said Roland, who liked to categorize, summarize, provide the concluding remark.

"The way I see it," said Lucas, closing his menu, "Elizabeth is our children's saving grace. I mean, her broader upbringing and experience provide some hope that our children won't turn out to be as unbearably provincial as the rest of us Parisians."

"Speak for yourself, dear brother," said Alix.

The waiter, dressed in a peasant costume that was too small, came and took their order; Elizabeth then excused herself.

She sat down on the loo and looked at the red ring on her left hand. *I bit my own hand. It was all I could do to stop from screaming. A man on fire right before my very eyes but that one the monk he just sat serenely you jumped and rolled and ripped off your t-shirt and put out the fire.* She stood up and went to the sink, ran her hand under cold water. *Leave it to Alix to bring up the fire, to pick that one moment in the film for the dinner conversation.* She dried her hands and looked in the mirror—but only for a moment—she could not bear the sight of her own bloodless face.

"They told us not to make a fuss," Lucas was saying when she came back to the table. As he spoke, his eyes were fixed on the blini that he was layering, first with a piece of smoked salmon, then some *crème fraîche* and a caper, constructing it with architectural care.

"Can one just ignore a fiftieth wedding anniversary?" asked Roland, folding his doughy hands. He somehow managed to look plump without actually being so. "Especially when it's one's parents."

"No, one can't ignore it," said Alix, returning the gaze of a couple at the other side of the restaurant. She and Lucas looked remarkably alike and the double vision of their powerful, intelligent faces, as well as their height, often made heads turn. They looked much more like twins than Gabby and Ariane. "Besides they don't really mean it. At least Maman doesn't." And she turned to Roland's plate and stabbed one of his herrings with her fork. "Wouldn't you agree, Elizabeth?"

"Don't ask me," she answered, feeling better now that the conversation had changed direction. "My parents ended their union after twenty years."

"It seems to me that there are three ways of doing it," said Roland, who could not refrain from employing the French civil servant's three points, even occasionally in his novels. "We could have a small gathering of immediate family. Or we could include the larger family. Or we could have an even larger party and invite all their friends and family."

"That would make an enormous event," Alix said.

"You might as well invite the entire Who's Who," said Elizabeth.

"We could restrict it," said Lucas, wiping his hands on the white napkin, looking at his sister.

"We could," Alix answered with a nod.

Not long after Elizabeth had met Lucas, she had asked him: "Why do you consider yourself Jewish, when you're half Gentile?"

"Why do you consider people with the lightest shading of colour to their skin black? It's always the difference that counts. That is counted."

She had immediately understood what he meant because at school in England she had been labelled an American. But by the time she went to college in America, she had acquired an English accent and manner that she was never quite able to shed or conceal. She knew that hovering sense of not completely belonging. Of always sitting on an edge that might, at any moment, give way.

The Teller sphere was large and composed of many intersecting circles. There were Gentiles even within the smaller family—Isabelle, Lucas and Alix's mother, was a Protestant like herself, and Roland was Catholic—but there was a core group of secular Jews. The bond, a sort of unspoken brotherhood, was formed by a shared history and was particularly strong in their father Claude's generation, based as it was on the first-hand knowledge of just how quickly things could indeed fall apart.

That was what Lucas meant by restricting the party.

Just as they were finishing the main course, a pair of musicians came in, one playing a balalaika and the other singing. They went from table to table with their Russian songs but played so loudly that conversation without shouting was impossible.

"Time to go," said Lucas.

"No dessert for me," said Alix, not quite glaring at the players.

Lucas asked for the bill but before it came, the musicians, sensing imminent departure and missed tips, honed in on their table and launched into a glass-throwing, plate-smashing number. The singer began to dance. Elizabeth tried to look pleased. Roland sighed loudly and muttered conspicuously. Lucas and Alix just sat there like two blocks of ice, but when they were finished, Lucas fished out a couple of coins, handed them over with a forced smile and bow of his head.

"So we'll be in touch about the party," he said on the street as they were about to part. "We'll draw up a list."

"I'll phone you beginning of next week," said Alix, kissing her brother good-bye.

"How shall we get home?" Lucas asked Elizabeth after the two couples had parted. "Shall we take the metro or do we tempt fate and walk?" The streets were slick and glistening with the umpteenth shower of the day.

"I could use a walk," Elizabeth said. "After all that sitting. All that noise and smoke." And they set out up the hill.

"How could Roland have taken us to that place?" he said shaking his head.

"Maybe the musicians had a night off when he was there before."

"But the waiters in those silly outfits, the food that tasted as if it had been prepared yesterday and pulled straight from the refrigerator. Really." Roland, who was the younger brother of an old friend of his, was on some level still a pesky intruder in Lucas' games. And Lucas could be very exacting.

"Come on," she said, looping her arm through his. "I thought Roland was very helpful this evening, providing us with definitions of words we already know and a three-point summary of our options for the party."

Lucas rolled his eyes and Elizabeth laughed: "But you must have a bit of sympathy as far as the restaurant is concerned. There isn't much choice on that street."

"I guess that's right." He looked up at the drizzle that was beginning to fall again; his glasses were already spotted with rain. "So much for tempting fate." He sighed, pulling his head into his shoulders. "By the way, I've been meaning to ask you. Who was that guy we met today at the Arènes de Lutèce?"

"Someone I knew in college." She slipped her arm out of Lucas' and pulled her collar up around her neck as the drizzle came down harder. The dinner conversation, a bit of vodka and some wine, had helped push Troy and even the film back into the shadows.

"An acquaintance or a friend?"

"I guess you could say we were friends. We shared a flat the last year with two other people."

"Quite a coincidence," Lucas said. Then after a minute. "Amazing face. Almost beautiful."

"Yes," replied Elizabeth slowly.

"An unusual person, or so he seemed."

It was now raining hard but as they were already more than half way up the hill and there wasn't a taxi in sight, they trudged on in silence, Elizabeth thinking how, in general, the company of other people, their different concerns and their distracting conversation, were vital tools in assembling the apparatus of forgetfulness.

"Are you all right?" Lucas asked as they walked into their building.

"Well, I'm soaked."

"No—I mean you seem a bit preoccupied. And you're very pale."

"I'm fine," she said following Lucas up the spiral staircase.

Later, as they got into bed, Lucas asked: "What did you think of that film? You didn't really say at supper."

"I don't know," she half mumbled, fussing with the pillow. Lucas waited—in general Elizabeth had an opinion on everything. "Strange."

"It certainly was that. Disturbing, in fact."

"Yes," she answered vaguely.

"So a strange film, followed by a loud meal and a wet walk," Lucas said, reconstructing the evening. "I'm too tired to read." He took off his glasses and folded them carefully on his night table. "Good night," he said, squeezing her shoulder.

"Good night," she said, opening her book to where she'd left off that afternoon. But she didn't see the words on the page. She saw snatches from the film: the two women, the actress and the nurse, moving about one another, one mute and inscrutable, the other bubbling over with confessional chatter, two opposing parts of one persona. She saw the mute, unhinged actress standing blank and alone in her stark hospital room, as she watched the monk on the television screen, sitting yoga-style in the middle of the street, on fire. Her heart was pounding so loudly in her ears, she looked over at Lucas to see if the noise weren't waking him up but he lay still, with his back to her and the white skin of the growing bald spot on the crown of his head glaring up at her.

Elizabeth looked down at her hand again. After the vodka and some wine, it had stopped throbbing, but it was still very red; she could still see the teeth marks. She closed the book and turned off the light but for a long time she lay on her back, eyes wide open, body stiff as a log, unable to push from her mind's eye those two women and the sight of a man on fire.

***

Weekday mornings, Elizabeth was on automatic pilot. So the following Monday, she was up at seven, emptying the dishwasher, putting out the breakfast things. The back door opened and Tristan stumbled through, still half asleep, hair tousled, towel draped low over his long, thin waist.

"Morning," Elizabeth said softly.

"Morning," he croaked, shuffling towards the bathroom.

She headed down the corridor, first into their bedroom, where she gave Lucas's shoulder a gentle shake. "Already?" he said, stretching, then putting his watch-face right up to his short-sighted eyes.

"Remember?" she said. "You wanted to get up early." And she kissed his forehead before moving on to Olivier's door. She knocked and listened—she was always wary of surprising adolescent boys. She knocked again and a muffled "What?" came back. She opened the door a crack. "Time to get up."

"Oh, no-o-o," moaned back at her.

She walked into the twins' room and shook each one of them gently, then returned to the kitchen where she buttered their toasted baguette. As she dug the knife deep into the jar of Nutella, she was once again reminded that she should be putting a stop to their chocolate-hazelnut spread addiction and start giving them jam, at least on one side. Well, she thought, not today. And as she did every day, she licked the Nutella off the knife before putting it in the washing-up machine.

After breakfast she couldn't find one of Gabby's shoes; Ariane insisted on having her hair plaited even though it wasn't quite long enough. They arrived at school just as the bell was ringing and the door was closing. Two other mothers greeted Elizabeth.

"We were talking about the new *directrice,* that Madame Forges, who slams the door in your face if you're a minute late," said Aurélie, lighting up a cigarette. She dressed in tight, flared jeans and high-top Converse, just like her skinny seven-year old daughter, only a size or two bigger.

"She'd be happy to keep us out, always and forever," said Martine, lighting up her own cigarette.

"With that *Vigipirate* anti-terrorism plan she might just get away with it," said Aurélie.

"I'm a little worried about our school fete at the end of the year," said Martine, looking at Elizabeth. Both were parent delegates. "I hope she doesn't try to cancel it."

"Do you think she would?" asked Aurélie.

"I don't know," said Martine, exhaling smoke.

"The *fête de l'école?*" said Elizabeth with a laugh. "Come on. It's is an immutable institution. She'd never get away with it. We should just go ahead and plan it."

"Shall we discuss it over a coffee?" asked Aurélie. Both she and Martine had stopped working when their children were born and they spent their days in cafés, museums and cinemas, via yoga, Pilates and dance classes.

"I'd love to, but…" Elizabeth looked at her watch: "I'm afraid I have to get going to the office," she said. "We'll e-mail."

And off she went, buoyed by the very need to hurry along. By the firm purpose of her existence, which allowed no time for idle morning chatter in a café. Her thoughts moved happily and gratefully to the busy week ahead: later that morning there was an editorial meeting; in the afternoon she needed to line up a translator. Tomorrow, lunch with a visiting editor from New York. Then Wednesday—she stopped dead in her tracks—as if someone had just stuck a gun in her gut and demanded all her money. That was the day Lucas had invited Troy to supper. *What are you doing here? Have you come to blow my life to smithereens? Are you planning to stand up in the middle of supper and tell Lucas how once we got back to the apartment you sat in that chair in the kitchen, under that pitiless neon light, sweating and swooning, half your hair burned away, and finally I convinced you to go to the emergency room, but that once we got there, I left you, abandoned you in every way?* She began walking again, picking up her pace and forcing her thoughts back into the less incendiary realm of the present.

Arriving at work, Elizabeth said hello to various colleagues and assistants and secretaries as she wound her way down the long, narrow corridor to her office. It was a small room, right at the back. Lined with bookshelves, it only had space for a large desk and a couple of chairs. Its one small window, set in the thick wall of the old building, looked out onto a jumble of grey Paris roofs, onto the copulating pigeons and the passing clouds. Small though it was, Elizabeth's office was her haven. It was the place where, on a Monday morning, she could put the crowded, chaotic weekend behind her and begin focusing on one thing, work.

Collapsing in her bouncy office chair, she reached to turn on the computer and caught sight of her hand. The red ring had turned into a purple bruise. At supper last night, Lucas had asked her about it. Having anticipated the question, she had prepared an answer—that while walking down the street, she had not noticed a metal post and had swung her hand right into it. "Ouch," Lucas had grimaced.

She leaned her head back on the chair, closed her eyes. *Two days later I was called in to the dean of students' office. He sat behind his desk and he had dark hair sprouting from his ears and his nose and his knuckles. He said, a serious crime has been committed, Miss Lyall. This kind of publicity we can do without...*

"Elizabeth."

"Yes!" She opened her eyes, jolted forward in her seat.

"Sorry to interrupt your reverie," said Gérard, her boss, from the doorway. "Could I speak to you? When you have a minute. No rush." It was unusually early for him; he almost always had a breakfast rendezvous of a professional or a personal nature and rarely arrived before ten.

Five minutes later, Gérard beckoned her in, while he talked on the phone. Leaning forward, receiver tucked under his chin, he reached across the many uneven stacks of paper on his desk and without the slightest hesitation snatched the very document he desired. Leaning back and swirling slowly in the black leather swivel chair, he ran a hand through his longish, carefully dishevelled hair. His voice was as smooth as his pink cotton shirt, still without a wrinkle at this time of day. Elizabeth looked at the family photo, prominently displayed on the shelf behind him. It showed his wife and four children on a sailboat. They were all tanned, smiling and windswept. It reminded Elizabeth that she had no idea who Gérard's mistress was these days, that once upon a time she would have been thoroughly *au courant*.

"*Ciao*." He put the phone down. "So how are you getting on, Elizabeth? Managing to keep home and hearth under wraps with all the work we pile on you?"

"I think so, yes," she said hesitantly. Being a fast reader, she didn't think her workload was unreasonably heavy and wondered who, exactly, he meant by "we". It suddenly occurred to her that Lucille might be his current love interest. Gérard made the moves on all the young, attractive flesh in the office, herself once upon a time included.

"I haven't seen many reviews on your last book. I thought maybe you hadn't had time to whet the critic's appetites."

"I'm working on it." *Sympa* rang in her ears and she reddened slightly. "As you say, it's just a question of time. Everyone here agreed it was a great book." That wasn't quite true: everyone but Lucille, who had systematically disagreed with every single one of her choices for the last year.

Gérard crossed his arms and leaned back again in his chair, silent and reflective. "We're getting a lot of pressure," he finally said. "From the new management. Sales so far this year haven't met expectations and they're grumbling. So I'm just checking." He pushed forward and stood up. "Let's have lunch sometime— it's been too long."

On the way back to her office, Elizabeth noticed that the door to Lucille's office was, unusually, shut.

There was nothing odd, she said to herself as she tentatively settled back into her desk chair, about Gérard wanting to speak to her. He often did. Or he used to anyway. Before the take-over, when they were all above such crude concerns as the bottom line. Before Lucille's arrival.

Of course, she reasoned, Gérard hadn't really said anything. But there was his tone, there was the fact that she was out of the loop on his romantic life. There was Lucille's closed door.

There was a change in atmosphere that had begun to make her feel that things were going on behind her back. That her star was falling.

***

Like many French mothers, Elizabeth stayed home on Wednesdays because the younger children did not have school. In the morning she went to the market on the place Monge, tried to catch up on her reading and took the twins to the Arènes de Lutèce. In the afternoon she took them to their sports and music activities and did more reading.

When they arrived at the arena this Wednesday morning, Ariane asked: "Is that man coming again to talk to you?"

"I don't think so, but he's coming to supper tonight."

"Do we have to eat with you?" asked Ariane.

"No. It will be too late."

"Good," she pronounced before skipping off to play with a little girl from her class.

Elizabeth exhaled loudly to herself. Her effort to pad out the evening with other people had failed. Any French friends, she knew, would not be able to resist slipping back into French and subjects only of interest to *Parisiens*. Their only two Anglo-American friends, Trevor and Béa, were busy. She had then considered using her children as buffers but she hadn't asked Troy until eight and in any case Lucas had a late meeting. So it was just going to be the three of them.

That afternoon Elizabeth got the housekeeper Manuela to

take the twins to their judo class while she prepared a lamb curry and baked a lemon tart. While chopping onions for the stew, she cut her finger on the knife she'd just sharpened. While making the tart she dropped an egg and it splattered all over the place. She tried to sponge it up but kept finding drips of yolk and albumen on the floor and on cabinet doors. *That's what I've been doing all these years, trying to wipe away the bad by being good. By being the perfect working-wife-mother. But nothing I can do now will wipe out what I did then, it's as simple as that. I am as rotten as a rotten egg and on top of it I'm married to a saint. Where do saints stand on the subject of forgiveness?*

At eight sharp the doorbell rang. Elizabeth was testing Gabby on the poem he had to learn for school the next day. She rolled her eyes and said: "Only an American would arrive on time like that."

"You're American," said Ariane from her desk.

"Not that part of me," she said and she got up to go answer the door, trying to steel herself for the ordeal ahead.

He was standing on the stoop in the dark, hands behind his back.

"You should have turned on the lights," Elizabeth said, swinging around the door-jamb to point at the illuminated button in the corner of the stairwell. She came very close to him and her skin tingled—his physical presence was that strong. She pulled back inside. "In Europe, you see, they have stairwell lighting on timers. To save electricity."

"Live and learn," he said, following her into the living room. "This place is quite something."

"I am married to an architect." The old wood floor and the ornate mouldings on the wall and ceiling, mixed with the clean lines of modern lighting, bookshelves and furniture often elicited comments, even from their more world-weary friends. "So. What can I get you to drink?" she had decided to adopt a breezy tone for the evening.

"I'd love a beer."

"Ah," she said, already feeling less breezy. "I'm afraid that's the one thing we don't have. But I can offer you a whisky. Or wine, red or white."

"You don't drink beer anymore?" he asked wryly, almost scornfully.

"No," she said. "But I'm sorry. I should have remembered."

"Yea, well. It *was* a long time ago."

"Yes," she said.

"I'll have some red wine," he shrugged, now looking around the room. "I am in France after all.

While opening the bottle in the kitchen, she peeked at him through an oblique angle in the doorway. He stood up and walked over to the bookshelf to scan its contents. Wearing black jeans and a slightly rumpled long-sleeved cotton shirt with the sleeves rolled up to the elbows, he shifted his weight from one foot to the other while examining the spines of the books. It was quite uncanny, she thought, how he had maintained the woodsy physical beauty of his youth, his agility and grace. He was every bit as attractive—magnetic, really—as he had been all those years ago.

She popped the wine cork; he turned away from the shelf.

"So what have you been visiting here in Paris besides *les Arènes de Lutèce*," Elizabeth asked as she set the glasses down and poured the wine.

"Listen to that French—*Arènes de Lutèce*," Troy said, again in that lightly mocking tone. He had imitated the accent almost perfectly and she remembered how he could imitate anyone, how it had made them laugh.

"I have lived here for twenty-five years," she said.

"Seems like you've made a real good life for yourself in this city."

"Yes, I've been…" she trailed off, now reminded how James Dean-ish she had found him at first, with his real-goods and close-fitting t-shirts and his cocky grin.

"Lucky?" he finished for her.

She nodded and cleared her throat. There was something irresistible about that blond hair and dark skin that needed no sun to look tanned, those muscular, hairless arms and that broad nose and face, those dark brown irises in the large corneas, like two black holes, sucking in everything that crossed their path.

Troy picked up a glass paperweight they'd bought in Venice a few years ago and turned it around in his hand, before tossing it slightly and catching it. Still balancing it in the palm of his hand, as if testing its weight, he asked: "Do you ever get any news from the old gang?"

Elizabeth looked down and shook her head, felt her face reddening.

"I've looked them up, over the years," he continued, putting the paperweight back on the table. "Sally's a teacher in a suburb of Washington and John works for an insurance company in Hartford. Exactly what I would have expected of them." He paused, sipped his wine. "You remember all those nights we played that card game, hearts?" She nodded. "How easy it was to stick them with the queen of spades and most of the hearts?" She nodded again. He took another sip of wine. "I guess you were destined for greater deeds in more exotic lands than the suburbs of America." He looked so intently at her that she twitched slightly. "You sure moved far away."

"I came back to where I came from," she said, blinking at the awkward half-truth of her phrase. "As did you, it sounds like."

"I guess that's right," he nodded. "I'm still living in the woods."

"How long have you had the tree business?"

"I got hired about twenty years ago as an employee. Since the owner's son was afraid of heights, he passed on the business to me. But it's just my front operation."

"That sounds ominous," Elizabeth said, disliking the false notes of good cheer in her voice,.

"I don't mean it to," he said seriously. "I just mean that I still consider sculpting my real work."

"I'm pleased to hear that," she answered quietly.

Troy cocked his head: "I'd say that English accent of yours is stronger than it used to be. Your manner too."

"I guess it's living back over here, this side of the Atlantic," she said, realizing that she was sitting on her hands and they were going numb. She pulled them out from under her legs and folded them on her lap, careful to cover the bite-mark, now a purple ring, going green around the edges.

"Anyway, I almost forgot. I brought you this." And he gently pulled a figure out of his pocket. The sculpture, about the size of his hand, was in a nut-brown wood. It was a monolithic human figure, part totem-pole, part African mask. The facial features, etched in finely, formed a melancholic expression close to a grimace. Beneath the seductive smoothness of the surface, it was disturbing and sad.

"How lovely. Really. Thank you." She set it down next to the blue and green swirls of the glass paperweight from Venice.

They both turned as the front door opened. "Sorry I'm late," Lucas called from the entry, putting down his motorcycle helmet, unbuttoning his jacket. "The meeting went on longer than expected." He entered the sitting room in a flurry, moving quickly, his back slightly bent. Breathlessly to Elizabeth in French: "I got the commission for Rouen."

"Well-done," she answered in English. Placing a nervous hand on his shoulder, she stole a look to see if he'd noticed the schoolmarm stiffness in her voice.

"Thank you," he said, too excited and flustered to notice anything. Turning to Troy, he explained in English: "I got a job to design an exhibition centre in Rouen. It's my most important project yet. Let me just say hello to the children." And he disappeared down the corridor. Before Troy could take control of the conversation again, Elizabeth launched into an overly detailed explanation of how architectural competitions worked.

When Lucas returned, he sat down next to Troy and poured himself a glass of wine.

"Look what Troy brought us," said Elizabeth. "It's his own work."

Lucas picked up the small statue, all his attention fixed on it, as he turned the figure around in his hand. "Very nice. The expression is…" he paused and the wandering blue vein at his temple bulged slightly, as it always did when he was concentrating or excited or angry. "I would say that the expression is inconsolable."

"Thank you," said Troy.

"Have you been very influenced by the American Indians?" asked Lucas, putting it down carefully.

"My mother's mother was Native-American."

"I can see that," said Lucas, nodding.

"German on my father's side. That explains the blond hair."

"It's an unusual combination," said Lucas. "I often find such unexpected mixtures intriguing and very—how can I say it— very successful."

"Well, thank you," Troy answered, raising his glass and looking approvingly at Lucas.

"Cheers," said Lucas, raising his own glass. "And welcome. You know, you are the only friend of Elizabeth's I have ever met from that college."

"Is that right," Troy said, looking at her with a curious smile, leaning into his arm which was braced on his knee. "Well."

"As I was telling you," she said," I haven't kept up with anybody." She looked sideways at Lucas, again worried he would notice strain in her voice. "If you'll excuse me, I have to see to supper."

She stood up abruptly and went into the kitchen where she poured the Basmati rice into the boiling water, put the lid on and turned the temperature down. *It's not that I never thought of you please don't think that.* She leaned into the counter and stirred the simmering lamb curry, put the spoon to her lips. *But ouch.* She added the last spices, took a deep breath and returned to the living room.

"Our street, *la rue Laromiguière*," Lucas was saying, "used to be called *la rue des Poules*—you know hens, girl chickens. It was the cemetery for persecuted Protestants who were not allowed to be buried with the Catholics." He had taken his Dictionary of Paris Streets from the shelves and the two of them were standing side by side, with their backs to Elizabeth.

"So we've got bones underneath us," remarked Troy, turning towards her as she sat down again, addressing his words directly to her. "Kind of like skeletons in the closet."

"Paris is like that," said Lucas, who was now absorbed in the subject, and had not noticed Elizabeth flinch. "One buried city built on top of another. Whenever they dig to build again, they find something from the past. For example in the east of the city, not long ago when they were digging to lay new foundations for new buildings, they found canoes and artefacts from thousands and thousands of years ago that had been preserved in mud. Then of course there are signs of the Roman city, Lutetia, everywhere. Walls, houses. Or as you have seen, a whole amphitheatre." Lucas turned his head and looked intently at Troy. "You have heard of the Musée Carnavalet, the museum of the city of Paris?" Troy shook his head. "You really should go there if you're interested in these things. Of course you can also borrow my books."

"Thank you. There is a lot more to see and do than I expected." The timer for the rice buzzed and Elizabeth returned to the kitchen, thinking that the consequences of all this book-lending would be the return of the books—more meetings—and she could feel tentacles of panic once again rising up from her gut and surrounding her heart.

After the three of them were seated around one end of the large table, Elizabeth said as she uncovered the pot: "I hope you like curry."

Troy stared at the stew, his face frozen in barely contained rage. "I don't eat meat. Don't you remember that? I don't eat meat."

42

"I'm really sorry," Elizabeth said, putting her hand to her mouth and remembering not just his vegetarianism but also that look. How sometimes it did indeed lead to an outburst of terrible anger. "I'd completely forgotten."

"Well we must have something else to offer you?" Lucas asked. "Some eggs? We don't have some eggs?"

"I don't eat eggs either, except in sauces and stuff where I can't see them." He waved his hand dismissively, as if making the eggs disappear. "Fish and cheese are all right but no meat and no visible eggs."

"I'll see what I can find," said Elizabeth, relieved for another excuse to escape to the kitchen.

"When I was in high school," Troy said, still with that look of simmering milk about to boil over, "I had an after-school job in the kitchens of an institution for disturbed and disabled children..." She went to the kitchen, rummaged in the fridge. *No meat just vegetarian pizzas and games of hearts that lasted all night and then there was that beast who rummaged in our kitchen and under our floor and in our walls. All those memories I'd buried now they are emerging they are coming after me like the beast out of that hole in the floor and even the films I go to pursue me give me nightmares I keep dreaming of fire and I'm always running away. Go away please go away.*

"Once a week," he was saying in the same grave tone as she re-entered the dining room—to Elizabeth it even sounding accusing—"the butcher came to deliver the meat. He was always dressed in a long, white, hooded coat covered in blood. He carried whole sides of cow slung over his shoulder. The cook had been there for a long time. Too long. His only remaining pleasure in the job seemed to be doing it as shoddily as he could. When he chopped up all that cow with his hatchet, blood and fat and bits of bone flew everywhere. It was my job to clean up the mess he made. Some days the butcher brought in crates of dead, plucked chickens. I had to gut them, lop off their wings and claws and heads, before the cook literally tore the bodies apart for cooking." He paused, lost in the memory, as if he were right back in that kitchen, and the look on his face teetered between rage and despair. "But that wasn't the worst. The worst was once it was all cooked—reconstituted might be a better word. Once the kids started eating it. Some shovelled the stuff into their mouths like starving animals. Some couldn't even feed themselves and needed to be fed like babies. Since they were always short of staff, I often had to help get that disgusting slop into their mouths." He shook his head. "I couldn't separate in my mind the floppy necks of those raw chickens from the kids who couldn't quite hold their heads up, the bloody meat and bone from the red, runny noses and eyes of the others." He paused and a defiant sneer came over his face, as if he had just been personally offended. "No one ever came to see them. It's not surprising they ate like animals. That's how they were treated."

"Wow," said Lucas, leaning forward towards Troy, mesmerized by this gritty exposé.

"I'm sorry," Elizabeth repeated quietly. "I'm sorry I forgot."

"I'm sorry to get carried away," Troy said, shaking his shoulders and rubbing his face with his hands, as if ridding himself physically of the story and the mood that it had engendered. "I haven't thought of that hell hole in a long time." Then turning to Elizabeth, "I guess you're not a vegetarian anymore."

"You were a vegetarian?" asked Lucas with a startled look at his wife.

"Only for my last year of college, really."

"You've never mentioned that to me," Lucas said. "Or for that matter anything else about your college. Except that you didn't like it."

"Vegetarianism was just a fad for me. Like baggy jeans, or whatever it was that I wore then." She shrugged. "None of us in the apartment ate meat."

Lucas continued to look at her. "But it is odd," he repeated, "that it never came up. That you never told me."

"It didn't seem important," she said. "I'd pretty much forgotten it myself." She adjusted her position in her seat, began cutting her meat.

"I was worried when I came over here," Troy said. "About what I'd find." Elizabeth froze and continued to fix her eyes intently on her lamb; Lucas cocked his head in interest. "Food-wise, I mean. But I've been eating like a king. In fact, it's all so much better than I expected that I've been thinking about extending my stay. Through the summer."

"What about your business?" Elizabeth asked, looking up abruptly. "Can you just drop it like that?"

"Most of my clients are rich people," Troy said slightly hooding his eyes and crossing his arms over his chest. "People who have chosen to live in the middle of the woods but who prefer to enjoy nature through their windows as if it were a painting in a museum from the city or the suburb or wherever they've all come from. They're people who can't split logs or mend fences or tell a beaver from a small bear. They're helpless. They're at the mercy of us manual workers." He looked maliciously pleased as he unfolded his arms and picked up his cutlery. "So the answer to your question," he looked from one to the other of them, a bite of food poised before his mouth, "is no, I am not worried about my business. What I am worried about is where to live here in Paris. The hotel is too expensive for the longer term. Do you have any ideas where I might find something cheaper?" He popped the food in his mouth.

"You should try and find a *chambre de service*," Lucas said.

"A what?" he said, his jaw muscles working visibly as he chewed.

Lucas looked to Elizabeth. She said: "They're rooms on the top floors of buildings where the servants used to live. Now students not servants live in them, mostly. Our son lives in ours."

"Look for notices in the *boulangerie*. Or Elizabeth, can't you help Troy find a room? Don't you think someone at the school has one available?"

"Maybe," she said.

"Didn't you say there's a meeting of the parents' association early next week?" Lucas asked.

"Yes," she said.

"You can ask there."

"Tell them I can help with repairs as well," Troy said, his tongue working loose a piece of food caught in the back of his mouth. "I can fix just about anything."

"Okay," Elizabeth said as she got up with a sinking heart to get the lemon meringue tart.

***

"We decided to limit the size the party," Lucas said to the children over dinner one evening. "There will be about fifty people."

"Sounds like a lot of people to me," said Tristan, who was leaning over his plate.

"Do we have to go?" asked Olivier.

"To your grandparents' fiftieth wedding anniversary?" Lucas laughed. "Of course you do."

"Do I get a new dress?" asked Ariane.

"Tristan," Elizabeth pleaded lightly. "Can't you sit up straight and bring the food up to your mouth, not your mouth down to the food?"

Tristan half sat up and said: "It's the small talk I can't bear at those things."

"Maman, do I get a new dress?" Ariane persisted.

"Probably," said Elizabeth. "Well if you don't make small talk, how can you get to know anyone new?"

"In any case," said Lucas with an affectionately ironic smile at his son, "there will be plenty of fellow revellers who won't be the least bit intimidated if you want to talk Kant or Descartes with them."

"That's for sure," laughed Elizabeth.

"Will there be music?" Olivier asked. "So at least we can dance?"

"No music," said Lucas. "No thrills, no frills. Just a quiet celebration of your grandparents' fifty years together."

"How many years have you been married?" asked Ariane.

"Almost twenty," said Lucas.

"You should have a party too," said Ariane.

"So you can have two new dresses?" Elizabeth smiled. "Let's take things one dress at a time."

"Exactly," said Lucas, pushing his chair back and standing up, "and in the meantime there's a mess to be cleaned up."

While the children began clearing the table, Elizabeth said to Lucas: "I have a long book to finish by the end of the week. I'll have to read all evening."

"I've got some things to finish up too," he said, turning towards his office, then, on second thought, turning back to her: "I've been meaning to ask you. Is your work going any better?"

"I'm afraid Lucille Darmon's still Gérard's darling."

Lucas put a long arm around Elizabeth's waist. "Well, you know Gérard. His darlings tend to be, shall I say, fly-by-night."

"True," she laughed.

"Nor does he always get the girl."

"True again."

"You don't want to imitate his mating dance for me again, like you used to?"

"Fortunately, I don't really remember the steps," she said smiling. "And it's late. I have to read to the twins and get them to bed."

"Okay. I'll see you later?" He kissed her.

"See you later."

After getting teeth brushed, hair combed and school bags ready for the next day, Elizabeth finished *The Flopsy Bunnies*, tucked in the twins and went back to hers and Lucas' bedroom. She sat down on her *chaise longue* but did not turn on the light.

After a minute, she scrunched up and lay down on it, tucking the cushion under her head and curling up on her side, wrapping her arms around her torso, the way she used to do when she had what her mother called cramps and everyone else around her called curse pains.

All through their dinner conversation, she'd been thinking about her own parents, and the morning when, almost eighteen and home for the Easter holiday, she had come down late for breakfast to find her mother in tears at the kitchen table.

The fair skin around Vera's pale blue eyes was puffy and red from all the weeping. A balled-up, overused tissue was gripped in one hand and from the other dangled a note. Elizabeth's heart started beating uncomfortably in her drowsy state; she wondered if someone had died.

The note, left on the kitchen table, was from her father, Andrew Lyall. It informed his wife that he was leaving. Moving out and on for the sake of real love. I can't go on like this, he said, before providing his new address, c/o Monica Peretti. Elizabeth stood for several minutes reading and re-reading the I-can't-go-on-like-this note in stunned silence. Until she realized that she should be comforting her mother. Because Vera Lyall was undone, completely undone, as if every part of her body had become unhinged. Every part of her minus the hand that continued to worry the tired tissue. Elizabeth patted her mother on the shoulder and wished that Molly were there, instead of in the country, staying at the grand house of one of her grand friends. If Molly were there, Molly would not be patting their mother on the shoulder. Almost three years younger but she would have known how to handle the situation. She would have taken Vera in her arms and cried along with her.

Until that morning Elizabeth had never questioned her parents' marriage. There had been no significant arguments, no complaints or grievances voiced or even insinuated into conversation as far as she could tell and now, after twenty years, that was it.

She thought of her father, the wavy black hair and the lively, glittering blue eyes, his greatest asset. She imagined those eyes seducing c/o Monica Peretti and suddenly the glint looked malevolent instead of charming. Calculating too: he waited to leave the note until his daughters were home, so that they could pick up the pieces. I can't go on like this anymore, not even until the end of the Easter holiday.

Finally she said to her mother: "If that's the way he's going to act, forget him."

The divorce was not long in coming. Vera was so diminished she put up little fuss. Molly was conciliatory with one and all, even agreeing to meet c/o Monica. But Elizabeth refused to see her father much less his lover. She was in complete turmoil. His departure had made her whole childhood, their whole family life, seem a lie. A fabrication. A stage-managed piece of theatre. Objects in their slightly untidy but hitherto friendly house appeared to be props, rather than items belonging to a real life. Other things took on a secret, somewhat sinister, hidden meaning.

She felt angry with herself as well. How could she have noticed nothing? How could she have missed the clues? Because of course once she knew, she saw a multitude of them. And she could not get her father's eyes out of her mind. Those charming eyes that could light up a room, an entire gathering of otherwise dull people. After that note, she'd begun to wonder if they weren't the very eyes of Satan.

***

At the end of the meeting at school, after all the details for the school fete had been ironed out, Elizabeth stood up and announced that she had an old friend in town, an artist, and would anyone have a room to rent until the end of the summer. A young mother stood up and said: "What good timing. Our student tenant has just run out on me."

Since Troy had come to supper and announced his prolonged stay, she had been considering what to do. As he was apparently not going to disappear anytime soon, wouldn't it be wise to say something to Troy before Troy had a chance to say something to someone else? Shouldn't she force herself to deliver some kind of apology?

On the way home from work the day following the school meeting, she stopped by the hotel. He came down to the lobby and they sat in two chairs with rounded backs and ugly flowered upholstery.

"The room is likely to be rather Spartan," Elizabeth said. "And not very spacious."

"I don't need much," he shrugged in the half-embarrassed, half-resigned way he always did, she remembered, when material comfort was in question. Troy's mother had died shortly after he was born and his father, who couldn't hold down a job, sent him to live with an aunt and uncle and their two children, before heading out west. Money was short and Troy was always made to feel a burden. He had been a scholarship student at the college.

"Maybe it has a nice view," she said, thinking this was unlikely. The building was on a narrow part of the street. "She suggested you come by tomorrow at about six. Here's the address. She says she speaks English well enough."

"I really appreciate this," he said, leaning forward to take the piece of paper. "Not having to worry about money so much makes all the difference."

She couldn't say anything here; the hotel receptionist was standing at the desk, stapling bills together, right behind Troy's back. "Have you got plans for your stay?"

"I just want to take in as much as I can of this incredible city," he said with those dark brown eyes, staring right into her. Then, as if aware how their intensity could be unsettling, he looked away and added with a shrug and a smile: "Just have a good time."

She nodded. In the small space of this lobby, his physical

presence overwhelmed her, made her pulse quicken, as it always had. It was the way his strong arms draped the chair; it was his measured grace as he walked her to the door.

The early spring evening bathed the Paris stone in honey yellow. It was the city at its best and Elizabeth found herself asking: "Would you like to join us for supper? The family?"

He turned towards her with his own look of surprise and a smile that exposed fully his crowded teeth. "Yes," he nodded. "I would like that very much."

"Come in an hour or so. We're having fish."

"Thank you. Thank you very much."

As she walked away, she could feel his eyes on her back as surely as if they were his hands, and her spine tingled from top to bottom. *Ah yes. There's one memory that springs back to life with pleasure not pain: your hands running up and down my spine, all over my naïve body. I could never forget that.*

***

The following week Elizabeth was walking to work and there was Troy, sitting at a café on the place de l'Estrapade. Hunched over the small round table, he was writing in a notebook, left hand curled awkwardly over the page, just as it had been the first time she'd laid eyes on him in the lecture hall, during their modern European history class.

She was thinking how, at the college, she'd watched him, week after week, never summoning the courage to speak to him —he was so cool; she was such a gawky English schoolgirl— when he looked up from the café table and waved. Today she felt somehow caught out and wished she could have slipped down the side street without being seen.

"How's the room?" she asked, approaching the table.

"As you said, not very big, but it's got a great view on the dome of the Pantheon and a little balcony, which makes it seem bigger when I open the French window. You can see it from here." He pointed up. "It's just perfect."

"Good. Well, I've got to get to work." She looked at her watch. "Editorial meeting."

"Okay," he said.

"I'll see you then."

The next day she sat down and joined him for a coffee.

"Lucas took me to the Tuileries yesterday to see the trees being trimmed," he said, satisfied, almost surprised. "Like he promised at dinner last week."

"He's usually good to his word," she said.

"Yea, like the guy's got nothing better to do." Elizabeth did not reply. "What a sight it was too. When I consider that my business is mostly helping people get rid of sick trees, dying trees, trees they'd rather live without." He shrugged, almost embarrassed by the lack of artistry in his work. "I do thin them out as well, but just so they won't fall on people's heads or houses and kill them. Nothing fancy. Nothing like what I saw there. I use a noisy, smelly chain saw and there they were, with those moving ladders and hand scythes and when they're done, there's not a leaf out of line. Incredible."

Lucas had reported to her the previous evening: "It's so refreshing to be with someone who shows *genuine* interest. *Genuine* curiosity and appreciation." He'd sighed. "Troy made *me* see the place through different eyes. Afterwards he even coaxed me into showing him around the Louvre. I ended up taking the whole afternoon off—I can't remember the last time I did something spontaneous like that."

"Well," Elizabeth said. "Good." They sat in silence for a moment. She was trying to muster the courage to say something but no words, no words at all, rose to the surface. They'd been buried too deeply, too long.

"I have a question for you," he finally said.

"Yes," she replied, hardly above a whisper.

"Why do they leave the flowers on the zucchini? That's how they sold them to me at that market."

"You eat them," she said, feeling as if a black cloud had just given way to burst of sunshine. "They're a delicacy."

"Eating flowers. Only in Europe," he laughed, exposing his teeth again, and she remembered how embarrassed he'd been by them, how angry and resentful that his uncle wouldn't pay for braces. "I bought some zucchini and threw the flowers away. I wondered if they weren't trying to trick me, to take advantage of a dumb American tourist. Too bad. Next time I'll know better."

The moment was past. Tomorrow. She'd say something tomorrow.

But the next day, after she'd rushed the twins to school earlier than usual, Troy immediately launched into an almost breathless account of the walk he'd taken the previous afternoon, concluding with:

"What a city, especially for a loner. You can walk and walk and never feel lonely. The architecture keeps you company."

"That's a nice way to put it," she said, charmed as Lucas had been by his enthusiasm for the city she too loved. "And you're right. It does keep you company."

"It's giving me the time of my life," he said with a beaming smile, crooked teeth unabashedly in full view, and she just didn't have the heart to get in the way of that smile.

So after a moment, she asked: "What kind of life have you got in Vermont? Have you got a lot of friends?"

"I *know* everyone—it's a small community. And I've had various lovers over the years. There was one woman I actually moved in with for a while. But things didn't work out. Her son convinced her that I was having an affair with someone else. The kid couldn't stand me." He crossed his arms tightly over his chest and got that look of simmering fury. "I certainly put any thoughts of marriage to rest long ago."

"I'm sorry about that," said Elizabeth quietly—that look always frightened her slightly and she knew what a sensitive subject marriage was for him, how excited he used to get over the idea of someday having a family of his own, of the chance to compensate for his parentless, loveless childhood.

"Yea, well, things have a way of not turning out the way you expect." Smiling now, he leaned his knee into hers under the table. "Sometimes worse, sometimes better."

"I guess that's right," she answered, returning the pressure of his knee.

***

Besides taking Troy to see the trimming of the lime trees in the Tuileries, Lucas also arranged for him to do some work around the rue Laromiguière, the repairs he himself never had time to attend to. After unclogging drains and re-gluing loose tiles, he fixed a door that wouldn't close and a window that wouldn't open. He lubricated a squeaky hinge and made the hiss in the stereo speakers disappear. He could indeed fix anything.

Troy usually finished the job early evening. He would stay on for supper and tell stories about his rich, helpless clients in Vermont that made them all laugh. Just when it seemed he might be overly dominating the conversation, he'd ask someone a question and listen to the answer with complete attention and concern. After the meal, he'd linger, unearthing common ground with every member of the family. Tristan he treated like an adult and the two of them, who shared a slow intensity of manner, could talk and debate for hours at a time. Olivier lent him his old guitar and the two of them played together. Gabby listened with wide, awed eyes as Troy told him about his black belt in judo. Ariane, who never stopped talking, he just listened to. She pronounced him *étrange* but flitted around him like a moth at a candle.

Most of the time, though, it was Troy and Lucas who sat down after supper. Lucas, usually not much of a drinker, would open another bottle of wine, and they'd settle in the sitting room, talking about architecture, about art, about books. Elizabeth participated sometimes and when she didn't, she'd hover nervously within hearing distance.

Lucas also took Troy to see his parents' collection of African and Asian art and arranged for Troy to do repair jobs there, as well as at his sister's.

"Your friend is gorgeous," Alix said to Elizabeth one day over lunch. "Only Americans have bodies like that," she sighed.

Elizabeth nodded, thinking of yeasty Roland. She said: "Yes, he has managed to stay very fit."

"Lucas seems to have taken quite a shining to him too. As an artist. As a fresh presence in our musty old world," she said, eating her last bite of salad. "But he's like that, isn't he?"

"Who's like what?"

"Lucas. Lucas is like that. Attracted to people who are out of the mould."

"Like me, you mean," Elizabeth said trying to sound amused.

"Well, yes, but don't take it badly. I mean, you're not one of a kind but you *are* a foreigner and therefore something of a rare bird among us."

"True."

"He's always been like that," Alix repeated, as if still trying to fathom this peculiarity in her brother. "Maybe it's just a fascination with Americans. When he was a little boy, he invented an imaginary friend called Steve. He must have got the name from a television programme or some American book in translation. Anyway, I was quite jealous. It was Steve this and Steve that. He'd go on and on about how he and Steve were going to travel from one exotic place to another."

"Did he?" asked Elizabeth. "He's never mentioned Steve to me."

Alix shrugged. "It was a long time ago." She paused then cocked her head and looked at Elizabeth. "What about you? Didn't you come straight over here after that little American college you went to?"

"I did."

"Is that the only time you lived there?"

"I was born there. We moved to England when I was six."

"So what do you feel? More English or more American?"

"I don't know," Elizabeth said with a twitch of her shoulders. Being with Alix, she often felt like an insect pinned to a mat. "I'm both and I'm neither. I've lived in Paris now for more than half my life so you have to factor in the French influence too. Maybe I should say," she added with an awkward laugh, "I'm nothing."

Or too many things, Elizabeth was still thinking as she walked back to the office. Like a colour wheel, spun around, all mixed up, yielding a blank. Or something like that. Whatever she felt, it was an amorphous, hybrid thing that was impossible to explain to anyone who did not understand it intuitively. Lucas understood perfectly—his empathy was one of the qualities she'd fallen in love with—but his sister clearly did not.

While walking down the corridor towards her office, she heard Lucille laughing. She tried to imagine Lucille Darmon, native of Paris, graduate of Brown University, feeling uncomfortable about her cleanly divided bilingual, bicultural self but it was a futile exercise. Instead of seeing a hesitant, questioning Lucille, she saw a Lucille crouching on the squash court, awaiting the serve, then whacking that little rubber ball into the corner, where it dropped dead, before her opponent could get anywhere near it.

***

Late afternoon, just before Claude and Isabelle Teller's anniversary party, Elizabeth had pulled Olivier's smart trousers from the back of his drawer. They were crumpled almost beyond hope and she had given a resigned sigh—the whole week had been like that. The day after lunch with Alix, there had been a disagreement at an editorial meeting over the strategy to follow in securing a recent British bestseller and Lucille had prevailed. Then the translator she'd hoped to get for an American novel was too busy and she'd taken someone she thought was second-rate.

While Elizabeth moved the iron vigorously across the fabric of Olivier's trousers, Tristan was playing a Chopin Nocturne he didn't know very well. There was much stopping and starting, along with the mistaken notes. She pushed the iron even harder.

"Doorbell!" he called, during one of his pauses.

"What? You can't answer it?" She put the iron down with a bang and marched to the door.

"I haven't got a tie or a jacket," Troy said, as Elizabeth let him in.

"Lucas' jackets would be too long for you," she said, trying not to sound annoyed at yet someone else to take care of before they could get out the door. "The boys only have one each. Maybe I can find an old one in the closet. Just let me finish these trousers. I'm not at all ready and we can't be late for the party."

"Sorry to be a bother," Troy said as she resumed pushing the iron over the resistant wrinkles. "I did mention it to Lucas," who at that moment walked in.

"As you are apparently already aware," Elizabeth said to Lucas in French, "Troy needs a jacket and tie for the party."

"Come with me," said Lucas. "We'll find whatever you need."

Despite Elizabeth's objections, Lucas had insisted on inviting Troy to the party. When they'd argued about it as recently as that morning, he had said: "He's looking for more odd jobs, and who better than friends of my parents, people who do not even own a screw driver."

She wondered if it was her bad week or Troy's coming to the party that was making her so cranky. Though she enjoyed, actually savoured, their morning coffees and his mild flirting—which she chose to interpret as a kind of pardon—she worried about his increasing intimacy with her family. And this evening he would meet almost everyone she knew in Paris.

"Can you cheer up a bit?" Lucas asked as they approached the eighteenth century *hôtel particulier* where the party was being held.

"I'm perfectly cheery," she answered defensively.

"You were rude to Troy, then silent and sulky in the car."

She did not reply. Although she found his prissy scolding intolerable, he was of course correct—she had been silent and sulky and curt with Troy.

They walked up the stairs and into the grand reception rooms rented for the party. Alix and Roland were already there with their two children, as were Isabelle and Claude.

"We really can't thank you enough for your help," Claude said to Troy. "It's so hard to find people to do the little things." Claude spoke to him in perfect English, with a very polished but old-fashioned English accent. His family had escaped to England just before the Germans marched into Paris and he had spent the war years at a British boarding school.

"Yes," added Isabelle, in an airy soft voice. "You've been a great help." Though over seventy, she was still a strikingly beautiful woman. Even the wrinkles hardly showed on her fine skin—until she smiled, and then they seemed to obey some strange law of nature by which they filled her perfectly proportioned oval face in ordered lines.

"No problem," Troy said. "It's given me the chance to get a good look at that art collection of yours. And that's given me some ideas for my own work."

The waiters bustled about in their white coats as they arranged glasses and laid out *canapés*. Guests started to arrive; the grand reception rooms filled up; groups splintered and reformed. The party was larger than originally planned by Lucas and Alix because once Claude and Isabelle got hold of the invitation list, they worried about causing offence and added substantially to the numbers. There were over one hundred people in the room. Not quite the entire Who's Who but a sizeable selection.

While Elizabeth chatted briefly to people as they arrived, she watched Lucas introduce Troy to one group, Alix to another, as if Troy were a rugby ball making its way down the pitch, with the brother and sister vying for position as his handler. Other revellers, fleetingly attracted to a novel presence, joined the scrum, eager to be introduced. Elizabeth thought Lucas looked as pleased as if Steve had come back to life, while Alix took Troy's arm as if he were her escort at Cannes. She noticed too that Lucas had lent Troy his favourite tie, the one she'd bought for him at the Met, while on a business trip to New York.

"There you are." Elizabeth turned to see Uncle Antoine, Claude's younger brother, who had first hired Elizabeth at the publishing house. He was not speaking to her, as she'd thought, but to Henri, a doctor who travelled from one trouble spot to another. "I've been given a manuscript on Afghanistan and was wondering if you'd read it. See how accurate a picture it is."

"With pleasure. It's great to know someone's still interested enough to write about the country. Most people see the war there as yesterday's problem and have forgotten about it. It's a disgrace how easily places of no seemingly immediate strategic interest can be forgotten..."

Elizabeth turned to get some more champagne. On the way, she saw that Lucas was now introducing Troy to some wealthy banker friends of his parents, people who, if they did own a screwdriver, would never have been able to find it in their cavernous apartment. Alix hovered nearby. And she, Elizabeth, try as she may, could not chase away a toxic mix of jealousy and anxiety at all this attention.

"Elizabeth. Hello."

"Laurent," she answered. "Sorry, I didn't see you. How are you?" She had almost walked right by Lucas' cousin, Isabelle's nephew.

"Well. Very well," he said, putting a hand in the pocket of his tailored grey suit. "Just busy. Insanely busy."

"With all those books to read..." Elizabeth said. Laurent was a television journalist with a weekly culture show.

"Indeed. And along with finishing *my* book—I haven't had a free moment." Like Roland, he was a part-time but prolific novelist. "If it weren't for Delphine—she's been perfect. An absolute star."

"Undoubtedly," Elizabeth said, trying to suppress a smile. Laurent had not always been so confident in the stellar perfection of his wife. In more diffident days when he and Elizabeth had long lunches and too much wine, Laurent would tell her, with flushed cheeks and worried eyes, that he suspected Delphine of having an affair with a painter.

"I hear it's tough going these days on your end of the fiction stick."

"Our new management is trying to inject a whole new value system," Elizabeth began stiffly, but Laurent, whose eyes had started wandering around the room, interrupted her:

"Who's that other American you've got there now? I've heard she's a powerhouse."

"Lucille Darmon and she was born and bred right here in Paris. But you're right: by birth she is half American. And yes, I guess you could call her a powerhouse. I'm going to get myself some more champagne—would you like some?"

"No," Laurent sighed, raising his glass. "I'll stick to water. The screen calls later this evening."

Elizabeth fumed as the waiter poured the frothing champagne. Did she even have to hear about Lucille here? And Laurent—what had happened to him? When she first met him and he wrote for the business pages of a daily newspaper, he dressed in rumpled shirts and patched jackets and had been natural and friendly enough to stop by her desk, the desk of the temporary archivist, and make bad jokes in terrible English. It was Laurent who had invited her to a party and introduced her to Lucas.

Really, he'd been so much nicer, so much more interesting and fun, when he was reporting on car manufacturers and supermarket chains. Literature had rendered the man insufferable.

She looked around the room, picked out the members of her family. Lucas had Troy talking to his father and an ancient distant cousin, the one who had lost her entire family—husband, parents and her own two children—during the War. She was slightly dotty and most people avoided her but never Lucas. Never Claude either. Certainly never Claude, because of his own lost sister. The flamboyant older sister Cosima, called Coco. Coco the artist who had ignored the warnings and her family's pleading and wouldn't come to London with the rest of them. The sister, the aunt, who was only whispered about, and rarely at that. All that was left of Coco, as far as Elizabeth knew, was the family photo, which sat next to the piano in the drawing room at the elder Tellers' apartment and one painting—abstract swirls of vibrant colours—displayed prominently in the entry hall.

Tristan was with a man she didn't recognize; it looked as though he'd survived the small talk and was enjoying himself. Olivier was entertaining his younger cousins and Gabby. Ariane was nowhere in sight. Elizabeth crossed the room briskly. From the landing, she saw her daughter climbing on the staircase railing.

"What are you doing?" Elizabeth asked sternly.

"I was bored," said Ariane. "I was looking for something to do."

"It's getting late," she said, looking at her watch. "The party must be almost over."

"Do you want me to take her home?" Elizabeth heard from behind her. She whirled around and there was Troy.

She paused, wondering if this wouldn't be the perfect way to get him away from the party, but said: "No, no, one of the boys can just take her down to the courtyard for a while."

"What—don't you trust me?" he asked, his face clouding over. That look always appeared to come from nowhere and almost made her jump, as if someone had just slammed a door.

"Of course that's not it," Elizabeth mumbled. "You're supposed to be enjoying the party." She went to look for the older boys. Tristan, who was indeed now deep in discussion and wanted to stay. But Olivier said he didn't mind and took both

Gabby and Ariane downstairs to play in the courtyard.

Having seen them off down the stairs, she walked back into the room to the tapping of glasses. There was a hush as everyone turned to its source, Lucas and Alix. Roland was standing just behind them.

"We'd like to call our parents up here for a moment," said Lucas. Claude moved forward with his head of white hair and sharp, deep-set blue eyes, his mournful, almost apologetic, expression. Given his highly successful career in government administration and industry, the look sat oddly on his face. Elizabeth always attributed it to the missing sister, to Coco, or to the more general burden of history. Now that his thin frame was at a bit of an angle, his head slightly tilted to one side, he looked even more solemn than when he was a younger man, as if the longer he lived the less he could bear it. Especially too with straight-backed Isabelle gliding along at his side. The couple joined their children. Their smiles hovered closer to forbearance than pleasure—they had not requested all this attention and their egos certainly didn't need it—as Lucas continued: "I want to thank you all for coming," he looked around with a slight, stiff bow. "We did want to take a moment and raise our glasses to Claude and Isabelle, our parents," he looked at Alix, with another little wooden bow, "who have instilled in us values of integrity, humanity and independence. Who have served as guides and inspiration to us both, without ever imposing a model or a muse. To you," he said facing his parents and raising his glass high, while the rest of the room followed suit, then broke into applause that was only a few degrees warmer than polite. Besides being averse to emotional displays, the revellers were, true to their reputation, largely unfamiliar with the pleasures of marital felicity and devotion.

"That was an eloquent little speech," she said, after she'd finally made her way through the guests to Lucas. Being left out had made her feel insignificant, dispensable—as if the role of perfect son was obviously more important to him than that of attentive husband.

"We thought it was important to say something. Where are the children? I only see Tristan."

"We?" she said archly. "What about me? I had Olivier take the twins down to the courtyard. Ariane was wandering."

"So they missed the toast?"

"If I'd known it was coming, I obviously would have kept them here."

"You know that something has to be said at these celebrations. How could you let the children go?"

"How could you not tell me you were going to make a toast? How could you not call me up there?"

"I couldn't find you."

"Sounded good, Lucas," said Troy, suddenly between them and shaking Lucas' hand, patting him on the back. "Even though I didn't understand a word of it."

"Thank you."

"You got the children under control?" Troy asked Elizabeth.

"Fine. Thank you." Out of the corner of her eye, she saw Lucas look with surprise from one to the other of them. "I think I've got a painting job lined up, Lucas. Thanks for introducing me. I should be set for the summer now."

"Good," said Lucas. "I thought this party might be a helpful source of employment."

"The party's been much more than that," he said looking down at the floor, hands in his pockets. "I don't want to be sappy or anything but I have to tell you I've never seen a gathering like this. When I think of where I live, of the people—even the rich ones—it's like planet of the apes. While this—" and he flung a hand out towards the room—"this elegance, this style, these people whose families have known one another for generations. I didn't even know such a way of life existed. Thank you very much for inviting me tonight. For letting me witness such an event."

"I'm happy to be able to provide you with some added

tourism," said Lucas with a satisfied smile, all anger with Elizabeth now seemingly forgotten. He put a hand on Troy's shoulder. "It is important for you to experience the social as well as the physical architecture of the place."

Troy laughed, his messy teeth flashing.

This exchange reminded Elizabeth how impressed she too had been by all the elegant, eloquent people. How lucky she'd felt to have fallen in with him and his sophisticated, confident friends. She had in fact been completely seduced, just like Troy, and Lucas had of course done the right thing by inviting him— he always did the right thing, said the right thing, in the eyes of the world. And tonight she found it unbearable.

The party wound down. After the last guests had left, the six Tellers went to eat a light, late supper at a nearby *brasserie*. Lucas asked Troy along but he declined.

When they were getting ready for bed afterwards, Lucas said: "I'm pleased Troy had a good time at the party."

Though she'd promised herself not to say anything, she replied: "How could he not, with the way you were attending to him."

"What do you mean by that?"

"Nothing. Just that he was bound to have a good time because you never left his side."

"First of all, that's not true."

"You're right. You switched on and off with Alix."

"You were certainly paying close attention to my movements."

She did not answer, told herself in fact, to shut up.

Lucas, however, continued: "I invited Troy. It was my job to make sure he had a good time."

"That didn't mean you had to ask him out to supper as well," she said, furious at his moralizing tone.

"It didn't seem right to abandon him."

Elizabeth stole a look at Lucas to gauge any underlying meaning, and seeing none, pulled back the duvet with a jerk. "I just don't see why he has to be with our family, nuclear and extended, every minute of the day and night."

Lucas made a sound of air being let out of a tyre as he turned out the light. Then, softly but not kindly: "What happened between the two of you? Were you lovers or something?"

Elizabeth paused a pause that could not go unanswered as she turned off the light. As she laid her head on the pillow, she said: "We had a fling once. You know, four of us sharing a flat. A few long nights. Everyone having too much to drink. That kind of thing. You know."

"No, I do not know what you mean by 'that kind of thing.'" They were lying distinctly apart in the bed, both on their backs, talking to the ceiling. "So what? You feel like a jilted lover, after all these years? Is that it?"

"Certainly not," she said sharply. Hot and angry, she threw a leg outside the duvet. "You know as well as I do that those were promiscuous times."

"Yes. But you did go to bed with him." He paused. "On some level, you're still in love with him. And you're jealous of the time I spend with him. That's the only explanation I can think of for your odd behaviour."

"Four children and a job fill my life beyond the brim already. I don't need extra work. Extra people around. I don't have time for it all."

"Don't have *time* for other people," he said reproachfully, huffily. "Even an old friend—an old lover. It's unbelievable." After a minute, he threw the covers off and grabbed the book next to the bed. "I can't sleep."

***

The next morning the twins were darting about in excitement as they waited impatiently to leave for the school fete. Each was dressed in a white shirt and blue shorts, as instructed by their teachers, for the singing recital. This was as close as Elizabeth ever got to dressing them like twins, and she couldn't repress a tweak of pleasure at seeing her little miracles turned out in tune.

As she walked them to school, however, her pleasure quickly dissipated as the previous night's argument crowded back into her mind. Elizabeth had lain awake for a long time, longer than Lucas' absence, though she had feigned sleep when he'd finally returned to bed. She was accustomed to Lucas' moral stances, to his implicit tone of impunity—on some level she believed he was in fact morally superior to most of the world, certainly including herself. But the vehemence he had displayed was new, and it had left her feeling bruised and very unhappy.

It was a relief to be at school, to be setting up the food and game tables in the courtyard with the other mothers involved in the fete. Elizabeth cut her homemade brownies into squares with ceremony. She laid them out with particular care, knowing that they would be remarked upon. Although brownies could now be bought at any *boulangerie* in the city, hers came with a stamp of authenticity and people would comment on them discerningly. Knowing a good brownie from a bad, after all, was an indication these days of one's broader international exposure and sophistication.

In complying with the *Vigipirate* security measures, Madame Forges, who had been patrolling the courtyard like the chief of police, kept the door to the school locked and the other parents waiting outside. She waited so long to let them in that there was an agitated rush when she finally did open the door. It took Elizabeth several minutes to find Lucas, Tristan and Olivier. The two older boys had been through the same school but had not been back since Olivier's last year, age ten. As they arrived, Elizabeth noticed that both had been careful to wear their images loud and clear that morning, leaving no margin for error about what kind of people they had become. Tristan, with his un-brushed curly hair, his loose khakis, a hands-in-the-pockets intellectual aloofness next to the cooler look of his brother Olivier—baggy jeans and oversized rock-band t-shirt. Lucas looked distracted and unhappy and Elizabeth avoided his gaze, busily cutting up a packaged marble cake in its aluminium container, sprinkling Smarties onto a paper plate. When the singing was about to start, she joined Lucas and the boys, purposely standing next to Olivier.

"So how does it feel to be back at the old place?" she asked them.

"Small," said Olivier.

"Proustian," said Tristan.

The first class was filing into the room and forming their lines. Ariane was in the front row. She searched the room frantically, but all the parents were waving and she had trouble locating her family at the back. When she finally did, the near panic melted from her face and she waved furiously.

"She's so embarrassing," said Olivier.

"She's sweet," said Elizabeth.

"Oh, God," said Tristan. "Look, Olivier, it's Mademoiselle Gouze."

It was indeed their old music teacher. She still had the same lank, mouse-brown hair in need of a trim, the same perpetually frazzled, harried look, the same scolding manner with children and parents alike. Turning on a cassette machine that looked and sounded as if it pre-dated Tristan and Olivier's era, she faced the children, hands suspended in the air. The children looked up at her expectantly. The taped music began and the hands fell; the little voices tried with limited success to oblige the rhythm and remember the words.

"Even the song is the same," whispered Olivier.

"Time warp," said Tristan.

"Shh," said Lucas.

Elizabeth thought she would melt with love for her daughter. Ariane's face was fixed on the teacher and her mouth was moving broadly, intent on showing that she knew all the words. In between songs she looked towards her family with flushed cheeks and a proud smile. After her class filed off, Gabby's class came on. Unlike his sister he nudged and poked his friend and had to be called to order by Mlle Gouze. He did not know the words by heart and had trouble keeping up but none of this bothered him, and Elizabeth's heart ached as much for his fumbling as for Ariane's ardour. She remembered that Tristan had taken the music seriously like Ariane, while Olivier had flubbed the words like Gabby. She remembered how those two hulks next to her were once small and adoring and she felt a sudden pang of regret that she would never be able to fold them onto her lap again.

The recital went on and on. The room got hotter and hotter. Mlle Gouze got more and more flushed and determined with each class, and it no longer seemed amusing but sad. There was a general relief when the final class sang their last off-key note.

"I'm going out for a coffee. I have to make a call," said Lucas, not quite looking her in the eye. "I'll be back in twenty minutes."

"Okay," Elizabeth said hesitantly. She was wondering if he really had a call to make—there was something furtive, suspicious in the way he didn't look at her—and he too was obviously still upset by their unresolved argument the night before.

The party moved outside into the courtyard, where Elizabeth manned the make-up stand. While she smeared small faces with swathes of paint, she looked up from time to time to see how Tristan and Olivier were getting on. They were older by several years than the other brothers and sisters, and they looked uncomfortable and unhappy in their difference. Seeing them tower over the others reminded Elizabeth that her children formed two discrete units. Tristan and Olivier were only twenty months apart but Olivier was seven years older than the twins.

This gap sometimes caused a fracture. A split down the middle of the family. Different needs, different registers. It meant that they had not been on many cultural holidays, the way they had before having children and what they were hoping to do again with Tristan and Olivier when the twins came along. It meant they did fewer things in general as a family.

It reminded her too that Lucas had not wanted any more children after Olivier and that she nevertheless had gone ahead, wilfully allowing herself to get lax with the birth control.

By the time Lucas returned from making his call, the fete was winding down. He went home with the children and Elizabeth stayed to help clean up. She walked home alone, seeing nothing but fissures and discord in her family, in her marriage.

**

"The Paris sewers don't look anything like the sewers of Vienna, but I couldn't get *The Third Man* and that zither music out of my mind. I kept expecting Orson Welles to appear out of the shadows at any minute," Troy was saying when Elizabeth walked in one evening from work. He and Lucas were sitting near the window, drinking beer.

"If you want a story with the Paris sewers, read *Les Misérables*. Inspector Javert is as sinister a figure as Harry Lime," Lucas said. Caught up in their discussion, they barely acknowledged her entrance.

Suey the cat jumped off the sofa and came to rub herself against Elizabeth's leg.

"No one's fed the cat, I see," said Elizabeth.

After feeding Suey, she went back to the television room. The twins were so riveted to a reality show they didn't even notice their mother entering the room. On the screen, a young man with a shaved head and elaborate tattoos up and down his bare arms was accusing a young woman, whose ears and eyebrow and lower lip were pierced and studded, of infidelities with various other members of their group, two of whom were kissing demonstratively in the background. The studded woman was saying that the tattooed man didn't pay enough attention to her. "Bastard!" she screamed. "You treat me like shit! Do you hear me —a pile of fucking shit!" He screamed back: "You're a whore! A lying, cheating cunt!"

Olivier meanwhile sat across the room at the computer playing a game that must have been lent to him by a friend—Elizabeth refused to spend money on such things. Looking over his shoulder, she could see, at the front of his screen, the end of a simulated machine gun. The screen gave the impression that he, Olivier, was directing the gun and moving quickly through eerily empty office corridors, coming around corners and discovering terrorists, whom he would then shoot and kill with his weapon. Bodies flew against the unmanned reception desk; blood spattered against the white wall, spilled over the blue wall-to-wall carpet.

"Okay," said Elizabeth, trying to control her voice, "that's enough. Off with the screens." The twins moaned and complained but looked for the remote control. Olivier didn't even hear her. "Off, Olivier," she raised her voice. "Off," she said again, even louder. When he finally pressed the pause button and looked up at her with glazed eyes, she added: "Too busy shooting people to feed the cat?"

"Oh. Sorry," he said dully, still under the influence.

"The three of you can lay the table for supper."

"Do we lay a place for Troy?" Ariane asked, skipping out of the room; Elizabeth did not bother to answer.

On the way home, she reflected while re-lining her eyes in the bathroom, she'd been drinking in the summer evening, looking forward to being with her family. Now she wondered why. Who but the cat would care if she stayed away? All the children needed was a computer or a television screen; her husband didn't even notice her arrival as he sat with Troy drinking beer, a beverage he usually eschewed. Next he'll be wearing a baseball cap and watching sports all Saturday afternoon on the television, she thought feeling very sorry for herself indeed.

Later that night she and Lucas had an all-out row.

"Can you tell me," said Lucas as he unbuttoned his shirt,

"why you've had such a sour look on your face all evening long?"

"I come home from work and while you're having a pleasant drink and a chat with Troy about the comparative enchantments of the Paris and Vienna sewers, Olivier's killing terrorists on the computer and the twins are watching a reality show that is completely inappropriate for children their age."

"Can't I sit down and relax for five minutes after a long and strenuous day? Give me a break." He paused sulkily. "You've never complained before."

"Yes, I have."

"Okay. But you've never blamed me before."

"I'm not blaming you now."

"Yes, you are."

"No, I'm not." They were beginning to sound like the children. "I'm just saying the twins need more supervision."

"I can't help thinking," Lucas said, throwing his shirt violently on the chair. "That this is really about Troy. Why don't you just admit it?"

"It's about our children's exposure to smut and violence." Elizabeth almost screamed.

"Then why are we always arguing about him?"

"Because he's around all the time."

"I enjoy his company; he enjoys mine."

"Why? Because he's interested in Paris architecture, right down to its very bowels?"

"As you well know, we talk about many things. Art. Books. His life, which has not been easy." Elizabeth looked up nervously from the mirror, where she had been brushing her hair.

"What?" he asked, standing tense as a rod, his crooked blue vein popping out on his forehead, his fists crammed into the sides of his naked torso.

"Nothing," she said, heart pounding.

Lucas dropped his arms to his side, before throwing them up in the air. "Why am I defending myself? It's ridiculous."

"Look," she said, throwing her dirty clothes into the laundry hamper and trying not to look at the small paunch that Lucas had developed over the last year. "I have nothing against Troy. Nothing at all. I just don't want an outsider quite so present in our family life."

"I know, I know, you haven't got *time* for other people," Lucas said.

"Not for someone who's practically become another family member, no," she said. The paunch looked like rising bread dough over the waistband of his boxer shorts.

Lucas paused while he tucked the legs of his trousers under his chin to re-align the creases. Then turning to the closet to hang them up, he said: "By the way, I've asked him to stay in the flat and look after the cat while we're away in August."

"Well," she huffed, as if that proved her point about his being around all the time.

"I thought you'd be pleased," he said. "You were just complaining about having no one to feed the cat or water the plants."

She didn't answer.

"Come on," he said gently, wrapping his arms around her. "This is really silly."

"Okay," she said, unable, however, to return his embrace.

They got into bed, and Lucas took her hand. Elizabeth closed her eyes but could not sleep. She saw Lucas standing topless, with his fists at his waist. She saw his new little paunch and the chest with the fine, dark hair that she'd always found too fine, too straight. She saw him meticulously tucking his fine-wool trousers under his chin so they wouldn't wrinkle.

Lucas was asleep and snoring almost instantly. Elizabeth slipped her hand out of his and got up. She walked down the corridor past Olivier's and the twins' darkened doors, back to the television and computer room. When she and Lucas were first married, this had been their bedroom and she had moved to their new one, even though it was bigger and lighter, with some regret. Back here now, though, she could not retrieve the feeling of comfort the room used to give her. Not only was it messy, it also had a slightly acrid smell of too many children spending too many hours in it. She turned and left.

In those days, she remembered as she walked back down the corridor, the apartment, bought for Lucas by his parents, was just the one wing of the horseshoe-shaped floor. It had stayed that way until a few years after Olivier was born, when the next-door flat came up for sale, not long after Elizabeth's grandmother had died, leaving her with just enough money in a conveniently depressed real estate market to buy it outright. How they'd laughed at their luck, she thought, entering the part of the apartment that was in her name, the part that now constituted the sitting room, dining room and kitchen.

The last four-room flat, on the other wing, had remained stubbornly in the hands of a cranky old woman. They'd had to wait until three years ago for her to die, at which point Lucas, again with the help of Claude and Isabelle, had snatched it up and converted it into his office, thus completing their kingdom.

In the sitting room, she sat down on the ledge of the open window, leaned her chin on the balustrade and stared at the night sky. At the few stars that managed to make themselves visible, despite the city lights.

They nailed us in with plastic and the world outside was milky and diffuse. There was no fresh air. We stopped going out we ate pizza we played cards until you got into one of your rages and slashed the plastic. We followed. We always followed you. You outlined a plan to get back at that sculptor that Hoyt Thorpe because it was all his fault we were living in plastic. It's a wooden sculpture, you said, an easy target. And it was, it just went whoosh--

She stood up, stepped back from the ledge. While Troy's continued presence in the here and now had made the worst of those unhappy memories fade, sudden flashbacks could still sear across her mind.

Settling back down on the ledge, she wondered if the argument hadn't been caused by the fact that she was no longer seeing Troy one-on-one at the café. Following the Teller's party Troy had, as promised, been hired to help paint an apartment and he started work at eight. These days, only seeing him with her family, meant that some kind of balance had been upset. Did it make her jealous—or was she just worried? Or was Lucas jealous, suspicious of the half-truth she'd told about herself and Troy all those years ago? There was no question that, as the pressure of their legs under the café table, the nudging of shoulders and the occasional holding of hands attested to, the attraction was still very much alive. And she always had the feeling that Lucas, sensitive Lucas, sensed something, even if he couldn't identify it.

Whoever was jealous or suspicious of whom, they didn't usually argue like this. She wished that Troy would just leave, that their life could go back to normal.

***

After that row, as if he'd sensed the friction he was causing, Troy did stop passing by the rue Laromiguière. Neither Elizabeth nor Lucas mentioned his absence, though it hung in the air with all the weight of an ugly and awkward piece of new furniture.

One evening as she crossed the place de l'Estrapade on the way home from work, Troy walked out of the *boulangerie*. He paused, tore off the end of the baguette and popped it in his mouth. He didn't see her standing under the shade of the leafy chestnuts and she watched him, one graceful knee bent, lost in thought, while he chewed. Then, sensing someone's eyes on him, he straightened, cocked his head and looked her way. She stepped forward, out of the shadows.

"Hey," he said smiling.

"I haven't seen much of you recently," she said, shading her eyes from the ray of sun.

"No. The paint job finished today." He showed her the bottle of wine he was carrying in his rucksack. "Would you like to celebrate with me?"

She looked at her watch. It wasn't that late. It was a beautiful summer evening; school was over; supper could wait. "Why not. I'd like to see your room."

"I think I'm the only person living up here right now. It's always dead quiet," he said as he unlocked the door. The dormer window was open; a chair sat on the small balcony. "Here we are. My little kingdom. It faces northeast and gets some good sun in the morning," he said, almost proudly.

"It's very light and cheery, even now."

There was a single bed, with a duvet spread neatly over the top. Some shelves behind, where Troy had lined up his books and folded his clothes. On the table were two of his sculptures, placed as if they kept him company while he ate his meals. Olivier's old guitar, which he'd lent to Troy for the duration of his stay in Paris, was propped up next to the window.

"The woman's been really nice to me, lending me bedding and kitchen stuff." There was also a corner with a tiny kitchen sink and electric cooker, as well as a shower stall.

"Is this a yoga mat?" she asked. "I thought you did judo."

"I switched to yoga. Thought something less combative would be better for my soul," he laughed, then suddenly serious: "I like to think it helps control that temper of mine. Let's have some wine."

While he took a Swiss army knife from his pocket to uncork the bottle, she looked at the books. Amidst several contemporary American novels were the Paris reference books Lucas had lent him. There was also a copy of *Swann's Way*.

"You've been reading Proust," she said.

"Lucas gave it to me." The bottle gave a soft pop as he pulled out the cork. "At first, I found it too precious—this sickly guy who's hung up on his mother. But then I got into the rhythm of it. He's also very astute."

"Mmm," Elizabeth said.

When he handed her a tumbler of wine, he stood very close.

"You've got paint in your hair," she said.

"Where?" he put his hand to his head.

"No, here, on the other side," she said putting her finger on a brick red glob. He put his hand on top of hers, pulled hers down and held on.

"Let's see if we can fit two chairs out here."

They sat encased by the zinc balcony, looking over the iron railing to the dome of the Pantheon.

"How incredibly peaceful," said Elizabeth. The din of traffic was well below them. Swifts darted and swooped silently across the summer sky.

"You know," he said, resting his elbows on his knees. "I don't think I've ever been happier than right here, on this little balcony. Everything's at a comfortable distance."

"And right now is the perfect time of day during the perfect time of year."

"It's hard to beat," he said, as he wrapped his arm around her shoulder and looked at her with those hungry brown eyes. "Did you know that you're more beautiful now than you were when you were twenty?"

"It's the soft light of evening, I assure you," she laughed.

"No. It's not." And he pulled her face toward his and very gently kissed her. The glasses of wine were put down; they stood up, the city humming beneath them, the birds darting above them. The kiss lasted a long, long time and the twenty-five intervening years melted away. Troy pulled away and said: "I'm going to Berlin in a few days."

She nodded, uncertain if this was meant as encouragement or dissuasion, but the pause sobered her up enough to think about the hour, about Lucas, about her four children waiting to eat.

"I should get home." She looked down, said very quietly: "But first I should say—"

He put his finger to her mouth to stop her. "This is my little moment in my little paradise," he said. "Don't ruin it."

At the door, they kissed again. Finally Elizabeth managed to pull herself away and stagger home.

***

Like all good French grandparents, Isabelle and Claude Teller did their bit to lighten the load of their working children by taking their grandchildren for a couple of weeks every summer. As they had done with young Tristan and Olivier, they were taking Gabby and Ariane to the house in the Lubéron, a house that had been designed by Lucas. Elizabeth was mightily grateful, since her own mother, who still lived in London, made noises about helping with the children but had never actually spent more than two consecutive hours alone with them.

She climbed the majestic stairway of the elder Teller's building on the rue de Tournon and rang the bell. Isabelle opened the large door onto their airy apartment and as always, Elizabeth had the feeling of being greeted not just by the person opening the door but also by the missing sister Coco: her painting, large and bold and vibrant, framed the person standing at the entrance.

"Hello, hello," Isabelle said, bending down to kiss her grandchildren, then her daughter-in-law. "Come into the drawing room. Alix and the children are already here."

"You can't just forget about his early life before he got to New York," Alix was saying into the phone. "He was steeped in the European tradition. He was trained here." She wandered out of the room.

"The editor is trying to cut out part of her article," said Isabelle, then to Gabby and Ariane: "Gaspard and Juliette are in the back." The twins scampered off to see their cousins.

"Here are the bags. There should be a week's worth of clothes for each of them."

"They won't need much. I imagine they'll spend most of the day around the swimming pool. It's supposed to be very hot."

"Now that they know how to swim, it should be easier for

you."

"They're never a problem," Isabelle said, looking toward Alix as she walked back in, punching the phone off with a stab of her finger. "So?"

"I've agreed to tighten up a section. But not to cut it out."

"Bravo," said Isabelle. The two of them sat side by side on the sofa. Though Alix had inherited the sharpness of Claude's features and therefore lacked her mother's soft beauty, the resemblance around the eyes and high foreheads remained strong. They were very close too; Alix appeared to tell her mother everything and at times—such as this moment—it seemed the two of them hardly needed words to communicate.

Elizabeth never told anyone in her family anything. Reticence, interlaced with the occasional innuendo, was the only known medium of communication among the Lyalls, and it was amazing, really, that she could have married into such an intense stronghold of a family. Today, however, her footing within that fortified unit felt shaky. She let her children go play during the party; she was not even standing with the rest of them at the toast. She was, after all—as Alix herself had pointed out—a foreigner. If she suddenly disappeared for one reason or another, wouldn't the Teller's refined world, after a short period of mild remorse, go on quite happily without her?

It was a terrifying thought.

It was a thought that she couldn't quite shake all afternoon as she tried to finish a book for an editorial meeting the next day, and it was compounded by how isolated she was feeling at work. Her little office at the end of the corridor, which used to feel so cosy and secure, now felt more like a storage closet everyone had forgotten about. It seemed hardly anyone came to see her down there anymore and when she emerged, she felt shy, almost intrusive. At editorial meetings, she would sit mutely at the large round table while authors she had not heard of or didn't like were praised and strategies for securing them were developed. When Elizabeth did dare open her mouth, her voice sounded small; she was afraid she might stutter. Meanwhile Lucille, who was consulted at every turn, looked more radiant every day and Elizabeth wondered once again about her and Gérard. When Lucille had first arrived, she had been a little on the stocky side. Was it *only* trips to the gym, a regular squash date and a French diet that were behind the new glow? In any case, one thing was certain: Elizabeth, who had given up the gym when the twins were born, went home every evening feeling a little older, a little more slumped and defeated.

The old fear that underneath it all she was a loser was raising its ugly head. Although she'd been a good student at school, had been considered a clever girl, she had never been first in her form and then had badly under-performed on her A-Levels, which she'd sat not long after her parents' separation. She had never been particularly popular either and had been miserable at the college until she met Troy. With him and Sally and John, things seemed to improve. Disaffected or not, they were a group and Troy showed her how to have fun. He exposed her not just to the pleasures of drink, drugs and sex, but more important, to the joys of mischief, of flouting rules and not taking things too seriously. When all that had literally gone up in smoke, she'd left the college once again feeling a loser—and a bad person to boot.

In Paris she seemed to have left that persona behind. In this city where she had no history, where not fitting in was the very definition of an ex-pat, she felt immediately at home. She quickly met other people, went out all the time, and after two years was introduced to Lucas. With his elegant clothes and long, strong face, his thoughtful intelligence and his well-placed connections, he'd appeared to be no less than a prince charming; she'd felt touched by a fairy's wand.

But magic spells can run their course, especially when they aren't deserved in the first place. With Troy's arrival, she worried that the bad-person-loser was back. As her good luck ran out, so her veneer of self-confidence was being stripped away, leaving her exposed and fearful.

To top it off, she and Lucas had not been communicating—disputes left dangling had not been resolved or forgotten—and she approached the fish restaurant where they were meeting for supper with trepidation. Lucas was already there, bent over the table reading, the bald spot on the crown of his head beaming at her.

"Hello," she said, and he looked up with a start.

"Oh," he answered. "You surprised me."

"Why? Weren't you expecting me?" she laughed as she slid into her seat.

"I was lost in this book." He removed his glasses and rubbed his eyes. "Faulkner." He held up a copy of *Absalom, Absalom*. Even his face looked a different shape—somehow even longer—without his glasses. "Troy bought it for me."

"Ah," she said, putting the napkin in her lap. She propped her elbows on the table, rested her chin on her fists: "What do you think of it?"

"Astounding," he put the glasses back on. "Absolutely riveting."

"You aren't having trouble with the style?"

"A little. But he bought it for me in French, which helps. And I cheated a bit. I looked it up on the internet."

"I'm glad you're enjoying it."

"I wouldn't say 'enjoying'. The story and the characters are too tragic."

"True," she said, opening the menu. "I'm surprised he didn't give you *The Sound and the Fury*. It's better known."

"He said he liked this one better."

"Ah." *Books about fires and family secrets—what does that mean? What in fact are you trying to do, kissing me and giving Lucas books? What am I doing…*

"Elizabeth," Lucas said as the waiter arrived. "Time to order."

"Sorry. Of course," she said.

As the waiter left, Lucas asked: "Did you get the twins off all right?"

"Just fine." Elizabeth paused. "Alix was there too, which reminded me of something she told me the other day. Something I never knew about you."

"And what could that be?" he asked with a wry smile.

"That you used to have an imaginary friend called Steve."

"Steve," he said, shaking his head. "I haven't thought about Steve in years and years."

"How on earth did a little French boy make up a friend called Steve?"

"He was a real person. Originally, at least. An American boy in my class for a year—then his family moved away again. His French was terrible but in the courtyard during recreation, he was a star. I remember he tried to teach us to throw a ball—you know how we French never know how to throw because we're too busy kicking footballs. I thought he was very cool. When he left France, I decided to keep him alive." Lucas, still smiling, shook his head. "Steve and I travelled far and wide together."

Their food came and as Elizabeth stuck her fork into the lemon and squeezed it over the thin slices of raw tuna, she asked: "With the twins gone and Tristan and Olivier leaving in a few days, shall we try to have some fun these next couple weeks?"

"I don't know," he said. "I've got so much work and I let my assistant go away for a couple of extra weeks. He just got married. It was probably a mistake." He leaned back in his seat, crossed his arms across his chest. "I shouldn't have been so generous. I've got a few small jobs to finish up, plus Rouen, and those people aren't happy with anything I give them."

"Have you tried to pin them down on exactly what it is they want?"

"Of course. But they don't really know what they want," he said. "There's the added problem that they have no taste."

"Like all politicians and town planners," she said with a smile at the complaint she'd heard so often.

"True," he nodded, throwing a long arm up in the air. "They keep pushing me to make more of a big, showy statement. But I want something that blends in," he smoothed the air with his hand. "Something that makes sense with the city's history, with the surroundings."

"Same old story," she said.

"Same old story," he said. "But this time it's especially important, given that the first exhibition, the one that's already on the calendar, is the history of Rouen, from the Celts to the Romans to Joan of Arc to the Second World War. You see, I want to mix a lot of wood and glass, to recall the city's half-timbered houses and the centre's position on the Seine."

"And they want?"

"Soaring concrete, preferably asymmetrically cobbled together." He flung his arm up in the air again.

"They did, after all, accept your project," she said.

"But now they keep pushing me from my original model. They seem to want something to tower obtrusively over the rest of the ugly post-war architecture."

"Despite the bombing it's still quite a charming little town, isn't it?"

"They've made the best of what there is with the old buildings in the town centre. But minus the Joan of Arc church, the modern stuff is dismal. I discovered an interesting fact, though." Lucas always read extensively about the setting for his work and now he leaned forward over his plate, almost as if he were about to share a tawdry bit of gossip. "Half the town was burned before any bombs fell on it. There was a fire at the beginning of the war, when a French and a German tank collided. It took ten days to extinguish. The city seemed destined for a fiery end one way or another." He wiped his mouth with his napkin. "Even the church spire somehow set fire during that big wind storm a couple years ago. Anyway, I'm going day after tomorrow for a couple of days."

"That's too bad."

"Yes, but they've given me an apartment to stay in. It's not a bad set-up. A bedroom, a sitting room and a kitchen area, plus it's got a terrific view over the Seine." He laughed. "The last time I was there, someone had even put food in the fridge."

"Tasteless but attentive to detail," she said. "The very definition of a dutiful bureaucrat."

"Exactly," he laughed again.

Their main courses arrived. Elizabeth began twisting the pasta around her fork, stabbing a shrimp. Lucas cut his sole down the middle and lifted the strips of fish gently off the bone.

"What about post-Rouen?" she asked.

"There's one competition in England and one in Berlin," he said. "I'm hoping. This Rouen project is getting a lot of attention." Somehow Lucas had not been able to break beyond the French market in any significant way. There had been several near wins and it had become such a sensitive subject that she only referred to it obliquely.

"You'll see. One day," said Elizabeth, who believed fully in his talent and knew that it was mainly his integrity that got in the way. In designing a building, Lucas never lost sight of its function or the fact that his primary responsibility was to the human beings who would use or inhabit it, and not to the glorification of his own artistic ego.

"There is a move, in certain circles, against flashy statements. A renewed interest in natural materials. Maybe you're right. Architecture has its fashions just like everything else."

The waiter cleared their plates; Lucas said: "But tell me what's happening with your work these days. Are you still worried about that other woman? What's her name?"

"Lucille. Yes. I'm still worried," she said, crossing her arms against her chest. "Worried, in fact, generally about losing my touch. Worried that maybe I'm, so to speak, going out of fashion."

"Why do you say that?"

"My last couple of books have not sold well."

"Everybody gets it wrong sometimes."

"But these days there's less room for error. Our new

management wants a one hundred per cent success rate."

"Every story has to have a happy ending?" Lucas said, with an ironic smile.

Elizabeth laughed. "Only the real-life story, that bottom line. The fictitious ones should end badly. A teenage shooting spree is always a good idea, especially if it allows for the revelation of an earlier case of child abuse. Terrorists sell well too."

"Good and evil in no uncertain terms, right?" Lucas laughed happily and heartily; Elizabeth felt re-assured. If they could just get through these next few weeks, fly off to Nantucket—by the time they returned, Troy would be gone and maybe everything would go back to the way it had been.

They made love that night with unusual appetite. Though it had been at least a month, that wasn't an overly long time lapse for them. Elizabeth attributed her urgency to that balcony kiss, which had left her body in a constant thrum, almost an ache, of desire. But she wondered about Lucas, what could be making him so predatory. She hoped it wasn't suspicion and jealousy, a semi-conscious attempt to re-assert his male authority.

**

Two days later Lucas went to Rouen. The day after that Tristan left for piano classes in the Alps and Olivier for a language programme in Hamburg. After saying good-bye to the boys, Elizabeth dropped a note for Troy with the building's concierge on her way to work. She suggested he come over for a bite to eat that evening, before he left for Berlin.

As she laid out the slices of smoked salmon, she reminded herself that this invitation had nothing to do with what had happened on that balcony. No. This was her last chance to apologize. To bring things out in the open.

Finally she was going to muster the courage to speak up.

The bell rang; she jumped.

He held a bottle of champagne and had a shy, almost boyish

smile on his broad face.

"Hey," he said, sticking it in front of him.

"That's a treat," she said, taking the bottle and kissing him on both cheeks, just as she would any friend. "You shouldn't have."

"I'm feeling flush. In fact, even after my trip to Berlin, I'm likely to go home with euros in my pocket. So I thought I'd spend a few tonight."

"I'll let you open it," she said, going to get the glasses.

They sat down on opposite sides of the coffee table. Troy pulled out the cork and the compressed bubbles made a deep, vaporous thud as they were released from the bottle. He poured. "Cheers," they said, raising their glasses slightly.

Elizabeth put her glass down on the table and looked across at Troy. These months in Paris had obviously suited him—he looked relaxed and happy, somehow looser. She picked up his sculpture from the table, rubbed her hand over its smooth surface.

"It really is lovely." She thought of the two sculptures she'd seen sitting on the table in his room. "Have you got a lot of work done since you've been here?"

"Not that much. Enough. I've had other priorities."

Continuing to focus intently on the sculpture in her hand and remembering the book he had bought for Lucas, she asked quietly: "Why did you come here?"

"Curiosity, mostly. To see how your life turned out. And maybe in so doing to bring things full circle, in my mind at least."

She put the statue back down on the table, then said in a choked voice: "I've been meaning to say," she paused, began again, barely audible: "I wanted you to come tonight... I wanted to say sorry. For then...for..." With her throat constricting and the tears welling up and spilling over her hot cheeks, she couldn't finish.

For a moment, face frozen and serious, he just twirled the thin stem of the champagne glass in his hand. "It's true," he finally said, "that when I first came here, I wanted to extract an apology. But then I started enjoying myself so much, I was no longer sure that I wanted to have the past dredged up." Suddenly seeming to cheer up, he said with a hint of playful smile: "So maybe I should be thanking you for letting me into your life like you have."

She wiped her cheek with the back of her hand, thinking about all her recent arguments with Lucas, and felt ashamed all over again. "I haven't done anything. Really."

"You've got, like, a perfect family. A perfect life." He shook his head: "I haven't been able to get enough of it."

"I know," she said quietly, "I know that you wanted something like this for yourself. I'm sorry it didn't happen."

"Yea, well..." he said. The empty champagne glass dangled from between his legs. He refilled his glass, topped up Elizabeth's, perked up again. "Really, when I think about this trip —it's been far above and beyond anything I could have imagined. I never thought that I could feel so free. Not just from responsibility and my whole real-life life. But also from memory —from all the bad stuff that's ever happened to me. It's like I've been floating around in a soap bubble."

"I'm glad of that, at least."

"Being here in Paris, you see," he stared at her with those black-hole eyes, "has helped me understand how you left things behind. This city seduces you, it lulls you into forgetting what is ugly and unpleasant."

"A fine excuse," she said. After a minute: "How did you find me? I managed to escape the tentacles of the alumni office years ago."

"How do you think? The internet. I remembered your father was a journalist. I found a Who's Who in Journalism site and looked him up. His entry conveniently had both your sister's and your married names—it even said you lived in Paris. I got the Paris phone book on line and then I had the addresses of Lucas' whole family. When I did a search with your married name, there you were on a list of literati. But the hotel overlooking the amphitheatre—that was just luck. I chose it from a guidebook and one day I looked out my window and there you were. I couldn't believe it."

"Well," she said quietly, "you certainly surprised me."

"With a minimum of information it's easy to locate people who succeed in the world." He put his glass down on the table. "It's nobodies, like me or my father, who can hide."

"What about your father?"

"Once I tried very hard to find him. I went all the way out to Mount Hood, Oregon, to the ten-year old address that my uncle gave me. It was a nice little house. I asked around. He'd been married again. I don't know if there were children. Other children, I should say. They'd moved on, with no forwarding address. Now my uncle's dead and my aunt's moved to a retirement home. My father, if he's still alive, would have no way of finding me, even if one day he suddenly decided he wanted to. Though I guess that's a stupid thought—he got another life and made it pretty clear that he wasn't interested in what happened to the old one."

Both of their glasses were empty. The bottle was sweating on the table. He looked up at her with a smile that half-exposed his crooked teeth: "But we're supposed be enjoying ourselves, not getting all intense." He slapped his knees. "I'm hungry. Let's eat."

He followed her into the small space of the kitchen. She poured them each more champagne, put the bottle in the fridge, cut some lemon for the salmon. Troy leaned against the other counter, arms across his chest, watching. While she was dressing the salad, he stepped the two steps across the floor and leaned into her, pinning her body to the counter. They were exactly the same height—they had measured once, back to back—and their two bodies fit together like jigsaw pieces; his lips were level with her ear when his breath tickled it, before his tongue entered it. "Liza."

She half sighed, half moaned and once again the time in

between melted away as he led her to the sofa in the living room. He didn't take his shirt off and she didn't object. She just let herself go, abandoning herself entirely to his transcendent sensuality, to his uncanny, almost feminine, instinct for the right places to touch.

"Wow," she said afterwards. "That was—"

He stopped her with a kiss and: "I'm leaving early tomorrow. I have to pack."

"You don't want to eat?"

"I don't think so," he said quietly. "Sorry. It's really time for me to go."

She walked him to the door where he kissed her one long, last time.

"Good-bye, Liza," he said, disappearing into the dark corridor.

Closing the door quietly, she leaned against it for quite some time. Then she went to throw away the food for which she no longer had an appetite either.

***

"How could they do that?" Elizabeth asked, standing in the entry hall, her bag full of books over one shoulder and her portable computer over the other, a white cardboard box containing a strawberry tart balanced on her left hand. "Nothing is supposed to happen in France during the month of August."

"I warned you about this months ago. Before I even got the commission."

"I guess that's right," she said. "Well, I certainly didn't think they'd ever really do it."

"The building has to be ready for the exhibition at the end of next year and we're already way behind schedule. So they've announced a meeting."

"But they've known about this holiday since the beginning."

He shrugged. "I'll get there a few days after all of you. At least they're paying the difference on my changed plane ticket."

Elizabeth dropped her bags on the floor while still balancing the tart on her hand. Until this moment, she'd been feeling a great lightness, despite the heavy summer heat. She was about to go on holiday with her family and Troy was about to disappear from her life, she hoped forever this time. Despite what had happened between them and her constant replaying of the scenes in her mind, her overriding feeling this evening on the way home from work had been immense relief that within twenty-four hours, this unnerving, nerve-racking visit would be over. Real life would go back to normal, without any real damage having been done. The good memories—the ones from the balcony or their living room floor—could be treated like a box of chocolates, dipped into and indulged in whenever she fancied, then closed up and put back on the shelf.

Now Lucas was staying behind with Troy and the idea of just the two of them, filled her with dread, made her want to collapse in a heap on the floor.

Half dropping the tart on the kitchen counter, she started putting the rest of supper together and reasoned with herself that Lucas would be working or in Rouen most of the time. *And if you had intended to tell Lucas something, wouldn't you have already done so? I don't know, I don't know—for some reason I can't quite explain, I have a terrible, terrified feeling about these extra days.*

She called Lucas and the children and while the family ate their meal and discussed preparations for the trip, she did her best to sound unaffected by Lucas' deferred departure, to mask how completely undone she felt by it. Just as Elizabeth had released the children from cleaning up so that they could go pack, the bell rang.

Lucas said: "I'll get it."

Elizabeth, who was slightly closer, said: "That's all right. I'll go."

There he was, rucksack on his back. "Hello," she said, sounding too jolly. "We've finished eating but we did save you some tart."

"Great," he said, bending his knees as he shrugged off the heavy bag onto the floor in the entry hall.

"You have a reprieve," said Elizabeth as she led him into the dining room. "Lucas has to stay on for a few days and there's really no need for you to come until then."

"But I have to be out of my room by tomorrow," he said. "I have to leave the keys with the concierge before she goes away on vacation."

"You can stay here," said Lucas. "There's plenty of room. You won't be any bother to me—I'm going to Rouen day after tomorrow anyway."

"Thanks." Troy was served a large wedge of tart, and he tucked into it hungrily. "This is good. Berlin was fascinating but German food, I have to say, doesn't hold a candle."

Lucas said: "I'm eager to hear about your trip. You can tell me about it tomorrow evening. Now I must get some work done. Excuse me." And with one of his formal little bows, he left for his office. At the door he turned around: "Come any time. I'll be here working all day."

When they were alone, Elizabeth tried to sound neutral, even business-like: "Let me show you what to do for the cat."

"Good idea," said Troy.

There they were, back at the counter, side by side. "You just give her some of these." As she lifted the bag of *croquettes,* Troy smiled at her. "And a small spoonful from one of these tins mixed in. And make sure she has some water."

"Doesn't sound too difficult." He picked up the tin. "*Terrine de poulet et aux légumes provençales.* Even the cat food here sounds like a gourmet meal."

"Wait 'til you smell it," she said. "Speaking of which," and she pulled away, went out the door, around the corner, to the even smaller laundry area next to the back door.

"This has to be cleaned out every couple of days." Elizabeth crouched over the cat's box and with a large plastic slotted spoon and scooped the excrement and urine into a plastic bag. Her haunch bumped Troy's leg. He did not back up and she made no effort to move forward.

Still crouched over the box, leaning against Troy's leg, she tied a knot in the plastic bag and stood up, faced him. "I just changed the litter and rinsed out the box yesterday. Would you mind doing the same once while we're gone? I hate to ask you to do that but even with daily attention it gets disgusting."

"I don't mind at all. Really."

"Good. I forget that not every male has Lucas' aversion to Suey's box."

Troy said nothing but looked at her so intently she felt every pore of her face was being individually examined.

"What about the plants," Troy finally said, pulling away.

"Easier than the cat but not as affectionate," she said, desperately trying to stay light-hearted.

As usual when they went away, she had regrouped all the plants by one window in the living room for the sake of whomever had been enlisted to water them during their absence.

"You've got quite a collection," said Troy. "I hadn't realized."

"Usually they're spread out around the apartment. It just looks like a lot all together."

"A real jungle," said Troy, bending over one and touching a leaf.

"They need water every four or five days in this summer heat."

Another moment of silence.

"So," Elizabeth finally said and they walked to the entry hall.

"I won't see you tomorrow morning," he whispered, stepping eagerly towards her, encircling her in arms that were solid as bars of steel. "So this is it." And they kissed one more time, until a noise made them pull apart abruptly.

"Good bye," she said, rather too loudly.

"Good bye, Liza," he whispered back.

Instead of feeling happy and relaxed on the way to Nantucket, Elizabeth was short-tempered and edgy, snapping at the children for silly things such as tapping their knees to the music from their Discmans or playing with their tray tables.

Liza Liza. Lies, lies, lies.

When she fell asleep on the plane, she dreamed that the engines had caught fire, that they were about to burn alive. She woke up saying: "What's happened? What's happened?"

"Nothing," said Olivier. "Chill out," he added in English. "We're supposed to be relaxing. We're on holiday, remember?"

While they were waiting to change planes in Boston, Ariane asked what that was on the television screen. "It's baseball," Gabby said proudly but with a thick French accent so it came out bai-ze-bowl.

"They have funny costumes," said Ariane.

"Uniforms," said Gabby.

"They look like pyjamas."

"It's a good game," said Elizabeth, feeling very far away, as she remembered how before, before everything had gone wrong, they had played softball at the college. It had always been a lot of fun. Although she could never quite remember the rules, she had liked the ritual, the way everyone came together in the spring air, drinking beer and milling about. She had liked watching Troy too, his fluid body when he threw the ball. Every time he came to bat, the fielders would scuttle way back, usually to no avail. He almost always managed to hit the ball between or beyond them.

Elizabeth's sister Molly was waiting for them as they emerged from the tiny plane at the Nantucket airport.

"How was the trip then?" Molly said in a pure English accent, not at all like Elizabeth's, which could veer from British to American within the space of a sentence and fluctuated according to the person she was with.

"Long," said Elizabeth, kissing her sister hello and smiling. Molly's remarkably pretty face and cheery, familiar presence were comforting, re-assuring. Suddenly she felt better. Maybe she didn't need to worry about Lucas and Troy in Paris after all.

"It's such a shame Lucas isn't with you," Molly said. "But look at you boys!" she said grabbing Tristan, then Olivier, who received her embraces like megaliths. "And the twins!" She grabbed each in turn. After the luggage arrived they walked out to the parking lot. Molly swung around to pick them up in the largest passenger vehicle any of them had ever seen. The deep green monster had darkened windows and a motor with a whir not unlike the four-engine jet that had just flown them across the Atlantic.

"I can't get in one of these things," Tristan whispered in French. "It is directly contributing to the destruction of our planet."

"I'd like to drive one of them," said Olivier.

"You can't drive," said Ariane.

"Would you all be quiet please," whispered Elizabeth, "and just get in the car. In the vehicle." To her sister she said in what she hoped was a jaunty tone: "Certainly no shortage of space here."

"You can't imagine how much time I spend in the car," her sister said. "It's my office." She pointed to the mobile phone installation next to the automatic gearshift.

"Even your Range Rover will seem positively minute when you move back," said Elizabeth.

"We'll adjust," she said, craning her blonde head forward. The great thing about Molly, Elizabeth thought as they pulled out into the main road, is that she will always adjust. When her husband Gerald had announced that they would be moving to the States for three years, she had thrown herself into the project, going over to look for a house and a school for Robin, Charlotte and Thomas, her three young children. The family lived in New Jersey and Gerald commuted every day to his job in New York.

Now they were planning to move back to England at the end of the next school year—just in time for Robin to go to boarding school—and Molly thought that was perfect too.

"So children," Molly called from the driver's seat. "Ready for some time at the beach?"

"Yes," the twins answered. Elizabeth could feel the older two bristling at being called children, at Molly's effusive manner, and she wished she could turn around and defend her sister to them.

"How's the house?" she asked Molly instead.

"Big. And clean. It's almost brand new."

"It looks like most of the houses are brand new," said Elizabeth. "There's building wherever you look. What a change."

"You know, I calculated that it was twenty-eight years ago the last time we were here with Mum and Dad," Molly said.

"Huh," said Elizabeth, marvelling at how easily Mum and Dad rolled off Molly's tongue, as if their parents were still together, when in fact that last trip to Nantucket had been taken the summer before the divorce.

As they drove down the long, straight Milestone Road, across the scrubby moor, Elizabeth got an uneasy feeling in her stomach. It was along this road that their mother had taken her and Molly to tennis lessons in 'Sconset and she remembered how both of them had hated tennis. Not only were all the other children better, more experienced players; she and Molly were also clad in white socks that came too far up their calves and Plimsoles rather than the Keds everyone else was wearing. She remembered a boy saying to them: "You talk funny." And Molly crossing her arms and retorting: "Well, so do you." At that moment, driving along Milestone Road, the flavour of the three Lyall summer holidays in Nantucket was reduced in her mind to the tennis. The fact that her parents didn't even play and that she and Molly were hopeless.

It struck Elizabeth now, as they turned down Tom Nevers Road, that it was typical of her family to choose a place no one had much liked. And that in making holiday plans for this summer, they all would have conveniently forgotten or ignored this vital fact.

They turned again, down a sandy lane with new houses and identical gardens on either side.

"At least the new houses all seem to be that cedar-siding style. At least they're not ugly," Elizabeth added.

"We're down at the end," said Molly.

"That's good," said Elizabeth.

As their vehicle swung into the driveway, Elizabeth saw her mother standing on the front porch, book and crossword puzzle tucked into her arm. Having recently been diagnosed with osteoporosis, Vera looked hunched and frail, tentative and startled, and Elizabeth wondered how it was possible no one had noticed that she had shrunk a full five inches.

"Hello, hello," she said as they all piled out of the car. "You've all grown even since Easter. Of course I've probably shrunk." Each child filed past with a kiss and a Hello, Granny—or in the case of Gabby and Ariane—a 'Ello G-r-rann-i-e. "What a shame about Lucas," she said to Elizabeth, who now had to bend over to reach her mother's soft, fair cheek.

"He'll be here in three days."

"In any case," her mother continued, "it's good to see you. You haven't come to London much recently. We've missed you."

"I know. I haven't been travelling much lately."

"Well I'll be interested to hear if you have any good books for me to read. This one," she said, raising the one in her hand, "is junk. I can't imagine why it's had such good press. Anyway, I'm glad you're all here. Cy has abandoned me."

"He's just gone to the golf course, Mum," said Molly.

"Any game that takes so long to play should be viewed as a form of abandonment," said Vera.

Baggage was unloaded and moved into the house. Downstairs there were several bedrooms and a television room. Upstairs was an open space going right up to the rafters, with only partial walls separating the kitchen from the dining and the sitting areas. There was one large terrace with a view over the moor and a smaller one with a barbecue and a picnic table. It was very light and spacious.

Tristan and Olivier were to sleep on the mezzanine above the dining room and Gabby and Ariane were to be separated, each sleeping with cousins of the same sex. Maybe, Elizabeth thought, some improvement to her children's English would occur. Maybe, as Molly said out loud, some family connection would be established. Because mostly when Elizabeth had gone to London and seen her mother and stepfather, she had been travelling alone for work. She had seen Molly a couple of times in New York and once in New Jersey but again during business trips. The last time the cousins had seen one another was briefly in Paris two years earlier and they'd acted like strangers. "They *are* strangers, Elizabeth," Lucas had said.

This was in fact the first time they'd tried an all-family holiday. All-family minus Elizabeth and Molly's father Andrew and his second wife, Pru, and her children. Vera's second husband, Cy's one unmarried daughter, Gretchen, was to be included in the present sub-group for a few days at the end.

"This looks great," Elizabeth said to her mother and sister as they stepped out onto the deck facing the ocean that they couldn't quite see beyond the low shrubs of the moor. She squinted in the sun and shaded her eyes. A sea breeze softened and cooled the air. She took a deep breath. "Wonderful."

"It is, isn't," said her mother.

"One good memory I have from here is long and peaceful walks," said Elizabeth. "On the moor especially."

"Well you'll have to be careful now," said Molly, her large blue eyes getting larger. "Apparently the island's full of ticks and lots of them carry Lyme disease."

"That's too bad," said Elizabeth.

"We just need to be careful and check the children and ourselves regularly. Listen," Molly looked towards the door. "That car must be Gerald and the children coming back from the beach. I told them not to linger."

The front door burst open and Molly's children exploded into the house. "Leave your sandy things out front," she called to them. Then to Elizabeth: "You'll see—keeping the sand out of the house is a constant battle."

***

"Here you go, sir," Gerald said to Cy a few hours later as they gathered on the large deck. "Nothing better for what ails you."

"Just what the doctor ordered," Cy said, with a slight bow, as he received the gin and tonic. "Thank you, sire." He was a banker who years ago had been sent by his Wall Street firm to London. When his wife had divorced him and moved back to New York with their daughter Gretchen, he had stayed on. Not long after, he had met Vera and the two had been married within a year.

"Just fruit juice for me," Vera said, closing her eyes with a long-suffering tilt of her pretty head. "Only a little wine with dinner. Alcohol doesn't mix well with my medication."

"Here you go, Mum," said Molly, "a glass of non-alcoholic apple cider, straight from Bartlett's Farm, right here on the island."

"Thank you," she said sanctimoniously, holding the glass in her knobby hands between her white-trousered knees.

"Cheers," said Gerald, whose face, with its ruddy complexion, cleft chin and strong nose couldn't have been anything but English. He was dressed, however, more like a New Englander, in Nantucket red trousers, a whale belt and tasselled loafers. "Wonderful spot," he continued, leaning back in his chair and crossing one leg on top of the other. His exposed bare ankle, usually smothered and abraded by a business sock, was as smooth and white as a scrubbed turnip. "So Lizzie. How's Paris treating you?"

"Well," said Elizabeth, shifting, almost wriggling, in her seat.

She'd forgotten how foreign she could feel when talking about herself to members of her own family. "Lots of work, as always."

"I have to say," said Gerald, passing a hand over his wavy, sandy hair, "from what we see on the telly, it's sometimes hard to imagine anyone getting any work done over there. The place looks perpetually paralysed by protests of one sort or another. And what's the working week now? Thirty hours?"

"Thirty-five actually," said Elizabeth tartly. "Still a classic nine to five day, if the French counted the lunch hour into the equation, as the Americans do."

"The way I see it," said Cy, dispensing dry-roasted peanuts in his mouth from his fist, "is that they're still a bunch of lazy, ungrateful punks. What they need is a Ronald Reagan. A Maggie Thatcher." Elizabeth looked at Tristan, who was sitting with the adults on the deck, rather than with the children in front of the television. He was looking at his step-grandfather's small round head with the thin grey hair plastered to it, in startled bewilderment.

"The children look great, Lizzie," said Molly. "I wouldn't have recognized Olivier. When's the last time I saw him?"

"Two years ago. He was still a little boy then, that's right."

"And you, Tristan," Gerald said sibilantly. "You'll be finished with school soon, won't you?"

"Yes, I will," Tristan answered, hardly above a whisper.

"Then you'll be off to university," said Molly. "You lot are all so clever." Neither she nor Gerald had been to university. Molly had done a secretarial course and Gerald had trained as a chartered accountant.

Tristan nodded and his cheeks reddened.

"He's hoping for a place in what they call a *prépa*," Elizabeth said, coming to his rescue. "They are preparatory courses that lead on to the best universities. Sort of—they're not really universities. More like advanced schools. *Grandes écoles*, is what they're called. The French system is complicated. It's hard to explain."

Cy harrumphed and swirled the ice around in his glass.

"Not going to follow in your mother's footsteps and go to America, then?" asked Gerald.

"We couldn't afford that," Elizabeth laughed. Then, because of course Gerald could: "He's happy in the French system, which is cheap and excellent in its way."

"Unlike the taxes and the labour, I guess," said Cy.

"Cy, please," said Vera.

"Liz knows I'm just teasing," Cy said. "Just poking fun at her soft spot for those bleeding heart liberals."

"New York's certainly got its share of bleeding hearts," said Gerald, shaking his leonine head. "Not surprising, I guess. The place is run and overrun by the bloody you-know-who's."

Elizabeth flinched but Tristan had fortunately gone inside.

"It's really surprised us," said Molly. "The children get all the Jewish holidays off from school but not Good Friday or anything Christian."

"Even Christmas is verboten," Gerald said. "For that I'll be glad to get my feet firmly back on English soil."

"The Israelis do a pretty good job of leading the Brits around by the nose too," said Cy defensively.

"Otherwise how are you finding New York, Gerald?" Elizabeth said as Tristan returned. "The commute sounds a bit rough."

"For the last year, I've been sharing a car and driver with another chap. It's made a huge difference. All in all, it's been a great couple of years."

"A lot of my partners who live in the suburbs have come up with the same solution as you," said Cy.

"Former partners," added Vera peevishly, still cross at him for threatening domestic tranquillity.

"Whatever," said Cy.

"I better get that gas grill going," said Gerald. "If we're ever going to eat."

They got through supper, thankfully without any further

reference to politics or religion. When the women had cleaned up the meal, Elizabeth said as delicately as she could:

"You know I'd appreciate it if you'd ask Gerald and Cy to keep their opinions on Jews to themselves. Given my husband's and therefore my children's origins."

"Sorry, Lizzie," said Molly contritely. "I just didn't think. Certainly I'll speak to Gerald and watch my tongue as well."

"We always forget," said Vera shaking her head. There was an awkward silence.

"And maybe we could hold back a bit on the French bashing too?"

"Cy just doesn't realize," said Vera. "He thinks it's just teasing."

"Well," said Elizabeth. "I have to get the twins to bed. It's been a long day. I'm tired too. See you all tomorrow."

"Good night, Lizzie," her mother and sister said at the same time.

The twins, it turned out, had put themselves to bed. After kissing their foreheads and adjusting their covers, she went into her own bedroom and sat in the dark.

When her father left, Elizabeth had been angry with her mother too; Vera should have suspected what her husband was up to. He was gone all the time—if it wasn't a business trip, then it was yet another interview over dinner. It was only later that Vera said to her daughters: "Your father used all the oldest tricks in the book. And I chose not to see."

She had felt betrayed by both of them for handing down such a false view of things. Because while she had learned about good and evil in books, at school and at church, she had been kept in the dark about the things real people can slowly and quietly do to one another, about the real-life ways in which even members of one's own family can be deceptive and treacherous and cruel.

Which in turn had made her angry with herself. For not seeing. For having been such a good and dutiful daughter. Until then the teenage rebellion train had left without her—she didn't even swear. But oh how quickly things could change. Suddenly she couldn't speak about either of them without a "my full-of-shit mother" or a "my fucking fucked-up father."

Since she'd stopped working, performance on her A-Levels was well below expectations, but she'd rejoiced in the disappointment she believed she was bringing them. She'd then continued her campaign to distress and annoy her parents by defying their wish that she stay in Britain for university. Instead she'd selected the most secluded American college she could find in upstate New York. She'd wanted to go all the way to California but Vera had forbidden it, saying it was too far from home. To which she'd replied: "And what, exactly, do you mean by home?"

***

When Elizabeth opened her eyes the next morning, it was just getting light. She lay in the huge, hard, king-sized bed with the no-wrinkle, polyester sheets, listening to the birds beginning to chirp and watching the thin nylon curtain billow in the sea breeze. Often these days when lying in bed, she allowed her thoughts to wander back to Troy. She would close her eyes, pull the covers tightly around her and re-run every detail of that balcony scene. From the way he took her hand, to the moment he put his strong arm around her shoulder, to their long, drawn-out kiss. Then she would fast-forward to that evening in the apartment. To his body up against hers in the kitchen, to his "Liza" in her ear and all that so blissfully followed.

This morning, however, she looked at her watch and saw that by now it would be late morning in Paris. Meaning that Lucas should be well on his way to Rouen—he'd said the meeting started at noon. Meaning that she should stop worrying.

But she couldn't, so she pulled back the covers and got up to the day ahead in Nantucket. Thinking about the day ahead, however, brought back the evening before. Their bigotry should have come as no surprise; she had heard racist, anti-Semitic slurs all her young life. But her Paris circle of enlightened professionals, her world of tolerant snobs had lulled her into thinking—what—that her family might have changed?

She padded into the bathroom.

When she had told her mother that she was going to marry Lucas, Vera had asked, with something close to panic in her voice: "You don't have to convert do you?"

"No, Mum, I told you. They're secular Jews."

"Well, what does his father do then?" she'd asked as if already certain of the answer: pawn-shop broker, money lender, rag trader.

Later came the conciliatory comments, the odd compliment. How distinguished and refined Claude Teller was. How considerate and soft-spoken Lucas was, really. How gentlemanly.

How could her mother read so much and remain so narrow-minded?

How could she, Elizabeth, always look forward to time with her family, then so quickly feel alienated?

While she was making herself some coffee, Molly rushed into the kitchen. "We have to be in and out of the supermarket by eight at the latest; otherwise the place will be jammed. We won't even be able to find a place to park," she said in a voice verging on panic.

And indeed, when Elizabeth and Molly emerged from the supermarket with two trolleys full of food at just past eight in the morning, over-sized vehicles were circling and circling the parking lot like famished whales. And later they waited their turn amidst those same vehicles to get onto the roundabouts on their way to the beach. Once near the water, they had their own trouble finding a spot to park.

"It's worse than Paris," Elizabeth declared. "At rush hour."

To Elizabeth, this new Nantucket was all flashy opulence and conformity. With one cedar-sided house after another, each surrounded by the same blue and pink hydrangeas and the same weedless lawns, the authenticity of the place, the sense of an island exposed to the harsh elements of the Atlantic, had been glossed over. To her eyes, Nantucket now looked like an American suburban development imitating Nantucket. And that made this little bump of land feel like a stage set on which her family was acting out its holiday.

So every morning Elizabeth played her part. She got up and sat on the deck drinking coffee with various members of her family. She helped her mother finish the previous day's crossword. She climbed into Molly's enormous vehicle and did more shopping or waited at the roundabouts to get to the beach. She helped prepare and clean up meals and in the evening she followed Molly's lead, checking the squirming, resistant twins for ticks, before going back out onto to the deck for gin and tonics and another barbecued supper.

She was pleasant and congenial with one and all but inside the real Elizabeth was a cauldron of conflict and anxiety. At moments, she longed for Lucas' arrival, longed to lean on him, let him bolster her against everything that was making her feel so alien. But at other moments, no matter how much she reasoned with herself, she could not help fearing the worst, that somehow alone in Paris with Lucas, Troy would have told her husband everything.

Finally Lucas came, flying in at mid-day from Boston after spending the night there with an old friend from his Fulbright year at Columbia. Elizabeth went to pick him up, armed with the twins, just in case. She watched with a pounding heart as her tall husband with his newly sprouted paunch unfolded from the small plane and ambled towards the terminal. With his serious, bespectacled face, his well-cut trousers and long-sleeved shirt and elegant lace-up shoes, he looked the very image of a French intellectual and almost risibly out of out of place amidst the shorts and t-shirts and Tevas. Though she normally would have rejoiced at this sight, Elizabeth was surprised to feel mild repulsion. Lucas looked dandyish and physically unfit—not someone she wanted to throw her arms around and kiss hungrily on the mouth.

"Everything okay at home?" She was trying with all her might to sound relaxed as they got in the car. He had not kissed her hello, causing her to feel a disconcerting mix of relief and panic. They had both, in fact, seemed happy that the twins were there.

"It's been a long trip."

"How's Suey?" Ariane piped up from the back seat.

"The cat is fine."

Gabby started telling him about the waves and the body-surfing, about playing paddle ball on the beach and how he would have to teach Lucas.

Lucas looked out the window.

"Houses are going up wherever you look," said Elizabeth, coaxing interest where normally no prompting was needed.

"I can see that. All the same style, all the same material?"

"An attempt to preserve tradition," she said in a lightly ironic tone to counter his stoniness.

"A noble goal, I guess."

"It's not the place I remember, that's for sure. Nothing looks genuine."

"Memory, of course, is not always to be trusted, is it?"

When she didn't answer, he added: "I mean, it can be highly selective, can't it?"

"Yes," she said, looking straight ahead at the road, while her stomach rose to her throat.

"Papa, when do you want to go to the beach?" asked Gabby from the back seat. "Can we go this afternoon?"

"Of course."

The six Tellers went to the beach alone that afternoon and found that the water was full of red gossamer algae. It lapped onto the shore and left large deposits. Elizabeth said: "Oh, no. It must be that red tide my mother told us about."

"There aren't even any waves," said Gabby.

"I hope the weather's not changing," Elizabeth said. "It's been sunny and breezy. Now it's hazy and humid."

"They told us on the airplane that fog and rain are expected," said Lucas, as if the weather forecast perfectly mirrored his mood.

"Let's go home," said Tristan.

"It's no good today," said Gabby disappointed.

"Well, I'm going in," said Elizabeth. "Doesn't anyone want to join me?" All four children shook their heads and made faces. "Come on, it's just a bit of seaweed." And in she waded. Once up to her waist, she bent her knees and sunk into the cold, clouded water up to her neck. As she paddled about, she could see her husband and four children, watching her from the safety of their white beach towels. The water lapped around under her chin, each a confirmation: *he knows he knows he knows*. Although she desperately wanted to go back to shore, to escape the seaweed that surrounded her, there was a tiny part of her that wished she could just disappear into the great big red ocean.

"O-o-o," said Ariane, hugging her bony knees to her chest as Elizabeth came dripping up the sand. "You've got it all over you."

"I told you. It's just a bit of seaweed," she said, trying to rub the stuff off with her towel.

"It's even hanging on the end of your hair," said Gabby.

"Are you sure this stuff isn't dangerous?" asked Lucas, looking distastefully at the deposits of red tide on her.

"Only for shellfish," said Elizabeth. "So my mother assures us."

Lucas glared at her through his glasses. "Clams and such."

"That's right," she said.

He nodded and looked away.

That evening everyone sat on the deck drinking gin and tonics, everyone except Lucas who had white wine and Vera who once again held her glass of apple juice between her knees.

"I'm very pleased you're finally here," she said. "Things

seemed incomplete without you." She sipped her juice. "What do you think of the house?"

"It is a very good construction for a holiday house," he said. "Very pleasant."

"It's not so pleasant when you're trying to sleep in the morning," said Olivier, who was joining the adult group now that his father was here.

"I would say the mezzanine was built expressly for adolescents," Lucas said, with an ironic smile at his son. "So that they don't sleep away their holidays."

"So now I'm too tired to appreciate them."

"Don't stay up so late watching television then," said Tristan.

Olivier opened his mouth to reply but Lucas just looked at him and he stopped, as if he sensed Lucas was in no mood for argument.

Elizabeth sat through supper, hardly eating a bite she felt so sick with apprehension as she watched Lucas maintain a silence that the rest of the family attributed to jet lag. He excused himself early and went to bed. Elizabeth, afraid Lucas might still be awake, took up Molly's offer to sit out on the deck under the stars. Or what there was of them to see. Fog was indeed arriving in eerie, wafting patches and they could hear the mournful lowing of a foghorn in the distance.

Molly remained uncharacteristically quiet, so Elizabeth said: "I hope this won't ruin our fishing expedition tomorrow."

"Hmm," Molly said.

"Are you all right?"

"Yes," she said in the small, tight voice she used as a girl when she'd done something wrong.

"Come on. I can tell there's something," Elizabeth said.

Molly sighed. "You know how the children have all these sporting activities."

"Yes."

"Well, while they're playing, the parents talk." She stopped again. "It's kind of their social gathering time."

"Yes," Elizabeth prompted.

"And because lots of men living near us have made enough money to retire at forty," Molly paused again.

"Yes…"

"Well." Molly began distractedly twirling her large sapphire and diamond engagement ring. "You know how Robin has lacrosse practice three times a week." Elizabeth nodded. "I've become quite friendly with one of those rich retired fathers."

"Quite friendly?" Elizabeth asked.

"Yes," Molly said, looking up at her sister with her large and limpid blue eyes. "One stands around for hours and hours and there's nothing else to do but chat and we talk a lot. His wife Tricia is impossible. But the children. You know." Yes, she knew. It was such a classic story she might have laughed, if her sister hadn't looked so earnest and distraught. "Nothing has happened and nothing will," said Molly firmly. "I love Gerald and our family too much." She paused again, turning her perfect face straight to the sky. "It's just that I think about him morning, noon and night. I can't wait to see him."

"Are you sure you're happy with Gerald?"

"Things have maybe gone a little stale. Isn't that normal, after more than twenty years of marriage?"

"I guess," said Elizabeth weakly.

"I mean, you've been married almost as long as I have. Haven't you ever been at least tempted?"

"Well, no, not really," she fudged.

Molly sighed. "I guess why would you be tempted—Lucas is too perfect," she said without even a trace of irony.

"I don't know about that," Elizabeth laughed, though she in fact knew exactly what her sister meant.

"He's has always rather daunted me, I'm afraid," she said. Then, obviously remembering her remarks from the first evening added: "I mean, I *like* Lucas. He's incredibly kind and thoughtful but he's so intellectual. And here I am—I didn't even go to university."

"You shouldn't let that bother you," said Elizabeth. "I know Lucas is very fond of you." Which he actually was. They sat for a few minutes, watching the puffs of fog slide across the sky.

Finally Molly said: "The thing is, I can't imagine life without Gerald. Nor do I want to. I feel guilty though."

"But you say you haven't done anything."

"Isn't thinking it almost as bad?"

"Nowhere near as bad." Elizabeth replied firmly.

"I still feel terrible." She rubbed her arms, considering. "Anyway, it's getting clammy out here, isn't it? I think I'm ready for bed."

As they walked inside, Elizabeth was thinking that her sister, with her limited intellect but generous heart, was the only one in the family who walked a straight line. Who was somehow genuine. She put her arm around Molly's shoulders. Despite their different interests in life, Elizabeth loved her sister very much: "Everything will turn out fine."

"I hope you're right," said Molly with a trusting smile.

"I know I am." Elizabeth smiled back.

In this, at least, Elizabeth was being completely sincere.

When Molly and Gerald had married, all Molly wanted was to have children. But no children came. They both had tests; nothing could be found out of order. They tried and tried, while Molly became more and more desperate. Not wanting to adopt and being too old-fashioned for science, Molly had finally resolved herself to a childless life. They sold their house for something smaller; she started a decorating business. A month later she was pregnant with Robin and the two others followed in quick succession. If they had survived that childless desperation, Elizabeth was sure they would survive this.

It was her own chances of survival that she went to bed less certain about.

***

108

"Is Lucas still asleep?" Vera asked as Elizabeth poured each of them a cup of coffee the next morning.

"No, he must have woken up early and gone for a walk." She put the mug to her lips and sipped. "He's still on European time of course." When she'd slipped into bed the night before, she'd had the feeling that Lucas was feigning sleep. And all night long he'd remained firmly positioned on his side of the large bed.

"The weather doesn't look great—can we go fishing?"

"Hard to tell," said Gerald. "We'll just drive down to the port and see."

Elizabeth woke up Tristan and Olivier and poured cereal for the twins and fretted that Lucas wouldn't be back in time for the fishing excursion; she hadn't mentioned it to him. But just as they were loading the cars with children and equipment, he arrived.

"Where have you been?" she asked.

"Wandering."

"I should have told you about the ticks."

"The ticks?" Lucas did not like insects.

"Apparently there are diseased ticks all over the island." He shook his head and rolled his eyes, as if diseased ticks really were the last straw. She said: "You only need to be careful in the brush."

"I've just been in the brush," he answered sharply. "You didn't tell me."

"I didn't know you were going," she answered, her voice raising. Then more softly: "Did you have a nice walk?"

"Not really." He stared at her defiantly.

"We have a fishing expedition planned," she said.

"This fog is thickening. I think I'll stay here and read." Then he turned to Vera, who was gingerly making her way down the stairs. "I hope it's all right if I don't come with you on the boat. I'm still a little tired." By now he had her by the arm and was helping her towards one of the two vehicles in their convoy.

"I understand," she said, looking at Elizabeth. "Maybe you'd like to stay too?"

"And leave the twins for you to watch?" she said, shaking her head.

When they got into the town, Molly went to ask about the boat.

"He says it should be all right," she reported.

"I hope his optimism is based on the weather forecast, rather than his desire for a morning's pay," said Gerald.

"Well, it's his life too," said Molly. "I'm sure he won't want to risk it."

The boat, which was just big enough for the twelve of them, was moored on one of the outer docks. Once they were all boarded, with Vera and Cy seated safely on a raised platform in the middle under a roof and the younger children kitted out with bright orange life jackets, the motor spewed out exhaust and revved them forward. Through the milky air, they sputtered past giant yachts and sleek sailboats and Vera shook her head, saying: "It didn't used to be this way." Tristan and Olivier were in a sulk; neither had wanted to come once Lucas had desisted. Gerald had severely dressed down his children in the car and Molly was annoyed at him for being so harsh. The twins, involved in some secret dispute, were scowling and sitting on opposite sides of the boat. Elizabeth couldn't help but feel, irrational though she knew it to be, that the collectively sour mood was an extension of Lucas' arrival and aloofness.

The boat headed out to sea and the air became thicker, damper, heavier. When they got beyond the point, the captain idled the engine and prepared the rods and lines. There were four swivel seats for fishing and everyone was to take turns, the youngest first. Without protection of the bay, there were more waves now and they rolled up and down as the boat cruised slowly to give the fish time to take the bait. Elizabeth ordered Tristan and Olivier to stand behind the twins, in case one of them got a bite. Molly and Gerald did the same for their children. Vera and Cy sat on their thrones, Vera still looking anxious, Cy with his faintly superior smile. Elizabeth leaned over the edge and watched the nylon lines cut through the water. *Lucas knows something. But what? Which one of my numerous crimes has Troy revealed? Arson? Abandonment? Adultery? What would Hawthorne do with me—adorn my chest with triple A's?*

The engine went dead. They all looked towards the captain with alarm.

"Fog's too thick," he said with his thick Massachusetts accent. "We'll have to drop anchor for a while." With the motor cut, they could hear the foghorn moaning and just make out the light going round and round at Sanketty point.

"A while?" asked Cy.

"The fog might be here for days," said Vera.

"Don't think so," said the captain.

"You don't think so," repeated Gerald, shaking his head.

"We should have known," said Molly.

"We should have known," said Vera.

"Have we got anything to drink?" Gabby asked his mother.

"Not a drop," said Elizabeth.

"A good cold beer is what I'm ready for," said Cy.

"I feel sick," said Ariane.

"Oh, God," said Elizabeth. "Lie down." And Ariane curled up on a bench and Elizabeth asked the captain for a bucket.

The fog began to encircle the boat too and the desolate moan of the foghorn was the only sound besides the slapping of waves against the boat, the snapping of lines against the mast. *Lucas has been snapping at me since his arrival, all those pointed little comments about memory and clams and no I didn't have a nice walk. But what can I do about it here on this strange island with all these people, my family, around?*

"Couldn't we just turn back to port?" Gerald asked the captain. "Wouldn't another boat hear the engine?"

"Best just to sit tight for now." And he started fiddling with the lines.

They sat there for over two hours. When the children started complaining, Molly got them playing Twenty Questions, as they had done on long journeys in the car when they were small. All of them except Ariane who was intermittently throwing up into a white bucket, and Tristan and Olivier who glared at their mother for dragging them into this. Olivier defiantly pulled out the Discman Elizabeth had told him to leave at the house and he and Tristan took one earpiece each and listened to music. Cy patted Vera's hand reassuringly, that faint smile never leaving his face. Gerald paced, hands in his pockets, and Elizabeth sat next to Ariane, smoothing her brow. The water slapped, the lines snapped and Elizabeth felt trapped, trapped, trapped.

Shortly after noon a pale orb of sunlight pierced the fog and the captain announced that they could return.

"Good timing," said Gerald. "He'll get back just in time for lunch with his mates."

As they set off in their two-vehicle convoy back to the house, Cy said: "That was quite an adventure."

Elizabeth, wedged between the continued ill-humour of her two older sons as they gedunked over the rough cobblestones of Nantucket Town, wanted to reply: *No it wasn't. It was like a trip to purgatory. Just like this whole holiday: a prolonged stay on the road to hell.*

Just as they drove up to the house, it started raining. And it kept raining for three days. Minus one excursion to the Whaling Museum and another to the Life Saving Museum, they were confined to the house, where the children bickered and went wild after too much television. Elizabeth ate and drank too much at meal-times and slept too much afterwards. It was the only way she could get through each day. Unlike Lucas, who seemed to have little appetite for anything but a French translation of *Moby Dick* and his own children. When he wasn't sitting and reading in the low-slung chair, one long leg crossed over the other, he was playing chess with the older boys or cards with the twins. Sometimes Elizabeth would catch him looking at her with confusion or disdain—she couldn't exactly tell—it was an expression that she'd never seen before on his face—and it made her want to shrink out of sight.

Gretchen and the sun arrived on the same day.

"Anyone here?" she called up the stairs, just as they were all sitting down to yet another lunch. Gerald had offered to pick her up at the airport, but Cy had replied: "Oh, no. Gretchen will want to get here on her own irrepressible steam."

Her Jack Russell terrier came bounding up the stairs ahead of her, his nails clicking on the pine steps. "Any food left for me? I'm starving. You no longer get fed on planes and I didn't have time for breakfast."

"Hello, Gretchen, dear," said Cy, as he pushed out his chair with a sharp scrape.

"Hello one and all," she said, kissing her father. "What a trip." She plopped down on the chair that had been saved for her. The little dog immediately jumped on her lap, panting and excitedly looking around him.

"What is 'is name?" asked Gabby.

"Ricky," said Gretchen. "Ricky, say hello to Robin."

"Gabby," said Elizabeth.

"This is Robin," said Molly, pointing to her son.

"I'm sorry. Gabby. Say hello to Gabby," she said, shaking the dog's little paw. Gabby stroked the dog's head with two fingers.

"Children," said Vera, "re-introduce yourselves to Gretchen."

After they'd gone round the table, Gretchen said: "Well, I'll do my best to keep you all straight." Then she reached a freckled arm across for some salad and a large chunk of farm cheddar. She was neither thin nor fat, too busy with life to overeat or to starve herself. Her dog and her job at a news agency in New York seemed to be all she needed. Boyfriends would occasionally enter the scene but they never stayed in it for long. "Chases them away," Cy said with a shake of his small, round head.

Chewing, Gretchen re-adjusted the pony tail of her ginger-blond hair, pulling it tight. Though the skin and colouring came from her mother, the sturdiness of her frame, the briskness of her movements, were all a younger Cy.

Lucas was smiling for the first time since his arrival.

"She is certainly a lively one," he said, when he and Elizabeth briefly intersected while getting ready to go to the beach.

"She is that," said Elizabeth, tossing her towel into the bag.

The first afternoon Gretchen took them to Madaket Beach. Driving out to the far south-western corner of the island, they eventually left the snarling traffic and the frenetic construction behind and something of that wild island could still be felt. At Madaket, the houses were simple and small, the little lanes sandy and the beach all but empty. The children, released from their foggy prison, dashed in and out of the cold water with shrieks of pent-up delight.

Over the next days, Gretchen infused the group with an energy that otherwise they seemed to sap out of one another. She showed Tristan and Olivier a shop in town where they could buy used CDs, she took Lucas on a tour of the clapboard colonial houses of architectural interest and historical importance. The younger children played endlessly with Ricky. On her suggestion, Gerald took Molly to Boston for a day and a night—"It's what all the Nantucket couples do!" Gretchen had said with a hoot—and Molly came back glowing.

As for Elizabeth, she tagged on to one group or another, tried to be pleasant with one and all but oh, how miserable and frightened and alone she felt. Lucas avoided her completely—always getting in and out from his side of that huge hard bed before or after her. She wished she could burst this poisonous bubble of silence and confront him, but how could she even begin broaching the subject of her multiple sins with him, especially here? He seemed, anyway, to be thinking the same thing.

Finally the holiday drew to an end. On the evening before their departure, when the twins decided at the last minute not to accompany their parents, Elizabeth and Lucas found themselves going alone to the sweetshop to buy some chocolate for the

French cousins and to fill up the tank of Cy and Vera's hired van. They drove in complete silence, making Elizabeth such a bundle of nerves that she dropped her change all over the counter in the shop. As they left the service station, her mind was racing, trying to formulate the question—what's wrong—what did he tell you —when Lucas said: "I can't stand this another minute. Where can we go? I don't want to sit in this car."

Her insides came crashing together, suddenly softened. She said in a wavering voice: "There's a big moor in the middle of the island. I don't think we're far. I can probably find it."

And through some unconscious memory, she took them right to the turnoff.

"I think the highest point on the island is up there," she said and they headed off single file.

"What about the ticks?" asked Lucas, suddenly swinging his head back towards her. "They must be all over the place here."

"We should be careful," she said. He pulled his head into his shoulders as if surrounded on all sides by disease-ridden parasites.

And Elizabeth trudged along behind Lucas as if on the way to the gallows. She looked at his hunched figure and the back of his head, where the round bald spot glowed in the dying light, and she too cringed, though not at the ticks but at him, her husband.

Overhead small planes were flying one after another. The incessant drone made Elizabeth want to scream, take cover. In her terror of the imminent, long-awaited confrontation with Lucas, she could not get the ridiculous idea out of her head that at any moment, the planes were going to drop bombs on them.

This is just the flight path to the airport, she told herself. It is Friday and these planes are not carrying bombs but rich New Yorkers, on their way to a pleasant weekend at the beach.

"Here we are," Elizabeth finally said, hardly able to breath, when they reached an area under some low trees.

Lucas' head was still sunk into his shoulders, as if a tick

might fall from a branch at any moment. Elizabeth remembered her mother, who had read up on ticks, telling her that they do indeed climb trees, where they can remain dormant for up to twenty-five years and this thought sent a shudder right through her. Too petrified to speak and not daring to sit down on the bench behind her, she pawed the ground in front of her with her toe, waiting for Lucas, who was staring straight ahead with his arms now crossed tightly across his chest, to take the lead.

"He told me," he finally said, his voice cracking over the words.

"Who told you what?" she dodged.

"You know what I'm talking about." He looked at her with such intensity she took a step backwards. "What happened all those years ago." Still she said nothing. "The fire."

She half fell onto the bench.

"He told me," Lucas repeated, "but I want to hear your version."

She nodded, tried to collect herself, tried to figure out where to start the story that she'd suppressed to the best of her ability over so many years. That she'd wished into near oblivion in her mind until Troy came back to revive it for her. She sat for several minutes with her ears ringing and her heart racing as she tried to put some order to her haunted snatches of memory.

There were four of us, John and Sally and Troy and I, and we were all angry about something. It was partly the times, the end of the seventies. The Vietnam War was over but a sour after-taste of insubordination still lingered in the air. The four of us also had our personal reasons for resentment. My parents had just divorced. Sally was overweight. John was very short. Troy of course was the one with legitimate complaints. With no parents and no money, there were no cosy corners in his life, no places to curl up and feel safe.

Troy was also our leader. We respected, envied really, his natural cool, his supreme disregard for authority and danger. The disregard that made him take down the American flag and fly a Soviet one at half-mast in its place. Or run naked in front of the administration building the day the board of trustees was meeting or scale the tallest building on campus and beat his chest like Tarzan. That mockery of authority was also what made the college administration and especially the dean of students want to get rid of him.

The lovely flat we found to live in our last year got taken away from us over the summer by an artist, Hoyt Thorpe, whom the college had hired to create a sculpture for the front of the art building. The only place we could then find to rent was a run-down apartment in a rickety old building. The floors sagged and slanted, the rooms were tiny. The only other people in the building, our downstairs neighbours, were chain-smoking alcoholics. Their cigarette smoke wafted up through the thin walls day and night, as did his screams and her moans. Some creature—The Beast we called it—rummaged leisurely in the kitchen rubbish after we'd gone to bed, until we covered its hole with a thick stack of newspapers. But for months it still scratched around under the floorboards or in the walls.

Despite the flat, we were actually quite happy those first months. We felt like a family, of sorts. Troy was particularly pleased, ironically because of the man who had pulled the house from under our feet. Unknowingly Troy had signed up for the one sculpture class Hoyt Thorpe was teaching and in no time fell under his spell. It wasn't surprising. Hoyt had everything going for him. He was confident and charismatic and successful. He saw that Troy had both talent and passion and he adopted him. The first term Troy spent much of his time at that house we were supposed to be living in. He even spent the Thanksgiving break with Hoyt instead of going to his uncle's.

After Christmas, though, things began to fall apart. Hoyt started having an affair with another art student and he completely lost interest in Troy. Just about the same time we came back one evening from the campus to find that balsa boards had been hammered around the inside of each window frame. They held in place sheaths of plastic, to hold in the heat, we were told when we complained.

It was then that we started losing touch with the outside world, which through the plastic appeared milky and diffuse. We went to our classes but stopped going to any parties on campus or off. Instead we preferred sitting around our place, eating and drinking alone. We laughed a lot but there was something unhealthy about our laughter, induced as it usually was by alcohol or drugs.

As the winter wore on, we got more and more derelict, no longer bothering to clean up, instead just kicking the clothes and the beer cans and the pizza boxes out of the way so that we could play cards. We played a game called hearts, the goal of which was to take as few heart tricks as possible and to avoid at all costs the queen of spades, because she counted many points against you. Often we'd play all night. Troy and I were better than John and Sally and one of them almost always got landed with the queen of spades and most of the hearts. The cards drew something of a line down the middle, John and Sally on one side, Troy and I on the other.

Spring finally began to appear but no one came to release us from our plastic prison. Troy started reminding us that it was Hoyt Thorpe who was responsible for our living in plastic with alcoholic chain-smokers and rummaging beasts. The same Hoyt Thorpe who had dumped Troy in such cavalier fashion. He was also, to our minds, an unpardonable oxymoron—a successful artist. The Oxymoronic, Troy started calling to him. He had sold out and walked all over everybody in the process. It made us sick, his success and his popularity. At first we jokingly planned ways of making his life miserable. Silly things, such as letting the air out of his tyres. Sticking chewing gum in the lock of his studio.

On a warm evening Troy got in one of his rages and took a kitchen knife to the plastic in his room. He cut great long slashes. The thing was in shreds but he kept at it, screaming that the plastic had blocked the light, had killed his two plants. Eventually we joined in until ribbons of plastic hung from all the windows. That destructive frenzy intoxicated us, made us feel we were ready to take on the world.

Our ideas for making Hoyt's life miserable became more sinister. We even talked about how we might cause him to have an accident.

Then Troy mentioned Hoyt's sculpture, how damaging it would really be the best way to hurt him. A ceremony to unveil it was planned for the week before graduation. The statue, Troy informed us, was made of wood; it would be an easy target.

The night before the unveiling ceremony, there was a party on the campus, and we decided to go. Having not been out in months, we were like a family of wild animals emerging from hibernation and we smoked and drank ourselves into a mindless, reckless state.

The rest of the night becomes a cloudy, patchy dream. We leave the party and follow Troy our leader to the campus maintenance buildings. He worked there his first year and knows that the key is kept over the door. He fills up a large container with petrol. We follow him to the art building. The sculpture is covered by a large tarp. It looks like a starving beast, beamy bones poking through sagging skin. No one is around. It is very dark and quiet. The art building is at the edge of the campus; the woods are just beyond. Troy starts splashing petrol all over the tarp. The three of us just stand there on our unsteady feet, watching. The smell of the petrol is making me nauseous. Someone gave me a lighter at the party and I pull it from my pocket. I lean down and set the tarp alight. There is a whoosh as the petrol catches.

The fire spread, we learn the next day. The art building is half destroyed, all their watercolour collection gone. A fireman has been injured. Troy too and he is accused of starting the fire. The dean pounces. Finally he can properly dispense with that troublesome pest. John, Sally and I are all questioned but not as accomplices, just as his roommates, and I carry out the charade as I suppose John and Sally do but I don't know because the three of us leave the apartment, skulking out the door with our heavy bags, not daring to speak a word to one another.

I tell no one what happened. Instead I run to London and then from London I run to Paris, hoping that by fleeing in space I can escape time. But here I am...

She looked up, not quite remembering where she was, or whether she'd been talking out loud or just in her own head. But there was Lucas, sitting on a rock with his elbows on his knees. His clasped white hands almost shone in the dying light but his face was in the shadows.

"So you lit the fire." He sounded devastated.

"Yes." Her voice felt completely detached from her person.

"Troy spared me that part of the story," he said bitterly. "Of course, he wouldn't have told it to me at all, if I hadn't walked in unexpectedly and seen him with his shirt off." He paused. "Anyway, he did mention he was with other people and of course I knew one of them had to be you. Because otherwise why would he have shown up in Paris?"

She did not respond; she had never heard him use such a sarcastic, almost spiteful, tone.

"He told me that he hadn't seen the point of dragging in people who were no longer there," he continued. "That no one would have believed him anyway," he paused again. "And now I discover that not only were you one of those people but that you also actually lit the match."

"Yes," she half whispered.

"He covered up for you, even now," he said with the same bitterness.

A particularly noisy plane groaned overhead. When it had passed, Lucas said: "Well? Haven't you left out a few things?"

A tingle rose at the back of her neck, stretched to her hairline but she didn't answer.

"Things about Troy?" he prompted. When she still didn't say anything, he continued impatiently. "Injured, you said, as if he'd come away with nothing but a blister on the end of his finger." His distraught voice went up an octave. "He was hospitalized for weeks. His back and upper arms were scarred for life." He paused. "And what about that other small matter?" Again she stayed silent. His voice went up even higher. "That while you were making a nice little life for yourself in Paris, he was sitting in a prison cell?"

"Prison?" she barely whispered.

"What? You didn't even know he went to prison?" he screamed.

She shook her head.

"Arson is a serious crime, Elizabeth."

"I know."

"Not only were an art collection and a building destroyed, you ruined two people's lives. The fireman was so badly burned he could never work again—who knows how he and his family got by. And as for Troy, besides being scarred for life, he wasted five years of his life in prison, where he was raped on a regular basis. His cellmate was too, until he hanged himself."

"I, I, I—" she stopped. Started again: "I never knew what happened afterwards. I never heard another word from anyone. I just thought—I don't know—that—" she paused, searching. Then in an almost inaudible voice: "I tried not to think about it all."

"Jesus," he said in total disgust. "Weren't you at all curious about what happened to your supposed friend? Didn't your conscience weigh on you at all?"

The tingling numbness had spread from the back of her neck throughout her body.

"How could you have abandoned him like that? How *could* you?" he waited for an answer. She just shook her head. He stood up and repeated: "You ruined his life." He started back down the path, and Elizabeth followed without a word, the recurring drone and blinking of small aeroplanes still overhead.

In the driveway Lucas looked away from her. "I can't come in yet. But I know you can come up with an excuse that your family will believe."

She took a deep breath before entering the house. The worst part was that she knew he was right; she would have no trouble making up a credible story.

***

121

They made it back to Paris without any of the children remarking on or even seeming to notice the lack of communication between their parents; all four of them were too excited about going home. At the airport, they got into two separate taxis, Lucas and the older boys in one; Elizabeth and the twins in another, and for the first time in her memory, she felt no comfort or pleasure when the odd domes of the Sacré Coeur came into view. Even once the taxi began navigating the one-way streets of the fifth arrondissement, even once they were back at the rue Laromiguière on this sleepy Sunday morning in August, she felt nothing.

The plan had been, after two days of rest and laundry, to drive down to the Lubéron and spend ten days with the Tellers, Isabelle and Claude, Alix and Roland, in the house built by Lucas. But Elizabeth could not imagine being with them for even one day, much less ten, because they would notice what hers had not.

"It won't be fun without you," said Ariane.

"The swimming pool will be just as refreshing with or without me. I'm sorry too. But something's come up at work. I have to stay here."

"But you'll be all alone," whined Ariane.

"Suey can stay and keep me company."

"We'll talk when I get back," said Lucas, not looking her in the eye. His anger seemed to have morphed into a desolate disappointment, which was in a way even more unbearable. "I'll have time to think down there."

And to discuss. Elizabeth imagined the five of them—Lucas, Alix, Roland, Isabelle and Claude—on the elegant flagstone terrace with the huge outdoor torches that always reminded her of a Greek stage. They would be sitting erectly around the table, discussing in all their complicity, her treachery, her morally corrupt character, her fatal flaw. Speaking in low voices so the children wouldn't overhear. She imagined them, Claude in particular, shaking his sage head sadly but all-too-knowingly.

Well, it was no more than the first murmurings of her long overdue punishment, that's what it was.

After her family had gone, she at first just sat, for hours, with the cat on and off her lap. During Troy's visit, she'd remembered the fire, remembered him dancing around and tearing off his t-shirt and rolling like a gymnast on the ground to put the fire out. She even remembered taking him to the emergency room—but she hadn't allowed herself to imagine how bad a scar that kind of burn was bound to leave, even when he hadn't taken off his shirt during their frenzied love-making. It was amazing, really, that she could have stubbornly kept his injury's lasting consequences just beyond the edge of her conscious mind. Just as she had never allowed herself to imagine what practical consequences Troy might have suffered for their crime.

But now prison, prison, prison resounded in her head, reverberated like steel doors clanging shut in her skull. How could she never have considered that? Lucas' words pursued her like harpies: arson is a serious crime, Elizabeth, he was raped, his cell-mate committed suicide, you ruined two people's lives—it was horrible—she was horrible—she wished she could peel off her skin—get out of her own vile person. How could she possibly have thought he'd escape the burning of a building and an art collection, the irreparable wounding of a fireman, with nothing more serious than a reprimand from the college?

Because it was easier, more convenient, and she hadn't wanted such troubling thoughts intruding on the nice new life she had made for herself in Paris.

Elizabeth wondered what had happened when Troy had tracked down John and Sally. If he'd wheedled his way into their lives, told their families about the fire. She somehow doubted it. They weren't worth it to him. They were people who were so easy to stick with the queen of spades and all but one of the hearts. It was she, Elizabeth, who'd mattered to him. Because they had not just slept together a few times, as she'd claimed to Lucas. After Troy had been dismissed by Hoyt, they had in fact shared the same bed for several months. So it was she who had caused the real damage, who had added hurt to hurt.

Sitting in that living room where she and Troy had recently been engaged in wild and prolonged sex, she wondered how she had allowed that to happen. True she found him physically quite irresistible—but she was married—and happily so—wasn't she? So she thought—but she also had to admit that since Troy's arrival, Lucas had often appeared to her in a less than attractive light, physically. His paunch, his long, thin arms and the straight black hair on his chest had on several occasions made her almost recoil. But to throw herself into the arms of someone else?

When Gérard had made his moves on her years ago, she had made Lucas laugh by imitating what she'd called his mating dance. But what she hadn't told her husband was that without actually succumbing to Gérard's soft shirts and smooth, easy ways with women, she had not rebuffed him entirely either. She had allowed a hand to rest on her hand, an arm to linger over her shoulders.

Well, both incidents were illustrations of her depravity, weren't they?

Tired of sitting, she wandered around the apartment, through her children's rooms and finally into Lucas' office, which she entered on tiptoe, as if she were an intruder or a burglar. Her skin tingled while she looked at his overflowing book shelves, his work table and his computer, his sofa, on which he had spent the last two nights. The only empty space was where the model for the exhibition centre had recently sat. He must have taken it to Rouen. She walked over to the window, to the view Lucas looked upon every day. It was practically the same view they had from their living room, just a slightly different angle, but it changed everything somehow.

It had always seemed to her that one reason she and Lucas were a good fit was that they shared the same values of personal responsibility, consideration for others, standing up for what is right. They'd both been brought up with those principles; there had been no disagreement between them in bringing up their children. But Lucas, it seemed to Elizabeth now, had taken those values more seriously, more to heart, perhaps because his childhood had been overshadowed by Aunt Coco, by the cousin who had lost all her family, and by the other people who had survived but still bore the traces on their forearms. Whereas in Elizabeth's family, the values had at the end of the day rung hollow. She had been taught the right way to behave and then had witnessed her father leave her mother, via a note on the kitchen table. A note conveniently timed so that his teenage daughters would be home from school to pick up the pieces. Then she herself, far outdoing her father and his flimsy missive, had abandoned Troy in his hospital bed and let him go to prison, while she skipped off to start a bright new life for herself a continent away. It seemed she had inherited and perpetuated her father's example, rather than absorbing any of the values she had been taught. Because otherwise, how could she have done what she did?

Again, wanting to flee her own person, she ran out of Lucas' office, back into the sitting room, where she stood stock still, for several minutes. The scene swam before her: the summer heat, Troy maybe watering the plants, his shirt off, and Lucas coming in earlier than expected, putting down his motorcycle helmet—

She whirled around as if both of them were still right there in the room with her and her first thought was that if only Lucas hadn't come back unexpectedly, she wouldn't have been found out. She probably would have been off the hook forever.

Here I am, once again trying to brush the guilt off my clothes like recalcitrant lint.

Unable to be alone with herself for one more second, she set off for the office.

Being August, it was eerily empty, with just the odd secretary maintaining a presence. And Lucille. Elizabeth had forgotten about Lucille. She tried to slip by her open door unnoticed.

"Elizabeth. What are you doing here?" Elizabeth stopped

dead in her tracks, Lucille's eyes on her like two headlights. "I thought you were taking in the Midi sun."

"I...I..." she hesitated—Lucille's sister-in-law was a friend of Alix. "No, I'm not, as you can see. You look healthy for someone stuck in the office." Lucille was wearing a sleeveless white t-shirt that set off her sun-tanned, gym-toned, squash-honed arms to model perfection.

"People have felt sorry for me and I've been inundated with weekend invitations," she smiled. Elizabeth thought of Gérard's large house near Deauville. Since he didn't like to be alone with his wife and children, he invited anyone and everyone to stay, lovers included. She and Lucas had been a couple of times.

"Has anything happened around here?" Elizabeth asked.

"No, not much," Lucille answered, her eye straying to a manuscript sitting on her desk. "Pretty quiet. And I guess it will stay that way until next week when everyone's back."

"Right. Well. I thought I'd just get a head start on my post and any other papers that might have piled up. See you next week," said Elizabeth, suddenly certain that Lucille would never be Gérard's lover; she was much too cagey for that trap.

When she opened the door to her office, it was stuffy and musty. She flung open the window and sat down at her desk. Surprisingly little paper had accumulated and she once again had the feeling of having been forgotten back here in her corner office. Except that someone had nicked her fan. The open window provided little relief to the airless, hot room and she felt none of the familiar pleasure at being here. She closed her eyes but saw Lucas walking in, saw Troy's naked torso. She lurched forward in her seat, wanted to leave, keep moving, right now, but couldn't bear passing by Lucille's office again. She looked at her watch. Noon. Lucille wouldn't be leaving for lunch or the gym for another half hour at least. She stood up. To think of Lucas seeing that scar. Lucas who squirmed at even the thought of ticks and cat shit. To think *that* was how he had discovered the truth.

Her eye ran along the shelves. Her first day at this publishing house, Uncle Antoine had brought her back to this office, dumped a pile of novels on the desk, and said: "Here you go. Do what you can."

Even she had been surprised by how naturally it came to her. She had picked up the books one by one and on the basis of the first paragraph and a quick random plunge into the middle, she'd made a pile of hopeful, not-so-hopeful and probable lost causes. In the first pile, the second book she read had captivated her completely; she had had no doubt it would sell in France. Its lyrical charm, its distinctive voice, had made her certain that it would please in any country, any language. Antoine had listened to her recommendation and sure enough just after the book came out in French the American film rights were sold. A year later, everything the woman had ever written was being reprinted and Elizabeth was given a full-time job which she had never stopped loving. At least not until she'd started feeling eclipsed by Lucille. Until she'd started worrying about losing her touch. The mood had changed. People wanted immigrants—but not WASPY ones like her. Or they wanted violence, preferably in the form of terrorism.

If you and I were disaffected students today we would buy automatic weapons and spray Hoyt Thorpe and our fellow students with a belt-full of bullets.

The voice of Lucille telling a secretary that she was off to lunch brought her back to her senses. She waited three more minutes and left.

II
Rue de Sèvres

The day her family was to return, Elizabeth waited nervously, the butterflies in her stomach causing her to flit ineffectually around the apartment. Since their departure for the Lubéron, she had spoken to Lucas on the phone about the children, but that was all. His voice had been flat, almost dead. When she spoke to the children, it pained her to hear them so happy. She wished they missed her more.

She picked up Suey and held her tightly, stroking the soft fur, letting the purr reverberate through her own chest. Though she told herself to expect the worst, she had not been able to snuff out hope entirely. The resilience of that little h word was astonishing: while his voice on the phone indicated exactly the opposite, she was at moments able to convince herself that Lucas would walk in the door with a smile on his face, having resolved his disappointment and forgiven her completely.

There was no smile on his face when he returned on a particularly hot afternoon. He did manage, finally, to turn up the edges of his lips, to put his arm briefly, stonily, around her shoulder. The children were hungry and tired too.

"You bent the cover of my book," Tristan said through gritted teeth to Olivier. "I told you to be careful."

"It's just a stupid book," said Olivier.

"It may seem stupid to you but…"

"Stop it," Lucas cut him off. "It's been a long journey. Things get bent."

"A-a-a-a-o!" Gabby screamed from the bedroom. Elizabeth

ran back. Ariane had thrown his favourite stuffed animal, a ragged little rabbit, on top of the armoire.

"I hate you, Ariane," he screamed. "I hate you, I hate you."

"Gabby, stop saying that right now. Ariane, why on earth did you throw his toy up there?"

"He called me a liar."

"You are a liar. You told me yesterday you held your breath under water all the way across the pool."

"I did."

"No, you didn't."

"Stop this at once," said Elizabeth. "Come into the kitchen. I made some brownies."

"I don't want any brownies," sulked Gabby.

"Then I'll eat his," said Ariane, skipping out of the room.

"Oh, no you won't." He ran out after her and Elizabeth was left standing alone, feeling completely out of synch with her family and therefore even lonelier than while they had been away.

Later, after a dinner where no one seemed to enjoy one bite of the food Elizabeth had carefully prepared, the twins were put to bed and the older boys excused themselves to their rooms. Lucas and Elizabeth finished the washing up in silence and went to sit in the living room. The sun was just going down but they did not turn on the lights. Instead, Lucas turned on the fan near the window. For several minutes they said nothing. Lucas sighed. He rearranged himself in his seat. The fan turned in its relentless semi-circle, a sudden gust of air on the face, then nothing.

"I'm having a hard time," he finally said. "I'm confused."

His glasses caught and reflected the remaining light from the window so she could not see his eyes at all. She looked down at her hands, interlaced the fingers.

"I think it's important to let time pass," he continued. She could see the twist of his lip, an expression he got when he was very unhappy. It was a look that both pained and repelled her. "To wait and see. Let's say until Christmas."

"You know," she finally managed to say, " how sorry I am. How much I regret what I did. And not telling you about it. You know me well enough to know that, don't you?"

Lucas nodded, moved uncomfortably in his chair. "I do."

When they got in bed, they tried an embrace and a kiss. It was awkward and it was hot. The mixing of their sweat was not pleasant to either of them. They gave up and lay, not touching, under the sheet while the bedroom fan blew over and back.

***

The bustle, the comfort of re-establishing a routine made *la rentrée* a relief to them all, even Gabby and Olivier who grumbled and groaned about going back to school. Elizabeth could not say that her children knew what was going on but the tension between her and Lucas put everyone slightly on edge. Spinning off into other worlds was just what they all needed and it gave Elizabeth some real hope that things might turn out all right after all.

At work this was the biggest time of year for the publishing houses. During *la rentrée littéraire*, hundreds of novels flooded the market and the critics began to leak their preferences for the Goncourt, the Renaudot, the Femina. There weren't quite as many prizes as books but the ratio was favourable. Elizabeth was less affected by this frenzy, since there were many fewer awards for foreign literature, but it was important to get one of one's books on the short lists and Elizabeth had missed the mark for two years running.

Lucille arrived, browned and beaming, at the first editorial meeting. She was praised by the president of the group that now owned them for the selection of books she was presenting. One of them was indeed expected to win a prize. Then finances and management were discussed. It was announced, as it had been for the last decade, that times were tough and tough measures were needed. The difference this year was that their new president laid out concrete steps meant to redress the situation, as he put it. Besides the tightening of accounting, the reduction of entertainment reimbursements, the closer scrutiny of office supplies and photocopying, he announced that there were to be other changes. "You will hear more about these in due course." Lucille looked serious and pleased, Gérard pensive.

"All I can tell you now," he said in response to the rising whispers around the room, "is that job security is not what it used to be and these modifications may also involve a reduction of staff." The murmuring stopped. He concluded: "I'm sorry to be bringing in a monetary bottom line to our higher purpose but the world is changing and we have to change with it if we want to survive."

As they stood up from the table, people formed chattering clusters. Gérard, the person with whom Elizabeth wanted to discuss these announcements was in a *tête-à-tête* with Lucille. So she spoke a few words to a few people, then left, feeling troubled and alone. Usually at such a moment, she would have phoned Lucas for a little chat, but that was no longer an option. Little chats out of the blue, she realized, were a quaint relic of the past.

Whatever pleasure Elizabeth felt at re-establishing routine quickly subsided. At home she struggled to act normally with Lucas, to keep the children unaware that anything was wrong. At work she felt increasingly isolated so that at the beginning of the third week Elizabeth arrived at the office with all the weight of a Monday morning and none of the relief. She closed her door, plopped down in her swivel chair and looked out the window. Next to the neighbouring chimney pots two pigeons were copulating. The male strutted and cooed, his chest puffed to bursting as he jumped on the staggering female. After a great flutter he backed off before running through the whole process again. She often sat and watched the pigeons. It used to amuse her.

She and Lucas had tried to make love three times since the end of August. Each time Lucas had been unable to maintain a half-hearted erection for longer than five minutes.

"I'm sorry. I just can't do it," he would say, turning his back to her in bed, before slipping silently out of the room. She would hear the door between the apartment and his office open and close. She would imagine him masturbating on the sofa next to his drawing board and she would wrap her arms around herself and stare helplessly into the dark.

He started slipping out other nights for no reason until one night, without a word between them, he began to spend every night on his sofa. Once on a Sunday when everyone else was out, she had gone in there and looked in the cupboard. A fitted sheet and a duvet were neatly folded with a pillow on top and she felt a physical pain in her chest at the sight of his tidy bedding.

The phone rang on her desk; she could see it was Gérard. She considered not answering but what good would that do.

He sat solemnly at his desk, elbows on the arms of his black leather chair, fingers pushed together, spread apart in front of his face. "I had forgotten that I was once elected personnel representative," he said.

"Meaning?"

"Meaning that the unpleasant task of speaking to my fellow employees falls on my shoulders."

"Which unpleasant task?" She wanted to make him spit it out, to be direct for once, but her scalp was tingling.

"The unpleasant task that was discussed in our management meeting." When she said nothing, he continued: "The task of informing you that, for economic reasons, we have to fire you. Of informing you that within five days you'll be receiving a letter to that effect."

"You're firing me. After twenty years. Just like that." She could hardly breath.

"I'm afraid so," Gérard sighed. "But it's not quite as bad as it seems."

"You mean because you're not being fired."

"No. I'm not. But no, that's not what I meant either. The

offer you will receive in the letter is that we put you on commission."

"Translation?"

"You will be put on a short-term contract whereby you will get paid a very small retainer fee, rather than a salary, and the rest of what you earn will depend on the books you bring in." He pushed some preliminary papers across his desk, where a path had been cleared amidst his calculated clutter. "Think about it," Gérard said. "It may be your best option."

***

She did not even tell Lucas what had happened at work. They had both retreated into their shells and really only spoke at mealtimes with the children or at dinner with friends, though those had been dramatically reduced, as had all other outings. Elizabeth's life became a series of mechanical steps, repeated day after day. She woke children up in the morning, made their breakfast, went to work and sat in an office until it was time to come back again to oversee homework, eat supper, read and go back to bed. She needed to execute her days in such a manner because every time she stopped to think there was a risk of a complete breakdown.

The children appeared, at least, to notice nothing. What they were really picking up on, she didn't know, though even the teenage boys seemed remarkably tin-eared to the change of key in the house. True, Tristan was preparing his Bac and working so hard he didn't seem to notice anything, whether it was the food he put in his mouth or the weather outside. Olivier had his first girlfriend and that seemed to be all he could think about, while Gabby was wrapped up in some football playoffs. And Ariane— weren't girls supposed to be more tuned into mood and atmosphere? No, Elizabeth couldn't say she noticed anything different about her daughter, except that this year she was turning into a voracious reader—was that a sign— her disappearance into fiction?

As for the larger family, her in-laws, she found no proof that Lucas had told them anything in Provence. But she was convinced that at least Alix was suspicious. Something about the way she looked back and forth between the two of them, as if she were at a tennis match. Roland, she realized one night as they sat down at a restaurant after the cinema, would never notice anything. Referring to the real-life depression of the leading actor in the film they'd just seen, he said: "What's he got to be so unhappy about?"

"I don't think, *cher Roland*," Lucas had said, "that depression is necessarily related to material wealth or professional success. You never know what's going on under the surface."

"*Mais enfin*," Roland the civil-servant-novelist had retorted. "He should just think about all he has achieved! All he has in life! It can't be that bad."

"Pass the salt, Roland," Alix had said tartly.

As for Isabelle and Claude—well, she never had any idea what they were really thinking—but they didn't seem to notice any more than the children or their friends did. It was amazing to Elizabeth that so much tension and disconnection could go undetected. That what was really going on could be covered up with such ease. Until, that is, she thought of her own cover-up act, which she had kept up effortlessly and effectively for a quarter of a century.

The only people who noticed, or at least noticed and said something, were Trevor and Béa, the couple Elizabeth had tried having to supper with Troy. Béa was an English woman who, though several years younger, had been to the same boarding school as Elizabeth. They had not quite overlapped, but their fathers knew one another and when Béa moved to Paris, Andrew Lyall had asked his daughter to get in touch. Elizabeth had rather reluctantly invited Béa to supper but much to her surprise, she had liked her from the moment she'd walked through the door. She managed to be genteel without being small-minded, the way

Elizabeth had found most of her schoolmates. And Elizabeth had discovered that just the fact of their having been through the same school, of being familiar with the same buildings and teachers and customs had created a bond that would not have existed with another tenuous acquaintance. That had been a few years ago. In the meantime, Béa, who was a painter, had moved in with an American photographer, Trevor.

"So what part of the snail are you photographing now?" Lucas asked, as they sat down to a glass of red wine in the sitting room of Trevor and Béa's Montmartre apartment. Trevor was taking pictures of Paris arrondissement by arrondissement and called the project *La Vie de l'Escargot*, because the city's twenty districts, which spiralled around, were often described as a snail.

"I'm in the eighth, which is infinitely better than its predecessors, the seventh and the sixth. They've become so prettified that from a photographic and sociological point of view, they're without interest."

"And our fifth?" asked Lucas. "How does it fare, from a photographic and sociological point of view?"

"It's still got its redeeming corners," said Trevor with an ironic smile. "Anyway in the eighth, once you get behind the bland horror of the Champs-Elysées, there's some really interesting stuff. Some streets with old shops that won't survive the retirement of the owner. Some courtyards that still give a whiff of their nineteenth century opulence," he said while stroking the ears of the black dog at his side. "That being said, this is the first arrondissement that has not agreed to give me a small grant for my efforts. Nor are they interested in one of my booklets to entertain people while they wait in the *mairie* to sign their children up for school or to register a complaint. And with their property taxes, they are more than able to afford some support."

"A classic case," Lucas said, "of those with the most being the least willing to part with any of it."

"The unhappy rich, right?" laughed Trevor.

"Something like that," nodded Lucas, who remained serious. "And the fact that they don't want people poking around behind their pretty façades, reminding them of the cobwebs in their corners."

"Let me help you with supper," Elizabeth said to Béa, who had just stood up.

As they sat around a pine table in the kitchen, the dog lying on its mat in the corner, the candles flickering against the dark window and the bracketed shelves they'd put up themselves, the food was good and talk was easy. Even Lucas commented on the way home how pleasant the evening had been. How natural, how unaffected, Trevor and Béa were. "It was relaxing," he said, "to be with people who are not competing at every turn to be the wittiest or the best informed about the latest scandal."

And yet, when Elizabeth phoned to say thank you a couple of days later, Béa asked: "Are you all right?"

"Yes."

"You seemed a bit subdued and Lucas was very edgy." Pause. "I thought maybe I imagined it but Trevor sensed it too."

"We actually had a lovely time." Elizabeth tapped her pencil on the thick manuscript in front of her. "Work's not going very well. And Lucas—well, you know, he's often a little pre-occupied."

"I didn't mean to pry."

"No, no. You're not prying. But everything's fine."

"Why don't we have lunch sometime."

"I have a busy few weeks. How about if I ring you early next month?"

"Any time."

After she'd put the phone down, Elizabeth got up, walked around her desk, sat back down again. She felt caught between being found out and being relieved that somebody had finally noticed. Why had she hedged like that? Why did she always have to be so English? Shouldn't she confide in somebody and who better than Béa? The pressure of her situation was crushing her.

She couldn't go on like this.

The trouble was she had little experience of sharing confidences. Her friendships were not like that. When she had lunch with Sophie or Caroline or Dorothée, they would talk about children and work and the challenge of holding it all together. But intimate, heartfelt angst or doubt was uncharted territory for these driven, successful women. On the occasion that she had heard the confessions and confidences of others—she had always found it easy to be a good listener—she had never offered any information in return. It wasn't so easy to reverse the order of things now.

That dinner was the end of October. Shortly thereafter, Elizabeth and Lucas began to row. Usually it was over silly things such as Elizabeth throwing away the leftovers that Lucas had planned to eat for lunch or Lucas forgetting to put the phone back on its post so the battery went dead. But like the proverbial pebble plopped into the pond, each seemingly small dispute reverberated in ever widening circles. Family meals became a strain.

"Why didn't you pass the pepper with the salt?" Olivier said to Tristan, whose curly head was hanging over his plate.

"Because you only asked for the salt."

"How many times has Maman told us to pass both at the same time?"

"I always pass both," piped in Ariane.

"No one is interested in your opinion," said Olivier.

"Who cares about yours?" she answered.

"I care what both of you think," said Lucas. "But not about the salt and pepper. Couldn't we find a more interesting subject for discussion? Tristan, pull your head out of your plate and tell me how that physics experiment is going."

"Fine."

"That doesn't tell us much," Elizabeth said. *Does Tristan ever stop slumping, does he always have such a taciturn frown?*

"If you two had been paying attention, you would remember

that I finished writing it up last week. I got it back today. I got an eighteen."

"Good. Very good," said Elizabeth. *Relief. Eighteen out of twenty. No one in France ever gets better than that. But his Bac isn't until June, well beyond Christmas.*

"What about you, Olivier?" asked Lucas. "What happened on your Victor Hugo test?"

"I have to learn one of his poems for next week," said Gabby.

"Get used to it," said Olivier. "You're going to be reading the guy one way or another for the next ten years. At least."

"And the test?"

"I ran out of time."

Is he the one falling apart? "What did you think about the answer you did manage to write?"

"Don't know." Shrug.

"We are living," Lucas finally offered one evening, "in a state of purgatory. We hardly speak. We do not even sleep together anymore." He gave Elizabeth that twisted smile. Over the last months, she'd seen that look often on Lucas' face, and it had made her wonder if he didn't know something about her other sins with Troy but she didn't dare test him.

Picking up the blue and green glass paperweight from Venice, he resumed: "Even though I keep trying to remember the good times."

Elizabeth nodded. Yes, that Venice weekend, when they'd left the children with Lucas' parents. The freedom had been wonderful, as had the food, the wine, the breathtaking frescoes, one after another after another. But at that moment, looking at the blue and green swirls on the paperweight in Lucas' hand, what Elizabeth remembered most about the weekend was their argument near the Bridge of Sighs. It had been about Proust. Elizabeth had maintained that the narrator finally visited Venice with his mother in the volume *La Prisonnière*; Lucas said the trip didn't occur until *Albertine disparue*. Since they had no way of resolving the dispute until they got home, it hovered over the rest of their weekend escape. "But don't you remember?" Lucas would say. "He was trying to get over Albertine." Elizabeth would answer: "He was always trying to get over Albertine."

He, of course, had been right and that had made her furious. Not just because she had been wrong, but also because she should have known not to try and get the better of him on what was so clearly his territory; she'd only read Proust, in translation, and not even all the volumes, for a course at her American college.

Now, too, she remembered that they had repeatedly lost their bearings in the warren of streets. That they had always seemed to be looking up at the dark windows of empty flats or down dead quiet canals in the dank January air. That a pall of melancholy had clung to the weekend like a cloying fog.

"The fire was Troy's idea," Elizabeth said.

"Ideas aren't punishable," he said dully.

"He was the perpetrator. It was he who threw on the petrol."

"You lit the match," he said, his voice beginning to rise. "But I agree that's not the real problem. It's that afterwards you not only went along with a lie, you had no concern for Troy's condition, no concern for his fate. You abandoned him. Skipped off without so much as a glance over your shoulder. I don't know how you could have done that. How you could have lived with such an act on your conscience all these years."

"You should know how easy it is to suppress what you don't want to remember," she said defiantly. "What you wished never happened. And then how it gets easier over time. You should know—you and your family should know. You live—thrive would be a more accurate word—in a country that sixty years ago—well, you know all too well what that country would have done to you sixty years ago. What it did, to a member of your own family."

"What?"

"You know who I mean. Your Aunt Coco. The one who never gets mentioned, even though what happened to her marks every trait of your father's face." Lucas looked stunned, as if she'd just slapped him across the face. She continued more calmly. "All I'm saying is that for a Jew to live here in France at all—that takes a certain capacity for forgetting and forgiving too."

"You're talking about a collective crime that occurred before I was even born."

"Well, you're treating me as if I participated in just such a collective crime."

He had two deep furrows between his eyes and it was if her words had got stuck there. She asked more softly, pleadingly:

"So why can't you forgive me for something that happened if not before you were born, before I ever knew you?" When he didn't answer she said: "I have tried, in my way, to make up for what I did then by being a good person. An extra good person." Still he said nothing. "Haven't I been a good wife, a good mother? Doesn't that count for anything?"

"Yes," he almost whispered. "But you also lived with me for over twenty years without telling me about what you'd done. And when Troy was here, you still didn't try to set things straight, with him or with me."

She said: "I tried. A couple of times I tried I sort of did but..."

There was no need to finish the sentence. Lucas had already disappeared through his office door.

***

They started leaving notes for one another.

"I called the plumber—he's coming this morning," she would write. "I told him to ring your office bell."

"I'm going to Rouen today—back tomorrow afternoon," he would write. He seemed to be going to Rouen all the time, or stretching his office hours.

When he was absent, Elizabeth thought the tension would depart with him but she was wrong. For the first time ever she had trouble talking to her children. They would sit at the dinner table and she would struggle to think of something to say. Lucas' absence was denser than his presence. Still no child said a word and Elizabeth began to wonder if there hadn't always been some level of tension that she had chosen not to notice, in the same way as she had suppressed uncomfortable memories from their trip to Venice. If part of the reason Lucas was having such trouble forgiving her had nothing to do with morality but with an inherent fault line in their relationship.

"No matter what people say," Gérard had said to her over lunch in the days when he was trying to seduce her, "love between a man and a woman is destined to wither on the vine."

"I don't believe that," she had answered, vehemently shaking her head. "It's been over ten years and I still love my husband. I don't see why that has to change."

Gérard hadn't replied but the smirk on his face said it all.

That troubling, baffling conversation had come back to her often. Each time she had wanted to protest, to convince Gérard that he was wrong. Now she wondered if she hadn't wanted to protest too much because the great seducer was seeing right through her. She had, after all, allowed him to play the seduction game; she had not protested at the hand on her back, the knee under the table. And then Troy—

When she imagined touching Lucas, it was a peck on the forehead, not her legs wrapped around him or her mouth hungrily in search of his. Most of the time, if she were being honest, she would have to say that they made love as if they were doing the washing up and part of her, if she were being honest, was not unhappy that they were no longer sharing the same bed.

***

They were going to lunch at the elder Tellers. The children were gathered in the front hall. They had all asked what time lunch would be finished. Tristan had an essay due the next day.

Olivier looked stunned; he'd been out late with his girlfriend and was planning to see her again that afternoon. The twins wanted to stay home and play.

It was a cold day for early December. The car was covered in white frost. Lucas scraped the windscreen and ran the heat high. Elizabeth did her best to rub a spot clear on the back window with her glove. The twins tried writing their names. With arms tightly drawn across their chests, the older boys slumped sullenly in the back seat, an attitude that would not normally have been tolerated by either parent. But today neither of them said a word.

The pale winter light filtered through the large windows of the older Teller's apartment and illuminated their ordered, cultivated life.

"This is a nice piece," Lucas said, bending over to get a better look at the new sculpture from Bali. It was a large stone hand on a pedestal, the thumb and forefinger brought together in a Buddhist lotus position.

"Yes," said Claude. "We bought it for a song, on the roadside."

Ariane, at eye level with the statue, said: "It looks like he's squishing a bug."

Lucas and Claude had already turned away. Elizabeth asked her: "Where do you get such ideas?"

Ariane shrugged, and skipped away after her cousin Juliette.

Behind the statue, on a table somewhat hidden by the grand piano, was the family photo, the one with Coco. Elizabeth had often looked at it but today she paused and looked again. It was a formal, studio photo—everyone dressed up and smiling stiffly. Everyone except Coco, who had a large mouth and big teeth and who looked as if someone had just made a good joke. That smile and the fact that she was quite a bit older than Claude and Antoine set her apart, even before she laughed off her parents' pleas to join them in London. Elizabeth turned away, wandered over to the large window. The rue de Tournon was very quiet on a Sunday, empty except for a young couple coming back from the market with a shopping basket and a homeless woman who was huddled against a building in a large coat and sleeping bag. She had flowing dark hair, streaked with grey and she must have been pretty before she'd gone to seed. Elizabeth was wondering how she'd ended up on the street and why she hadn't been in a shelter on such a cold night, when Isabelle announced it was time to eat.

Elizabeth turned back towards the room, rubbing her arms.

"Cold?" asked Alix.

"A bit. The winter air comes right through those big windows."

When they were all seated, Isabelle turned her perfect face Elizabeth's way as she passed the quiche around. "We saw Antoine the other night," she said. "He told us a lot of you in the fiction department have been put on commission."

"Yes, that's right," said Elizabeth, feeling put on the spot and wishing she'd sat at the other end of the table, near the children.

"Fiction is a tough business these days," said Roland, whose latest novel had come out in the September torrent.

"If fiction is suffering," Claude said, "it may be because the real-world spectacle largely surpasses any credibly imagined one." He looked at Elizabeth. "As for these short-term contracts, they're all the rage these days. They're a way of getting around the thirty-five hour working week and the inflexible labour laws."

"So I've been told," Elizabeth answered, wondering if Antoine had informed them it was either that or get sacked. When she'd finally told Lucas about the new arrangements at work, she had left out that detail.

"I was wondering," Alix looked at Lucas and Elizabeth. "If you've had any word from your friend Troy."

"I've had a couple of e-mails," Lucas said. Elizabeth couldn't stop herself from staring at her husband in astonishment. "In response to mine." He fiddled with the stem of his crystal wine glass. "He's fine."

"I wish he were still here," said Alix.

"He fixed so many annoying little problems for us all," said Isabelle.

"He did that," said Alix. "But he was also an interesting person to have around. An unusual person."

"I actually thought he was a little strange," said Roland. "He seemed troubled. Not quite normal."

"You're just jealous," said Alix.

"Huh," grunted Roland.

"Well," said Lucas. "It's true he's had a difficult life, without all our advantages. And of course he's not quite *normal*. He's an artist."

"I'm glad I at least bought one of his sculptures," said Alix. She looked at Elizabeth. "Do you think he'll visit again? He seemed quite taken with the city."

"He was. But no, I doubt he'll come back," she said, looking at Lucas out of the corner of her eye. "As Lucas said, his means are limited." She was thinking how it would be just like Lucas to keep up contact, as a way of compensating for her deplorable behaviour.

"Too bad," said Alix, looking from Lucas to Elizabeth.

"Yes," mumbled Lucas, looking very uncomfortable. He wiped his mouth with his napkin and turned to his father. "How's work on the committee going?" Claude had recently been named to a *Comité des Sages*, a commission of admired, often retired, brains. Their task was to come up with the latest final word on the integration of minorities.

"The work is fascinating," he said, lining up his knife and fork side by side on the plate and looking up at the table, one bright blue eye slightly larger than the other. "We have heard many revealing testimonials, read pages and pages of razor-sharp analyses. Ideas abound. We will write an intelligent report suggesting some potentially very useful, constructive reforms." He laced his fingers together and smiled thinly. "Like its predecessors, it will result in a few newspaper articles, maybe even a television interview, before being shelved and ignored."

He picked up his knife and fork again. "Unless the social affairs minister is silly enough to listen to us, in which case he will soon find himself out of a job."

"But what's to be done?" Lucas asked his father. "The foundations of the whole system are shuddering. Education does not answer the needs of the poor immigrant children, yet the teachers are determined that nothing should change. Even if the children manage to get a degree, employers won't hire anyone called Mohammed. And everyone continues to live in crumbling blocks because the municipalities do nothing to provide better housing, better living conditions in general." He was quite red in the face now. "But I guess none of this is surprising since the political system regurgitates the same old tired men, election after election, and the best civil servants are jumping ship in droves for the private sector."

"Since when do you get so exercised about politics?" asked Roland.

"Since when do you get so exercised in general?" added Alix, eyes wide.

Elizabeth could feel her mother-in-law looking at her, questioningly. Or could she? She could feel Alix's eyes darting back and forth between her and Lucas. Or could she? She could feel Claude, with his frighteningly sharp eyes, staring, accusingly, at her alone. Or could she? She did not dare look up from her plate.

"This isn't just politics," Lucas continued. "It's the whole society that's falling to pieces."

"Though I presumably qualify as one of your tired old men," Claude said with an amused smile at his son, who still didn't seem to be aware of having insulted his father, "I have to say you are exaggerating the cataclysmic state of affairs slightly. Though I do agree that a realignment of priorities, of choices, is necessary. Our civil service, brilliant and prestigious as it is, cannot solve all the problems or offer a sufficiently attractive financial incentive to the best and the brightest." He himself had worked in government-owned industry, as well as having been hired many times over the years by private companies that wanted access to his inexhaustible address book and his invariably reasoned and intelligent advice.

"Change is ineluctable," said Roland with a harrumph.

"Thank you, Roland," said Claude.

"There are certainly lots of tremors under our feet," said Isabelle. "That always makes people unsteady."

"And generally brings out our darker side," said Claude, getting that look he sometimes got, as if the weight of the world —or at least of the twentieth century—were sitting squarely on his shoulders. "Fear of the unknown, of change, that is."

There was silence around the table. Knives and forks clicked against the porcelain.

"Well," Isabelle finally said, "we're not going fix it all today. Let's go next door for coffee."

***

Christmas, the date Lucas had set for a decision on their future, was almost upon them and since nothing had improved, Elizabeth had acquired physical symptoms of strain. Besides a nervous tic in her eye, she had also begun to start at the smallest unexpected sound. She had trouble speaking fluidly. At the same time, she was wondering how on earth they could spoil the holiday season with talk of separation and divorce. And beyond Christmas, there was Tristan's Bac just months away. How could they, his parents, jeopardize his performance on that by breaking up the family? When, Elizabeth wondered, could one ever find a convenient moment for a divorce?

Lucas was obviously having similar thoughts. Their infrequent conversations now took on a note-like quality.

"I hope Tristan's all right."

"Yes, he looks worried."

"And withdrawn."

"I hope he's getting on with his work."

"So do I. It's hard to know."

"Yes. It's hard to know."

Presents for their secular Christmas had to be discussed, since notes might be discovered.

"Gabby's easy. He wants a football."

"Ariane will be happy with a pretty dress or a book."

"Olivier is impossible. I wouldn't dare buy him clothes."

"No. Nor Tristan. He's no easier."

Silence.

"And what would you like?"

"Oh, nothing. And you?"

"Nothing."

"Some time early next year?"

"Yes, early next year. The holiday season is no time…"

"No, no time."

In a way they had never been communicating better—so few words and so much said.

***

In January Olivier's German class was taking a trip to Munich. The students would stay with different families at night, and during the day they would tour the city together. It was too late for the Oktoberfest, the teacher had joked, but they'd visit the Glockenspiel and the Residenzpalace and the Peterskirche. At the end a visit to Dachau was planned. In a letter from the headmaster, parents had been warned about this part of the trip and had been advised to discuss it with their children. The letter said that with anti-Semitic incidents and intolerance on the rise, the school felt it was important to remind students of the not-so-distant past. It was their contribution to the collective memory.

"Good," said Lucas, as he finished reading the letter aloud. The whole family was together in the sitting room. "It's important to see things firsthand."

"Is it like that other place we visited?" asked Ariane.

"Which place?" asked Lucas.

"I think she means Verdun," said Tristan.

"Where she threw up," said Olivier.

"I couldn't help it," said Ariane.

"No", said Lucas. "Verdun was the First World War. The concentration camps were the Second."

The twins nodded. They already knew about the War and the concentration camps and the six million Jews. About how lucky their grandfather had been because his father had had the good sense to leave for London in the nick of time. They also knew about Aunt Coco in the photo and about how many cousins and family friends had not been so lucky or perspicacious.

"But remember that what you're seeing at Dachau," Lucas continued, looking particularly stern, "happened only a generation after Verdun."

He looked stern because the family trip to Verdun a couple of years earlier had proved something of a disaster. Lucas, who had stopped there once on his way to Metz, where he was designing a school, had insisted the family take a detour via the First World War battle sight at the winter break, on the way to skiing in the Alps.

"It's a little more than detour," Elizabeth had said.

"It's east and the mountains are south-east."

"Sort of. I'd say Verdun is east and the mountains are south."

"Close enough," he'd said.

Because it was going to take an extra day and a half for this "detour", there was resistance right from the start. Tristan had a couple of friends in Chamonix that he was eager to hook up with. Olivier was borrowing a snowboard and was desperate to try it out as soon as possible. The twins were only four at the time. They left home late. There was heavy fog, followed by sleet, on their way through Champagne.

"We won't be able to see anything," said Tristan, looking grimly out the window.

"This is just the way to experience it," said Lucas. "On a dark and gloomy winter's day."

They left the main road, driving past bleak shopping malls and cheap new housing, until finally they were winding their way up a hill into the forest.

"Look in there," he said.

"Watch the road, Lucas," said Elizabeth. "It's slippery and full of sharp turns."

"You see all that undulating ground?" he pointed. "The result of the relentless shelling."

"The ground underneath the trees does roll unnaturally," said Elizabeth, trying to compensate for the children's sullen silence behind them.

"I feel sick," Ariane said.

"Don't throw up on me," Gabby said, moving closer to Olivier.

"Get off me," Olivier said.

"Last time she threw up it landed on me," Gabby said, starting to cry.

"Where's that plastic bag I gave you, Ariane?" asked Elizabeth.

"I don't know."

"Open the window," said Lucas.

"I feel really sick," said Ariane.

"Pull the car over, Lucas," said Elizabeth.

"I can't. There's no place to stop. There's another car right on my tail."

Up it came, before Elizabeth could locate the plastic bag or the paper towel. Ariane was now crying, along with Gabby, who was screaming "My leg! My leg!"

By the time they got to a lay-by, all four children were complaining loudly. Elizabeth felt peevish too, wondering why the trip to Verdun couldn't have waited, as she cleaned up Ariane and Gabby and the seat as best she could. But the car still stunk, and no one was shy about pointing it out, again and again and again.

Lucas, however, was not deterred. As they drove by the vestiges of trenches, he said: "Imagine all those young men—not much older than you two boys—stuck out here in the cold and the rain, up to their knees in muck, not knowing when a shell might land in their sodden trench, or worse, when they might be ordered to leave it, to slither along on their bellies in the mud and amidst the barbed wire under direct fire. It's really a shame the museum is closed. You could see it in the film." They had arrived just as the museum was closing for a long lunch.

No one responded.

"Yea," Tristan finally muttered.

"Imagine," Lucas went on, "that in 1916, the ground all around us was completely scorched. No grass, no trees—not a single living thing."

He took them to the Fort de Douaumont, an imposing fortress with many dank corridors built right into the side of a high hill, a place that normally would have interested the boys at least. But they all marched across the undulating ground that covered and camouflaged its roof, staring blankly, hands in pockets, unyielding in their determination to be bored and apathetic.

They climbed back in the car and Lucas drove them to the ossuary and cemetery. "This is the last stop," he said.

"I'm cold," Ariane whispered to Elizabeth.

"All those people are dead?" Gabby asked as they gazed over a sea of white crosses.

"Yes," said Lucas. "There are fifteen thousand graves of French soldiers here. In the ossuary there are the remains of one-hundred thirty thousand French and German soldiers. So many dead that they had to build those wings on the building. And they're all mixed up because the bodies could not even be identified. The best that could be done was to bury them by area of the battlefield. Just bones piled on bones."

"It's really cold," said Olivier, finally. "Can't we go back to the car?"

When they'd stopped for the night near Dijon, Lucas, completely disheartened, said to Elizabeth: "How could they have been so unresponsive? Not even Tristan seemed to take a bit of interest in what he was seeing. You try and teach your children lessons from the past and they don't listen. It's no wonder we keep making the same foolish mistakes over and over again."

"They're children," Elizabeth had said. "You can't expect them..."

"What do you mean—I can't expect them to understand? They need to understand and the sooner the better."

When they finally arrived in the Alps and the children exploded with joy in the snow, Lucas became even more morose. "Pleasure. Enjoyment. The here and now. It's all people care about," he had grumbled to Elizabeth, who had laughed and said:

"Come on, Lucas. Lighten up. The snow's wonderful. Let's ski."

***

Olivier had insisted that he was too old to be picked up by his parents, so at the end of the Munich trip, he came home alone from the Gare de l'Est. When Elizabeth and Lucas greeted him at the door, he fell into his father's arms. Elizabeth had not seen him cry for several years.

"What is it?" Lucas asked softly.

Olivier shook his head but didn't speak.

They got his coat off and sat him down in a comfortable chair.

"What happened?" Lucas asked.

Olivier's eyes darted about as if they were too sickened by everything they saw to rest on any one object. Finally he fixed them at an oblique angle on a pair of Gabby's shoes that had been left on the floor. After a few minutes of silence, he began:

"It was what happened yesterday. At Dachau."

"Come on," said Elizabeth softly, putting her arm around him. "Tell us."

"We went on a bus out there and first the driver got lost. The place is impossible to find, like they did everything they could to hide it or pretend it wasn't there." He paused, shook his head in disgust. "Once we finally did get there, everybody was wild. It was the last day, we'd been living with strange families all week. I don't know, everyone was feeling kind of crazy. These two guys, Philippe and Jean-Marie, started imitating Nazis. They were goose-stepping and saluting and barking orders at one another. No one paid any attention or said anything. Then Jean-Marie took out one of those disposable cameras and they started taking pictures of one another. In front of the barbed wire, one of them pretended to escape. Near the shooting range, one of them pretended to be shot."

"Didn't the teachers say something?" Lucas asked sharply. "Order them to stop?"

"They didn't see. Philippe and Jean-Marie were lagging behind. But we all saw. And we didn't say anything. There must be seven Jewish kids in my class and not one of us opened our mouths, told them to stop. We were such cowards." His voice cracked and the tears started rolling down his cheeks again. "The thing is normally, they're not bad guys." He shook his head. "So how could they do that?"

And finally he looked up, from one parent to another.

"I'm going to phone the school," said Lucas.

"Don't do that," Olivier said, panic rising in his voice. "Everyone will know I snitched."

"I do not consider bringing brutish, insensitive, possibly dangerous behaviour to light as snitching," said Lucas.

"But I didn't have the guts to say anything then. You should just keep quiet now."

"Keeping quiet killed millions of people," he said, standing up and leaving the room.

"Maman, please tell him not to call the school," Olivier said.

She looked at her pleading son. A year earlier she might have obliged him, argued with Lucas that it was just kids acting silly but now her moral capital was spent and gone.

"I'm afraid I can't. Your father is right," she said.

It was Sunday, meaning the call would have to wait a day. At supper Lucas made Olivier repeat the story for the benefit of the other three children and even the twins were disturbed by it. They stared at their brother with wide eyes, while their food got cold on their plates.

"But why did they do that?" asked Ariane.

"I don't know," said Olivier miserably. "They were just being stupid."

"That," said Lucas, pointing his knife at his son, "is exactly how it can start again."

"What do you mean?" asked Ariane, in an increasingly worried voice.

"What will start all over again?" asked Gabby.

"Nothing," Elizabeth said to the twins. "You don't need to worry about anything."

"Can I be excused?" asked Olivier, though he had eaten little.

"Yes, go ahead," answered Elizabeth quickly. "You too," she said to the twins. "Go get ready for bed. I'll be there in a minute."

When the others had cleared their plates and glasses, Lucas turned to Tristan:

"Tristan have you heard any anti-Semitic remarks around school?"

He shook his head. "It's not that kind of place. There are lots of Jewish kids."

"That's what I thought too. And I'm sure it's generally still true, which makes this incident all the more shocking. That the children of educated, enlightened parents could act in such a way is more frightening than similar behaviour in a less privileged environment."

The next morning Olivier tried again to prevail upon his father, arguing that he would suffer untold humiliation if everyone knew who had informed the school, but his protests had no effect on Lucas' determination to bring the story to light.

First the parents of the German class were called in with their children. A "Photo's Quik !" plastic bag containing the evidence —the used camera and developed photos—was held up before them. The photos were distributed, while the two culprits, Philippe and Jean-Marie, stood in front of the group, heads hanging. As Lucas himself said later, the photos were more tasteless than shocking but that did not detract from or qualify the boys' misconduct. Then the two teachers who had accompanied the class stood up. They looked more ashamed than the boys when they apologized for their negligence. There was a discussion as to whether or not the whole school and therefore the larger public should be informed; many thought not—they were worried about the school's reputation. Lucas argued vigorously that for just such a reason, the school's high standing, it was vital that the truth be told. Before a decision could be made, the news leaked and it wasn't long before the whole country knew what had happened.

Within the school itself, Holocaust discussions were carried out in all classes. Students were instructed to be honest and candid, an attitude not normally encouraged in the French classroom, and some grabbed the occasion as a one-time offer not to be missed. A surprising number said that they were sick to death of hearing about the Holocaust, that it was a subject for old people and had nothing to do with them. "This is a new millennium, and it's not our guilt trip," one boy in Tristan's class was quoted as saying, "so why can't you stop shoving this stuff down our throats?"

As Olivier had predicted, word got out that it was his and Tristan's father who had spilled the beans, but besides the odd cold shoulder, there was little fall-out. Olivier did break up with his girlfriend shortly thereafter and though he blamed his father, disagreements had begun before the trip to Munich.

Lucas and Elizabeth were the main beneficiaries of the incident. It gave them a new focus, a temporary distraction, from their own troubles. Lucas threw himself into making sure the incident was widely reported and denounced, and Elizabeth, on the surface, supported his every effort, was pleased to be able to ride on his moral coattails. As if making right prevail in this instance would somehow discount or outweigh her earlier wrongs. But underneath she found Lucas' crusade irritating. Of course it was admirable but he was acting like a religious zealot, a proselytiser, and she did not like it.

Once the national fervour died down—and it did, remarkably quickly, given the initial uproar—the reprieve came to an abrupt end—their relations were worse than they had been before. Though they managed to hold out through Tristan's Bac, by early July the tension between them had even elicited reactions from the children.

With Tristan it was slouched shoulders, sighs and disappointed looks, from one to the other of them. "I'm going out," he would excuse himself from the table after gobbling his food.

"Can't you two stop glaring at each other?" Olivier said.

"Can't both of you come to my football match?" Gabby asked.

"You don't look very happy." Ariane proclaimed. "And you don't tell us funny stories anymore."

On one level or another they all knew what was happening. Therefore, when separate summer holidays were announced, no one protested or even commented. Lucas would go south to his parents' for two weeks. Elizabeth would take the children for a week in Scotland with her father and stepmother.

"You're going to Scotland alone with the children?" asked her mother on the phone.

"Lucas can't get away," she fudged.

"What a shame," said Vera.

Lucas was more forthcoming with his family and Elizabeth even got a call from Claude, who she thought only vaguely knew of her existence. He said: "These things happen. I'm very sorry for you both."

Alix said: "What a shock. Let's have lunch first thing in September."

Unusually, Lucas had obviously not told his family a thing about their troubles until now. Instead of feeling relieved by his discretion, Elizabeth was peeved. Everything might be easier if Lucas weren't so damned irreproachable.

Summer got under way. Tristan started his work experience in a newspaper and Olivier went not to Germany, as originally planned, but to the Pyrenees on a hiking trip, and the twins left for the Lubéron. Between her and Lucas even the notes had stopped. It was amazing, really, that two people could occupy the same space and intersect so infrequently.

They came together once, near the end of July, after having fixed a formal appointment with one another: six o'clock at a café, to ensure Tristan didn't come home and hear something. They could at least begin on a positive note:

"Tristan certainly did well on his Bac."

"As expected."

"True."

"Still, it's a relief."

"Yes, it is."

"So."

"So."

"It isn't getting any better."

"No, it isn't."

"We can't go on like this."

"No, we can't."

"I was thinking," said Lucas, sitting with his arms and legs crossed, as if he'd tied himself in a knot, "that maybe we should consider a trial separation."

Although Elizabeth had thought this herself, his saying it

aloud still felt like a physical pain. She sighed and nodded by didn't reply.

"Giving it time hasn't seemed to have helped," Lucas continued.

She shook her head in agreement.

"The thing is," said Lucas, un-knotting his body and leaning his elbows on the table, "I don't see how I can move. With my office right there and the amount of work I have at the moment."

Now she was dumbstruck. It had certainly never crossed her mind that separation might mean her leaving. "And the children?" she finally managed, hardly above a whisper.

"We can't afford another large flat."

"Don't you think that they need their mother?"

"Yes. But look, one of us has to move. I don't see how, right now, it can be me."

"Your office has another door."

"It wouldn't be right for me to be working right next to where you're living," he said. "And it looks like I may well win that competition in Berlin that I mentioned. I've taken on another assistant. I'm working flat out."

"But you can't expect me to live without my children."

"Why should you expect me to?" he answered, his voice rising. As a young, struggling architect, Lucas had often taken care of the children while Elizabeth was at the office, making most of the money. But didn't he intend this plan as the ultimate form of punishment for her treatment of Troy?

They sat in awkward silence for several minutes.

"I propose," Lucas finally continued, quietly again, "that we agree to a year's separation. That we find another place with enough space for the children to spend every weekend with you. After a year we will revisit everything."

"You're way ahead of me," she said. Not wanting to leave the café with him, she stood up quickly. "I have to think about it. I cannot sign my fate away over a cup of coffee."

She walked briskly back to the rue Laromiguière, thinking

she had to fight this, had to find some solution that would allow her to stay with her children. Why, she wondered, couldn't Lucas just move into his office? There was plenty of space and he was practically living there now.

Despite all this tough talk to herself, when she walked into the apartment she felt as if she were the one who didn't belong. She couldn't say why but the place felt like his. Maybe because Lucas had lived there first. Maybe because all but the living-dining room and the present kitchen did in fact belong to him. Maybe because it was and always would be his country more than hers. Maybe too because her head was telling her she deserved to be sent away, even while her gut screamed back in protest.

***

While Lucas was in the Lubéron, Elizabeth felt as if she'd just stepped off the train at the Gare du Nord, almost twenty-five years ago. Her solitude, the empty streets, the smell of the stone in the oppressive heat, the knot in her stomach—*I have just escaped to London. To Mum's new flat. She has just started seeing Cy and is acting like a schoolgirl and I want to scream at her to stop it —she is almost fifty. My father I can't scream at; I'm not even speaking to him. Although Monica, the Italian journalist he ran off with, has dumped him, he is now seeing Belinda. I am sure that I could never cotton to someone called Belinda, just as I am reasonably certain that Belinda will not last any longer than Monica so why even try to make an investment. And Molly is gone. Having saved up from secretarial work over the last couple of years, she has just left on a tour of Africa with two old school friends. It is where she will meet Gerald, who is working for a company in Nairobi for a couple of years.*

In London I feel paralysed, numb. My gloom and inertia are obviously driving my love-struck mother crazy and it is she who suggests: "Why don't you give Paris a try? You studied French and lived with that family for a couple months when you were sixteen. What were they called? The Blanquettes?"

"The Blanchards."

"Well, you came back from that trip absolutely beaming. It's such a romantic city. You're young and unattached. Go. I'll help you get started."

The Blanchards have sent a New Year's card every year, and I had lunch with them once in London when they came to visit. And I did enjoy those months in Paris, when being completely foreign gave me a sense of lightness and freedom that I have never felt in England or America.

A few weeks later I am on the hydrofoil crossing the Channel. Water is crashing against the many windows, as the low-slung boat is bounced brutally by the waves. A man across the way is being sick into the bag provided. I close my eyes to calm my own mild nausea. It is like crossing the Channel in a washing machine, I think, and indeed later, when I step off the train at the Gare du Nord, under the wrought iron and the slanting glass roof, it's all so new and exotic, I'm feeling fresh and new. I've already started forgetting.

The Blanchards have a comfortable three-room apartment on the Left Bank. Their children are grown up and they spend most of the time in the country, so I have it all to myself until the end of the summer. It seems too good to be true. When I'm wandering the streets in broad daylight and surrounded by the urban bustle, I feel like a cat, beginning another one of my multiple lives.

Nights are different. Nights I am seized by a persistent, nagging anxiety that I try to soothe by turning on the Blanchard's television. But it is like a worrisome, subcutaneous lump that I can't stop fingering.

Soon the Blanchards are coming back. I must act. I find a flat. It is a dingy place on the avenue des Gobelins, owned by a sinister man who wears shiny suits and works in a dark office off the courtyard. Asian men come in and out and since Paris' Chinatown is just minutes away, I am sure my landlord Monsieur Cros is involved with the Asian mafia. The two rooms smell of wet plaster and *mould, from a leak in the upstairs bathroom. Sitting on the loo, I am often surprised by a piece of paint or plaster dropping from the ceiling onto my head. Monsieur Cros meets my complaints with a smile under his brown hairpiece: "I'll see to the problem." But he never does and finally I just get used to it.*

*By the time the money my mother gave me is running out, no decent job has materialized so I decide to try some temporary secretarial work. I have always been a very fast typist. Now that I am busy and surrounded by people all day, unwanted thoughts are out of my mind for long enough stretches of time that I can push them aside even at night. Plus I am meeting people and my evenings are often busy too. My past recedes as my new life takes form—*the memories came back to her with such force, it was as if the intervening years had been a dream.

***

It was a relief to get the four children on the plane to Edinburgh, to pick up the hired car and drive to Killin, where her stepmother's family had an estate with several houses on it. The setting was breathtaking: ancient, worn mountains plunged into the long and winding Loch Tay, clouds clung to the hilltops and weather came and went swiftly, unpredictably.

At the family gathering, there were all sorts of step-cousins and second step-cousins and step-cousins-once-removed. Meals were chaotic groupings of people whose names Elizabeth couldn't keep straight. But there were lots of children and hers, surprisingly, got caught up in the pack, in the games and in the music the older ones listened to and then endlessly discussed. Having her children happily occupied allowed Elizabeth to explore her surroundings.

On her first stroll through the village, she wandered into the local sports shop and came out with hiking boots and socks, a small rucksack, and a map of the area. After that she spent every afternoon walking the hills. She climbed peak after peak amidst the bleating sheep and the long low walls of flinty stone. When she reached a summit, she could see well-worn tracks that stretched along the hilltops for what seemed forever, but she always turned around and made her way carefully back down the steep slopes.

All the walking made her feel fit and strong. At moments it seemed that the regenerated exterior only highlighted her irredeemably weak and rotten interior. But at others the fresh, clear air, at a healthy distance from Paris and all her troubles, made her wonder if what she'd done was really so bad. Why couldn't Lucas forgive her? She wished she could talk to someone, get another perspective.

Her father was the obvious choice. She had long ago forgiven him for leaving her mother and had in fact come to admire him a great deal. He was still a trim, active man, who after retiring from journalism had transformed himself into a high-fee political consultant. But what Elizabeth admired most about her father was the way he had become more, rather than less, tolerant with age. She could probably tell him anything and he wouldn't flinch. If there was anyone to turn to, it was Andrew Lyall.

One evening near the end of the holiday, she engineered a moment alone with him. They sat behind the house having a drink, the long evening sun slanting across the grass.

"Lovely evening," Andrew said. "Nothing like this northern light."

"Exquisite," said Elizabeth. They gave the evening a moment's silent admiration. "You've probably been wondering about my being here without Lucas."

"Naturally. But I didn't want to pry."

"Things between us haven't been great-great."

"I'm very sorry to hear that," he said in that deep, seductive voice of his. "Though I obviously suspected something."

"In fact," she said in a small, strangled voice, "we're considering a trial separation."

He leaned back gravely in his chair, folded his bared forearms. "Is this your decision or Lucas'?"

She hesitated, looked out at the hills, over which a cloud with a ridiculous silver lining hung. "It's complicated."

"Yes, of course."

"It seems to be the right thing."

"Good."

"Yes."

"Has he found another flat?"

"Actually," she said, looking down at the watery dregs of her drink, "with his office right there, I might be the one moving out. Just for the time being. Until we figure out the next step."

"Is that really the best for the children?" her father asked quietly.

"His office is attached to the flat and he's got a lot of work right now. He took care of them a lot when they were small."

He sighed. "I guess in this age of feminism, you can't expect to have it both ways."

"As I say, it would only be a temporary solution."

Her father nodded gravely. "`Well—"

"Andrew, Lizzie" Pru called from the kitchen. "Sup's on the table."

That was the beginning and end of their exchange, but even if Pru hadn't interrupted with her annoying familiarities, her "Lizzie" and her "Sup's", Elizabeth doubted she actually would have been able to say any more to her father. It just wasn't the way in her family.

***

"I've found an apartment," Lucas said when they got back. "It belongs to a friend of Alix's. Do you remember Sybille? She's just moved in with her new boyfriend but she wants to hold on to her place."

"In case things don't work out."

"Yes, in case things don't work out."

"A temporary sublet," she said, nodding slowly. "Where is it?"

"Rue de Sèvres. Not too far away."

"How many rooms?"

"It's only got two bedrooms. But the sitting room is quite big. There's a pull-out sofa bed. It's available from the beginning of October."

A large lump of silence sat between them.

Finally Lucas repeated what he'd said in their first discussion: "My career is finally going somewhere. I've got too much work. I don't see how I can move."

"Why couldn't you work here during the day and then go back to the rue de Sèvres at night?"

"I'm working day and night. Our paths would be crossing all the time. It wouldn't be good for the children."

"You and your concern for the children. You make me sick." And she stormed out the room, barely able to restrain herself from breaking everything in sight. He was a self-righteous prig—how could she ever have married him in the first place, she wondered as she paced back and forth in their bedroom.

But that night, lying in bed, unable to sleep, a new wave of guilt washed over her and she felt deserving of punishment. Deserving of some equivalent to the prison sentence she had never served.

Over the next week, there were terrible arguments about who would move. With the children close by, they managed to keep their voices down but the words were venomous and wounding. Their disputes were so intense that afterwards, Elizabeth could not quite remember what had been said. Except for the moment the last evening when she'd finally consented to one year, not a day more and she'd hissed: "I hate you, Lucas. I hate you."

When Tristan and Olivier were told after supper the next day, Elizabeth told Lucas he could do all the talking, since this was his plan.

"You have undoubtedly noted some tension in the house

these last months," he began. Tristan blushed and looked down at his hands; Olivier nodded. "Things have not been going well between your mother and me." He shifted position in his seat, adjusted his glasses between his forefinger and his thumb. The zigzag vein at his temple was bulging and Elizabeth turned her head, repulsed by it. "We have decided that it is best for the family if we separate."

"Why? How?" Tristan blurted out, unable to contain a second longer the rage that had been brewing for months. "How can you be happy one day and spitting angry the next and the next and the next?" He looked desperately from one to the other of them, as if afraid he might miss some look, some expression, that would provide him with an explanation.

"People can grow apart," Lucas said. "It's not always easy or even possible to explain why."

Both boys sat, frozen and silent.

Lucas continued: "Since I have my office here and a great deal of work, your mother has agreed to move out, for the time being." Olivier looked up, mouth dropping open; Tristan hung his head as if it were being pushed down from behind. "Not far. Just to the rue de Sèvres."

"What about the twins?" Olivier asked.

"The twins will stay here too," Lucas said. "Manuela will work some extra hours. You can go to the rue de Sèvres at weekends."

Now both boys looked at Elizabeth, who managed a defeated nod.

"What are you going to say to them?" asked Tristan, all anger now drained from his voice. It was unbearable to see the older boys being protective of their younger siblings.

"About the same thing we've told you," said Lucas, with an uncomfortable shrug.

They all stood up. The boys left silently for their rooms. After hearing the doors click shut, Elizabeth wobbled back to the bedroom and lay down on the bed, holding one pillow in her arms while her head rested on the other. She had not thought it possible to feel this miserable. One year, she kept telling herself. Not a day more.

The next evening they told the twins. Elizabeth had expected tears and hysterics but there was nothing of the kind. The twins just fidgeted, showing little reaction. Of course, the announcement was less blunt:

"Maman and I have decided that she is going to go live in another apartment for a while."

"Why?" asked Ariane.

"Sometimes adults argue. Like you and Gabby," he said.

"But we don't move apartments," Ariane said.

"But you aren't adults," Lucas answered. "And you'll spend every Friday, Saturday and Sunday night over there. Almost half the week."

Ariane nodded blankly, as if she had something else on her mind. It was Gabby who finally spoke:

"Can we go now?"

"Yes. Get ready for bed," said Lucas and it made Elizabeth furious all over again, this assertion of parental authority of which she was soon to be deprived.

***

The flat on the rue de Sèvres was on a courtyard in a tired, old building. The outside walls were thick but they sagged; the apartment itself had been redone on the cheap. The walls and doors between rooms, not part of the original structure, were paper-thin. The kitchen counters had gaps and the drawers didn't quite close. Yellow-brown tiles, so ugly they must have been a last mark-down bargain, had been used both here and in the bathroom. There was a stained wall-to wall carpet in the sitting room, covered by a worn Persian rug. Sybille had taken most of the knick-knacks and paintings, leaving blank surfaces and pale spots on the dirty walls. Elizabeth was surprised that a friend of

Alix's would have lived here, but she told herself it had probably been nicer, fresher when she'd moved in. And naturally she would have stopped noticing the decline.

Alix had offered to drive her over to the rue de Sèvres and though Elizabeth would have preferred not to further involve her sister-in-law, she felt too diminished and unhappy to refuse. The day of departure, they all stood in the front hall. She was only bringing one large suitcase and the cat, who mewed and scratched so desperately at the sides of her wicker cage that it was rocking back and forth on the floor. Elizabeth kissed her children good-bye at the front door, trying to pretend to herself and to them that she was just going on a short trip, saying simply: "See you on Friday."

"Are you going to be all right here?" Alix asked when they'd lugged the suitcase and the mewing cat up the four flights of uneven, narrow stairs. "I don't remember it being quite so...so... grim."

"She must have taken a lot of stuff."

"That hid the dirt."

Elizabeth lifted Suey from her basket. The liberated cat began sniffing suspiciously, her nose haughtily and resentfully in the air, just barely concealing the underlying panic at being deposited in this unfamiliar place. "It probably just needs a good clean."

"That's probably right."

They stood awkwardly. The apartment seemed to belong more to Alix, since it was her friend.

"This is just a temporary solution, right?" Alix finally asked.

"Isn't a sort-of furnished sublet by definition temporary?" Elizabeth answered.

"Yes, I guess it is," said Alix. "But I was just wondering..." she trailed off. "Well, let's see if she didn't leave something to drink in the cupboards."

They found some tea and put a saucepan of water on the gas. They walked around the place and discussed possible improvements. When the water had boiled, they took their cups and sat one on either side of the sofa. Alix slid off her shoes and tucked her long legs underneath her.

"How's your work going?" asked Alix.

"Okay. It can be a little hard to concentrate these days."

"I can imagine."

Elizabeth, doubting that she could, changed the subject: "How are the children?"

"Just fine."

They sipped their tea. Already they seemed to have nothing to say to one another.

"It was really nice of you to bring me over here," Elizabeth said.

"I'm happy to do what I can." Alix looked at her watch: "Well I'd better get going or my car will be ticketed. The police are everywhere these days."

"Thanks again," Elizabeth said.

"Give me a call when you want to bring over the next load. Or for anything else."

"I should be able to manage the rest by myself. But thanks."

Alix paused at the door. "You know, it's been a great shock to all of us," she said. "None of us understands your separation at all. It seems...senseless. A complete mystery." She stared hard at Elizabeth with her sharp green eyes looking to pierce that mystery, coax an admission.

Elizabeth could not contain a slight wriggle. "I..I don't know what to tell you," she said, reddening.

"Lucas doesn't either," she said, peeved at this unusual reticence on the part of her brother. "But I'd be happy to talk, any time you feel like it."

After the first few moments of relief at being released from her sister-in-law's difficult questions and untroubled life, Elizabeth turned around in terror at her solitude. The silence had a ring to it. She looked at the stereo; the CD cabinet was empty. Sybille must have taken her music. She sat back down on the sofa. She looked at the indent in the cushion where Alix had been sitting. Suey the cat was still sniffing and padding around the place indignantly. Elizabeth sighed and got up to feed her and set up the litter box. Suey rubbed against her leg.

She sat back down again on the sofa. If Lucas had been there, she would have jumped at him, fists flailing, nails clawing. How could he expect her to leave her children? To live apart from them, even temporarily? She stood up too quickly and her head began to spin. At the window she leaned her forehead against the pane and looked up at the sky. Daylight was slipping away earlier and earlier, now that it was October, and a sliver of the moon was already etched into the deepening blue. The thought that it might be on the wane, that it might be about to disappear completely, made her gasp for air. She moved away from the window.

Sitting on a wooden stool, Elizabeth tried to focus on the kindness and interest people had shown since word had got out about their separation. Many friends had phoned, suggesting lunch dates, and she was just as happy to stick to a midday meal. For the moment a dinner party without Lucas would make her feel like an amputee. But everyone wanted to see her—concern overflowed—Elizabeth was amazed. Of course, everyone also expressed the same surprise as Alix; everyone wanted to know whatever in the world could have happened and how it could be that the children were staying with Lucas.

It was a Wednesday. On Friday evening the four children would come for supper. The twins would stay until Monday morning, when Elizabeth would take them to school. Tristan, however, would not sleep there—he was too old and had too much work. Olivier, they'd see about. Already her time was chiselled away, yet all the arrangements made sense; she couldn't dispute that.

She went into the first bedroom, where Sybille's daughter had slept. There were bunk beds and the twins would find this exciting until they started arguing over who would get the top bunk first. They might notice the peeling stickers of Disney characters on the bedposts but not the chipped paint and the dirty smudges on the walls.

Sybille's room was dominated by a bookcase, with sagging shelves and books going every which way. It gave onto a shaft and was very dark. Olivier wouldn't like it. She could hear him saying Maman, this place is creepy. She in fact already knew that Olivier would never spend the night here.

Elizabeth collapsed on the bed and stared at the ceiling.

Today was only Wednesday. How could she possibly make it until Friday? How could she even make it through the evening?

She got up and began to unpack her suitcase. Tucked into the folds of the clothes were the photos of the children she had brought along, one of each individually and one of the four of them together, when the twins were still babies. She took them out to the sitting room and tried to fill up some of the empty surfaces by spreading them out but this only highlighted the general bleakness, so she grouped them together on the mantle and went into the kitchen. In the back of a cupboard she found a half bottle of whisky and a bag of corn chips. The alcohol burned her empty stomach and then shot right up to her head and it felt wonderful.

While she consumed the entire bag of chips, she looked at the book she was supposed to be reading and felt a physical revulsion for it. The writing was flawless—the man had clearly attended any number of writing workshops—but to her mind it had no more soul than the phone book. Unlike that novel she'd read at the end of the summer and liked so much. The one Gérard had rejected—after, she suspected, consulting Lucille. The look on his face when he'd handed it back still made her wince. It was almost a look of pity.

Elizabeth turned on the television and as soon as she sat down, Suey jumped on her lap. The eight o'clock news began. Her family would be sitting down to dinner without her. The cat extended its claws into her thighs while she sipped another glass of whisky.

Alternating between watching television and pacing the apartment, she got through the evening, with the help of the whisky. After kissing the glass on each of the children's photos, she went into the bedroom, ready to drop. She pulled back the cover, only to find that the bed was of course unmade. Unable to face finding a sheet, she grabbed a duvet from the child's room and slept on top of the cover.

Or tried to sleep.

To read.

To lie still.

The first light of day came as a great relief; she could give up trying.

Coffee in hand, she couldn't stop looking at her watch every five minutes, the way she did when getting the household underway each morning. Except now she could see Lucas, back in their bed for the first time in months, waking up. She could see him shaking the twins awake, making their *tartines*, spreading the Nutella—or had he already got them onto jam. In any case, he would not lick the knife before putting it in the dishwasher. The vision of Lucas carefully wiping off the knife on the lip of the jar made her want to punch something.

She had to get out of here—to a café for something to eat, then to the office. And once at work, she'd no longer be alone. That there would be other people around was about the only positive thing to be said about the place right now. Several editors had left; departing secretaries were not replaced. Morale had suffered badly as a result. People were secretive, suspicious. Phone messages and e-mails frequently went unanswered, alliances were formed and then re-formed.

Given the atmosphere and her new commissioned status, she needed to be a bundle of energy and initiative but unfortunately she was acting more like a factory worker. She went to her desk, carried out tasks that were put in front of her. But not much else. Or so it seemed. In her memory of the last year, time and thought appeared shapeless and muddled. Every day was sort of the same hopeless exercise.

But she wasn't going to dwell on that this morning. Her main concern now was getting out of this dingy apartment that had nothing to do with her, was in no way a home nor ever would be.

Once dressed, she put on her raincoat, tied the belt tightly around her waist, and headed outside. She breathed in the cool early autumn air. The rising sun glinted bright orange on an iron balustrade. The first leaves on the plane trees were beginning to shrivel and fall. The morning bustled with people going to work, and it was a relief. The lives of others carried on; the pace of the city did not slacken because she, Elizabeth Teller or Lyall or whoever she now was, was unhappy. It was too bad the scene also had to include parents taking their young children to school but she tried to keep her eyes focused upwards, her thoughts forward to the day ahead. On work. Maybe now that she and Lucas were actually separated, she could throw herself into the job, make up for her perfunctory performance over the last year.

Elizabeth stopped at the café next door to the office and ordered a double espresso and a croissant. As she tried to read the newspaper someone had left at the next table, she heard a voice, felt a presence. "Elizabeth. I'm so sorry." It was Lucille, who didn't hesitate to pull back the other chair and sit down and wave for the waiter.

"Sorry about what, Lucille?" She was too tired to understand what Lucille might be referring to, at least until Lucille's incredulous eyes brought her to her senses. "Oh. Thanks." Of course she would have known through her sister-in-law, friend of Alix. Other people's bad news always travels at lightning speed. She looked down at her half-eaten croissant and the sight of it suddenly sickened her.

"I mean, you've seemed a bit...off your game," she paused. "But I thought it must be the atmosphere at work these days."

"I'm surprised you've noticed, Lucille. Everything's going swimmingly for you isn't it?" She instantly regretted her sour words.

"I know you've being going through a bad patch and I'm sorry. That's all I wanted to say."

Elizabeth drained her coffee cup. "I'd better get going," she said, searching the floor for her bag: "Oh, God. I forgot my bag. My money."

"I'll get it, don't worry," said Lucille.

"I'll pay you back tomorrow."

"Really. Don't worry about it."

And Elizabeth left, feeling more humiliated than she thought possible.

The missing bag upset her whole morning. It seemed to funnel her sense of all that was missing: her family, her home, her professional edge. She felt lop-sided, incomplete, unequipped. During lunch she'd planned to go to the Bon Marché and buy new bed linen but instead she went back to the rue de Sèvres to get her bag. Arriving in the middle of the day, she felt even more of an intruder. A guilty intruder. Lonely Suey rubbed up against her leg like an abandoned animal. Back at the office, Elizabeth slipped a note and the money owed Lucille onto her desk while she was still at the gym. But all afternoon she could not shake a sense of missing property. Although she went through the motions of making phone calls or writing e-mails, she felt she had lost all her bearings. Was she coherent when talking to that literary agent in New York? Did that long e-mail she wrote to the prickly editor make sense? As much as she dreaded returning to the dingy flat, she was, at the end of that endless day, relieved to leave the office.

Just before she left, she phoned the children. Or tried to. In the half-hour she rang every two minutes, she kept hearing her own voice saying: we're already on the line; please leave a message. Like some post-modern ghost, her recorded voice still haunted the rue Laromiguière. Why hadn't Lucas changed it? On the other hand what if he had? When it kept being engaged, she finally left a message to her own message. Miss you. Can't wait for tomorrow.

Friday evening finally came and the four of them filed in the front door. Tristan and Olivier stood with their hands in their pockets. The twins made a fuss over Suey. On discovering the bunk beds, they were indeed excited but they didn't argue about who would get the top. They negotiated a solution. Ariane would get it the first night and Gabby would get it the second; the next week Gabby would get it the first night. Elizabeth wished they'd bickered; even tears would have been welcome. Tristan tried to be polite but it was obvious he was counting his lucky stars that he wasn't staying in this place overnight. Elizabeth said to Olivier:

"I've been thinking. It doesn't make much sense for you to spend the night here. With school. Your friends on Saturday night. Won't it be easier for you to stay at the rue Laromiguière?"

"Yea, probably."

She had fixed the family favourite for supper—spaghetti with tomatoes, mozzarella and basil. She'd bought San Daniele ham, sliced paper-thin, the way they liked it, and dried sausage from Lyon. For dessert she'd made her brownies, undercooked and gooey, the way they liked them. Though everyone put a good face on it, the food just didn't taste the same off the chipped plates Sybille had left behind.

"So how have you all been since Wednesday?" Elizabeth tried to sound jovial. "I had trouble getting through on the telephone yesterday."

"Olivier has a new girlfriend," said Ariane.

"Oh? What's her name?"

"Philomène."

"That's a stupid name," said Gabby.

"It's old-fashioned," said Elizabeth. *Ultra-Catholic. I'm gone a few days and already he's going off the rails.* "Does she come from a large family?"

"No, she just has two brothers."

"Smaller than our family," added Ariane helpfully.

"Yes. Tristan, are you surviving the work?"

"Yea, but it's pretty tough. Not far from torture, actually."

I know these things are gruelling but he's never complained before. "What about your friends? How are they doing?"

"Don't know," he shrugged. "Who has time for friends when you're being worked like a slave."

"And how about you two?" she turned to the twins. "How's school going?"

"My teacher's mean," said Ariane, her eyes filling up with tears.

Why hasn't Lucas told me she's upset? "You didn't think that at the beginning of the week."

"We have a replacement. The other one is having a baby."

"Well, maybe she'll get nicer."

"No, she won't."

"Stop complaining," said Olivier. For the first time ever, Ariane obliged an order from an older brother.

"Gabby, have you got a football match tomorrow?" Elizabeth asked. *I should have made both him and Ariane stick to judo this year. I can't deal with this extra complication.*

"Yea. At three."

Thank God. Something to do. But what about Ariane? I'll have to drag her along and listen to her complain. I have no housekeeper anymore.

"But you just have to drop me off at two. It's an away game." And so they got through the meal.

"That was good," said Tristan. The others nodded.

"Well, I guess you two need to get on with your evening," Elizabeth said to him and Olivier.

"I have to work," said Tristan.

"I've got school tomorrow."

"Yes, you two run off." Then she looked at the twins: "For you two, I've got a video."

Though she hated kissing her two older boys good-bye at the door, it was something of a relief to have them gone. Their departure reduced the awkwardness by half. Even Ariane and Gabby seemed to feel it. They went into the bedroom they would be occupying and both climbed up to the top bunk, where they pretended to be on a ship in the middle of the ocean. Gabby was captain while Ariane used a rolled-up magazine as a telescope, through which she looked out for sharks, rocks and other lurking perils in the dark, choppy sea. Elizabeth cleaned up the supper.

She put Beauty and the Beast into the video player and sat down on the sofa, with one twin tucked under each arm, the cat on her lap, and thought everything would be fine if she could just stay like that for the rest of her life.

***

Twice during lunch hours Elizabeth went back to the rue Laromiguière. She would let Lucas know she was coming by e-mail; Manuela the housekeeper would let her in. On both occasions she took more photos of the children, as well as mementos: a little dish Tristan had once made for her in a pottery workshop, an etui with a lock of Olivier's very blond hair when he was a baby, a mother's day card Ariane had made in nursery school and a piece of volcanic rock Gabby had brought back from a class trip to the Auvergne. One day she also took the little sculpture Troy had given them—she wasn't even sure why —all she could think was that she didn't want Lucas to have it. Holding it in her hand, she thought how over the last year, Troy had constantly lurked in the sphere of her semi-conscious but not often much closer. She felt too bludgeoned by the here and now to dwell on the past.

These visits to the flat were very painful, so she decided the third would be her last. She brought two large suitcases and ordered a taxi to pick her up.

This time Lucas answered the door with a wan, ironic smile that looked almost apologetic. But the shock to Elizabeth was so great he may as well have been wielding a dagger.

"What? Isn't Manuela here?" she asked, pushing past him and making her way back to the bedroom.

Lucas followed her. "She's here. But I wanted to see you. Talk a bit."

She was tossing shoes into one of the bags as swiftly as she could. "Talk about what? Hasn't it all been said? I acted despicably and you can't forgive me. Now I'm paying for my crime by living in a grotty flat without my children."

"Come on," he said, hardly above a whisper.

Tossing the last shoe into the bag, she straightened and answered more softly: "What do you want to talk about then?"

He didn't reply immediately. Then: "I thought I'd feel better once you were gone." He did look awful, at least there was that. "Or that I'd be able to see more clearly. Instead I'm even more mixed up. Do you know what I mean?" And gave her that twisted smile and a look that was expectant, accusatory and probing, all at once.

She sighed; put her hands on her hips and looked around the room. Lucas had left clothes all over her *chaise longue*. Her desk was piled high with lots of unpaid bills and a stack of Lucas' current reading material. She turned back to the closet and began throwing things, unfolded, into the large suitcase. "No, I'm not sure I do."

He said nothing for a moment, then, so quietly she almost didn't hear: "This isn't just about forgiveness."

"Well, I did behave despicably, didn't I," she said, zipping shut the bag and glaring at Lucas provocatively. "I don't think I told you that when the doctor in the emergency room asked me what happened, I said: 'I have no idea. He just came back to the apartment like that.'" Lucas gave a pained sigh. "Do you mind if I take some CDs? There's no music over there." And she lugged the two full suitcases out of the room.

In the taxi several minutes later, she was surprised to feel an odd sense of relief at having hammered what was perhaps the last nail in her own coffin.

***

Evenings, when she got back to the flat, she fed the cat. Suey, who was still not used to being alone all day, would purr so loudly the whole kitchen seemed to vibrate. While the cat was eating, she'd put on some music and pour herself a glass of wine, which made her hungry. She'd eat a handful of peanuts. Before she knew it, she was pouring another glass and eating more nuts. After she'd eaten her meal, she would take a large scoop out of the Nutella jar she kept for the twins. Or she would not be able to stop herself from opening one of their biscuit packages. While she ate, she looked lovingly and longingly at the children's photos, at the little things she had brought with her. Before going to bed, she would have a little weep and kiss the glass on each of the photos.

By then, she had not only eaten too much, she had also effortlessly finished off the whole bottle of wine. Every morning when she woke up and looked at herself in the mirror, she looked worse than the day before. Her face, with the eyes that were slightly too close together and the rather pointed nose and chin, could not accommodate these pudging cheeks and puffing eyes. She would resolve to buy no more peanuts, no more wine.

But every evening, hungry and tired and oh, so lonely on the way home from work, she would relent and buy more nuts and more wine.

Not unlike my first year at boarding school when I was homesick and couldn't stop eating. Sweetened condensed milk, yummy. I spent all my pocket money on it and I became plump. No one in my family was plump. My father was too busy to notice; my mother acted as if nothing was wrong but she looked at me in horror every time I put a piece of food in my mouth. The next year I grew several inches and I was happier. I thinned out, became in fact gawky. All elbows and knees. It wasn't until the college that some curves finally started to form, that I no longer felt like an ugly duckling.

She decided that she needed to get out and see some other creature than the cat, to stop thinking obsessively about her children. Over the last weeks, as the separation became old news and people lost interest, even her lunch invitations had fallen off. Some, Elizabeth suspected, viewed her being alone as a contagious disease, something they might very well catch, if they weren't careful. She wondered about Lucas, then decided it was unlikely he was undergoing the same quarantine. Single men would forever remain a commodity and his life-long friends wouldn't let him down. He wasn't a foreigner.

One Tuesday morning she got on the phone and arranged a series of lunches in the hopes that dinner invitations might now follow. She phoned Sophie the diplomat, Caroline the management consultant and her old pal Laurent, now the television journalist, cum novelist. All of them sounded happy to hear from her; all expressed their profound sympathy for her situation. Since they were busy people the lunch-dates were set weeks away. Except Laurent. "Isn't that perfect," he said. "My lunch today was just cancelled. Meet me at one-fifteen at Le Pompadour."

That morning she felt brighter than she had in months. Laurent would cheer her up, make her feel part of the world again.

Le Pompadour, being not far from the main publishing houses and the National Assembly, attracted the high and mighty like fly paper. Laurent obviously came here often: when she uttered the name Monsieur Mandille, the waiter turned from dismissive to obsequious before she even got to the last syllable. He escorted her to a large table set apart but visible.

It had not occurred to her that Laurent would be late—in the past he was always punctual—and she had not brought a book or newspaper. This meant she had nothing to do in the half hour she waited but to nod at editors, writers and journalists and wonder how many of them knew that she was separated from

Lucas. She turned to counting National Assembly Deputies. She was on the verge of getting up and leaving when he finally swept in the door.

"Sorry. I was held up," he said, kissing her hello with the harassed flourish of someone constantly in demand.

"No problem," she answered curtly. "I've memorized the new menu. Quite a make-over." Le Pompadour had recently been bought by a smaller, trendier restaurant and the décor had gone from stubbornly old-world and provincial to assertively modern.

"Have you found anything decent to eat?" he asked, pulling out the red reading spectacles he had begun sporting on television. After consulting the menu, he whisked them off and dangled them from his forefinger in the same expansive gesture he used on television, when he'd finished citing a passage from the book he was discussing. Once they'd ordered, he popped his glasses behind the silk handkerchief of his jacket pocket and acquired a concerned air. "So. How goes it?"

"Not great. As I'm sure you can imagine."

"Delphine and I just couldn't believe it. Really. What on earth happened?" He poured Badoit into their two glasses.

"Well," she said shrugging her shoulders, thinking how his round, boyish face used to redden when they drank wine with lunch, how that face was no longer flushed but a little fleshy. "It's probably not very interesting, is it?" When he did not answer, she continued: "Tell me about how you are. I haven't seen you since when? Since Isabelle and Claude's anniversary. I couldn't make your last book launching."

"Which one was that? Oh, yes. *La vie de l'autruche.* I get confused. I've got another en route now," he said, sounding like an industrious Catholic mother, pregnant yet again.

The waiter put down their plates. The cuisine, along with the décor, had gone from copious and traditional to spare and nouvelle. Sitting on Elizabeth's large rectangular white plate with the corners turned up was a small mound of mixed greens with two langoustines intertwined on top. A stiffened chive in the centre curled vertically to dramatic effect.

"But I must say," Laurent continued, "progress on the writing front has been slowed by the television show. I have so many books to read that I really only have time for my novel-writing during the holidays."

"Must not make for much of a holiday," said Elizabeth.

"I always manage to carve out a couple hours when I come off the slopes or in from the beach umbrella. Fortunately," he finished chewing and dabbed his lips with the white napkin, "I have no fear of the blank screen."

"I'm not surprised," she said with a smile, remembering the two flimsy novels she'd breezed through. "But doesn't it bother you that your television show is on so late?" She popped the second langoustine in her mouth.

"No. The people who matter watch. Because they want to see what other people who matter have to say."

"I guess people who matter don't need much sleep." She laughed. "Eleven to twelve-thirty's past my bed time." Laurent did not seem to hear her. He was nodding at someone Elizabeth couldn't see. She continued: "Now that I think about it, it's funny how all the people who were on at prime-time twenty years ago today have those late slots."

"Yes," he said vaguely, before launching into a list of the authors he had lined up over the next weeks.

The rest of the meal was constantly interrupted. People on their way out needed to stop for a word with Laurent Mandille who, like a Michelin starred restaurant, was now worth the detour. On the street they said good-bye. Laurent had an important interview and was in a hurry now to leave. No mention of a dinner invitation or even a future cup of coffee was made.

***

One night she was drinking her wine and eating her peanuts

and the phone rang.

"Hello. It's Lucas."

"It hasn't been that long. I know who it is," she said.

"I'm phoning about Tristan." He paused.

She waited.

"His school called."

"And?" She was losing patience with the slow delivery.

"He hasn't handed in all his work over the last month. He slumps sullenly and absently in class."

"Have you noticed anything?" she said.

"He's been quiet but he's never very talkative." Lucas paused. "The other night I came home and noticed him on the street talking to the homeless people who linger around the metro exit."

"Did you say something to him?"

"No. I just watched for a few minutes. He gave all three of them cigarettes."

"He's started smoking?"

"It would appear so."

"And then what?"

"He took a couple of sips from one of their beers."

"He what?

"He took sips from their beers."

"And you didn't phone me immediately?"

"I thought you'd be upset."

"Not half as upset as I am at your not telling me." She wanted to hurl the phone against the wall but that would have deprived her of the mouthpiece for her ensuing tirade: "Have you decided to cut me out entirely? Because you're afraid of my bad influence? Afraid if I knew what he's been doing I might go join him, encourage him? You're so God-damned morally superior it makes me sick. You're treating me like some kind of pariah. Or like a child. All because of a moment of weakness years and years ago. All because you, Lucas Teller, are above and beyond fault."

He answered in almost a whine: "Stop it, please. I told you —" He collected himself and said more firmly: "This is not about you, or about you and me. It's about—"

She put down the phone on him. "Insufferable prig," she hissed to herself. Then she pushed in the number of Tristan's mobile and his recorded voice came back to her. "I'm not here. Beep."

"Hi Tristan. It's me. Can you give me a call when you get a chance?" sounding as casual and natural as possible.

Why wasn't he answering his phone? What was he doing, and with whom? She was not naïve; she knew what teenagers got up to. But usually they got up to it casually with friends, not in the company of homeless drunks and drug addicts. Tristan, however, had that kind of extreme personality whereby he threw himself completely into what he was doing. Up until now it had been constructive activities—schoolwork, piano, books. But there was no reason he couldn't veer in the opposite direction and become just as assiduous with drugs and dereliction. The line between high achievement and active self-destruction would be easy for him to cross.

She had last seen him two weekends ago. A Saturday night. Elizabeth had taken the four of them to a new bistro her friend Sophie had talked about when they'd had lunch. But the restaurant was noisy. Olivier was sulking because Philomène was going out to the cinema with his friends—"probably falling in love with somebody else," he'd grumbled—and the twins wouldn't stop playing with the cutlery and she'd got cross. And Tristan. He had been quiet, very quiet, but she knew he hated noisy places. Still, hadn't there been something else? Yes, it was his hair. He never combed it but he hadn't washed it either. It was filthy, and she remembered refraining from the urge to say so. She remembered now too that he hadn't eaten very much. That as they were parting, she had asked what he was doing that evening. "Seeing friends," he'd said with a defiant look that she had interpreted as anger at her for meddling in his affairs or for no longer living with his father. Is that what he had done afterwards? Gone to sit on the ground at the place Monge and share beer and cigarettes with the homeless drunks?

And what about Lucas? He had never, ever, as far as she could remember, hesitated to confront one of the children with a concern, a criticism, a question. It was unlike him to lurk in the shadows and watch Tristan revel with tramps, to sneak away and say nothing.

Suddenly, he seemed a complete enigma. As was her son—as was she herself, for that matter.

**

Tristan did not phone her back. Elizabeth imagined him slumped in a gutter, his wallet stolen, his identity unknown and his absence unnoticed.

"He's around," said Lucas when she phoned the flat.

"Have you talked to him?" she asked.

"Yes, I've talked to him. And I've just talked to the school as well. We have an appointment next Tuesday at three. I'll make sure he phones you."

She paced the room like a caged mother tiger, so that when the phone rang, she could not summon the calm voice she had intended.

"What is going on with you?"

"Nothing."

"What do you mean nothing? You're hanging out on street corners with homeless drunks and drug addicts."

"They're not all drunks and what's wrong with that anyway? They're human beings too."

"Look, Tristan," she said, softening. "Your father tells me you've stopped working at school. You're smoking and drinking on the street. These are not things you used to do."

"People can change."

"Of course they can. But it's possible to change in a

186

dangerous direction."

"I'm tired of people who think about nothing but direction. Nothing but success. I'm tired of the only kind of people I've ever known my whole life."

"Can I see you?" asked Elizabeth. "Before your father and I go with you to talk to your school?"

"I guess," he answered, with a weary tone indicating that he had placed her clearly in the camp of those he found so exhausting.

"Why don't we meet at that Café de l'Epée on the place Contrascarpe, that one you used to like so much. Tomorrow at seven?"

"Okay. If you want."

The next day she got to the Café de l'Epée a little early. This was the café Elizabeth used to bring the children to on their birthdays. The tradition had begun when Tristan was about eight. He had solemnly requested, as a birthday present, dispensation from the dreaded *cantine*, the school cafeteria, that day. From then on, each child had been spared the *cantine* for lunch on his or her birthday. Although the food in general was not particularly good, they all contended that the Café de l'Epée had the best *frites* in the world.

Tristan came around the corner, stomping out a cigarette, exhaling his last drag. He scuffed at the ground angrily, shoved his hands into his pockets. When he walked in the door, he hardly seemed to know where he was or what he was doing there. His eyes eventually located Elizabeth, and he made his slow way over to the table.

"What would you like?" Elizabeth asked. Seeing him like that, seeing him for the first time with a cigarette, felt like a slap in the face but she tried to keep her tone light: "It's a little early in the evening for *frites*."

"I guess," he answered, with his gaze distractedly fixed on some distant object that Elizabeth couldn't see. It was almost as if he'd had to work very hard to understand her words at all.

The waiter approached the table. "What would you like to drink?" she repeated, enunciating as if she were speaking to a foreigner.

"Um. I'll have a coffee."

"I'll have a tisane, please," she said, though she would have preferred wine. She sat back in her chair and looked at him. He looked disturbed. More than disturbed. He looked as if he were suffering from some cognitive disorder. "Tristan. Tell me what's wrong."

"Nothing's wrong."

"You've completely changed in the last two months and you're telling me nothing is wrong." She paused and then mumbled: "You're allowed to be upset, you know. It's normal."

He finally looked her in the eye. In fact he glared at her. "Thank you. Thank you for your permission. But you misread the situation. Let's say your separation has just made me take a new perspective on things. Isn't that *normal*?"

"What kind of perspective, then?" she asked.

"I already told you. One different from what I've always been surrounded by." He hunched his shoulders, as if cringing from the high-achieving hordes.

"You don't find it worrying," she said, trying a different tack, "that your different perspective involves the complete margins of society?"

"I don't see it that way."

"Well then how do you see it?"

"I see that I'm branching out and trying to understand different parts of the world, different types of people. That I'm trying to widen a vision which up until now has been very narrowly focused."

"But why these people?"

"Please don't refer to my friends like that."

"All right then. Why not artisans or athletes? Firemen or factory workers?"

"You don't even know who you're talking about. Benoît

doesn't drink or take drugs. He used to be a social worker but he decided he liked the other side better. He gets a little pension and earns enough other money begging so that he can travel once a year. He's even been to South America."

"Look. I'm not trying to dictate your choice in friends. I'm just worried about you, about your sudden lack of interest in your life. What about your work? Apparently you aren't keeping up. Are you trying to get booted out?"

"No. I just don't care about that stuff anymore."

"But you might change your mind again and by then it might too late. What you're doing now can have consequences for the rest of your life."

"You sound like Papa," he said.

That stung. She did not want to sound like Lucas. She took a deep breath. "Maybe I sound like him because he's right. Actions you take or don't take now *can* affect the rest of your life. Especially in France," she added. "You know as well as I do that there is little room for deviation. If you derail, it's hard, if not impossible, to get back on track."

He did not reply. After a minute, she asked:

"Tell me what you have been doing, if you're not working."

"I don't know. I pass the time."

"I'm not being facetious. What are you up to?"

"Reading. Walking around."

"Do you see any of your old friends?"

"Not really. No one has any time. They're boring."

"Are you playing the piano?"

"No. I haven't been going down to the apartment much."

"What about meals?"

"I manage," he shrugged.

"Will I see you this weekend?" Elizabeth asked as she kissed him good-bye outside the Café de l'Epée. His clothes smelled unwashed, his skin like cigarettes and stale beer. "Lunch on Sunday maybe?"

"Yea, sure," he shrugged again, looking past her down the

street.

"You and your father and I have a meeting at your school next Tuesday. Don't forget that."

"No, I won't."

As she walked back to the Pantheon to catch the bus, she felt a disquieting mix of panic, guilt and relief. Panic at seeing him so close to the edge, guilt for her role in his precarious position and relief at having the encounter over.

***

Tristan did not come to lunch Sunday, and the next time she saw him was in front of the school before the meeting with the director the following week. He and Lucas were already there waiting. Her heart gave an unwanted leap when she saw those two tall figures. Lucas looked—there was no other word for it—noble. In her fury at being ostracised, she'd forgotten what a striking figure he could make and she felt a new wave of remorse for what she'd lost.

They were kept waiting in a small room with nothing to read. Lucas, after looking in Elizabeth's direction, said:

"By the way, is there anything we should know, Tristan? I'd rather hear it from you."

"I don't think so," he mumbled without looking up. He was slumped in the chair, arms folded tightly across his chest.

They sat there. There were no windows and the silence had a dull ring to it.

Monsieur Aubert, the director, finally showed them into his office, a large room with big windows and gilt mouldings on the ceiling. He was a very thin man with a large head that tapered at his chin. Hair sprouted from his droopy ears. "It is unusual for us to deal with parents," he said in a nasal, barely audible, drawl from behind his substantial desk. "But Tristan is still only seventeen, a minor."

"Of course," said Lucas.

M. Aubert sighed and opened up a large ledger, the only object other than a lamp on the vast expanse of his desk. He ran a long, thin, hirsute finger along the left-hand column, found Tristan's name, and held his fountain pen underneath it: "As you know," he began, "the students are ranked constantly, on their assignments and on frequent exams, both written and oral. Until a month ago, Tristan was ranked third in his class. His current rank is twenty-four. Out of twenty-four." He looked from one to the other of them, then fixed his gaze on Tristan with a mixture of distaste and patronizing pleasure: "Have you told your parents about yesterday's oral interrogation?"

Tristan shook his head. Lucas looked at him furiously.

"Well," M. Aubert continued in his nasal whine, "when questioned on the ideas of the Enlightenment, Tristan regaled his examiners with a discourse on the irrelevance and futility of book-learned knowledge. Which of course begs the question of why he is here in the first place." He paused; Lucas nodded solemnly. "Surely you of all people, Monsieur Teller, know that *prépas* are not long on patience and understanding. There are too many bright, capable young people as it is." He turned and looked at Tristan: "It's really up to you. You can take the work seriously and have a chance of success, or there will be no place for you here."

"There's no question," Lucas said, " that this behaviour is unacceptable. That such antics are completely inappropriate. I hope this will be the last of it."

"The real problem," said M. Aubert, "is that if he doesn't keep up, he will never be able to catch up. There is simply too much work. Tristan, do you understand what is at stake here?"

"Yes."

"Are you determined to make an effort from now on? With your present performance, you will not be asked back next year. Do you understand that?"

"Yes," he said, looking earnest, or pretending to look earnest. There was an unmistakable note of challenge in the set of his jaw.

"Why don't we revisit your standing at the end of January. If there's not a significant improvement, I'm afraid it won't be worth your continuing."

"Thank you for your time," said Lucas as they walked out the door.

When they got out on the street, Lucas turned to Tristan, and Elizabeth thought he might hit him he was so angry. "I asked you if there was anything I should know and you chose not to inform me of your efforts to, shall I say, enlighten your teachers?"

"I didn't tell you because I thought they'd appreciated it," shrugged Tristan. "They told me it was well-argued."

"For God's sake, Tristan," Lucas almost screamed. "Have you completely lost your senses? These people don't have time for such childish flights of fancy."

Tristan hung his head, looked at the ground.

"Do you understand," Lucas continued, enunciating his words very carefully, "that you're in the process of throwing your life away?"

"Yes," he said.

"I certainly hope so."

"I'm going to try and work. I have to go back in. I have class."

They both watched his rounded back, his scuffing step.

"That was incredible," said Lucas.

"But that man," said Elizabeth indignantly. "He sounded like an off-key oboe."

"He's just doing his job."

"Why didn't you tell him about our separation?"

"What business is it of his? What difference would it have made?" Lucas shrugged with disdain. "These places do not care about, do not have time for, personal crisis."

"But he's a boy."

"So what? You know the system. It does not provide second chances at almost any age and certainly not in these *prépas*, which are expressly designed to narrow the numbers, to discard the bottom of the barrel. The important thing is to help Tristan get over this." He paused. "My cousin Raoul has given me the name of a good therapist."

"Old cousin Raoul," she said with tight smile. "Soul healer for the rich and famous."

"That's right. But he does know everyone. I thought I'd phone the woman this afternoon."

"A woman?"

"Yes, her. Brigitte Dax is her name. There's nothing wrong with him seeing a woman is there?"

"Nothing. I'm sure it's the right thing. Keep me posted."

As she walked away, Elizabeth tempered her indignation that her son was no more than a number in the rank by reminding herself that until now she had bought wholeheartedly into the system. It had been easy to do because all the children performed, if not as well as Tristan, well enough. She had felt proud when the school suggested Tristan skip the first year of primary school, and even prouder when she'd discovered it was a talking point among ambitious mothers. That it was the first step on the coded route to success in the Byzantine French system. Olivier hadn't been asked to skip but he was very young for his year. With the twins, the *directrice* had said Ariane could jump but not Gabby. It was Lucas who had flatly refused to separate them.

When no one was threatened with failure, when she was comfortably within the circle, she could laugh at people like Monsieur Aubert. But now that Tristan was floundering, the circle looked smug and heartless and Elizabeth could almost rejoice at Tristan's rebellion, at his resistance to becoming a Roland or fifty other people she could think of who never asked a question to which they could not provide a three-point answer. People for whom the idea of soul-searching was a quaint, misguided occupation for the incurably naïve.

Only now did it occur to her the similarity between her son's situation and hers at the same age. He was so much like Lucas that she could sometimes forget she'd had anything to do with producing him. But here he was turning eighteen, furious at the world as he confronted his parents' separation, just as she had been. Even stranger was the repetition of events, as if they were part of some inevitable familial pattern, as if history were bound to repeat itself in any number of peculiar permutations, over and over again.

***

Béa Fairbank had invited Elizabeth for supper on a Saturday evening. She'd felt almost giddy that day; this was her first night out in months. And Tristan had agreed to stay with the twins, meaning he would not be spending the evening with the homeless but with his brother and sister. She would wake up on Sunday surrounded by three of her four children; it was almost possible to pretend life was normal. Before getting into the bath, she was even able to take off her wedding ring, the way Lucas had removed his, she had noted during the meeting with Monsieur Aubert.

"Bye," she called to the children. Tristan had brought over the Disney film of Robin Hood and the three of them were watching it. "Bye," she called again, louder. "Bye," came back distractedly. "Don't forget to listen for the pizza man," she said.

On her way out the front door, she caught a glimpse of herself in the entry mirror. She'd stopped bothering to put on make-up at the weekends, and she could see that her rounder face now more than ever needed to have its eyes lined and its lips rosied. Fortunately the mirror was small and she couldn't see her bottom half, clad in an old pair of jeans that used to be too big and a large jersey. Most of her other clothes had become uncomfortably tight; she had taken the belt off her coat, the belt she used to tighten expressly because she knew it highlighted her long, formerly thin, waist.

If the children had noticed her widening girth, they hadn't acknowledged it. But Béa and Trevor would notice. As she got closer to the place, the day's giddiness fell away and she felt frightened. About what they might think, how they might look at her. About what it would be like without Lucas. About other people who might be there.

Béa opened the door with a smile. She had a face with pronounced features—slightly bulging eyes, a prominent nose—and tonight they looked bolder, more attractive, than usual.

"I hope you don't mind," she said as they walked into the sitting room. "I haven't invited anybody else. If it's possible I'm even less organized than usual these days."

"No. I don't mind at all," she said, relieved. Their black dog came towards her with its eager tail wagging. "Hello, Dog." She leaned over to stroke its head and the whitening muzzle lifted up to lick her face.

"Cassie," said Trevor, as he turned from the table where he was putting down three plates. He kissed her hello. "No social graces, I'm afraid. Good to see you."

"And you," said Elizabeth.

"A glass of wine?"

"I'd love one. Thank you." They sat down in front of the small fireplace where a fire burned. The dog sniffed Elizabeth with great interest.

"Cassie, stop it. I'm sorry."

"I don't mind. She must smell my cat." Elizabeth stroked the dog's soft ears. "She's beautiful. Such soulful eyes."

"All the better to beg with. Béa, are you coming?" he called with an edge of doubt, as if were worried that she actually might not be coming back from the kitchen.

"How's work going?" Elizabeth asked. Much as she liked him, she found small talk with Trevor difficult.

"Never quite good enough," he answered in the same tentative manner. "Same old story."

Béa came in with a bowl of pistachios. "Sorry to be gone so

long."

"Have you done something different in this room?" asked Elizabeth.

"Trevor painted it recently," said Béa.

"It's a nice salmony-brick colour," said Elizabeth, thinking as she always did how inviting this small, modest flat was. Tonight, having come from the rue de Sèvres, it seemed particularly warm and welcoming.

"We're in the process of re-arranging generally," said Béa.

"That's right. The table used to be in the kitchen." Elizabeth remembered the last time she had been here, with Lucas.

"Would you like a nut?" asked Trevor.

"No thanks," said Elizabeth, eying the two of them to see if they were looking at her or at each other.

"I'll have some," said Béa, who grabbed a handful.

No one spoke. Béa was working very hard on her nuts and the silence began to weigh. Trevor finally said:

"Aren't you going to tell her?"

Béa reddened. "Well. It's no big deal for you—you've got four of them," she said, tossing shells into the extra bowl nervously. Of course. The radiance, the loose shirt. The glass of water.

"Wonderful," said Elizabeth, changing her mind on the nuts.

"I'm thirty-nine," said Béa. "Sneaking under the wire, really, but..." she shrugged. She looked at Trevor with glistening eyes. Elizabeth took a large sip of wine.

"Everything will be fine," she said.

"I'm getting a test next week," said Béa. "To be sure."

"Are you feeling all right?" asked Elizabeth, pulling a pistachio shell apart with her thumb-nails.

"Not too bad. There are some foods I simply can't stand the thought of. Leafy things, like cabbage and salad. Just talking about it makes me nauseous. Speaking of which, I better go see how our non-leafy supper is getting on."

When she'd gone back into the kitchen, Trevor said: "She

thinks she's old. I'm forty-seven."

"Careful—I'm not far behind."

"Except you've already had four children. And I'm just getting around to one now."

"There are lots of men much older than you who have children." She thought of Lucas, imagined the younger wife, the new and better family. She reached for more nuts.

"And they're dead before the child becomes a teenager."

"Don't be silly," Elizabeth tittered to hide a half wish that all men over the age of forty-five would indeed be dead. "There are spry seventy-year-old fathers all over Paris. They practically constitute a caste of their own."

"You know your social strata well," he nodded slowly, then looked up curiously. "How many years have you lived here? Either I can't remember or I've never known."

"For about twenty-five years. And you?"

"Since I was eight. My mother moved over here with my brother and me. After my father died."

The expression on his face changed. His mouth hardened and his eyes fluttered ever so slightly.

"Did you ever go back to the States?"

"We used to go in the summer. And I went to an American college for a year."

"I went for four. How strange I didn't know that."

"I don't talk about it much. It was a mistake I realized almost the minute I set foot on the campus."

"If only I'd been as perceptive."

"Here we go," Béa said as she came back in with the food. While serving, she asked Elizabeth: "How are you managing?"

"All right." Elizabeth took a sip of wine, hoping to reverse the direction of the tears that were prickling her eyes.

"We thought, you know," Béa said, "the last time we saw you that something was wrong." She paused. "And what about Lucas? How's he getting on?"

Elizabeth flinched slightly at hearing the name pronounced

so casually, as if Lucas were just a friend in common, as if of course smooth relations had been maintained all around. She knew Béa hadn't meant it unkindly but it stung nevertheless. "I don't really know. I'm sure he's still seeing the friends he's always seen."

"It's a funny thing in divorces," said Trevor. "People so often take sides. As if staying friends with the two parties were unnatural, impossible. Even unethical. Of course people take Lucas' side," Trevor continued, "because he's Lucas Teller."

"It's not really a question of sides, is it?" asked Béa.

"Yes it is," said Trevor. "In most cases, people choose the husband or the wife."

"Our inviting Elizabeth," said Béa, "had nothing to do with sides."

"You invited me because you knew me first. Just as 'our' friends knew him first," said Elizabeth, still unable to pronounce Lucas' name out loud. "I moved into his world, his group of lifelong friends."

"If it's any consolation to you," said Trevor, "if Lucas lost all his clients or his grand family somehow suffered an ugly twist of fate, those lifelong friends would drop him too. In a second."

"I'm not sure about that."

"Yes they would. For all the beauty of its façades, Paris is a cold and cynical city."

"It's a big city, with lots of different façades," Béa said.

"The façades I'm talking about," said Trevor, "are all the same." He looked at Elizabeth: "Come on, you're a literary person—think of the French novel. From Dumas to Balzac to Stendahl and on. The list is long but the story's always the same. Nothing's changed. From century to century. From fictional rendition to real life."

"You're both right," Elizabeth answered, sensing a growing tension. "About the city. And I really should bone up on my French fiction. I've been too busy reading books for work to read the classics. All I've really read is Proust. And that was in translation, for a class in college. Before I ever came here."

"If you want to understand the world you live in, just read him again, this time in the original, and your real-life education will be complete."

"Or talk to you," Béa said quietly. Trevor reddened. "Let's move on to cheese."

Elizabeth helped clear the table while Trevor poked the fire.

In the kitchen, Béa almost whispered: "He does get carried away with his opinions sometimes."

"I don't mind," said Elizabeth.

Béa stopped stacking the plates and turned to face Elizabeth. "You know, don't you, what happened with his brother and sister-in-law?" Elizabeth shook her head. "Well, I probably shouldn't dredge up his past sins but he shouldn't pontificate like that. Trevor had an affair with his sister-in-law and that was the end of his brother's marriage."

"Oh," peeped Elizabeth like a startled bird.

"She was American and moved back to the States, leaving the children with Edward, his brother. Who also, by the way, got all the friends."

"Oh," Elizabeth peeped again.

"In his case it seems understandable. But with you—it doesn't seem quite fair that Lucas should get both the children and the friends."

Elizabeth turned toward the sink, began scraping the plates into the bin underneath. The dog looked up at her hopefully, a long string of drool stretching from its mouth. "It's a trial separation. A temporary solution. His office is right there, you see. And it's best the children's lives are as little disturbed as possible."

"That's very noble of you," Béa said.

"No. Really. It's not. Here, let me take that cheese." Béa looked startled at her abruptness, and Elizabeth paused at the doorway, cheese platter in hand: "Does Trevor's brother still speak to him?"

"For five years, no. Not a word. Then Edward got more happily remarried and they started seeing one another again. But they've never been very close."

"Doesn't the whole thing bother *you*?"

"It all happened before I knew him and he told me about it straight away so it's always just seemed a part of him. I know what he did was pretty awful, but no, it doesn't keep me awake at night."

"So you're the noble one," Elizabeth said. Béa laughed.

Back in the sitting room, Béa took Trevor's arm in a kindly way and said: "Maybe we should have our cheese in front of the fire."

"Good idea," he said contritely.

They sat around the low table in front of the fire with the plate of cheese and a bowl of fresh figs and plump dried dates and the dog looking on hopefully. Elizabeth provided them with advice on how to cope, on the wonders of how children change one's life. She told them stories about her own children when they were babies. Her face became flushed from the fire and the wine. She talked more than she would normally have done and once out in the street, she wondered what sort of impression she'd left. A somewhat deranged middle-aged woman whose happy moments were all behind her? That's how she felt, so wouldn't that have been how she came across?

The cold night air sobered her up and the good feeling of the evening evaporated. She had made a fool of herself. Like a starved person, she had gobbled up their company to excess. She had held forth, the great expert on children, lavishing them with loud and confident advice while she drank too much. While Béa sipped at one glass of wine and Trevor not much more. She imagined the two of them soberly discussing the now large and loud Elizabeth as they washed up.

At the Pont Royal, she looked over the edge. The streetlights twinkled on the rough water of the Seine and illuminated the men along the quayside. There were some couples on benches, flirting or engaging in earnest conversation. There were solitary men, leaning alluringly against the wall while others walked along, examining the possibilities, shopping. Elizabeth wondered if generally these cruising men were looking for everlasting happiness or just a night of pleasure. They seemed very far away, those men, but of course they weren't. All it would take was to have a gay family member or a good friend, and she would know all about the scene.

She thought about Tristan. She thought about herself and Lucas. The distance between the known and the unknown, between being well or unwell, loved or unloved, was frighteningly narrow. It was no more substantial than that thin little ring of gold she had so proudly removed from her finger earlier that evening.

***

"Gérard would like to see you," his secretary said to Elizabeth, standing in the doorway, not looking her in the eye.

"Is he too busy to tell me himself?"

"I don't know. He just asked me to call you into his office."

"Elizabeth," said Gérard, extending the palm of his thin hand, a few minutes later. "Sit down. Please." He leaned back in his leather chair, his carefully arranged clutter on the desk between them. Like a doctor with a practised bedside manner, he continued in a hushed, calm voice: "We've had bad news from the powers that be."

"I thought you were the powers that be," said Elizabeth.

"You know I'm not in charge of the purse strings." He paused, pressing his fingertips together in front of his mouth. "I know you've been going through a tough time." She found his tone patronizing. "But your performance is way down, in both number of books published and in sales."

"This has been something of a difficult year," said Elizabeth with what she hoped was a modicum of dignity.

"I know that. And I wish…" he trailed off, gazing up, as if that elusive wish had floated up to the ceiling.

"You just wish what, Gérard?" said Elizabeth, her voice rising uncontrollably.

"If it were up to me…" he trailed off again, now looking wistfully at the photograph with his wife and children on the sailboat near the edge of his desk.

"What exactly are you trying to say?"

He sighed. "When your contract expires at the end of the year, it will not be renewed."

"Just like that?"

"You received the letter, saying your contract runs out at the end of the year." And he held up the slip she had signed from the registered letter.

"I thought that was just a formality. That it would be renewed, as you said it would be."

"I'm sorry, Elizabeth. I'm just doing what I've been ordered to do."

"So you're just firing me, or should I say re-firing me, like that?"

"No. Technically we're just not renewing your contract."

"I've worked here for twenty years, and you're talking about the technicalities of termination?"

"I'm just saying that our only *legal* obligation to you is the contract that expires at the end of this year. But since you *have* been with us for so many years, we propose to pay you what would have been, last year, three months of your salary."

"Plus three months notice."

"Not under our present agreement."

"You want me to leave, just like that, after all these years?" she repeated.

"By the end of the year."

"That's a month away, Gérard, and the place is all but closed between Christmas and New Year. What about the work I'm in the middle of?"

"It will be taken care of." He paused. "There's really only enough work for one person. Or so we're being forced to believe. As you know, you're not the only one…I'm very sorry, Elizabeth."

She stood up and walked unsteadily from the room.

Though she had felt the uncertainty of her situation ever since she had been put on commission, this apprehension did not reduce the shock. As Elizabeth settled slowly in her office chair, her ears were ringing and she felt speechless, as stunned as if she had received a physical blow to the head.

The previous occupant of this office had once upon a time been an important author. He lived in the country and the publishing house provided him with an office for his visits to Paris. When she was hired, Elizabeth was told that he no longer needed the office. But by then he had come to be considered old and stale and something of a pest. Until now she hadn't given it a second thought but maybe he hadn't wanted to give up the office at all. Maybe he'd minded a great deal, having to relinquish his space to a young upstart.

An image came to mind of the children's game where all hands are piled on the table, one on top of the other, with the object being to pull your hand from the stack and slap it on the top. And she began to laugh. It was as pointless and ridiculous as that game, trying to stay on top.

***

The apartment on the rue de Sèvres, Elizabeth had discovered over the last weeks, was impossible to keep warm. Heat came from a few ancient electric heaters that never managed to take the edge off the air and since the onset of cold weather, she'd started spending most of her time in bed. In the morning, she drank her coffee and ate her breakfast there. In the evenings, even if she tried to settle on the sofa, she quickly ended up under the covers with a drink and her supper.

The bed became the one place where she could find a semblance of contentment. Besides feeling warm and covered, she was eating and drinking and reading, the only activities she now enjoyed. Suey usually joined her, purring. After consuming too much, Elizabeth would pull the duvet tightly around her body, eventually falling asleep like a caterpillar fattening in its cocoon.

On the day she was fired, a particularly cold day, she came home to what felt like a meat locker. After quickly turning on the heaters, she got out her thick cardigan. She fed poor, lonely Suey and poured herself a whisky, which now preceded the wine, and a bowl of nuts. As she sipped her drink and ate her nuts under the duvet, the purring cat on her lap, she wondered what would happen after leaving her job. The option of staying in bed all day and night until her money ran out was not unattractive.

Eventually of course she would have to find another job but tonight, with the wound still fresh, she was not going to think about that. It was not a time to think about anything, she reflected, licking the peanut oil and salt from her fingers. When she'd drained her glass and finished the bowl, she padded back to the kitchen and poured herself a tad more whisky and a small handful of nuts while waiting for the large portion of Chinese noodles she'd bought at the take-out to warm up. When they were ready, she took a glass of wine and the plate and went back to bed. Although she tried to be careful with the noodles, a short one escaped her fork and fell on the sheet, leaving a trace of soy sauce not far from the tomato sauce she had dripped a couple evenings before.

Once replete, Elizabeth pulled the covers tightly around her and turned to her book. The day after her dinner with Trevor and Béa, she'd dipped into Sybille's chaotic but well-stocked bookshelf. Because she did, as Gérard had been so prompt to point out, have less work. At first, with the same abandon she was applying to food and drink, she read whatever struck her fancy amidst Sybille's wide scope of fiction—everything from trash to classics. Her reactions to what she read proved extreme. The trash novel—her first ever—made her itchy. The overwrought writing blocked enjoyment of the racing plot and she couldn't stop herself from taking out a red pen and trying to improve the flabby prose. A more serious novel, with a happy ending, had enraged her. After finishing the final, uplifting sentence, she had thrown the book across the room with such force that the binding had split in two.

***

As Christmas loomed, Elizabeth tried to turn her thoughts from her impending unemployment to her children. She wanted to make the day festive for them, perhaps even return to some of the Lyall Christmas traditions, of which she had fond memories. They all went to church and belted out carols. Elizabeth and Molly chose the tree with their father and helped their mother bake cakes and cookies while listening to Christmas music on the record player. And at Vera's prompting, they gave a Christmas party for Andrew's family. Because he was forever trying to ignore or forget his lower-middle class start in life, there was little contact the rest of the year. While Andrew suffered through it, the Christmas party gave Elizabeth at least a passing feeling of belonging to something larger than her isolated nuclear family.

The trouble was her children only knew the Teller version of Christmas, a Jewish-Gentile compromise where the day was tolerated rather than celebrated. Concretely this meant that the extended family would eat Christmas Eve dinner together but there was no tree and only one, modest present given to each person.

Try as she may, she could not see how to make the event joyous, especially in this dingy, foreign apartment. She imagined the five of them sitting around their Christmas lunch morosely, with nothing to say, nothing to be thankful for or content about. As for presents, already this year the children would get two, one from her and one from Lucas, and if she wanted she could go even further, return to her family tradition of slightly overdoing the gift-giving. But how could she? Having abandoned so summarily her family traditions, she couldn't just pick them up now. She would appear to be taking a stand against the Tellers. The children would be embarrassed and so would she.

In the end she settled for one nicer-than-usual present each and a small Christmas tree, which she decorated with lights and ornaments bought at the Bon Marché. She made turkey with stuffing, instead of leg of lamb.

When the four children walked in just after noon on Christmas day, they all stopped dead in their tracks and stared at the tree.

"It's so pretty," said Ariane, mesmerized. Gabby eyed it suspiciously. Olivier looked astonished and Tristan ironic.

"I know we've never had a tree before," said Elizabeth. "But I thought it might do something to cheer up the place."

"It's cool," said Olivier.

"Is it real?" asked Tristan.

"Of course it's real," said Elizabeth, incredulous, that one of her children could suggest she would have anything other than real pine. Then again, what could she expect, given their poor education in the matter?

"When can we open the presents?" Ariane asked.

"What do you think? Now or after lunch?" Elizabeth said, looking at the meagre littering underneath the tree.

"Now," said Gabby. The teenage boys shrugged apathetically but couldn't take their eyes off the tree.

"All right then. Let's open them now."

"Me first," said Ariane.

"No, me," said Gabby.

"Don't be so greedy," said Tristan. "I'll hand them out."

For Tristan she had an expensive leather-bound edition of *Les fleurs du mal* that she'd found at an old bookshop on the rue Dauphine. Olivier got the video game she knew he wanted—

unlike the ones he borrowed from friends, it had no office terrorists, but such a present was still a serious deviation from her former principles. She gave Gabby a new football tucked inside the number ten jersey of his hero Zidane, and Ariane a hand-smocked dress. She'd even wrapped up a tin of *Timbale au saumon sauce aux épinards* for Suey. They were all pleased and it did warm up the room. Elizabeth went into the kitchen to check the turkey and the mashed potatoes and when she came back out there was a present sitting on the glass coffee table.

"This is for you," said Tristan, embarrassed.

"It's not stuck, like usual," said Ariane. "We couldn't find the tape."

She pulled the red bow on the poorly folded tissue paper and a shawl spilled out. It was blue-grey, made of cashmere and fine wool. "Thank you. It's gorgeous."

"Papa bought it," said Olivier, shrugging and looking at the floor.

"It's just what I need in this cold," she said, wrapping it tightly around her shoulders and disappearing into the kitchen to whip up the gravy and collect herself. She had not needed Olivier to tell her who had purchased the scarf. The exquisite taste, the choice of colours she would love—who else but Lucas? Yet even this mutual, intimate knowledge of one another's likes and dislikes was apparently not powerful enough to see them through. It was unendingly painful.

"We don't usually eat turkey at Christmas," said Gabby as they sat down to their lunch.

"Or mashed potatoes or stuffing or gravy," said Elizabeth. "This is what my mother used to make for us on Christmas. I've been negligent in your education. You need to know more about how things are done in England and America."

"You're not going to move over there are you?" asked Ariane.

"Would you keep quiet?" said Olivier.

"Of course I'm not moving away from Paris," said Elizabeth. "It's my home as much as it is yours."

"But you're not French," said Gabby.

"Well, neither are you, completely."

"Yes, I am," he said, defiantly, confidently.

"Well…" she started again, uncertain how to explain to a boy his age where the laws of genetics and nationality met and parted ways.

"You're always partly what your parents are," said Tristan grimly.

"That's right," she said. "In any case, I would not move away from you. Though I'm not sure how long I'll last in this flat."

"But where will you go?" asked Ariane, her nose pinching in concern.

"I'll find some place else. Paris is a big city."

They all concentrated on their food. Elizabeth said: "Don't you like the gravy?" All of them had politely taken a tiny bit; all of them had pushed it to the side. The twins shook their heads. Tristan said:

"It tastes a little, I don't know, English."

"That doesn't mean it *has* to taste bad," Elizabeth said.

"Maybe it's one of those things you have to eat early on in life," said Olivier. "Like Marmite." That's what Elizabeth had told her stepmother Pru when she'd once served it to the children and Olivier had actually retched.

"That's probably right," she said. "I was thinking—maybe if you're not going skiing at the winter holiday I'll take you to London. We haven't been in a while." Though she had not discussed it with Lucas, she had also begun thinking about British university for Tristan, if an option to his *prépa* became necessary. "It would be a nice way to spend time with all of you."

"What would we do there?" asked Gabby, who did not look happy about being deprived of the mountains.

"We could go to some museums," said Tristan, with a taunting smile. Gabby frowned but didn't say anything. Tristan tried again. "We could go to the theatre."

"Or we can go on the big wheel—the biggest in Europe,"

said Elizabeth. "And the aquarium. And of course we'll see your grandparents."

No reply. There were no cousins they wanted to see. Though Molly and Gerald had moved back to England, they were at some distance from London. Their children would not be on holiday and in any case, what would Olivier and Tristan do in the country? And there were no children of her old friends because she had no old friends. She had wilfully allowed her entire past and her heritage to wither on every branch; she had passed on nothing, except an imperfect knowledge of the language. The number of ways in which she had failed her children appeared to her at that moment incalculable.

At least she had foreseen that they might be at loose ends after lunch and had rented a video. As always it had been a struggle to find something that would appeal to all four and she had finally settled on a very silly French film, *Le Père Noël est une ordure*—Father Christmas is a Scoundrel—knowing that the older two would chuckle nostalgically, while the twins would roar at its puerile humour. And once again, all that mattered to Elizabeth was being able to hold on to her children, so the video box informed her, for another one hour and twenty-three minutes.

***

"I don't see the point," she said when Gérard's secretary asked about a good-bye party. "People take me for dead already." In the days since her dismissal, everyone in the office had given her increasingly wider berth. The few remaining secretaries seemed to evaporate when she walked past. Lucille's and even Gérard's doors were closed most the time.

She spent the last week cleaning her office. Faced with all those files, she at first considered just throwing everything away. But once she started reading the memos and the letters and the e-mails, she couldn't stop. It was the story, her story, of the last twenty years. She was reminded of all the books she had excitedly uncovered, then watched through to translation and publication. She was reminded too that some of the writers and editors and agents she had worked with had become almost friends. And how recently those relationships, just like her sort-of friendships with everyone else, had atrophied.

Reading her memos and letters and e-mails also reminded Elizabeth that she had been considered an intelligent, competent person. That she had held other people's fates in her hands and had exalted in this power. It was important for her to remember who she was—or had been—because while reading, she was time and again surprised by the control, confidence and professionalism exuded on these pages. It honestly seemed to her, with her diminished ego, that she was reading words written by someone else.

Waking up on New Year's Eve, her last day of work, she had a vague headache and a minor case of indigestion. It had been difficult to get out of bed. In the harsh light of the bathroom mirror, her fair skin was disturbingly waxy against the messy dark hair. The narrow-set eyes were puffed. The lines from the edges of her nostrils to the edge of her mouth seemed to have deepened since the previous morning. Even her upper arms, she noticed, were getting thick and dimpled and the little bone that used to protrude from her shoulder had disappeared in a layer of flesh. All the litheness, all the sharpness was gone. She looked frightful. From a chair, she picked up the trousers she'd worn the day before. They were really the only ones she was still able to squeeze into but as she wiggled them on, she remembered that the button had popped off the day before. Tossing them aside, she put on jeans. She ate a large slab of bread and butter and Nutella and set off.

In the eerily quiet office, she was taping shut the last box of books for storage when the phone rang. She jumped, having grown unused the sound.

"Hallo."

"I've just heard."

"I'm surprised it's taken so long. News usually travels faster in the vicious circles of this incestuous city." She wondered about the circulation pattern. Lucille to her sister-in-law to Alix? Antoine to Claude, via Isabelle?

"What are you going to do?"

"Finish cleaning up and leave."

"Come on, Elizabeth."

"How should I know, Lucas?"

"I'm sorry." Pause. She wondered with whom he was spending New Year's Eve. "I hope…I hope you find something else quickly."

"I do too," she said.

"Well, as I said. I'm sorry. That's all I wanted to say."

"Okay."

And they hung up. This show of sympathy did not lift Elizabeth's spirits at all. Quite the opposite, in fact, because she did not consider it sympathy but pity and that was unbearable. Pity came down at one. There was nothing eye-to-eye about it; it had nothing to do with love or forgiveness. She pulled the last piece of tape savagely across the box top.

The time had come. Since the beginning of her clean-up, she had been dreading the moment when she would have to drop off her on-going work in Lucille's office, dreaded the one last self-satisfied smirk that Lucille would be unable to suppress. She picked up the folders and trudged down the corridor. Lucille's door was open for the first time in weeks. She walked in, then couldn't resist her own small smile: Lucille had a bad cold. Her nose was red, her eyes watery, her voice clogged. From the superior position of good health if nothing else, Elizabeth dropped a stack of folders on the desk.

"Here you go, Lucille. Enjoy them."

"T'anks," she said, as a sneezing fit seized her. Elizabeth walked out while Lucille was blowing her nose, without so much as a good-bye.

The day before Elizabeth had taken the boxes of signed books that she wanted to keep in a taxi to the rue de Sèvres. Today she walked out empty-handed, speaking to no one and feeling as if she might never even have been there in the first place.

Back on the rue de Sèvres, she spent New Year's Eve with the cat, eating and drinking. Even the twins had been invited to spend the night with friends. As she munched her nuts and downed her whisky and looked at her children's photos, she imagined Lucas re-marrying. She imagined the wedding and the woman moving into the rue Laromiguière. Once the children had a stepmother—and she would surely be not only young and beautiful but kind and generous, nothing short of a saint—no one, not even the children, would have any more use for her at all.

***

By the time Elizabeth reached the top of the stairs, she was gasping for breath and uncomfortably warm in her winter coat. She took a minute to compose herself, then rang the bell. A very pretty, compact blond, about her age, answered the door. This was her first meeting with Brigitte Dax, Tristan's therapist. Leading Elizabeth into a room that smelled of rose water, she pointed to a chair opposite the desk. Elizabeth took off her coat and settled on the chair. As Brigitte Dax sat down on the other side of the desk, Elizabeth looked at the woman's ring finger. Two white gold rings, one a wedding band, the other an engagement ring clutching a largish diamond. Elizabeth had hoped she would be unmarried and childless.

"I have seen Tristan three times," said Brigitte Dax, folding her thin hands over a lacquered-covered notebook. "It isn't enough for much of a diagnosis. But I do like to meet the parents early on, hear what they have to say. See if they can fill in any gaps." She took up a lacquered fountain pen between her delicate fingers and opened a notepad holder.

The woman had not a hair out of place. She was not a gram overweight. She was dressed in a short but not too short leather skirt and a grey wool pullover that hugged her thin but not too thin shoulders, her shapely breasts and flat midriff. Elizabeth shifted her overcoat on her lap and tried discreetly to cover the gap that was surely forming between the buttons of her shirt over her newly enlarged chest. "I'm glad you've called me in. As you can imagine, I am a bit more distant from the situation than I would like." The sound of her own voice made her feel even more ungainly. She might have been talking about her bank account rather than her son. "I'm very worried about him. He is a determined boy, no matter which direction he is heading."

"He is also a very sensitive young man and what has been happening between his parents is very painful to him."

"Obviously," Elizabeth prickled.

"I know I'm stating the obvious but it's important to start there. To take things from the beginning. So," she steadied her pen over the pad of paper. "What about the conception?"

Elizabeth started slightly. After a moment: "That was a long time ago. I can't really remember." In fact, she remembered perfectly: Tristan had been conceived on a night when Lucas had thrust himself upon her. She had been furious afterwards, had lain in bed fuming.

"Well then how would you characterize yours and M. Teller's physical relations in general?"

"Adequate," Elizabeth said so tersely, she almost reduced the word to one syllable.

Brigitte Dax scribbled earnestly. Then: "And the pregnancy? Any problems or complications there?"

"No. None."

"The birth itself?"

"It was the happiest day of my life," Elizabeth smiled to herself, remembering the utter joy and wonderment she had felt at that little ball of wrinkled flesh. His birth had made her feel— suddenly, from one minute to the next—a bigger, better person.

"Yes, but did the birth occur smoothly? How long did the labour last?"

"It went fine. About eight hours, I think."

"How would you describe Tristan's personality as a baby?"

"He hasn't changed much. He was always intense—from the start he could occupy himself for hours—first looking at whatever object was within his vision and then with his toys. Maybe he was a little too serious. It was sometimes hard to get him to laugh. But really until recently, he's never seemed unhappy. He loved school, the piano. He's always had friends."

"Did he have tantrums?"

"Yes, he did," Elizabeth coloured, as if they were her fault. "Not very often but when he got into a screaming rage, he was inconsolable. The more I would try and comfort him, the louder he would scream. So I started leaving him alone, letting him get over the rage by himself. It seemed to work better." Mme Dax continued to scribble away with her expensive pen. No matter what you say to these shrinks, Elizabeth was thinking, you feel you've done something wrong. You've come up short.

"There are people for whom the sympathy of others is an extra burden," Mme Dax said, looking up.

"Only when he was angry."

Then came questions about potty training and the age at which Tristan had started crawling, walking, speaking. Elizabeth couldn't quite remember and again felt inadequate. She made up answers that sounded plausible. The scribbling went on. When the long list was finally finished, Mme Dax leaned back in her chair and said: "Tristan is an adolescent, who until now has not showed any rebellious behaviour. In that sense, his acting up now, especially given the circumstances, is normal and healthy. But there's more to his troubles right now. He's convinced that something is being hidden from him. He cannot understand why you and his father broke up. To him it was sudden and wholly unexpected."

"Isn't it normal for children to be surprised?" asked Elizabeth.

"Not necessarily. Some sense tension and have been expecting a separation for as long as they can remember. But this, according to Tristan, was not the case with you and Lucas."

"When I was eighteen my parents separated and I hadn't suspected a thing."

"Yes, Tristan told me. But your father left for another woman, as I understand it. That isn't the case here, is it?"

"No. But things can happen between parents that the children are unaware of. That was my only point."

"Tristan, I believe, has begun frequenting this *demi-monde* at the metro because subconsciously, he thinks he can find the answer among the lost, the fallen."

"Well he's not going to find any answers there." Elizabeth said rather too loudly. Then, more quietly: "I worry about the alcohol and the drugs. As I mentioned, Tristan has always been someone to live a situation to the extreme."

"He's less interested in the substance abuse than he is in understanding, empathizing with, his new friends. He says they're nicer, more interesting and unusual, than what he's used to. He says he likes being a drop out."

"But that doesn't make it good for him."

"No. But Tristan will be eighteen soon and an adult. I agree with you that it would be better for him *not* to be making friends with street people but we can't make decisions for him."

Mme Dax then looked at her watch. The fifty-minute hour was up and the two women stood and shook hands and Elizabeth left feeling that, on top of everything else, she'd just been laid off as a mother.

***

Much of her early days of unemployment were spent in bed, lost in a book. The weather was cold and clear and the flat was so chilly, she had trouble leaving the duvet and *Les Misérables*. Sybille had a three-volume paperback edition and the story was as addictive as the chocolates she often consumed while tucked up and reading. Jean Valjean and Cosette became her companions. The cold dreariness of her flat made her feel as if she were practically living in Marius' unheated lodgings next to the dastardly Thénardiers.

I used to lie in bed with that little light, and my mother would read Peter Rabbit and Benjamin Bunny to me. I wanted a bunny or some kind of pet to keep me company. I pretended my stuffed rabbit was real. I put him in Molly's playpen and gave him cut-up strands of yarn to eat. Later Nancy Drew was my friend—too bad for Bess —Nancy wanted me to help her solve the mysteries now. I sat under the table and spied on my parents' dinner parties, taking notes on the conversations, on possible leads. Later still, I walked around the school with Elizabeth Bennett at my side. She kept me company and I liked her so much, I started speaking the way she would speak; my essays took on an Austen-like cadence.

Books stopped inhabiting her in such a way as an adult and a professional reader but now here she was, as if Jean Valjean were reinventing himself time and again right in her own bedroom.

It's fiction. It means nothing to my real life. I'm not a child anymore; I can't play these games, can't mix up the real and the imaginary.

But real life at this point was an extremely unpleasant subject. Real life meant thinking about a new job, an income. During the last weeks she'd asked around the other big publishing houses but staff was being cut everywhere. In this threatened atmosphere there was little room for generosity; many people she considered friends never even phoned her back. She decided to give it until the end of January—maybe someone would return a call—and if not, then she'd have to come up with another plan.

Elizabeth and Lucas had rather proudly lived with a Bohemian disregard for money. As long as there was enough of it, it was below the radar of their higher purposes in life. This meant that accounting practices and domestic finances were somewhat haphazard and confused. Having maintained separate bank accounts, they had divided up bill-paying as evenly as possible. Elizabeth paid the housekeeper and the phone bill; Lucas the electricity, which was always higher than the phone, and all bills relating to the motorcycle and the car. Generally he covered house repairs as well. They divided spending on food, etc., as best as possible.

The system worked well enough until the months leading up to their separation, when money had been a constant source of chafing. One of them always felt hard done by, and this was usually communicated through one of their notes: "I had to pay for Tristan's piano lesson two weeks in a row—don't we usually trade off????" When Elizabeth moved out, it was agreed that she would pay the rent on the rue de Sèvres. Lucas would pay all the bills, then ask Elizabeth for a quarter of the sum in return. At first that clarity had provided a feeling of relief; now, when there would soon be no more money coming in, it was a worry. A very big worry. Not just for herself but for the children. She was still determined to get them back after a year and that meant she had to have a job and a place big enough to house them. She wasn't going to be able sit in bed and read forever. But when the end of January arrived, she still had no idea what to do. Fortunately by then she had another excuse for putting off action:

"I'm planning to take the children to London for a week over the winter holidays," Elizabeth said to Lucas over the phone.

"I'm taking them skiing the first week."

"It would have been nice if you'd consulted me."

"It would have been nice if you'd consulted me."

"Right. Well, then I'll go to London the second week. I see the twins all the time but Tristan and Olivier hardly ever. And my father's offered to pay."

"Okay."

"Any news on Tristan? The few times I've seen him he puts on his act. I have no idea what's really going on."

"I can't say I do either. He comes and goes up the back stairs most of the time. Joins us for supper only at the end of the week when his spending money has run out."

"I've been thinking," said Elizabeth gingerly. "Maybe I should have him look at some universities in Britain, while we're over there. Just in case."

Silence. "You're probably right. Yes, that's a good idea."

"How did your meeting with Brigitte Dax go?" she asked.

"Fine." He paused. "Did you say anything?"

"No. Did you?"

"No."

"Good. We agree on that."

"Yes."

***

In the end, Tristan did not come with them to London. Just before the holiday, Monsieur Aubert had informed them by letter that Tristan's ranking had improved considerably—he was now fifteen out of twenty-four—and he said he wanted to stay home and work. So Elizabeth met the other three children at the Gare du Nord and boarded the Eurostar. The train was very crowded and there wasn't enough room for the voluminous and cumbersome luggage of their fellow travellers.

"Are they moving over there for good or what?" Olivier asked, after a particularly large man squeezed past with his oversized suitcase.

"I thought this was a special train," said Ariane.

"It is," said Elizabeth. "Maybe that's why it's so crowded."

Gabby and Ariane now argued over who would get to sit next to the window. Olivier, who was sitting next to her, was singing along—softly, but nevertheless singing—to whatever music he had blaring into his ears. Her three children suddenly seemed like an annoyance. Her nerves were out of practice and she had to use all available restraint not to shout out loud. She pulled out a magazine and flicked the glossy pages with a snak as they began

218

to hurtle through the French countryside.

Later Elizabeth fell asleep. She was woken up by Gabby tugging her sleeve. They were in the tunnel underneath the Channel.

"How long does this last? I don't like it. My ears are funny."

"Didn't they make an announcement? Usually they tell you. I think it lasts about twenty minutes. Don't worry. Many trains do exactly the same thing every day."

"But there's all that water on top of us. All around us. Just think how far it is to the air." He hunched his shoulders and looked around as if the water were already beginning to seep through the roof of the train and drip down the back of his neck.

Elizabeth said: "Sit on my lap." Gabby awkwardly folded himself onto Elizabeth's lap; he was getting too big for lap-sitting.

"You're taking up all the space, idiot," said Olivier.

"Have some patience. Just until we get through the tunnel," said Elizabeth. As she tried to make Gabby as compact as possible, she got a smell of his clothes. They smelled different—Manuela must have changed washing powders—but it made her feel a foreign being was in her lap. As if Gabby were no longer Gabby. Or not her Gabby anyway. That was what was happening. In a million little ways her children were being detached from her, thread by thread. Maybe, just maybe, this trip to London would put a stop to the fraying.

Once out of the Tunnel, Gabby hopped off Elizabeth's lap. She rested her chin on her hand and looked out the window as the train rolled through the Kentish countryside. Suddenly they were no longer on high-speed, state-of-the-art transportation but British Rail. Old British Rail, which had taken her to and from school for six years.

The train rocked back and forth. Not fast enough. I wanted to get back to London. To get home, be with my things again. To have the homesickness melt away. How grim those end-of-holiday Sunday nights going back were, how lonely and lost I felt. Until things reversed. Until school felt more like home and going to London meant boredom, lethargy. Waking near noon with nothing to do and no one to see, since my school friends lived in the country. I read books, lots of books, but the satisfaction they gave me was somehow shameful, embarrassing. Unlike the other girls, I had not gone to any parties and had no stories to tell about boys and fun when I got back at the end of those book-filled holidays.

The screech of the train's brakes as they neared Waterloo made her jump.

"Get your things together," Elizabeth told the children vaguely, still half in another world.

Her father was there to pick them up. He was driving a sleek and gleaming new Peugeot with leather seats and an automatic transmission.

"Hello," he said cheerfully, stepping out of the car. Elizabeth noticed an almost imperceptible widening of the eyes when he saw the size of her.

"You're very kind to pick us up," she said, kissing him hello. "Will we all fit in this fancy new car?"

"Absolutely."

"What happened to that beat-up Vauxhall you used to drive?"

"Junked it. Quite a number, isn't it?"

"Indeed," she said. It was powder blue, and Elizabeth wondered if Pru had chosen the colour as well as footing the bill.

He drove them to a mews house in Belgravia. It was made of brick and painted white and belonged, Andrew informed them, to Pru's sister and brother-in-law who now spent half the year in the south of France. The place was full of the expensive porcelain that the couple collected. "You'll have to be careful," he said to Elizabeth.

"We will," she said. "And it can't be that bad."

"Has it a television?" asked Ariane in her best English.

"We didn't come to London to watch television," said Olivier in French.

"That doesn't mean we can't watch any," the sassy one replied in French too.

"It help our English," added Gabby earnestly, unaware of his conjugation error. Elizabeth had delivered strict orders not to speak in French when with family.

"Any other plans besides the BBC while you're here?" asked Andrew.

"We'll see Mum," said Elizabeth, annoyed at her father for continuing to airbrush her mother out of the picture.

"Of course," he said opening the front door. The small house smelled of soap. It was immaculate and there were indeed bits of porcelain everywhere. Elizabeth wanted to tell her children to freeze. Not to move, not to touch anything. She hoped the upstairs would be less fragile.

"I see what you mean about being careful," she said.

"It is a bit of a minefield," Andrew said. "With children."

"We'll do our best not to move and see you this evening. Thanks again for coming to fetch us."

The five-day visit she had been looking forward to was weighing on her like five large, heavy stones. Besides never being able to relax here in the china shop, she was going to be juggling people and languages the whole time: when to see her mother, when her father, forcing the children to speak English yet trying to keep them from getting bored and cranky.

"Let's look at the bedrooms," she said. The stairs were covered with soft, off-white carpet. Elizabeth imagined dirty shoe marks. She imagined Olivier going against strict orders and carrying something to eat and drink up the stairs, dribbling a little along the way. The three bedrooms were only marginally less cluttered with porcelain than downstairs.

"Where did they get all this stuff?" asking Olivier. "It's creepy."

"They're collectors," said Elizabeth. "Zealous collectors, whose children must be grown up. If they ever had any. What we'll do up here is take some of this stuff away. Downstairs will be off limits. No food or drink up here under any circumstances, do you understand?"

"You don't have to scream at us," said Ariane.

"I'm not screaming. I'm trying to convey a firm message."

"You're always screaming now," said Gabby.

"No I'm not," she said, all too aware of the shrillness she could not keep out of her voice as she put little statuettes, cups and saucers and bowls up as high as she could reach on the bookshelves.

She took them to the King's Road for something to eat and then they walked towards Buckingham Palace. They passed a music shop and Olivier said he would rather look at CDs than "some random palace." She acquiesced. The twins were suitably impressed by "the Queen's house." Afterwards they picked up Olivier who stunk of cigarettes. As the afternoon progressed, the twins went into their exclusive mode, where they stuck together and whispered to one another, making others feel as if an impenetrable barrier existed between them and the rest of the world. Olivier was showing teenage disdain for everything and complaining it wasn't fair that Tristan had got to stay home.

They went to Andrew and Pru's for supper. Or to Pru's, was the way Elizabeth viewed it. Andrew had moved into her house, the house that had been part of the settlement in her divorce from her wealthy first husband. What her father had done with his own belongings, Elizabeth never knew but not one stick of Andrew's admittedly shabbier furniture had been moved into Battersea.

"Come in, come in," he said, greeting them at the door and leading them proprietarily through the foxhunt prints in the front hall to the narrow but richly fabric-ed drawing room. Pru came to greet them, still in her apron. She was a fair-haired woman, and though slightly overweight, looked more sturdy than fat in her ample skirts and frilled blouses. She was thirteen years younger than Andrew and even though it wasn't quite true, Elizabeth always felt somehow Pru was closer to her in age than to her father. This feeling of proximity did not, however, help her to overcome an aversion to her stepmother. Nor did efforts at a mature and reasoned analysis of the many qualities that made Pru so right for her father.

Pru was good at things like cooking and glass blowing, things that were creative, *interesting*, but that did not challenge Andrew's substantial but complicated ego. She was in fact very good at them. Pru and her best friend had written a cookery book called *Granny's Kitchen*, with recipes for such forgotten delicacies as nettle soup and elderflower cordial. It had sold well enough to earn them several magazine and television interviews. Beyond her unthreatening talents, Pru also allowed Andrew, once and for all, to forget that his father had been a municipal employee of a small city slightly too far to the north of England, something he had not quite been able to achieve through his American wife or his Italian girlfriend. With Pru, he had finally landed firmly and safely in the lap of the upper-middle classes. She anchored Andrew and satisfied his need for flair, while never once dredging up his lower origins, probably because she was as eager to forget about them as he was.

"Hello-o-o," she said, embracing them one by one. "You've certainly all grown. Lizzie, I've got a couple of films for the children to watch. I thought they'd be bored sitting at table too long with us. Is that all right? You don't have any objection to electronic entertainment on special occasions?"

"No. None at all. Even on ordinary occasions." Elizabeth answered.

"What can I get you to drink, Lizzie?" Andrew asked. "A little whisky?"

"That would be great." At least he and Pru always had good scotch.

"And you, Children? A beer Oliver? Juice for the twins?" asked Pru. "Why don't you come with me to the kitchen and choose what you'd like."

"So how are things going?" asked Andrew when the three had followed Pru downstairs. "You look strained."

"Losing one's family and one's job all in one year can take its toll."

"Of course." He paused, looking how to phrase it. "It makes me more worried about you, though."

"No need." She blushed.

"That really is bad luck about the job," he shook his head. "Though I can't say I'm surprised. One gets no slack for personal problems—in fact, people are generally only to happy to stomp on you when you're down."

"It would appear so," said Elizabeth with a sigh. She felt grateful for her father's understanding, could actually feel tears beginning to well up in her eyes.

But then the children returned and attention moved to them. Their grandfather asked them questions that the twins had trouble answering in English.

"Sounds like you two need a week in Britannia," said Andrew.

"They just need a day or so to adjust," said Elizabeth, now aware that she'd not only allowed them to speak in French all day; she'd also been speaking it back to them.

Dinner was served and it was, Elizabeth had to admit, delicious. After the main course, Pru got the children going on the film; she'd managed to find a comedy that would amuse all three. She came back to the table with cheese and salad, saying: "In honour of your visit, I'm serving the cheese before the pudding. How's that?"

"Thank you," said Elizabeth uncomfortably.

Pru then smoothed the folds of her skirt and said: "Lizzie, do you ever think about moving back here?"

"My children, as you have witnessed, are too French. I could never take them from their life in Paris, even if I wanted to."

"But you are living in a foreign country," Pru persisted.

"I do not consider France a foreign country. It is my home. I have lived there for over half my life." She could feel her voice rising, her blood beginning to simmer—Pru invariably had that effect on her.

"But what are you going to do about work, Lizzie?" her father asked.

"I don't know. I've made the rounds at the publishing houses. No one is hiring."

"How about trying to work as some sort of correspondent for an English company?" asked Pru.

"Doing what?" asked Elizabeth.

"Finding French books."

"Pru," said Andrew, "her speciality is Anglophone literature."

"Couldn't you just switch?"

Elizabeth took a deep breath. "I haven't read much contemporary French fiction but from what I have read, I have no interest in becoming a specialist in the field."

"How about translating?" asked her father. "At least to tide you over."

Translating. The thing that every ex-pat is supposed to be able to fall back on. She thought of all the translators she'd worked with over the years. How hard they laboured and how little credit they usually got and just the idea of it made her feel tired and hopeless. She said: "Translating is actually not that easy, either to do well or to earn a living from. Unless you get a job with a company or a service, translating annual reports and things."

"It's just hard for me to imagine how you will be able to reinvent yourself," said her father, shaking his head. "If you really can't find another publishing job."

"Maybe you should write your own book," said Pru.

"On what topic?" asked Elizabeth, realizing that she had practically spat out the last word.

"On your life in Paris. You know some very interesting people. Those books about living abroad have worked well from the south of France. From Italy. Why not Paris?"

"I'm afraid my local colour is too subtle for that kind of success."

"And one can't write a book just like that," said Andrew. "Lizzie needs a payslip."

"Well," said Pru, pushing her chair back and standing up. "I'm just trying to help." And she began collecting the plates as if each one had personally offended her. "I've made a trifle for pudd'."

***

"Lizzie, what on earth are you going to do?" her mother asked fretfully, during the first visit to Holland Park, where Vera and Cy lived among other American ex-pat lawyers and bankers, now the only class of people able to afford the area.

"I don't know," said Elizabeth.

"It's a tough world these days," added Cy, who in his entire career had known only one employer, the investment firm that had hired him straight out of Yale, that had then made him a partner, thus allowing him to retire at sixty-five with his millions.

"Indeed," said Elizabeth.

"The children seem well," her mother said.

"We're all fine," Elizabeth said.

"You look strained."

Elizabeth looked down. Even after all this time apart, her mother and father sometimes chose the same words, took on similar facial expressions or tones of voice, that attested to their twenty years of marriage. And it still pained her.

"That's one way to put it."

"Are you going to the gym? I've been reading that exercise is the best way to combat any adversity, from depression to dementia to osteoporosis."

"I gave up the gym long ago." Though never quite attaining Lucille's muscle tone, she used to go to the gym religiously. Since the twins were born, most of her exercise had come from always being in a hurry. "For the moment it's an expense I can't afford."

"It's important not to be penny wise, pound foolish, Liz," Cy laughed.

"Cy," said her mother. "Lizzie is not in the mood for such impertinent jokes."

And that was the extent of their discussion of her physical and financial challenges, except that her mother never stopped looking at her, just as she had done all those years ago when she'd come home plump from boarding school.

The trip was not going well. Olivier was bored most of the time and told them so continually, before imagining out loud all the fun his friends were having in Paris. The twins bickered more than usual. At the house, she was after them all the time not to move, not to eat anything, anywhere. Every tourist sight they visited meant throngs of people and long queues. She angered quickly with the children; she railed against the crowds. The only time she really enjoyed herself was when she put Olivier in charge of the twins for a couple hours so that she could have lunch with Molly, who'd come up to London for the day to see her. And even then, it was with resigned pleasure that she listened to her sister's enthusiasm for her life back in England, for her marriage, back on track, as Elizabeth had predicted.

Mid-week her father said: "Why don't you take them on an excursion, away from London? I was thinking of Stonehenge. I haven't been there myself in a dog's age, but I doubt those megaliths have changed much. You can spend the night in Salisbury. Visit the cathedral. I'll lend you our second car."

Getting out and moving on. This struck Elizabeth as a wonderful idea. She was even pleased to learn that the second car was a pedestrian affair—a not so new, manual transmission, Volkswagen. It was raining when they piled into it. "Just the weather for Stonehenge," said Elizabeth jauntily to the children, who were quite giddy at being released from the porcelain prison, by the lure of the Druids. They rolled off, waving happily to Andrew and Pru.

They went directly to Stonehenge, with Olivier navigating. "The road goes right by it," he said, looking at the map.

"Then we won't get lost," said Elizabeth. She had only visited Stonehenge once, many years ago, on a school trip, and all she could remember was seeing it from afar, from the top of a hill, the megaliths standing alone in a field on the Salisbury plain. In her memory, it was romantic, poignant, unforgettable.

But had she imagined this memory? Could things now really look so different? Because here they were, the busy road indeed zipping right by. Two busy roads, in fact. There was something undignified about it: such an ancient ruin deserved more respect, more distance from the ugly, rushing modern world, than this. They parked their car amid the tour buses and took the passage under the road to the site. Even now in February, there were throngs of people. School tours, a large group of Chinese and another from Poland.

"Kind of hard to imagine the Druids carrying out a religious ceremony with all these people and the noise from the road," said Olivier. "It's a little like an airport."

"It certainly is," said Elizabeth. "Ariane, Gabby—keep close." The twins were dancing and running about, oblivious to what was around them. "Let's see if we can get a guide book."

They bought a small pamphlet that described what little was known about the origins of the huge stones.

"It's like Asterix," said Gabby.

"How do they stand up like that?" asked Ariane.

"How does anything stand up in all this traffic?" said Olivier. "When you look between the stones, you can see the cars and lorries whizzing by."

"Your grandfather was right that the megaliths haven't changed," Elizabeth said. "But everything around them has."

They did not stay long—the magic in the mystery, in the history, was impossible to feel in the surrounding commotion. Elizabeth then made a wrong turn going into Salisbury and they drove around and around. Everyone was hungry and grumpy and no one's humour improved, even after they finally found their way and something to eat. The hotel, which Elizabeth had found in a guidebook, had no charm and not much hot water. The cathedral, which she dragged the children to see, did not interest them at all.

The trip was a complete failure. The idea of getting away was an illusion. Even her memories of Stonehenge and the Salisbury Cathedral felt somehow violated. Or completely fabricated. She had no retrievable past. The best that could be said about the excursion was that it got them closer to the end of the holiday, when the children could happily return to school and their friends, and Elizabeth to her bed and her books.

***

Lucas wanted to talk to her. They met again at the Café de l'Epée.

"I hear the trip to London was a success," he said, his large hand looking gigantic as it turned a small coffee spoon around in the espresso cup.

"Who told you that?" she asked suspiciously.

"The children."

"All three of them?"

"Yes. When I asked them how it went, they all said they'd had a good time."

"Oh," she said, quite taken aback at how quickly history could be rewritten.

They sat in awkward silence for a moment.

"Tristan seems to be doing better," Elizabeth said, turning a cylindrical packet of sugar over and over on the table. Her throat was constricted and she felt her voice small and high as a mouse.

Lucas nodded. "He does seem to like this therapist woman."

"But you don't," she said, with a tight smile at Lucas' elliptical confession.

"I wouldn't want to confide in her," he shrugged.

"I got some information on the University of London. Just in case."

He nodded slowly again. "How about you? Any news on the job front?"

She shook her head. "No one seems to be hiring. Most people don't even bother to return my call."

"I'm sorry to hear that," and he looked down. Lucas, who always returned calls, knew that in general, his friends would not in a situation that might be awkward or unbeneficial.

"What did you want to see me about?" she asked, impatient now to move along.

He tapped his coffee spoon on the side of the cup, laid it on the saucer, shifted uncomfortably in his chair. "We've been separated for over six months now."

"I guess that's right."

"I know we agreed to wait a year. But I wonder if dragging things out is in anybody's interest."

"Have you got some reason to precipitate the situation?" Elizabeth asked with an attempt at indifference.

He shook his head, the blue vein swinging her way. "Only that I find this limbo unbearable."

"I thought we were giving things time to settle, making sure —"

"I just don't see any hope, any reason to keep waiting." The coffee spoon was back in his now empty cup and he was distractedly scraping at the dregs with it. "Nothing's improved over the last year and a half, either before or after the separation. I feel trapped. I don't want to feel trapped anymore. I need to do something, to act, so that maybe, just maybe, one day I won't wake up wondering why the hell I should bother to get up."

"Have you met someone else?" she asked, looking him straight in the eye, trying to detect even the smallest twitch.

But he didn't flinch. He was deathly pale and he actually looked as if he were about to cry, when he said very quietly, almost in a whisper, so no one else could hear: "This is not about someone else. It's about us. About how I feel towards you. It's a very hard thing to think, much less to say, but I don't love you anymore. And nothing I've tried to do or say to myself over the last eighteen months has been able to change that."

"Is that because you still haven't forgiven me?" She too was almost whispering.

When he shook his head, he looked like a caged and crazy animal. "I don't know. I don't know anything anymore except that I feel nothing and the vacuum makes living an exercise in torture."

For a moment she did not speak, trying to think clearly about what *she* felt. Time and again over the last months she had felt irritated and put off by him, most recently just now, the way he'd tapped his coffee spoon on the edge of the cup. Did *she* love *him*? She could not answer that question. All she knew was that because he was making the decisions, pushing things forward, she felt trapped and powerless. The mere fact of being on the defensive made her want to resist him.

"But shouldn't we stick to our year agreement?"

"I can't live like this," he answered, swaying his head again.

"What do you suggest then?"

"I've talked to someone. A lawyer."

Given what Lucas had already said, this should not have surprised her. But it did. She felt stunned. While she had been sitting in bed, eating and drinking and reading, living in a suspended state of inertia, Lucas had already got up and gone out the door. "Oh," Elizabeth said. "I need some time to think about all this."

"I understand," said Lucas, fishing money out of his pocket. As he put the coins on the table, Elizabeth saw that his hand was trembling.

Outside the café, they muttered awkward good-byes and headed their separate ways but she was still muddled and smarting when she got back to the rue de Sèvres. She phoned Béa Fairbank and invited herself to supper.

At the end of the meal, she helped Béa clear up while Trevor took out the dog.

"I'll wash," said Elizabeth. She filled up the sink, squirted in the washing-up liquid.

"Are you all right, Elizabeth?" Béa asked, taking the tea towel. "You hardly ate a thing."

"Not really." She did not look up as she finished washing a glass, rinsing it, putting it in the rack. "Do you remember what you said to me once? That I was being noble? Because I was letting Lucas keep the flat and the children, and he was also getting to keep the friends?"

"I remember thinking it didn't seem quite fair," said Béa.

"Well," Elizabeth said, putting another glass in the rack. "There's more to the story."

"Ah," said Béa quietly.

"Noble is the last thing I am." Elizabeth's hands dropped into the soapy water.

"Come on," said Béa softly, pulling her away from the sink, handing her a tea towel, guiding her to a chair. Pulling up another chair, pregnant Béa sat across from Elizabeth like a Buddha with her huge belly resting on her small lap.

And so Elizabeth told Béa the story of Troy Ross and the fire, of the burn and the prison sentence and the way she walked out on him. And how Lucas had seen Troy's scarred back. "So in a way," she finished, dabbing her eyes with a Kleenex, "it seems I'm getting everything I deserve."

"It *is* quite a story," said Béa. "But no one died. It wasn't *that* unforgivable."

"He's said he isn't sure whether or not it's about forgiveness but I don't know. He's such a moral person."

"Were there other tensions, things that this might have brought to the surface?"

Elizabeth fiddled with her tissue. "Until Troy came, I thought we were happy enough, even if things simmered sometimes. But we were so busy with everyday life—our jobs, our children. I didn't have the time or the inclination to sit down and analyse our overall happiness." She blew her nose. "It's true that the sex was never great-great. You wouldn't have called our marriage passionate."

"That can certainly create tension," said Béa.

"It did a long time ago." She continued to worry her tissue. "But it seemed just another thing one learns to live with, like snoring or dirty socks on the floor."

"Well, primitive as it may sound, I think sex or let's say a physical connection, is the foundation. It's what you can fall back on when things get tense or troubled."

Elizabeth paused, weighing if she should tell Béa the other part of the story, the part that Lucas didn't know, but before she had made up her mind, Béa asked: "You don't think Lucas is seeing someone else, do you? That would explain his hurry."

She shook her head. "I asked him. He said no. Or he said it was about us, not about someone else." The Kleenex was now in shreds. "A little elliptical, I guess."

"Could he have been having an affair before? That could affect his feelings for you even now."

"I don't think so. He's always despised infidelity in others."

"Well then," said Béa, shaking her head, "there must have been more underlying tension than you were aware of. What you did all those years ago was a moment of weakness and we all have those." She paused again. "I guess what I'm trying to say is that if you were both as happy as you thought, the crime doesn't seem to justify the punishment."

"Maybe you're right—maybe we weren't happy enough in Lucas' mind and when he learned about what I did, it tipped him over the edge. In any case," she said sitting up straight, collecting herself, "he's determined to go ahead. So there's one other thing I wanted to ask." Elizabeth stood up as the front door opened and the dog bounded in. "Do you think Trevor could get me the name of his brother's divorce lawyer? And then I'll let you two get some sleep."

III
Pigalle

On an unusually warm day in early March, Elizabeth was roused into a spring clean. She had wiped every surface, even the walls, and was just beginning the window-panes, when the phone rang. It was Sybille, her proprietress.

"Sorry but things aren't working out. I need the apartment back. Mid-April is my limit."

Elizabeth put down the phone and the window cleaner. It was Friday afternoon—what could she do about it now? She crawled back into bed. Since the children were going to a wedding of a distant relation in Alsace for the weekend with Lucas, for three days she read *Le Rouge et le noir* and hardly moved.

Running out of food and whisky and wine just as she finished the last depressing pages got her up and out. While replenishing her supplies, she bought a copy of Le Figaro and consulted the property pages. Every day, in an almost trance-like state, she bought the paper and looked for another place to live. Although she knew from the start that places in *les beaux quartiers* would be beyond her means, it quickly became apparent that if she wanted to stay within the city limits at all, she would have to find a job quickly too. By now she had completely given up hope of hearing back from any of the publishing houses and she interviewed at various temp agencies.

Within a month she had a new temporary life. The apartment, another short-term, furnished rental, was on the rue Pigalle. It was in a nineteen-seventies' building and its ageing concrete had no charm whatsoever. It belonged to a highly-strung air hostess who was going to be in Germany for three months' training for some position on the ground. Or maybe six months—nothing was certain—except that a cat would not be welcome for any length of time. "They get their claws into the furniture and shred it to pieces," Carole said in such a flutter that it was hard to imagine that she could have been permitted to work on any airborne vehicle with passengers. The apartment looked as if not even a human had lived in it. Or that many had; it felt more like a hotel than a home. Elizabeth was surprised to find this impersonal functionality a relief. She felt no ghosts, no spirits, lingering in the mass-produced corners of IKEA furnishings. After the first night she realized how much Sybille's place had weighed on her. How much she had felt she was living in someone else's life. How uncomfortably close yet shabbier that life felt to the one she'd been forced to give up. Her continued inability to house the children, and returning Suey to the rue Laromiguière, proved her only regrets in leaving the rue de Sèvres.

The area around Pigalle did, however, take a little getting used to. Prostitutes with short skirts and inflated breasts lingered in doorways. There were many "clubs" with darkened windows and men slinking in and out beaded entries. But it didn't take her long; once again, the very difference from her old *quartier* was actually a relief. And the prostitutes, generally, were really very friendly.

Her first three-month employment contract was at an international law firm, where she was replacing a pregnant bilingual secretary. The American firm Barker, Baker and Mudge had recently merged with the British firm Campbell and Cutler, a phenomenon, her father informed her, that was occurring throughout the legal world. The combined firms now occupied a large *hôtel particulier* on the place des Etats-Unis that had been completely gutted and remodelled inside for the newly merged lawyers. Elizabeth worked for two partners, one Briton and one American. Mr Hadley and Mr Green were so archetypically true

238

to form that at times she had trouble believing they were real. Mr Hadley was upright and trim. He combed his light brown hair neatly back and wore an immaculately tailored pin-striped suit and a signet ring on the wrong hand. Mr Green's paunch made it hard for him to button his sports jacket and his large bottom made the single vent in back splay open. As for the work, she found it not much different from running a household: she helped them keep tidy and manage their lives. And for this, she was pleased to learn, she would be earning slightly more than she had ever earned at the publishing house, even in her pre-commission days.

In fact Elizabeth found she spent much of her time on the lawyers' personal lives. She arranged the travel for Mr Hadley's children to and from their boarding schools in England and for the frequent family holidays taken by the Greens. She paid household bills for both of them and Elizabeth wondered what their wives did all day. Mrs Hadley didn't even have children at home and Mrs ("call me Jane,") Green had a full-time Filipina cleaning lady as well as a Czech *fille au pair* for her two young boys. Elizabeth, of course, knew these details because she prepared the pay slips and wrote the cheques for Mr Green to sign, as well as arranging the plane ticket from Prague to Paris. Both Mrs Hadley and Mrs Green made Elizabeth happy that, if nothing else, she had avoided this particular form of ex-pat hell.

Money was coming in again and that was a relief. She was no longer spending days alone and that made her feel less savage. But the work was blindingly dull and she had little in common with her co-workers. Lunch, if she didn't manage to sneak off alone, she ate with her fellow secretaries at a sandwich and salad bar. She rarely contributed to the office talk and became mute when personal subjects such as children were discussed.

She was seeing even less of hers. The older boys didn't like having to come all that way and given the Pigalle low-life, Elizabeth didn't try to change their minds. As for the twins, Sunday nights had been abandoned some time ago and

Wednesdays she now had to work. They stopped coming Friday night as well. When they had school on Saturday morning, Elizabeth would pick them up there at eleven-thirty, where she continued to run into other mothers, former colleagues on the parents' association, from which she had withdrawn some time ago. It didn't seem to get any less awkward but it was better than picking up the twins when they didn't have school at the rue Laromiguière, where the smell of the place and a glimpse of the sitting room made her ears ring and her eyes sting.

Where seeing Lucas, even briefly, stirred up more confusion and pain. She had thought a lot about Béa's theories on physical closeness and existing tensions. Her friend was undoubtedly correct, that there had been too little of the former and more than she'd realized of the latter. That Troy's presence and their subsequent relations had subliminally awakened her to these fault lines, and it had been naive or deluded of her to think that once Troy left, the two of them would return to life as it had been.

At moments Elizabeth convinced herself that she had misjudged her husband entirely and that all the while he had been seeing another woman—it was common enough among their friends—but then she would remember how he had always despised their hypocrisy, vociferously and emphatically. And no matter how much she combed over the past few years, she could find no clues to indicate he had been having an affair. Nevertheless, Béa had agreed that not being able to forgive her involvement in a crime that had occurred years and years ago, did not seem to make sense either. So had he met someone else in the meantime? It was the only explanation she could think of.

When she picked up the twins, she would try to read his grave demeanour. But she couldn't, which made her think: I don't know him anymore—and maybe I never did.

So she went ahead and contacted the lawyer Trevor's brother had suggested. At the first meeting, since she had no intention of telling the lawyer the truth, Elizabeth pulled out the phrase she often read in the newspaper, when movie stars or industry magnates were getting divorced. Elizabeth told Natalie Surmon that there were irreconcilable differences between her and Lucas. Then she outlined the situation: the four children, at present living with Lucas, and the inconvenient distribution of their property, the flat that had been cobbled together, two parts bought by Lucas and his parents, the one in the middle by her.

At the second meeting, Natalie said they needed to try and keep things simple. "Simple," Elizabeth nodded. The property was indeed complicated, Natalie allowed, but she thought they should propose something of a package deal whereby Elizabeth would sell her part of the apartment to Lucas and have the option to take certain common belongings when she eventually settled in more permanent accommodations. There would then be no further financial obligations or transactions between them. Since for most of their married life, Elizabeth had earned as much or more than Lucas and because this was France, there would be no question of alimony.

As for the children, Natalie asked delicately: "Are you sure you are content for the children to continue living with Monsieur Teller?" Elizabeth told Natalie that it was her intention to have the children live with her again as soon as she was able to provide the necessary space but that for the moment they should not be uprooted from their settled life in the fifth arrondissement and should remain with their father. She said that he too favoured joint custody, as far as the settlement was concerned.

Since moving to Pigalle, her former life had begun to take on a dream-like unreality in her mind. The old buildings, the narrow, charming streets themselves seemed part of a dream too. Part of a fairy tale she had lived in another life.

Tristan of course could bring her back down to earth and remind her that even the fifth arrondissement had its share of grit. His ranking had plunged again and he had actually been asked to leave his *prépa,* thus giving him more time to hang out on the corner with his homeless friends. His therapist Brigitte

Dax was strongly suggesting a change of scene and time away from the broken home that was crippling him, and it was decided that Tristan should go to England. With his Baccalaureate results he could have gone to Oxford or Cambridge but now it was late in the game and he'd be lucky to get a place at the University of London. Elizabeth scrambled to see what might still be available.

For his eighteenth birthday Tristan announced that he wanted everyone around the same table, the request for solidarity being another of Brigitte's therapeutic suggestions. Tristan planned the whole thing with an attention to domestic detail that was unusual for him—every item on the menu, a precise list of gift requests. It saddened Elizabeth to see him forcefully asserting authority over this one event because the larger picture was so wholly beyond his control but she agreed to come to supper and bake his favourite chocolate cake.

She hadn't baked anything since the first days of moving to the rue de Sèvres and she could barely remember the ingredients, much less the execution. Her cookery books were still in the cupboard above the sink at the rue Laromiguière. As she clumsily began to prepare, little bits of shell got in the egg whites and since they were very difficult to extract, she eventually just left them there. She let the melting chocolate get too hot and it began to curdle. By the time she got the batter in the oven, she was running late but that didn't deter her from letting the cake burn around the edges while she was trying to find clothes that both fit and made her look less fat. She arrived at the rue Laromiguière overheated and flustered.

Tristan opened the door. His cheeks were slightly flushed. "Hello," he said with a childish smile. "You brought the cake."

"I did. But that oven up there at Pigalle is very hot and it burned a bit around the edges."

"That's okay," he said but his face deflated, in much the same way as the centre of the cake had when she'd belatedly pulled it from the oven.

She walked tentatively into the living room, part of the apartment that was technically still hers. Suddenly feeling the large drink she had downed while getting dressed, she was afraid she might topple over. But she couldn't bring herself to sit down either.

"Hello," said Lucas, with a formal, vaguely embarrassed bow of his head. Despite an effort to smile, he looked as if he were attending a funeral. He was dressed in a dark grey shirt and black khakis. The small paunch he had developed before their separation was completely gone; he was now cadaverous. It was difficult indeed to imagine that he was in love.

"Hello," she answered.

The twins came running in, giggling with excitement over the party, over the reunion. "Would you take the cake into the kitchen?" she asked them. In arguing over who would carry it, they almost dropped it. "Let me take that," said Lucas, disappearing briskly.

Olivier came from his bedroom with Philomène, who was leaving. This was Elizabeth's first glimpse of the girlfriend, who moved her small, fine frame like a dancer. She kissed Elizabeth's two cheeks without hesitation then looked her straight in the eye and Elizabeth felt a pang of jealousy for the girl's youth and composure, for her place in Olivier's life.

Lucas returned from the kitchen. "Tristan wanted chicken and I tried to follow Manuela's instructions and make the sauce, the way Tristan likes it," he said. Lucas had never been much of a cook. "Would you mind looking at it? The rice should be done in ten minutes."

She walked carefully into the kitchen, still feeling unsteady. She opened the oven, spooned sauce over the chicken. The kitchen and the chicken and even the family meal made her think of Troy. Troy leaning into her, Troy's breath tickling her ear, his tongue, his strong arms, his Liza. The sensation was so strong that she shuddered.

She tossed the salad and realized it had no dressing. While

the timer ticked away the last minutes for the rice, she whisked a *vinaigrette*. Despite all that had happened, thinking of Troy could still arouse her, whereas when she thought of Lucas, the pale, thin man next door, she felt nothing, except perhaps mild aversion. As she pulled the cooked chicken from the oven, she actually had trouble imagining that they had ever been to bed together. On the other hand, the thought of his finding a new wife could still send her into a tailspin. What did that mean?

Suey walked into the kitchen and stared at her indignantly. Elizabeth bent down to stroke her but the cat switched its tail and turned away huffily. "Come on, Suey," she said, close to tears. "It's not my fault. I didn't *want* to abandon you."

They sat around the table. Elizabeth noticed that they'd all shifted from their old places.

"I get a leg," said Ariane, raising her hand, while Lucas carved.

"I get the other one," said Gabby.

"It's not your birthday," said Olivier.

"Let them have the legs," said Tristan. "I like white meat better anyway."

"There's plenty of light and dark for everyone," said Lucas as he pulled a wing off the body.

"Have you had a nice day on your birthday, Tristan?" Elizabeth asked, thinking she sounded like a vague acquaintance, rather than his mother.

"Pretty good," he nodded. "Some friends took me to lunch. And it's Saturday. I'm going out again after dinner."

"We're going out too," said Ariane. "We're coming with you, Maman."

"That's right," said Elizabeth. Because of the birthday dinner, she had not picked them up at school today and what a relief that had been. She sipped her wine and noticed her glass was almost empty. Tristan's too. Not Lucas', not Olivier's.

Tristan, knife and fork poised over his plate, said: "Remember that time we drove back from the south in the snowstorm?"

"Yes," said Lucas slowly. "But why on earth would you be thinking about that on a beautiful spring day like today?"

"Just came to mind," he shrugged, looking down at his plate. "It was a really cool night."

"I remember too," said Ariane.

"No, you don't," said Gabby, a concentrated knit to his brow as he searched his memory. He did not like his recollection of the past to diverge from hers.

"I do so. I remember lying on the floor of the car."

"You remember that because you've been told," said Olivier. "Both of you were lying on the floor and Maman was afraid Tristan or I would fall off our seats and crush you."

"It was a really cool night," repeated Tristan and the other children all agreed.

They'd spent New Year at the elder Tellers' house in the Lubéron, just the six of them. The day they were to leave, a terrible ice and snow storm was predicted. They had debated staying on another day but the bad conditions were supposed to persist. Elizabeth had an important meeting in Paris on Monday; the children had to go back to school. They dithered, took a long time to pack up, but finally set off late morning when there was no sign of snow at the house. The radio reported trains cancelled and the *autoroute* closed as far as Valence but they drove on, not seeing a flake of snow until just past Orange, where they were suddenly pelted with freezing rain. The tree branches were coated in ice; the children marvelled and the parents took a deep breath as they joined the other cars moving in slow motion along the ice rink, trying to avoid using the brakes. They changed roads and conditions improved. But only for a few minutes. The predicted snow was now falling heavily. Suddenly they found themselves in a long, long line of stopped cars. Lucas walked up to see what the trouble was and came back with a report that a lorry had skidded and turned over at a roundabout. It was blocking the entire road. They waited and waited. The children began to bicker. It was cold. Lucas, who had been silently consulting a map, suddenly started the car and did a u-turn onto the car-less side of the road. "I'm not going to sit here like a lemming all night," he said. "We're taking the back roads."

He took the first right and they went up and up on a small, winding road into the steep hills of the Ardèche. The snow got heavier and heavier as they climbed. The road got harder to see. Both Lucas and Elizabeth leaned forward, tensely alert, expecting at any moment they might skid on one of the endless curves or simply be blocked by the accumulating snow. In two hours of driving they did not see one other car, even in the stone villages they passed through like ghosts. Near midnight they pulled into one village and stopped at the main square. It was eerily quiet, the snow having muffled what little sound there might have been. "There's a hotel," said Elizabeth.

"It's all closed up," said Lucas. "We'd have to pound on the door."

"Do we dare go on?" she asked, looking back at the children. Only Tristan was awake.

"This is amazing," he said, almost in a trance.

"You should go to sleep," said Elizabeth.

"I think we should keep driving and try to pick up the *autoroute* at Lyon," said Lucas.

"Assuming it's open."

The two of them bent their heads over the map in the dim light and planned the route. "Let me drive now," Elizabeth said.

"At least try to lie down," Lucas said to Tristan as they drove slowly out of the village. Tristan stretched over two seats and draped his legs over some luggage but kept looking out the window.

Not long after he did fall asleep. As did Lucas. Elizabeth was the only one awake when they finally started down, out of the hills, toward Lyon and the snow began to let up. They began to pass other cars. A policeman at the entrance to the *autoroute* said: "The road's closed."

"What are we supposed to do?"

"Where are you going?"

"Paris," said Elizabeth.

"Go ahead," and he waved her on, his illogical response perfectly in keeping with this dream-like night.

"It was a very difficult drive," Elizabeth said, remembering that as she'd driven down the hill and finally begun passing other cars, seeing signs of life, she'd thought: we're safe and now this night will become a fondly evoked memory for all the children, part of our family lore.

"I remember waking up at one point," said Olivier, "and feeling like we'd been transported to another world. It was like the car was rolling on clouds it was so quiet in the snow."

"Exactly," said Tristan, looking from one parent to another with his cheeks now even more flushed from the wine. "I remember thinking: maybe we've died and I'm waking up in heaven."

"Can we have some cake?" mumbled Olivier.

"You're right. It's getting late," said Lucas, pushing his chair back and standing up.

Elizabeth stood up too to help clear the plates and thought: now that memory just causes pain to one and all. Family lore has been blown to smithereens.

Besides being overcooked, the cake had no birthday candles. Elizabeth hadn't thought of bringing any and none could be found in the kitchen. Instead one was taken from its brass stick, a relic from the days when Lucas and Elizabeth entertained by candlelight. It was inserted awkwardly into the cake. Tristan would not allow happy birthday to be sung but he did ceremoniously make a silent wish as he blew out the single flame. The cake was rock hard around the edges but everyone made a good show of eating the moister parts near the centre. When Tristan opened his presents, he cheered up slightly. Presents open, the evening was finally over and they could all go their separate ways.

"I've got the application information for you," Elizabeth said when she met Tristan a week later at the Café de l'Epée. Since moving to Pigalle, she'd taken to meeting him and Olivier here after work. "We have to move quickly—there will only be the odd left-over, last-minute place at best—but you can do it all on-line. And I've asked your grandfather to help in any way he can." When he still didn't answer she said: "You do want to go ahead with this, don't you?"

"I guess so," he shrugged, slumped in his chair, arms folded across his chest.

"Have you got any other ideas?"

Another shrug and a barely discernible shake of the head.

"Brigitte thinks it's a good idea too," Elizabeth coaxed, then immediately regretted evoking her rival.

"That's the only reason I'm going through with it," he said, looking at her for the first time since they'd sat down.

"I hope you also view this as the right step," she answered prissily.

"Right step, wrong step—I've told you. I'm tired of all this walking in the right direction stuff. I'll go because Brigitte thinks it's a good idea. Because I don't know what else to do." He snatched the plastic folder from the table. "*C'est de la merde, tout ça !*" he half screamed and left.

Elizabeth was so stung by this encounter that she didn't even realize where she had walked until the avenue de l'Opéra stretched out in front her. As she neared the Opéra itself, the naked green bronze body of Apollo on the roof came into clearer focus. The casual grace of his bent knee and the glinting golden lyre held high above his head seemed either to beckon or challenge the entire city. It was close to eight and people were streaming into the entrance. Others were waiting, eyes out for friends or spouses. She thought about Apollo's bent knee and she decided to go in. While buying her ticket, she discovered that it was a Stravinsky evening, with *The Firebird Suite*, followed by *Petrouchka*, and ending with *The Rite of Spring*, being danced by the Paris Ballet. Music she had heard but never seen performed. She took her seat on the second balcony. A corner of the stage was cut off from her view but she could not be spoiling herself with front and centre anymore.

The string section was already tuning up. There was a gentle buzz from the audience. The Chagall ceiling, with all those incongruous modern bodies, floated above the Baroque gilt.

The Blanchards had brought her here for the first time, not long after she'd moved out of their flat. They had wanted her to meet their son Xavier, who had been doing his military service the months Elizabeth had lived with the family as a teenager.

Xavier had cropped, dirty blond hair. His hand, damp when she'd shaken it, sat stiff and motionless on his grey trouser leg throughout the entire first half of the opera. She'd sat stock still next to him, watching Carmen flounce around the stage and wishing, with Xavier next to her, that it were *The Magic Flute*. During the interval they had gone into the foyer for a glass of champagne and she'd dribbled a sip down the front of her only dress. She'd tried to hide it with her arms over her chest but the wet line on the silk was too long. No one had commented. Xavier had made an attempt at conversation and then they had thankfully returned to their seats for the second half. Afterwards there had been an awkward scene on the pavement, an air of disappointment and discomfort from every side as they'd said good-bye.

The conductor came out; the clapping rose and fell.

The overture began, the music so quiet no one in the theatre moved. As the music got louder and dancers appeared, she strained to see as much of the stage as she could. She watched the emerald green bird dance and then the evil ogre lunge in and out of her view as the music became more and more fraught. She watched, riveted, until the prince's soul was released from its egg, whereupon the theme was taken up again, at first almost inaudibly, but then rising to a raucous finale of brass and percussion that made her heart pound uncomfortably.

Petrouchka, the doll who wanted to become human, reminded her of Pinocchio, a story that had frightened her as a child, one she had avoided reading to her own children. The carnival air and the hints of dissonance in the music were nightmarish and she closed her eyes. She was relieved when it was over. During the interval, she wandered amidst the chattering, champagne-drinking crowd with her glass of red wine. She kept moving, not wanting to stand still by herself.

That's what it was always like, when I was young. Whenever there was a party, I wandered because I had no one to talk to. Things began to change in Paris and then from Laurent's party on, everything was different. From the moment I saw the tall, well-dressed man with the rimless glasses, with the distinct rather than handsome features. I watched him because he looked interesting, kind. Who's that, I asked Laurent. My cousin. Let me introduce you. He has recently returned from New York. From a Fulbright, at Columbia. Lucas did not turn away when I told him I was working as a replacement archivist. I'm temporarily a temp, I joked. What do you want to do, he asked with a gentle smile. I don't know, I said. I studied literature. I like to read but what can you do with that? I bet you want to write a novel, he said laughing. No, not me, I said. What are you reading now? I have been reading Tolstoy, I said. I believe Anna Karenina is the best novel ever written. Sorry, he said, nothing beats Crime and Punishment, except maybe Proust.

The bell called them back to their seats.

I had almost forgotten what it is like, the near humiliation of standing alone.

The music from *The Rite of Spring* was what she knew best of Stravinsky and she had always liked its nervous energy. But tonight, hearing it live and seeing it danced on stage, she felt a sort of panic rising up in her, right from the very first pure strains of the bassoon. As she watched the young girl who was to be sacrificed in a pagan celebration of spring dance in and out of her truncated view of the stage, she moved to the edge of her seat. She looked around at the other spectators. No one looked remotely disturbed—one man's head even bobbed sleepily on his chest—and she told herself to calm down. But as the bassoons whined and the percussion crashed, panic rose up uncontrollably. She could *hear* barbaric frenzy, almost *see* flesh being ripped from the bone—she could hardly believe that music and dance could evoke such palpable physical brutality—how had she never felt that on the recording. Afraid that she might scream or faint, she stood up—she fled—running down, down the stairs to the exit.

She paused on the front steps to catch her breath, take control of herself. *I should have known better. I should have known better than to be lured in by Apollo's golden lyre and bent knee. I should have known all that fire and sacrifice would be too much for me.*

***

By the time Elizabeth walked in the door at the rue Pigalle, she was panting and perspiring. All the way up the hill she hadn't been able to get the music out of her ears, the flouncing bodies out of her mind, no matter how fast she walked. She stood for a moment amidst the bleak furnishings of crazy Carole's flat and tried to recall the deep breathing she had learned in some exercise class long ago. After a moment she walked into the bathroom, peeled off her sticky clothes and stood under a cold shower for many minutes. Finally the music and dancing began to recede.

Dressed in nothing but a sleeveless satiny nightdress, she poured herself a large Noilly Prat vermouth and cassis on ice, the drink that had replaced whisky when she'd moved up to Pigalle. It had a bittersweet coolness to it and she'd become quite addicted to the stuff, having two large glasses, sometimes three, every evening. She got out her fountain pen and a sheet of white paper and sat down at the table in front of the window. Cocking her pen, she felt both exhilaration and apprehension at the blank page. She took a sip of her drink and began to write:

Dear Troy, I went to the ballet tonight. Stravinsky. Fire and sacrifice. I was terrified and once again I ran away.

Her heart began to race again and she stopped, took another sip of her drink. She looked at his sculpture, which sat on the table next to her. She took a second sheet of paper and wrote:

Dear Troy, I am sorry. Sorry for what I did and didn't do all those years ago.

Now what? She looked at both sheets of paper. She sipped her drink again and looked out the window at the rue Pigalle below her. It was warm and she had to leave the window open, though the noise and sometimes the smell were unpleasant. All her other apartments in Paris had been on a courtyard or a quiet street and Elizabeth hadn't even suspected that the din could be so irritating. On these warm nights she had begun sleeping with one pillow under her head and another on top. It worked quite well, except for Fridays and Saturdays, where even corking of the bedroom walls would not have protected her from the commotion outside.

She sat for a long time, drinking one drink, then another, and watching the people pass. Guessing which prostitute a particular man might choose could be entertaining, almost suspenseful. It reminded her of watching the pigeons on the roof at the publishing house.

That night Elizabeth went to bed with the two sheets of paper, lying side-by-side, unfinished.

The next evening when she returned from work, she got her drink and sat down at the table and took a third sheet of paper: *I was thinking about you today when I walked by the guitar shops on the rue de Douai. That's where I bought both of Olivier's guitars, the one he lent to you and the new one...* Just the act of sitting over that paper the previous evening had made her think about Troy all the next day, made her feel as if she were carrying on a conversation with him. It had also brought on a slew of memories. Of Troy picking and strumming quietly in the dark while she and John and Sally listened. Of the four of them laughing until they cried over something ridiculous, while they sat on the floor playing cards.

Elizabeth recalled these memories to Troy and then described the guitar shops on the rue de Douai. How the same store had shops in several buildings. How in Paris expansion often occurred in pieces like that. She thought he would be interested in this peculiar practice, until she paused, fountain pen in front of her mouth, wondering if all that curiosity he had shown about the city hadn't been a ploy. That with Troy one could never be certain what was really there. Troy's ploys, she thought with a giggle and a sip of her drink. Until she thought about it again. One could never be sure about anyone, even one's self. And she went back to describing her neighbourhood.

After she'd finished that, she got herself another drink and looked at the two sheets of paper from the previous evening. She wasn't sure what she could add to that awkward little apology so she took the other page, the one about the ballet, and continued writing:

The ballet was absolutely terrifying. Fire without heat but it burned right into my ears, the dissonant sound of suffering. Fire and dancing, like we danced around the fire, round and round, with greater frenzy as the flames leapt higher and higher and then oh, it's still such an untouchable memory. For a long time I couldn't close my eyes in the dark.

Her heart was racing and her hand was slippery with perspiration. She stood up, unable to go on, and turned on the television.

But the next evening:

I had too much to drink, too much to smoke, that night and as you tossed the gas on the tarp I imagined that the sculpture underneath was The Beast from our kitchen, its beamy bones poking through sagging skin because we'd blocked off his access to food so long ago. I lit The Beast on fire, put him out of his starving misery and then John and Sally were gone and we started to dance like the Indians we had seen on television and at the movies, that's how I remember it. The flames leapt and grew. We could feel the heat; we were illuminated. The wood snapped and crackled and pieces of the tarp flew up flaming and one of them must have landed on you because when I turned around, you were on fire. I froze but you rolled like a gymnast over and over on the wet grass and then finally you stood up and ripped off what was left of your t-shirt.

Back at the apartment the fire engines went by and by, and in the pitiless white light of the kitchen I smelled your burned hair and saw your back, your back was red and black, over-under-cooked meat on the grill, and I turned away so I wouldn't be sick. You couldn't sit still, couldn't stop moaning and there were beads of sweat on your forehead and your head was lolling like one of those dead chickens and I said we must go, we must go to the emergency room. To help you to get you off my trembling hands. We waited and waited with the broken-nosed drunk and the pale woman whose hand was wrapped in the white tea towel, the blood seeping through. By then you were sweating all over and swooning. I thought they'd never come for you where are they. Come and take him away take this whole night away. Hurry please hurry.

Later, when the doctor comes out, he looks grave and says he is very badly burned what happened and I say I don't know he just came back that way and the doctor walks away shaking his head leaving me alone with my treachery in that hollow hall with the yellow walls.

Again she had to stop, drink her drink, look outside at the tawdry life in the street below.

Until the next night:

My stomach drops, my scalp tingles, my heart pounds. The man, the dean of students, sits on the other side of the desk, with dark hair sprouting from his ears and his nose and his knuckles. He calls me Miss Lyall and tells me the college wants to wind this case up as quickly as possible; this kind of publicity we can do without, he says with a smile. He even thanks me for taking you to the hospital. For my sense of responsibility. I do not demur. I allow him to lead me through the story of your sole culpability like a lemming over a cliff: We haven't forgotten his earlier escapades. He's always been a troublemaker. Throughout his entire time with us, professors have noted an attitude problem, a tendency to insubordination, even sullenness, most recently in the case of Mr Thorpe, against whom he seems to have harboured some sort of grudge. Given his difficult childhood and complicated background, his behaviour is not overly surprising, is it? The dean squares the police report on his desk and continues: In his current fevered state, and under the influence of the morphine, he can't tell us anything. But it's not difficult to fill in the details. A jerry can is missing from the maintenance building where Ross worked his first year at the college and the police found his burned t-shirt near the scene of the crime. The dean shakes his dark head but can't suppress a satisfied smile that says: finally, justice will be meted out to that undeserving and insolent agitator. And I do not even ask: will he be all right?

By now, on her third large drink, with moist eyes: *How could I have done it? Leave you like that, let you take all the blame? To shrug my shoulders, how should I know, he just came back that way. Why can't I go back and do it all over again? At least have a second chance to stand by you, to tell the truth. To take my part of the responsibility.*

Eventually writing into thin air no longer satisfied her and one evening she unfolded the piece of paper on which Troy had noted his e-mail address. Since her laptop had been reclaimed by the publishing house and the family computer was still with her family, at the rue Laromiguière, she had used internet cafés a few times to check her dwindling number of e-mails but she found it inconvenient. At the office, personal correspondence on professional e-mail was forbidden for the secretaries, but she didn't care—she'd send a quick note from work. The next morning she arrived early and wrote the following from her desk computer:

Dear Troy, I'm sorry I never really said sorry.

She deleted this nonsense.

Dear Troy, I'm sorry for everything and I think about you often. Elizabeth.

She quickly pushed the send button and turned around to see if the whole office hadn't been drawn to her desk by the sound of her thudding heart.

She didn't really expect him to answer her note. Part of her believed that right from the start, despite his claims, he'd come to Paris with the sole intent of ruining her life, of paying her back. But she was wrong. A few days later he sent a short reply: *Liza, Thanks. I appreciate your writing. I'm sorry, too, about the mess I left in Paris. Hope you're OK. Troy.*

One day Mr Green, her American boss, asked her to start making travel arrangements for a family holiday to the Seychelles. Instead of going to lunch, she wrote an e-mail:

Dear Troy, Do you remember our island utopia? Our perfect world had to be on an island, you said, or it would be too susceptible to the outside world—"nefarious influences" you called them. We pored over the atlas and after several evenings of heated debate you and I agreed upon the Seychelles as the location for our paradise. Do you remember? The islands were far enough away from a corrupt and reprehensible America, and there were lots of little islands to choose from. Plus we liked the name. We said: she sells seashells by the Seychelles. As always, we won out over John and Sally, who were lobbying for the safer, closer waters of the Caribbean for our retreat.

We planned for two weeks. What we'd bring, who would fish or collect wood or climb palm trees for coconuts. You even drew up plans for the construction of a village.

As Elizabeth wrote, she remembered how much fun they'd had imagining a better life, until Troy had started reading about Easter Island for one of his classes. It had sent him into one of his rages. "There's no use trying to make a perfect life, even on an island. We the people, we destroy every possible paradise."

But Elizabeth nevertheless dwelled on the memory day after

day as she spoke to Mr Green or to the travel agency about times and prices, as she wrote the confirmation letter to the hotel where the Greens were planning to stay. She'd looked on the place's web site and carefully examined photos of sea and surf, as if she were the one about to take the trip.

A pattern formed: at work she wrote Troy informative e-mails about her present life. Because she was not allowed to be writing these, she tried to arrive early or to stay in the office during lunch hour when few people were around. He often didn't answer and when he did, it was always just a sentence or two but that did not deter her.

In the evening she continued to sit at the table overlooking the rue Pigalle, with Troy's sculpture and her vermouth-cassis next to her, and to rehash the past and her conscience. Writing and writing words that never got sent. The paper piled up on the table and distant Troy became her only companion. Although she knew that she was using him in much the same way as a lonely child creates an imaginary friend, she didn't see the harm. Even if the real world around her was becoming somewhat diffuse.

Often she forgot to eat—food no longer interested her and neither did her appearance. She had barely noticed that her clothes were fitting again, that some were even growing baggy. She no longer bothered with make-up and rarely looked in the mirror.

On her better days she thought she should get out and see other people. She had gone to visit Béa and Trevor once, since they'd had their baby, a little girl called Lily. But in the way of many first-time older parents, they were overwhelmed and had therefore been overly doting. The whole evening had revolved around the baby and she hadn't enjoyed it.

It occurred to her that she could try and have an affair with one of the lawyers. They were not all as risible as Mr Hadley and Mr Green. There was Mr Howe, who was attractive in an ursine sort of way. He had gentle, kindly manners and none of the stiff pretensions that seemed to plague so many in the profession. There was a French lawyer, Guy, the only one who insisted she use his first name. He drove a convertible sports car. That might have been fun. But he, like all the others, was married. She'd end up the loser and she still had enough sense to know that she couldn't afford that.

So she stuck to Troy. To Troy and the written word.

And the children. Always the children. Tristan and Olivier she saw sporadically; the twins still came every Saturday night. She was finding it harder and harder to occupy them. There was no nearby park, no one for them to play with. And the less she took care of her children, the more difficult she found it. Discipline, direction, distraction—she had no patience for any of it anymore.

***

The divorce proceedings were advancing and as part of the process, the French administration, forever taking its role seriously, made its own attempt to reconcile Lucas and Elizabeth. The couple was required by law to meet the judge handling the case. On the day of the meeting Elizabeth waited on the street for her lawyer in front of the Palais de Justice and wondered how many potential divorces judges had managed to avert over the years.

As she was wondering, Natalie Surmon called to her from the courtyard on the other side of the wrought iron bars. She was dressed in her black robe with the white ruffled collar, having just pled someone else's case in front of the court.

"I'll meet you on the other side of security," she said, pointing towards the entrance at the side.

Elizabeth walked to the side door and in the small entry hall took out her coins and her phone, put them in the plastic tray. When she walked through the metal detector and forgot about the keys in her other pocket, the guard on the other side

258

continued to stand stock still, with glazed eyes. He was chewing gum and his jaw rotated like a cow with its cud.

"Security," Natalie said. "What a joke." As they walked up the wide steps of the building, she continued: "The best thing is to say as little as possible." At the top of the stairs Elizabeth paused and turned, remembering all the times she'd seen barristers in their black robes on television standing right here as they commented to the television cameras on trials for unusually gruesome murders or sex crimes. "Don't provoke any extra questions," Natalie added.

"I can assure you I won't do that."

"It should go just fine. I've spoken to Ilse. She's generally not the contentious type."

Ilse—could she be the one, the new, perfect wife-to-be? Elizabeth felt jealousy rising as she eyed the tall, confident blond waiting in the corridor outside the judge's office. But once again she was struck by how pale and unhappy Lucas looked and it was difficult to imagine him in love.

They were called in without their lawyers. The judge, a stocky woman in her mid-fifties, looked tired. Tired of too many efforts at reconciliation, of too many divorces, to be overly interested in anyone's particular circumstances. Elizabeth wondered if she were single, married or divorced. Single seemed the most likely. She wore no ring and her face was pinched.

"How long have you been separated?" she asked, peering over her reading glasses.

"Nine months," said Lucas promptly.

"And how long married?"

"Twenty-one years," said Lucas.

"That's a long marriage and a short separation," said the judge, crossing her stout arms and leaning back in her chair. "Are both of you certain that divorce is the only solution?" She looked right at Elizabeth, who looked at the floor. The judge continued with the tone of an impatient parent: "What would the two you say is the underlying problem?"

Neither of them spoke. Elizabeth had decided to follow Natalie's instructions to the letter, to sit as an observer and offer no information unless forced. Lucas shifted in his seat. He finally said:

"One cannot always explain these things. Why people love or don't love one another is not only an intensely private matter, it is also, often, impossible to put into words."

"What measures have you taken to address these inexplicable problems?"

"We have talked," he said. "We have given it time."

"Not much time. Have you sought professional help?"

"No."

The judge raised her overly plucked eyebrows.

He added: "Not everyone's problems can be solved through the intervention of a professional."

"I suppose that's true," said the judge with a wry look at Lucas. "But it's not unusual for couples to seek outside counsel as they try to resolve conflicts. To understand complicated situations. Emotions." The word seemed to stick in her throat.

"The trouble with emotions," said Lucas rather sharply, "is that they are not something which can be manufactured, like steel or pencils. Or repaired like a car. In which case outside assistance is of little use."

She shook her head, not at all pleased with Lucas' elliptical but implacable responses.

"And what light can you shed on this situation, Madame?" The judge gave Elizabeth a challenging, almost resentful, look. She would have known who Monsieur Teller's family was; that fact alone perhaps accounted for her persistence.

"None. I agree with...with Monsieur." She was still looking intently at the floor and wondering who had decided on such an ugly shade of brown for the carpet. "On the underlying problem."

The judge sighed and shuffled some papers on her desk. "I see here that there are still some questions in your settlement that need to be agreed upon. Your property appears to be rather inconveniently distributed."

"Yes," said Lucas. "We are formulating an agreement whereby I will buy the middle portion of the flat. Then financial arrangements between us will be more or less settled."

"You have children..." she peered over her reading glasses. "Four of them."

"Yes, we do," said Lucas. "We want to request joint custody. We want arrangements to be flexible."

"I have to say," the judge responded sharply to Lucas' imperiousness, "that I am not much convinced by what I've heard here today. You're rushing into an irrevocable decision that will affect not just yourselves but also your four children, yet you have not sought outside help. You have not been able to answer my questions directly." She paused. While she clearly found this reconciliation business tedious, she did not like the procedure to be treated so summarily, especially by the likes of Lucas Teller. "However, your determination is clear. The court date is likely to be in October."

***

Behind the polished manners of Mr Hadley and the beefy joviality of Mr Green lay many demands. Mr Green wanted a presentation he was going to give the following week typed up. He wanted charts and tables put onto transparencies. Mr Hadley, who still used a Dictaphone, needed a long letter to a client transcribed.

It seemed they could do little for themselves and were rarely pleased with her first efforts. Or was it that Elizabeth was slipping? Sometimes she found that she'd forgotten to phone her children. One Saturday she forgot to pick up the twins at school and Lucas had phoned, furious, after the school had phoned him about the forgotten children.

Is this what they mean by falling apart, she asked herself,

before her mind wandered off into thoughts of what she would next write to Troy.

Arlette, the head of the secretaries, spoke to her. "Elizabeth, your hair needs to be cut. If you are going to wear trousers, they need to be part of an outfit."

Since Arlette was a woman who thought about little else than her physical appearance, letting one's self go was as incomprehensible to her as the legalese of her employers. Elizabeth began finding self-improvement magazines on her desk. Cards for nearby beauty and hair salons. Once she would have found this either funny or infuriating. Now she distractedly pushed aside the documentation.

At the end of her three-month stint, Elizabeth overheard Mr Hadley saying to Mr Green: "Thank God Denise is coming back next week. Even part-time she'll get more done than this one."

"With one hand tied behind her back," Mr Green had replied.

The woman from the temp agency said to her: "What's happened to you? You don't even look like the competent person we took on three months ago. And read this report," she said, pushing the paper across the table. Elizabeth's eyes ran over words such as distracted and disorganized and disaffected. The agency woman was not unkind. She said: "We can give you one more chance. Something with less responsibility." She pulled out two folders. "We have a couple of receptionist positions on offer. Which would you rather—an insurance company in the city centre or information desk at the airport?"

She thought for a moment. "I think I'd prefer the airport. Yes, definitely the airport."

"You start next week and work until the end of July. You'll wear a uniform. You'll have to go through the terrorist vetting. We'll see how you do. There will be a large cut in pay."

At least this is how Elizabeth remembered the encounter. As the report indicated, she was finding concentration increasingly difficult. Her mind would tune in and out of a conversation, veering uncontrollably towards Troy and what she wanted to tell him. *I stood outside the school near my apartment today and watched the children. They were mostly from poor immigrant families, not like my children, on that lofty hill in the fifth arrondissement. Isn't it spookier up there, much spookier, really, than my new quartier, with its hookers and workers, its immigrants and shop-keepers?*

Then she would snap to, as if emerging from a trance.

The children were about to finish school and would be scattered. Tristan was going to work in London, to bone up on his English. Thanks to the Latin and ancient Greek he had studied at school, and a few phone calls made by her father, he had been offered a place to read ancient history at the University of London in the autumn. Olivier got a job in the bicycle shop once owned by their friend Trevor. The twins were going to tennis camp and then straight to their grandparents'. Elizabeth assumed she'd get another job after the airport, or such was the reason she gave for not being able to take the children in August.

She arranged to see Tristan and Oliver at the Café de l'Epée, just before Tristan was leaving for London. It was a hot evening and there were a lot of people on the square. No one wanted to be inside. Elizabeth, who had arrived early, was sitting on the terrace and the sun was shining on her. She felt crowded by the people and the tables and the chairs, oppressed by the heat and the unrelenting bright light. The sun was at such an angle that there was no shade anywhere. Just as she was finishing her second glass of wine, she saw her sons walking up the street. Tristan had cut his lovely curls to the scalp. The hair on his head was about the same length as the stubble on his face and Elizabeth thought he looked disturbingly like a convict. Olivier had let his hair grow and it was very unkempt. In fact his head looked like a bird's nest, a comparison that she would formerly have shared with her son. Today she was not even tempted to comment.

The two boys were not really boys anymore. Tristan was

eighteen and Olivier almost seventeen. While she ordered her third glass of wine, they both ordered beer, not the bottled pineapple juice they used to drink in cafés. Tristan was beginning to look like a man. The hair on his arms and hands was thickening. It was fine and black and looked just like his father's, even the way it whorled over the wrist. Olivier, who had been a shy boy, now had a direct gaze in his green eyes and an open manner that put people immediately at ease.

Elizabeth asked them about their weeks, about the end of school. She asked Tristan if he were still happy about going to London, if he had passport and pounds prepared. She asked Olivier if he was going to put the money he earned in his postal account or under the mattress. The joke fell flat, so she asked Tristan about his banking arrangements for London, during the summer and afterwards at university. Practical matters needed to be addressed before a long departure but of course Lucas must have taken care of all that so she didn't much listen to the answers.

She took a deep breath. The red wine and the people and the sun were making her head spin. Her fingers felt swollen, her feet too. The heat was as unbearable as the silence between her and her sons.

"I want to tell you a story," she finally said. "A story that happened to me, when I wasn't much older than you." She shifted; her legs were sticking to the chair. "It was just after my own parents had separated. I was furious with them and I wanted to run away." Both of her sons now had their eyes fixed on the ashtray that Tristan was turning around and around on the table. They both knew, had known all along, subliminally, that something unpleasant was behind all this. "So I left London and went to college in America. It didn't help. I was unhappy there too. After a while, I met Troy. You remember Troy?" Saying his name out loud felt odd, as if the name in itself were a secret or a lie, her own invention. "In my last year I shared an apartment with him and two other people. We were all unhappy and so we got angry. Just before our graduation, we set a brand new wooden sculpture on fire." The ashtray was no longer turning; both of them were staring at her, eyes wide. "It was Troy's idea—he didn't like the sculptor." She paused, unstuck her legs again from her seat. "But I was the one who actually set the tarp that was covering it on fire." Olivier's mouth was now hanging open; Tristan's was clenched shut. "A burning piece of it flew up and landed on Troy's back. He got very badly burned, as did a fireman and the art building. The college accused Troy, who was in hospital, mostly unconscious, of acting alone. And we went along with the story. We said nothing. We just moved on with our lives and Troy took all the blame." A rivulet of sweat ran down her back; she wriggled to stop it; wiped her upper lip with the back of her hand. "I never told anyone. Not my parents. Not my sister. Not your father. But then Troy came to Paris and your father discovered what I'd done. Your father is a very moral man and he was angry and disappointed. Though he tried to forgive me, he couldn't. Not just for what I did but for not telling him during all those years we were married."

Now it was her turn to look at the ashtray. No one said anything.

"I asked you," Tristan finally croaked. "I asked you. Brigitte asked you too. She told me."

"It's not easy to admit guilt, to confess past mistakes to anyone, much less to your own children."

Tristan pushed back his chair violently and stood up jerkily. "You make me sick," he said. Pushing aside other chairs, he left the café terrace and stormed down the street on stiff legs, his oddly cropped skull disappearing around the corner.

Olivier was looking intently at his half-finished beer. He finally said: "It's kind of a hard story to hear about your own mother."

"I know. That's one reason I didn't want to tell you. To protect you."

"And yourself," he said looking up at her, his broad mouth

tightening and twisting like Lucas' when upset.

"Yes, myself too."

"Can I go now?"

Elizabeth nodded. Unlike his brother, Olivier stood up slowly, deliberately. He shuffled through the people and the tables and down the pavement as if his feet had suddenly turned to wet clay. When he got to the corner, he glanced back, a confused, hurt expression on his face. Elizabeth looked down at her empty glass, at the bits of dried foam stuck to the insides of her sons' half-empty glasses.

Stunned herself by this confession that she'd had no intention of making, she left the café, walking in the other direction from her sons, to the Arènes de Lutèce. The place where she used to bring her children, where one warm spring day Troy Ross had appeared in the pit, looking up at her and smiling, as if he'd been waiting twenty-five years to pounce and finally the moment had come. She climbed to one of the stone benches and looked down. There were some old men playing *boules* and the last children were leaving their ball game, going home to supper. The pit was not that far away but she had the sense of looking the wrong way through a telescope, seeing in the distance what was lost and gone forever. She saw Elizabeth Teller, book editor, proud wife of an architect and mother of four good-looking, well-adjusted children whose lives she structured and organized and followed almost as closely as her own. Elizabeth Teller had a book on her lap, a book she might decide should be bought, translated and sold for the French market. Or maybe not. She was a person whose address book was full of important names, the people who made France tick. People with whom she had serious and in the end hollow discussions about life and love.

The Elizabeth Lyall who sat on the stone bench at this moment was still the mother of four children but as of twenty minutes ago, two of them were no longer speaking to her. The other two could hardly speak their mother tongue. Their daily lives were in large part a mystery to her. This Elizabeth Lyall was a secretary, soon-to-be receptionist, who no longer made decisions but instead took orders, most recently from self-satisfied men on whom she wished if not tragedy then at least a moderate dose of misfortune.

The sun had not quite disappeared below the horizon and it was still hot here on the bench. She got up and walked amidst the trees, in the small park that had been landscaped in the early twentieth century to prettify the ruins, to provide a semblance of wilderness. The paths and the landscaping had an artificial, imposed feel but it was cooler there in the shade. Her old life was irretrievable, and it was hard to imagine that a new one could ever provide any genuine pleasure or satisfaction.

***

When Elizabeth tried contacting Tristan and Olivier the next day, their phones were off and they weren't at home. Her messages went unanswered. Tristan left for London without a word to her. She finally cornered Olivier at his bicycle shop, just as it was closing. He was laughing at something his boss said and she watched the laugh evaporate at the sight of her.

"Maman, this is Piotr," he said looking at the ground.

"Hello, I'm Olivier's mother, Elizabeth," she said, sticking out her hand too forcefully.

After the requisite questions about how Olivier was doing, Piotr departed. Olivier looked as if all he wanted to do was go with him but Elizabeth said:

"You can't avoid me forever. Talk to me."

"What am I supposed to say?"

"Whatever's on your mind."

"Nothing's on my mind." He shrugged, as if something itched inside his shirt.

"How's Tristan?"

"He's okay," he said with the same itchy shrug.

"Can I walk you part way home?"

"I guess."

So she accompanied him down the boulevard St Germain, asking unthreatening questions about his job, about what friends he was seeing, about Philomène and about the films playing at the cinemas they passed. She tried to make him laugh by telling him about her new job at the airport. She was supposed to help people find their way to connecting flights or into Paris. To give out maps and point people in the right direction. She got a lot of stupid questions, usually in bad English, sometimes in worse French. She told him about the group of Japanese who asked her for a list of all the Japanese restaurants in Paris and who looked at her in horror when she suggested they try some French food. About the Russians who wanted to know where they could hire a stretch limousine to drive them into and around the city. About the Americans who whispered their request for information on the Lido and the Crazy Horse. By the time Elizabeth had left him at the corner of the rue St Jacques, he had smiled, once. She said she'd try to come every Tuesday when she worked an early shift. He said okay.

The new job turned her into a commuter, going the wrong way. Every day she walked to the Gare du Nord and took the train out to the end of the line, Aérogare 2 of Roissy Charles de Gaulle Airport. The line ran through suburbs that were largely populated by immigrants and their children. Minus some air travellers with their pull-along suitcases, Elizabeth's fellow voyagers were mostly residents of these suburbs. Every morning she watched from the window as the train left the Sacré Coeur behind and ran by the small houses abutting the tracks. Or by the shabby tower blocks and worse—patches of shacks that looked as if they belonged in third world shanty towns.

In her life on the hill, she had managed to avoid ugliness, as well as underground or train transport, almost altogether. From the rue Laromiguière to work she had walked or taken a bus from the Pantheon, along the Luxemburg Gardens and the Senate, down picture-postcard streets. From the rue de Sèvres, even closer to the office, she walked by the Bon Marché department store, the Hotel Lutetia, the Eglise Saint-Germain-des-Près and the Deux Magots café. Many of the people piling on the train with her now, she supposed, had never even been to St Germain des Près, much less heard of the Deux Magots café, of Jean-Paul Sartre or Simone de Beauvoir or any one of the other intellectuals who whiled away the hours there, solving the problems of the world over coffee and cigarettes. The resigned faces Elizabeth saw every morning and evening suggested they didn't stray much further than the route between their rundown lodgings and their low-paying jobs.

Terminal 2 had six subdivisions, A through F. Elizabeth was stationed in Terminal E, the newest of the six, the one where a year before a whole section had collapsed early one Sunday morning, killing a Chinese man. The undamaged part had recently been re-opened, and while the effect of light and air under a huge, curved ceiling was quite spectacular in the departure area, she worked downstairs near the arrivals exit, where the ceilings were not high and the light was artificial. She sat at a desk behind a Perspex window and if she had been claustrophobic, it would have been unnerving as well as belittling. By the end of the morning and all that sitting, Elizabeth badly needed to stretch her legs, so during lunch hours, instead of going to the employee cafeteria, she walked the long passages with the moving walkways that connected the terminals of Aérogare 2. Dressed in her blue uniform, with her ID tag swinging around her neck, Elizabeth would walk all the way around, through all six of them, without every going outside. It became her only form of exercise.

Once she was familiar with the place, she thought how much it resembled a village. Food, of course, was available everywhere. There were book and newspaper shops, a post office and a pharmacy, showers and places to pray. One would never have to leave and some didn't. Although she never ran into him because he was in Aérogare 1, there was the famous man without a passport who had been living there for years. He was periodically written up by journalists or interviewed for television, and then even a Hollywood film was made about him starring Tom Hanks. The movie gave his story a preposterous turn, a happy ending in the form of true love with a stewardess. Elizabeth shook her head at the idea of it. From the homeless people she did run into, it seemed they did pretty well for themselves—travellers often left almost complete meals uneaten on a table—but still—none of them remotely resembled Tom Hanks and she could not imagine any employee of the airport, much less a pert and pretty air hostess, being attracted to such generally grizzled, unwashed persons.

Contact with the other two women at the information desk was limited. They staggered their breaks and were usually too busy answering questions for chatter. The worst part about the job was that Elizabeth now had no free access to a computer. The one on her desk was for gleaning traveller and tourist information only. She had no professional e-mail address and had no time or freedom to consult her personal mail. Occasionally she still went to an internet café in the evening but she'd been spoiled at the lawyers' office. After a week, she was becoming desperate.

Until her desk computer froze and a technician was called in. He did not look anything like the computer technicians who serviced the publishing house. They generally wore short-sleeved shirts, tight trousers and nauseating scent. This man had large hands, dressed in baggy, slightly rumpled clothes and did not smell of anything. He moved slowly and his patience in locating the problem with the computer mesmerized Elizabeth. When the machine balked at one manoeuvre, he would try another. And another. And so he fixed it.

"In real life I am a musician," he told her with a smile, when she probed a bit. "But not a very successful one. I do this to pay the bills."

"Oh," she said. "You don't know how I could get a cheap

computer, do you?"

"Sure. How much can you spend?"

"Not that much," she said. "I just need something to write with. Word processing. Something I can use for e-mail."

"I'll see what I can find for you."

Jean came back the next day just as she was getting off work. Once she had changed out of her uniform and they had both taken their tags off, they had a drink together at one of the airport bars.

"So how did you end up here?" asked Elizabeth.

"I was going to ask you the same question."

"The temp agency I work for sent me here."

"Are you always posted as an information desk clerk?"

"No. Two weeks ago I was a replacement secretary," she said.

"Okay," he answered slowly.

"And you? You don't look like a computer technician. At least not the ones I've encountered."

"A hobby turned into a good way to earn a living. I like working here because I live in a village to the north of Chantilly. It's easy to get to."

"What about your music?"

"I play the piano and keyboard and do some improvisational jazz."

"Have you got a band?"

"I play for several bands, here and there. The problem with the job, of course, is that it doesn't always leave much time for music. But it's okay. I can't complain."

She looked at his broad-set grey eyes, the regular features of his face and wondered how old he was. Late thirties, she guessed. "Have you always lived up there in the country?"

"Oh, no. I grew up in Lyon and came to Paris to university. I studied law but didn't want to be a lawyer. I didn't much like Paris either. Underneath all their finery, the people can be quite barbaric."

"That's harsh," laughed Elizabeth.

"Obviously it's not true across the board," he said with no trace of resentment or dislike on his mild face.

"Why didn't you go back to Lyon then after university?"

"Too provincial." And he gave a smile that would have softened the heart of the fiercest barbarian.

Elizabeth didn't see Jean again for a few days, when he stopped by to tell her he had found an abandoned computer on the street. "There doesn't seem to be anything much wrong with it," he told her. "Give me a few more days and it should be ready." They were having lunch together. He told her that his father was a doctor and his mother a teacher. He had two sisters who had both married doctors and still lived in Lyon.

"So you're a renegade?" laughed Elizabeth.

"Yea, I guess," he said with his melting, infectious smile.

The next few days he stopped by often to say hello, tell her he was working on the computer. The following week he told her it was ready.

"I've completely uninstalled and reinstalled everything. It's a little slow but it works fine."

"That's really kind. I can't thank you enough," Elizabeth said, turning red. Not only had Jean refused to let her pay anything for the computer or his time, he had insisted on delivering it to her. They were standing in her hot, tacky apartment and she was suddenly embarrassed by the mess, the fake leather furniture, the stupid posters on the wall, the fact that she was a replacement information clerk at the arrivals desk, Roissy Charles de Gaulle Airport, Terminal 2E. She wanted to say: This place isn't mine; I'm just subletting for a while. This work is not me; I'm just trying to get by right now. But such declarations would have begged questions that she did not want to answer. So she just said:

"Let's put it here, on this table." And she quickly began to clear away the pile of notes and letters to Troy, before he could possibly read any of the words. "Sorry about the mess."

"Looks as if you have quite a writing project underway," Jean said.

Elizabeth kept her head down over the piles of paper to conceal her disarray: "You can't imagine how much I have to say after a day at my exciting job."

He laughed and lifted the computer screen onto the table.

In his methodical, patient way, Jean began connecting the various bits and pieces. "It's amazing," he said. "The whole thing, cables still attached, was just dumped. I didn't have to buy a thing. Not even the plug strip."

"Where did you find it?"

"In Paris, on the Left Bank, where I always look when I need something. People who live in *les beaux quartiers* often just toss what they no longer want onto the street. Usually once they've got the newest model, out goes the old."

She did not dare ask which arrondissement of the Left Bank.

"All you have to do is get your internet access organized," he said.

"How do I do that?"

"I can get you modem, if you like."

When he'd attached the last cable, Jean turned on the computer. The two of them sat side by side as he showed her how the various functions worked. When he reached forward to use the number keys, his shoulder leaned into hers. When she was wiping dust from the screen, he pointed to a corner she'd missed and his hand brushed the tips of her hair.

Afterwards, in the crumpled sheets that she hadn't changed in weeks, she couldn't stop crying. Not sobs, just streams of tears down her face which fell onto his bare chest. He ran a large, gentle hand through her hair.

"Who are you Elizabeth?" he asked. "Why do you work at the airport? Why do you live alone in this funny little flat?" He had undoubtedly noticed the photos of her children amidst the mess.

"I don't know," she whispered, overcome by a fresh wave of tears.

Later, at the door, with his hands cupping her face, he gave her the most tender kiss she had ever received. For a long time after he was gone, she sat in the droopy black leather sofa, her knees collapsed together, satisfied and spent, almost happy and irrevocably sad. He was an excellent lover. He was too young; she was too old. Too tainted. She couldn't let it happen again.

***

When she saw Jean the following Monday, he smiled. "I got you a modem."

"That was fast."

"If you want to use the computer for e-mail, it's not much good without one," he said, holding up the box.

That evening he drove her back from work. The traffic was terrible and they had a long time to talk. Without going into the messy details, Elizabeth told him about Lucas, about her four children, about the job she had lost. He listened, lifting his foot on and off the clutch, slowly changing gears from first to second, second to first, as they inched along the motorway. When she'd finished, all he said was:

"Doesn't sound very good."

"No. But what about you, Jean? Don't you at least have a girlfriend?" She had thought and thought about this, how it could be that a nice-looking, gentle man his age—he was, she had discovered, actually forty-two, only five years younger than she—could be alone.

"I was living with a woman until last summer. It didn't end very happily. She said she wanted more out of life than I had to offer. I was very hurt. You're the first woman I've felt attracted to since."

It was the first comment close to a compliment she had received in many, many months and she felt a tears pricked the corners of her eyes.

When they got to Elizabeth's place, the modem and the

requisite software were quickly installed and they were back in bed. Despite declarations about not allowing the scene to repeat itself, she had tidied up and changed the sheets; that morning she had made the bed, just in case.

Afterwards they ate pasta with garlic and olive oil and drank red wine. Elizabeth felt happier and more expansive than she had in a very long time. Jean was easy to talk to. She told him how hard the separation had been, how disappointed she had been by people she'd thought were friends. He shook his head: "I can't say I'm surprised." When she asked him about his friends, he said in his slow way:

"I've still got one friend, my best friend, from when I did my law studies and most of the others I've met through music. It helps, you see, the music. A common interest creates an immediate connection. Unless you've known your friends all your life and history forms the link."

"Well, in my case, it's too late for history," she said. "And it's not looking too good on the common professional interest front either."

***

Elizabeth didn't know what to think about Jean, except that she had begun to think about him all the time. As she got ready for work, while she sat on the train, at quiet moments behind the information desk, even as she continued to write to Troy. Though she now had all the equipment, she found herself writing more rambling messages by hand that did not get sent.

I have met a man, she wrote one evening, *who reminds me of you. He is a loner and a wonderful lover.*

She paused, took a sip of her drink, thought of Jean again. *I met a man like you but less wounded.*

Why was she telling him this? Why was she writing to him at all? Especially given that Troy had stopped answering her rambling messages altogether some time ago.

And what about Jean? If he walked in the room, right here and now, and saw her with pen in hand, or fingers over the keyboard, vermouth and cassis at her side, what would he say? Maybe nothing. Or would he say to himself, when he noticed the large window that needed cleaning and the books that lay helter-skelter on the sofa and the half-empty glass on the table: this place needs a good tidy. A good scrub. The wall-to-wall carpet needs a good hoover. Or was it vacuum? That's what her mother said. Your room needs a vacuum. But everyone else around her talked about hoovering.

She wrote:

I am a chameleon. I adapt myself to the people around me. Hoover-vacuum, loo-bathroom, lorry-truck, flat-apartment, gas-petrol. The list is endless and I am not even consistent. One minute American one minute English and I can change not only the words but my accent too. Is this a good or a bad thing? A sign of strength or of weakness? An indication of adaptability or complaisance? Chameleons are reptiles. Reptiles are not, generally speaking, trustworthy creatures.

She paused again and thought about Jean's house, which she had visited the day before. It was an old stone cottage at the edge of a village, and a surprisingly homely place for a single man. The bedroom window looked out over a walled-in garden and a field of sunflowers.

She looked again at the clutter around her sitting room. At papers and more papers on the table next to the computer, paper full of words not really to Troy but to herself. She sipped her drink, which by now was warm and watery. *If Jean walked in right now, what else could he think but that I'm crazy. And a drunk to boot.*

***

Although the pay at the airport was considerably lower than it had been with the lawyers, though the "offices" and the travel were considerably less attractive, Elizabeth found she preferred it. Not the job itself—answering questions all day required patience she did not have and frequently she could not stop herself from giving a curt or sarcastic response—but the circumstances. She liked going out and away. She liked the constant flow of new faces, not the mugs of Mr Hadley and Mr Green to confront every day. Being surrounded by so much anonymity and movement made her feel, at moments, that she herself had ceased to exist and she found this both liberating and oddly comforting.

A couple of Saturday evenings, she took the train out to Chantilly. Jean picked her up and as they drove through field and forest, Elizabeth would stick her head out the car window, intoxicated by the sun-drenched smells of summer in the country. While they ate supper in his small garden, he often made her laugh and with each spasm, she felt as if more toxic waste were leaving her body. When the evening light finally faded and the wine, which here she drank with moderation, was done, they went to bed in his bedroom under the eaves and the next morning she felt almost hopeful, almost healthy. After breakfast they read or walked; after lunch they would go back to bed. At moments, she wondered if she shouldn't tell him her story—but she couldn't do it. As with Lucas in the early days, she didn't dare. Didn't dare jeopardize her fragile happiness.

Then Jean went to Lyon for ten days. When Elizabeth woke up on the following Saturday morning, slightly hung over, she realized that she was completely alone, that her children and the three people she had come to think of as her friends were away: besides Jean in Lyon, Béa and Trevor were in Britain with the new baby for the summer months.

It was odd, to be completely alone. She spent the weekend sitting in her flat and wandering the hot streets around Pigalle and by Sunday evening she was feeling very strange—as if she were invisible, as if she had ceased to exist as a physical being altogether. As if only her mind and her thoughts had any reality.

She sat down with her vermouth-cassis and turned on the television for company, staring blankly at the cable news.

Eventually she got bored hearing the same stories over and over again and she began channel surfing, pausing at Arte, which sometimes showed un-dubbed films. But there was a history programme on instead. Of course—she almost laughed—when Arte isn't showing serious films, it's airing depressing black and white documentaries on the barbarities of the twentieth century. She was about to switch again when she recognised Paris.

It was a show on the *Rafle du Vél d'Hiv,* the round-up of over twelve-thousand Jews in Paris the 16th and 17th of July 1942. Because no footage of the day exists, the films consisted of contemporary interviews and old photos, of Jewish children and their mothers; of French policemen, who were solely responsible for the round-up, looking duty-bound; of the bicycle stadium, the Vélodrome d'Hiver, where many of the Jews were taken; and of the internment camp at Drancy, where Jews were held in unspeakably squalid conditions before being shipped to Auschwitz.

The train Elizabeth took every day to work went through Drancy—she'd never made the connection. When this disturbing programme was over, she searched for Drancy on the internet. It was indeed the same place. Not only that: she learned that one of the buildings was still standing. Using Mappy, she tracked the route—she was surprised by how far the place was from the station—and told herself one day, she'd get off the train and see for herself.

That night her dreams were troubled. She was being chased by a group of men who wanted to arrest her and she was trying to hide behind an armchair but it wasn't quite big enough to conceal her whole body. The next day at work one of her colleagues was not there and she could not even take a lunch break. But as she sat answering one needy person after another, the nightmare clung to her conscience; it was still there when she was finally released at six in the evening.

As the train back to Paris emerged from the tunnel, she noticed that the cloudy, humid morning had cleared into a beautiful summer evening and she suddenly wanted to be outside, walking, taking in the day she'd been deprived of in her underground information box.

At Drancy, she got off the train.

Outside the station, she walked over the bridge spanning tracks, twenty-wide. Old freight trains stood empty. The former station house, a small building with Le Blanc Mesnil-Drancy in quaint ceramic tiles, stood abandoned. It reminded her of the gingerbread house in Hansel and Gretel. Then again maybe it was more like the forlorn station-house in *La Bête humaine*, another book she had read while lying in Sybille's bed. Was it from here that they left, she wondered. Were they bussed over here by the lorry-load and herded into freight cars like these?

Despite her directions, she missed a turn and ended up walking down the rue Sacco et Vanzetti, past the cemetery. Just inside the entrance there was a plaque:

In remembrance of the Drancians
Dead for Independence
And for Freedom
In the Nazi extermination camps
LET US NEVER FORGET

Behind it were several rows of graves topped with tall white obelisks. To whom did the plaque refer? To the bodies buried under the white obelisks? These were presumably the graves of *Résistants* because the exterminated would have no individual graves, no personal plots, with name and year and messages from loved ones, like the ones she was looking at here. So what did they mean by those who had died for independence and freedom? What about those who were just hauled off and slaughtered before they had time to consider any such lofty Enlightenment ideals?

She moved on, but when she got there, she didn't realize she had arrived. The building looked too much like a nineteen-sixties council housing block. The gaunt structure, its salmon and beige concrete slabs stained and chipped, stood in a dilapidated, eerie silence. The odd person passed by. Another stared blankly out of a window at a group of white, Arab and black boys, as they drank beer and smoked cigarettes in a dull-eyed huddle around a bench.

She stood frozen, unable to believe that the building, which had imprisoned up to five thousand terrified Jews at a time, was still used as housing. After what had happened, how could they expect people to go on living in such a place, surrounded by such ghosts? Is this what they meant by never forgetting? Or had she made a mistake?

No, it was unquestioningly the right place. She recognised its horse-shoe shape and the pillars along the grubby ground floor doors from the film. And there was a tired sign indicating it as a *monument historique*, pointing towards the entrance of a commemorative association. Except that when she walked around, she saw no sign of the association that she had read about on the internet, the *Conservatoire historique du Camp de Drancy*. Maybe it was the invisible association what was meant by never forgetting.

Yes, this was the place. At a certain distance, there was the sample cattle car on a section of sample rail tracks and the memorial statue, tidy remembrances that did not speak as loudly as the place's name: *Cité de la Muette*, City of the Mute.

She walked back to the train another way, through post-war Drancy. There was very little traffic, pedestrian or otherwise, on these quiet streets. Just one little *pavillon* after another, each surrounded by a tiny tended garden and a secure fence.

And which side of the fence would you have been on, Miss Elizabeth Lyall?

No wonder Lucas can't forgive me.

Returning to Pigalle, she felt hollowed out and utterly

irredeemable.

***

The twins were back in Paris, just for the weekend, and they were to spend it with Elizabeth. She'd almost forgotten, just as she'd forgotten to stop by and see Olivier the previous Tuesday after work. It had taken her three days to realize and then she'd been too ashamed to phone.

She had asked Lucas to put them in a taxi that she would meet.

"I'd be happy to drive them."

"No, I don't want you coming here," she said quickly, as she always did when he made that suggestion. "Just phone when they've left and I'll be waiting."

"If that's what you want..." his voice trailed off.

While Elizabeth waited on the pavement, she greeted the hooker who always lingered in the next doorway and with whom she often had a short exchange about the weather or the sorry state of their street.

After a moment, the woman, in a skirt the size of a tea towel, eyed her and said: "Not changing professions, are you?"

"In these clothes?" Elizabeth asked, looking down at her wrinkled shirt and shabby jeans, her sensible flat shoes.

"I guess not," the woman gave a gravelled laugh and lit up a cigarette.

"I'm waiting for my children," she replied, just as the taxi rolled up. "How are you?" she said, embracing the two small bodies that emerged from the back seat. Maternal instinct surged at the sight of them, at the smiles on their tanned faces, at Ariane's relieved "Maman" and Gabby's "I can jump from a high dive now." For a moment she thought: I can do this. I am happy to have them back. She waved good-bye to the hooker and took her children upstairs.

For supper Elizabeth had made them tuna melts and tomato

salad and they seemed comforted to have food only their mother made for them. Both children bubbled with stories of life in the Lubéron, the life that she was no longer a part of. A year ago such stories had pained her; now she sipped her vermouth and yawned and had to stop herself from slouching in the chair.

"What are we going to do this weekend?" asked Gabby.

"What would you like to do?" she asked. A few times she'd thought about making a plan. But she'd never got any further than the thought.

"I don't know," he shrugged. "Something fun."

"What about you Ariane?"

Shrug. She was fiddling with a ring on her finger.

"Where did you get that?" asked Elizabeth.

Ariane looked up, as if caught out in a crime. "Lise," she said quietly.

"And who is Lisa?" she could feel her voice rising.

"A friend of Papa's."

"You can watch some cable television tonight. How's that?" Elizabeth said, draining her glass and getting up to clear the table.

The twins hopped over to the fake leather sofa and began arguing over the remote control. "I got it first."

"No I did."

"Stop it," Elizabeth said shrilly. The twins froze. They looked at their mother with terrified eyes. "Take turns," she said, almost as brusquely, before turning towards the kitchen with the stack of dirty plates.

She stood over the sink. *I knew it I knew it I knew it and her name is Lisa, is it?*

She poured herself a third glass of vermouth and cassis. She'd left the ice tray out and the cubes had melted. The drink was tepid. She shoved the plates in the sink but only one broke. The sound went down on the television next door. She threw the shards of the white plate in the bin. Washed the other two.

"Can I have a glass of water?" she heard Ariane's small voice behind her.

"Of course."

"Are you okay, Maman?"

"Fine. Thank you." She wanted to grab her daughter by the shoulders and interrogate her: *who is this Lisa? Tell me everything you know about her.* But she turned back to the sink. Ariane lingered. "What is it, then?"

"Can I have a glass for Gabby too?"

"Yes, of course," she said, handing over another glass. She had forgotten that when Ariane asked for water, she meant it for both of them.

The next morning she woke up with her usual hangover, her musty head that spun when she moved. When she'd been eating too much, the food must have absorbed some of the alcohol, but now that she was eating so little, the alcohol was more or less on its own as it travelled through her system and its effects were amplified.

It took a minute to come back to her. She rolled over, wrapped the duvet tightly around her, put the second pillow over her head and tried to go back to sleep. She could hear the cartoons already on next door, where the twins were sharing the sofa bed.

He told me there was no one else and now I hear about Lisa. What hurts most is the idea of him trading me in for a better, purer model. This Lisa woman is undoubtedly bursting with all-American confidence and competence, none of this Anglo-American, Franco-fried mishmash that constitutes my own impure self.

When she walked into the living room, there were Gabby and Ariane, tucked up side by side in the folded-out bed. Gabby was sucking his thumb. He pulled it out quickly when he saw Elizabeth. *Shouldn't I say something? Didn't he give that up over a year ago? Well, why should I. If it makes him feel better, who am I to comment?*

"Ready for some breakfast?"

Two heads nodded. They hadn't forgotten her fierceness of

the night before; they were huddled together protectively. *They'll always have one another, I've always told myself that that is one good thing about twins, one reason to be happy they came out two instead of one. They can't get divorced—then again, now that I think about it—they could still grow to hate one another, just like any two people. Having spent the first nine months of existence crammed into the same small space could just as easily, in the longer run, engender animosity and resentment as love and fidelity.*

"Shall I go out and buy some croissants?"

"Have you got any Nutella?" ventured Ariane, pulling the duvet up around her chin.

"Of course."

Elizabeth put on her clothes and went out into the late July morning. It was bright and clear but the nights always lingered in these streets, a bit like her hangovers. She bought two croissants for Ariane and a croissant and a pain au chocolat for Gabby. Then she stopped at her corner shop to pick up some Nutella and another bottle of vermouth. The day stretched ahead of her like an immense, flat field that needed crossing. *How the hell am I going to do it? The television will soon start to make them edgy and argumentative. But I've done all the kid stuff I can think of with them. Take them to a park? Which one? Not the Arènes de Lutèce—it's too far away, too close to Lucas and now Lisa, and none of their friends would be there anyway.*

When she got back upstairs, Gabby was trying to walk around the room on the furniture without touching the ground. Ariane was in the kitchen, trying to heat up milk for hot chocolate. She had the gas on but no flame.

Elizabeth chose not to say anything but: "It stinks. You're going to asphyxiate us." It was getting close to eleven; she hadn't noticed. They were probably starving. But at least the day was almost half gone.

"Can we go to the Tuileries?" asked Ariane as she licked buttery crumbs from her fingers.

"I guess so. Why?"

"There are lots of rides there now. Papa told me."

"Of course. Yes. It's summer. There's the fair. That's a wonderful idea." Elizabeth was surprised not to have thought of it herself. When Tristan and Olivier were younger, before the twins were born, she used to take them there every year.

The sun on the white clay surface of the Tuileries was blinding and made Elizabeth's already light-sensitive eyes water and sting and her stomach churn almost to the point of retching. The twins ran over to look at the fair. Nothing had changed, not one single ride. The huge, hairy gorilla was still next to the water slide, there were fun houses, a haunted house, elevated swings and bumper cars.

"You get four rides each," Elizabeth said. It was easier to assert authority when there was a focus. When the day ahead didn't look quite so bleak. "Two before lunch, two after. And at the end we do the wheel." When Tristan and Olivier were smaller, she'd always insisted they go on the big wheel with her, even once they'd begun disdaining its limited thrill value, because Elizabeth had loved the view when the wheel paused at the top. The Paris roofs stretched for miles, right at eye level, and she'd always felt perched on the top of the world.

At lunch they ate greasy hamburgers and *frites* and discussed the rides. Gabby liked the bumper cars and Ariane the big swings in the air. For all her motion sickness, things that went high and fast did not bother her in the least. Gabby got scared going down the water slide—Elizabeth probably shouldn't have let them go on it alone.

At the end she took them up on the wheel. The cars were open saucers that could be made to go round in a circle by turning the pole in the middle. They went up and around three times. The wheel paused at the top, the saucer car swung slightly. The city's uneven jumble of grey roofs stretched before them and the geometrically arranged gardens were spread below. *Why did I bother? This view no longer touches me at all. Just some random zinc, slate and stone, as Olivier might say.* She tried spinning the saucer the third time but Gabby asked her to stop.

I've just got to get through it; I'm almost half way there.

In the evening, she made them have a bath, mostly because it helped kill more time. Ariane got soap in her eyes and cried; Elizabeth shrieked at her to shut up and she did. Neither of them uttered another word. She poured herself a vermouth and cassis. She'd get through it.

The skeleton in the cartoon on television gave her an idea for the next day: she'd take them to the Catacombs. She'd never been there herself. That would be fun. Exciting. Different.

"Where are we going?" they asked on the metro.

"It's a surprise," Elizabeth said.

When they got to the entrance at Denfert-Rochereau, she told them: "This is called the Catacombs. It's where they used to bury unimportant people. People they didn't know what else to do with."

They had to wait in a long line; this subterranean mass grave was a surprisingly popular tourist destination. Once they'd wound down the steep, deep stairs, they walked and walked through sinuous corridors lined with meticulously arranged tibias and femurs, behind which the rest of the bones were thrown helter-skelter.

"Well, that was quite something, wasn't it," said Elizabeth, as they climbed back up and back out on the street, where the three of them shielded their eyes against the bright summer sun. She felt pleased that she'd come up with an original plan for the day. "Better than the cinema."

"Where are we?" asked Ariane.

"I have no idea," said Elizabeth. The exit was on a small street. There were no signs, no indication of where they were or how to get back to the entrance. A group of tourists was twisting around a map, trying to get their bearings. "Let's just walk this way." She turned to the left.

"But we don't know where we are," whined Ariane.

"Oh, stop whining," said Elizabeth, marching ahead with her

children running to keep up. The first big cross street they came to was the rue de la Tombe Issoire. "Ah, yes. I know this street. Now if I can only remember where it goes." At a corner there was a café. "Would you like an ice cream? Something to drink?"

The twins shook their heads.

"We'd like to go home," Ariane said, with Gabby eagerly nodding.

"What time is it?" Elizabeth asked Gabby, who had received a watch for his last birthday.

"It's…"

"It's seven minutes past four," said Ariane, impatiently looking over his shoulder.

"Will Papa be there?" asked Elizabeth.

"Yes," said Ariane. "He'll be packing for Brittany."

"Of course," said Elizabeth, remembering that they were leaving the next morning for the house Alix and Roland had rented for a month.   Seeing a pedestrian sign for Sainte-Anne, she said: "Let's go this way. Hospitals always have a taxi stand."

Elizabeth opened the door and watched the twins scamper up the stairs. She too hurried, away from the building, from the *quartier*. She remembered that the rue Laromiguière, formerly the rue des Poules, had once been a cemetery too. The whole city was founded on the bones of the anonymous dead.

Later, back at Pigalle, her drink had never tasted so good. She felt quite giddy, at having the twins gone, at no longer needing to plan, to accommodate. She sat down at her table, turned on the computer and began an e-mail: *Didn't you once visit this place? The underbelly of the city. Full of dead people. Bones. We walk over them every day without a thought.*

She paused, took a sip of her drink, and then began writing on paper:

Did I really think I could get away with it? Did I really think no I didn't think I acted like an animal, on instinct. In order to survive. Truth or lies, lies or truth—it stopped counting. Everything was blurry wish wash wooshed I just wanted to be away from what I did. From what I didn't. From thinking wait I should wait stick by him see how he is see him through tell them what happened. But I don't wait stick by see through. I turn and walk away like the dog in that story, walking away from his frozen dead master.

I am an animal, that is what I should have said when that divorce judge asked what Madame is the underlying problem.

She stood up abruptly, went to fix herself another drink, returned to the writing table.

Afterwards my clothes smell of fire and I shove them in the washing machine but you can't get rid of that kind of smell except by being a good person. An extra good person. That's what I'll try to do. If I can accumulate goodness it will wipe out at least outweigh the bad. I was an attentive wife. To my children an attentive mother. A parent delegate and a baker of brownies from scratch there is The Beast again I can hear him in the kitchen. Please don't think I never thought of you. But ouch it hurt it sent electric currents through my gut and prickles up the nape of my neck and I had to sit down or maybe fall over or faint. Fear and guilt, fear of being found out by that husband I was so good to. By those children—let's think about something else, yes, let's read a story how about the gingerbread man says Ariane, no says Gabby, he gets eaten. Now I am a good person so now, now, children, don't argue, let's read The Flopsy Bunnies instead you both like that and whatever that bad thing was from before it must have been done by another person, another person who was bad but who is now dead and gone because now I can open my eyes in the dark because now I am good.

But scritch scratch that worry is always there. That some day, no matter how good I am. Gotcha it grabs me on the street like an armed robber, gun in my gut. My heart pumping in my ears. Keep people at a safe distance, that's the answer. Even my husband. It was a formal, respectful waltz between us, never like our frantic dance. But we were happy enough with things that way—weren't we—I don't know anymore I don't anything anymore except that you can't forgive me so I must have been wrong. Wrong and wrong again. Luck runs out and you have to get stuck with the queen of spades sometimes.

Now he's found the queen of his life. I hate him how you must have hated me. My freedom, my presumed innocence. Did you grind your teeth, imagining the happiness I had surely found, the way I do now about him? What goes around comes around.

She put down the pen and turned on the television. She couldn't write any more. While watching the cable news, she ate the half croissant that Gabby had left without even noticing its crusty staleness and then went to bed.

The next morning she was late for work. Her supervisor looked angry.

"Sorry," said Elizabeth. "The electricity went out in my building over night and my alarm didn't go off." This was not quite true. She had inadvertently pulled the plug on the alarm clock and that was why it didn't go off. Once a liar always a liar, she almost said to the woman.

Jean was back from Lyon and stopped by at lunch-time. The moment she saw him, with his open, hopeful face, she cringed like a frightened animal.

They bought sandwiches and sat in their usual corner, behind a concrete pillar, next to a window. "I missed you," he said. "Can I drive you home tonight?"

"I don't think so," she said, staring at the ID tag around his neck.

"Are you all right, Elizabeth?" he asked.

She nodded slowly.

"You look really thin."

"I guess haven't had much of an appetite recently," she said, looking at her uneaten sandwich.

"Why?"

She shrugged.

"Maybe you'd like to come to my place tonight. An evening in the country."

She shook her head. "I need some time to be alone."

"You've just been alone. I've been gone for ten days." She

shrugged again. He went on: "I'm not asking anything of you, Elizabeth. I don't want to become the stepfather of your children or anything like that."

"I know," she said, reddening. "But I can't."

"There's something you're not telling me." The baguette had a hard crust and made a lot of noise as Jean pulled off pieces of the sandwich with his teeth. He wiped his mouth and said: "Do you remember I have a gig on Friday? On a boat next to the new library?" She shook her head. "Just because you don't want to sleep with me anymore doesn't mean you can't listen to my music, does it?" She tried a smile. "I hope you'll be there. The singer is American."

"Thank you," she finally managed, in not much more than a whisper. "I'll try to come," almost asking if the singer's name wasn't Lisa.

***

On her way home, she noticed that Lucas had left a message on her mobile. His voice sounded urgent—he said she was to phone him that evening in Brittany. He even repeated the number, slowly, and gave specific instructions not to phone on his own mobile, which was on the blink. That evening when she came in she looked at the telephone but couldn't bring herself to call. What if Alix or Roland answered the phone? She hadn't spoken to either in many months. She couldn't risk it.

With her vermouth-cassis, she sat in front of the television. The phone rang.

"Is there some reason you couldn't phone me back?"

"I didn't know you'd called."

"I left you a message." When she didn't reply, he continued: "What do you mean taking two sensitive children to see all those skulls and bones?"

"You don't have to shout. I thought they enjoyed themselves."

"Gabby woke up in the middle of the night screaming from a

nightmare. Ariane can't stop asking me questions. 'Why are there so many bones? Are there really six million people buried down there? Were they dead when they went down there? Where are their mothers and fathers?'" He paused and then asked, sounding sadly perplexed rather than angry: "What were you thinking, taking them there?"

"They watch all those spooky films without flinching."

"They're films, Elizabeth, not real bones of real people. Does the figure six million ring a bell with you?"

"I didn't think," she said and despite her recent trip to Drancy, it was true that she hadn't. "Once you've done the sewers, it's not so easy to find new things to do with them." Lucas didn't reply. She said: "Anyway, you insisted they see Verdun and then they were only four."

"That was a different time," Lucas said quietly. "And there were no dead children. According to the twins, you tagged on to a tour guide who helpfully informed you that the first bones in the Catacombs were from the Cemetery of the Innocents, named for the Holy Innocents, the children killed by Herod. That the cemetery was thus named because it was full of so many dead children. Children whose parents hadn't taken care of them properly, or children whose parents had come to Paris with the express purpose of abandoning them. Paris in those days, you were told, had a reputation for abused and abandoned children wandering its streets. Why did you put them through this?"

"I don't know," she mumbled and could feel tears rising in her throat. After a long silence, during which she collected herself, she said: "I'm sorry. I didn't notice they were upset. I thought they looked interested."

"Are you all right, Elizabeth?" When she didn't answer, he asked very softly: "Do you want to talk to them?"

"Maybe not. Maybe it's better if I call back in a couple of days," and she put down the phone.

The next day was Tuesday, her early day, and she went by the bicycle shop to meet Olivier after work.

"Not here," said Polish Piotr in his truncated French. "Last week his last week. He is on the holiday with his father."

Had she known this, or was this yet something else that was happening without anyone bothering to tell her? She couldn't remember. She could hardly remember what she'd talked about to Olivier two weeks earlier when she'd stopped by. That's right. He was saving up to buy some new piece of musical equipment. He was hoping to get contributions for his birthday. He would be seventeen in November. Or was it eighteen? She had to do the calculation—she had always known her children's ages better than her own. Are you all right, Elizabeth?

Back at Pigalle, she sipped her vermouth and cassis. She turned on the cable news. Hearing the same stories over and over again now comforted her. When she finally fell into bed, she dreamed that she was back at the Arènes de Lutèce. The pit was filled to bursting with skulls and bones. Gabby was standing at the edge, crying because he couldn't play football. Ariane was squeezing Elizabeth's hand and pulling her down, whining that Gabby was crying and that things weren't very good anymore and where were Papa and Lisa? And she, Elizabeth, didn't know what to do. The panic was rising up in her, mostly because she knew that the people who were responsible for all these bones were right at the gate, would be there any moment, and she had to find a way to get out but if she chose the wrong exit, she would run into the killers or into Lucas and Lisa and she wasn't sure which was worse.

The alarm beeped, beeped, beeped and she sat up, with a pounding heart and no idea where she was.

***

Friday afternoon the agency told her that they would not have any work to offer her, starting next week.

"But give us a call in September and we'll see."

Elizabeth knew this was an excuse but instead of feeling

slighted, she was relieved: she wouldn't have to do anything, all month long. Lucas was keeping the children, since she was supposed to be working. Why not just leave things at that.

Jean stopped by too on Friday. "You haven't forgotten about our gig tonight, have you? Here's a little flyer with the place and time." His eyes were hopeful and his mouth was set in resentment and hurt. She answered: "Thanks. I'll see."

Elizabeth had indeed forgotten. Nor could she imagine going. For the last weeks, since Jean had gone to Lyon, she had spent every evening sitting at Pigalle, drinking vermouth and cassis. Each time, when she poured her first drink, she had experienced a feeling of relief that bordered on elation—she had finished with another day, she could sit down and have one drink and then another and do nothing else for the rest of the evening. Day-time and people she found distressing; here alone with her drink and her reams of words and the droning television, she felt safe, almost happy. She could not imagine finding that same sense of comfort and enjoyment with other people ever again.

Back at the apartment that evening, there was a message from Molly. "No one's heard from you in a donkey's age, Lizzie, what's up?" Beep.

Recently there had been messages from both her parents. Her mother was threatening to come to Paris and her father had asked her to accompany him to a conference in Majorca because Pru couldn't go. Elizabeth had not returned either call.

She poured herself a drink. She looked out the window. She looked at the paper piled up on the table, at the computer Jean had fixed up for her. Her sister would phone again this evening, she was almost sure of it, because Molly would have been put up to the task by their mother. Vera would be worried by Elizabeth's silence but would not know what to do except solicit help from someone else. And Molly could always be counted on. Unlike her, Lizzie Liza Liz, the contrarian, the rat, the coward.

If she went to the concert, she would miss the call again. If she went to the concert, she would not think about how she should phone her children.

To get to the boat on which Jean was playing, Elizabeth took the newest metro line for the first time. It had been built to link up the recently developed eastern side of the city, where the new Ministry of Finance, the Bercy stadium and the new national library stood. Although the place de la Madeleine station where she got on was strikingly modern, it stunk of the sewers. The smell was so strong Elizabeth covered her mouth with the sleeve of the cardigan she had draped over her shoulders. She looked around but everyone else seemed immune to the smell. *If they take this line every day, they don't notice it anymore. That's what always happens. We get used to the stench.*

These trains, she remembered, as the door closed and they began to hurtle through the tunnel, had no drivers. This at first filled her with panic. *Trains without drivers could end up anywhere. Or maybe not. Maybe it is better to remove human intervention. To trust an invisible hand at distant controls. It's like believing in God...what's the difference, really, between religion and technology? Invisible hands at distant controls, it's all the same thing.* She got so lost in these thoughts that she almost missed her stop and when she did get off the train, she felt weak and confused— as if she were suffocating—even when she emerged from the station into the evening air.

The metro exit was on the edge of two worlds. On the right hand side was an old Paris street, with modest, low buildings, each one different from the other. To the left was an endless stretch of bare grey, identical concrete pillars and platforms, part of some as yet unidentifiable construction project. Up an escalator and the mix continued. An old bridge over railroad tracks, a warehouse in the distance, but recently rebuilt streets and a line of new buildings in the direction of the new library. At the corner of the ensemble was an Irish pub, which reminded her that she hadn't eaten all day and no wonder she was feeling faint. She still had plenty of time before the concert.

After a jug of Bordeaux and a bowl of pasta at the Irish pub, she moved towards the towers of the library. The only time she had been here was on a family excursion, not long after it had been built. Such architectural outings were frequent in the Teller household; Lucas insisted the family be aware of the new Paris as well as the old. The day with her family here at the library had been a happy one, despite Lucas' disappointment with the architectural results. "Books in towers. What an idea. I can almost hear the bindings crack." And once they had arrived, the vast spaces between the four towers had further depressed him. "The scale is completely overblown, inhuman." The twins had run gleefully along the long wooden planks, their arms out like wings on the exposed, windy platform. Olivier had imagined what it would be like to skateboard here, if only the planks had been smooth. Tristan had railed against the wood, which he contended had been taken from the trees of a depleted tropical forest. *I was happy that day. Happy to comfort Lucas and Tristan, to be with my family.*

Or was I? Didn't Lucas' way of criticising the architecture begin to annoy me? The way he clucked about, like a disapproving old woman inspecting someone else's inferior kitchen. I walked away so I wouldn't have to listen to him anymore. A cold wind swept across that bleak wooden plain; there was a taste of the sea in the air, just before a big rain. After a short time all six of us, in that unfriendly space, disappeared into our own lonely heads.

Tonight as she surveyed the area, she noticed everything had been battened down, buckled in. The bushes, perhaps because of that wind, had been caged with metal wiring. The huge trees in the pit had been trussed up like Gulliver and birds had been painted on the windows to stop real ones from flying into the glass. Despite the precautions, some of the birds must have been inattentive, must not have heeded the signs, because several lifeless pigeons were visible in the foliage at the bottom of the pit.

She sat down on a bench, feeling bloated from the meal that had been too large for her shrunken stomach. Even a couple of large burps didn't relieve the situation.

She wondered if it was time yet. Having abandoned her watch when the battery went dead some time ago and having left her phone at the flat, she did not know for sure, though from the waning light, she supposed it must be getting close to ten, when the concert was to begin.

She walked to the edge of the complex. The steep, wide stairs were as vertiginous as the steps at one of the Incan or Mayan temples they had been modelled on. It was easy to imagine falling. Letting herself fall. *What would happen if I closed my eyes and stepped forward into thin air? I might break some bones, even my back—it might even kill me. Whatever the fall would to— injure, paralyse or kill—I cannot fathom the prospect of either the pain or the nothingness. I am, I must remember, a coward.*

Across the road she saw lit-up boats docked along the bank. The one on which Jean was about to play was made of wood and painted green and yellow. It rocked sweetly on the waves created by a passing barge.

She turned around, towards the smelly, driver-less metro and the more enticing prospect of a vermouth and cassis, alone in front of the cable news at Pigalle.

***

Now there was nothing and no one. A clean slate ahead. It rendered her incapable of locomotion, almost of coherent thought. She did ask herself, for a moment, where Tristan was. Had he come back from London and gone to Brittany? She had had no contact with him for six weeks and she wondered if he would ever speak to her again. But she wondered these things from a distance, more as abstract concept than visceral worry, as it would have been some months ago. Lucas would take care of it. Of him.

Elizabeth's days were spent mostly in bed or stretched out on the fake leather sofa. Though she was not aware of how much time passed, for hours on end she did nothing but allow her mind to wander. Things came to her from long, long ago.

Molly is going to be born, so I must be almost three. Mum is sitting on a kitchen stool and waiting to go to hospital, pale and round. The sight of her makes me panic. What is wrong with my mother and why is she leaving? Will she come back? Yes, my parents are walking in the front door together, bearing a bundle that is Molly. They are beaming and standing very close together, as if the bundle's weight requires the two of them to hold it together. My excitement turns to alarm. I do not like to see my parents looking so radiant, so unified, over someone who isn't me.

If indeed these are really memories. I was very young. Perhaps they are just inventions that I have developed over time. How can I know? The pictures are as clear as if I were looking at them in the family photo album yet there are no such photos. Then again: does it really matter if I have simply imagined these images, put them together from things I have been told? What difference could it possibly make, if my memories are real or imagined?

Later, after we have moved to England from Washington, where Mum and Dad met and were married and where I was born, my memory is on more solid ground. I'm at my new school and initial interest in my accent turns to teasing. There are two girls in particular who try to imitate me, before breaking into peals of laughter. Once the teacher even intervenes. I like my teacher, Miss Redmond. She has blond hair and what at the time I consider a large bosom. Looking at Miss Redmond's bosom often distracts me from the lesson. I have one friend, Alison. Alison comes from South Africa but she talks like everybody else and although not teased, she is treated as something of a different animal too. But Alison doesn't seem to mind the way I do. We are friends until we are sent to different boarding schools. During the first year away we see one another during the holidays but then Alison's family moves to Bristol and that is that.

At boarding school I am hopelessly, cripplingly homesick. There's a real memory because I feel sick even now, remembering that smell, that smell of old wood polished too many times. But I never tell anyone. I am a good girl and don't complain and my parents are content to believe I am fitting in just fine.

Pretending, I discover, is the secret. I make a great effort to hide the real Elizabeth. Hide her because the consensus among my schoolmates from the other school was clear: Lizzie Lyall is an oddball, a person to be taunted and teased and when we get bored with that, ignored. If that's what they all thought, mustn't there be some objective truth to it? Mustn't one put some stock in consensus?

The strategy certainly seems to work. Sometime during the second year I start to make a few friends. And my teachers seem to like me better and so I work harder. By then of course I can make my accent thoroughly British, though just after the holidays and time with my mother, I have to be careful. Still I now know: Lizzie will be all right if she can just dissolve, like salt in a glass of water. If she can just keep that inside self to herself.

Except when I go back to America and there I am, oddball again. By now I can't completely get rid of my English accent. A certain English way of being. Even turning myself into Liz doesn't help. It's hopeless.

But wasn't that the seed of my future concealment policy, that moment when my inside and outside selves began to separate?

***

She began dreaming of tunnels. Sometimes the tunnels seemed to be in the Catacombs but they got confused with the connecting passages at the airport or the corridors at the publishing house. She would be running along moving walkways or through narrow passages, sometimes above ground, sometimes below. There were never any windows. Her terrified children were often waiting for her or she was trying to find them. Bad or dangerous people lurked everywhere. She would wake up with a start, heart pounding, only to fall back asleep into the same dream.

It's no wonder those dreams keep coming back to me. That's what you get for trying to slam the doors of history: haunted houses in your head.

***

And now August is ending. People are coming back there will be questions I cannot answer calls I cannot make faces I cannot see. The telephone is a loaded gun and take cover when it rings. Letters pile up give them a frightened kick under the table sight unseen. Sweep all this paper away away out of my sight. Eyes are open senses shut what's done cannot be undone. Some things are unforgivable. Fingers stuck stuck in knotted hair where are those kitchen scissors. That's better but now the phone keeps ringing leave me alone. My heart pounding in time pull out the plug, pull out the plug, but time is running out who will come and get me take me away lock me up. My turn. But who can see me I have disappeared poof like steam if I talk no one will hear a tree falling in the woods.

Invisible to you too in that large auditorium where I first see you sitting alone left hand curled over your notebook on the small desk. Awkward hand on a graceful person in jeans and t-shirt, god-like is what you are, with that blond hair and dark skin, those muscular, hairless arms and that broad nose and face, those dark brown irises in the large corneas that draw me in, that draw everything in, like a black hole. I try to be places you are but I am so shy thank God Modern European History is a year-long course and finally one day you ask to borrow a pen and at the end you give it back and ask my name.

Finally you have come all the way into my bed, finally I get what I've wanted since the beginning and your hands and lips are running up and down and never did I think anyone could know so well where when how...is this love I ask and ask but I don't know in bed yes but out of bed it's different. You are different you are wounded even before you were wounded and you say real good like James Dean and I loved that at first but in the longer term? Well, in the longer term we like James are dead it's in the meantime I cannot see us settled within the thick safe walls of a house.

One day it's spring and suffocating and stale and why don't they let us out no fresh air can get through to us. They do not come and you get into one of your scary rages, saying we'll have to take matters into our own hands around the kitchen knife, you show us the way, you always do, and ah that's better, shreds of milk hanging from the balsa boards they nailed us in but you're still angry, ready to nail someone and how about that oxymoronic artiste, you say. It's his turn. And then you imitate him you could imitate anyone we laughed when you did the dean of students. We laugh and laugh all the time all year long and now we are free and at the party I ask that silly very drunk boy for a light, take this in remembrance of me, he says with a stupid grin—why didn't I give it back. If I'd given it back—

Whoosh shush too late keep the lighter hidden it can talk it can tell on me it's my fault. If I throw it in the pond, they will dredge it up. If I bury it a dog will find it. The dean has hairy fingers. Hide it deep in my drawer. Stop it's just a plastic lighter. Millions and millions of people own plastic lighters but not ones with fraternity logos on them so take it in that heavy bag all the way back to London and go underground into the Tube and when no one's looking quick—Bic in the bin.

And quick—to Paris in that washing machine that walks on water and before I know it it's wet and mouldy and plip plop plaster white paint on my head. My towel never dries but I brush off my guilt until I am so happy so lucky Lucas is too good to be true his family too, a fortress, a famous fortress that people admire from a distance, and I am inside it and uh-oh now my luck's run out it's my turn to pay. Lucas is frowning brooding I am an ogre and have been cast out of heaven. Is that a knock on the door? Loud and leave me alone I will pull the pillow over my head and lie perfectly still, not making a sound, like when there's thunder at night. When God is bowling or is it logs he is rolling logs down mountains he sounds so angry up there his beard and his gown must be getting in the way. If I don't move he will not hear me he will not be angry he will not come after me in his fury. I cannot breathe I am hot itch behind my ear itch itch itch but lie still still still. Until I am certain the rumbling has gone away but the room around me is spinning going round and round forever...close my eyes it doesn't help...what's done cannot be undone.

And then one day I wake up a little less muddled. My head has cleared, the way it might after a long night of high fever. I prop my head against the pillows and look at the poster on the wall that makes no sense. Around the edges are scraps of music sheets, old posters, bits of newspaper, imitation Braque or Picasso. They surround a Paris street, or what is meant to look like one. A street sign says RUHE NAPOLEON, with the H half ejected from the word but there's no rue Napoléon in the real Paris anyway. The style in the centre becomes more imitation Dada or Surrealist; the super-imposed nostalgic icons of a quaint old city are re-arranged nonsensically. It is an IKEA attempt at post-something and has no artistic value whatsoever.

What really went wrong with Lucas? Was I, am I, *that* bad?

I turn on my side. The sitting room is an unspeakable mess. A tip, that's what Matron at boarding school would have called it. Paper litters the floor and I do have a vague memory of sweeping my arm across the surface of my writing table. There are traces of leftover food, plates I didn't bother to wash. My jeans, which I pulled on to go buy more vermouth, are on the floor in a heap where I last shed them.

I get out of bed and hobble into the bathroom. My legs are stiff from middle age and little use of late. It's amazing, really, how quickly one starts to fall apart. The kitchen scissors are still lying on the side of the basin; there are clumps of the knotted hair I cut off on the floor. My head now looks like a poorly cropped bush.

After clearing some space amidst the empty bottles on the kitchen counter, I make some coffee and get back in bed and consider the last couple of months, the stages of my unravelling. What I can see clearly now, is that I am not crazy enough and probably never will be. Because here I am rationally analysing the poster on the wall and my unbalanced behaviour. I could not in good faith show up at Sainte Anne the psychiatric hospital and request internment. Which in one way is unfortunate. Going crazy—or better yet, becoming a drunken, homeless ranter of nonsense in the streets—would turn me into something of a victim too, wouldn't it? As would throwing myself down the stairs at the national library. But I couldn't do that either.

Or perhaps—put another way—I don't ultimately *want* to be a victim and what's wrong with that?

After the food and the bottles and my hair have been dispensed with, I turn to the paper. All my confessionals, my attempts at expiation or at least explanation. The writing started off all right, with dated pages and Dear Troy and full sentences. Then everything begins to break down. Thoughts unhinge, sentence structure is abandoned and even my hand-writing starts to wind up and down the page, which, when I consider how much I'd had to drink most of the time, is not surprising. As I reread these pages, it seems very important to put some order to all this rambling. To reconstruct it.

By late afternoon I've almost finished, when there is a knock at the door. It is a terrifying sound. But that raven-like rap rap rapping doesn't stop and I can't stand it. It is probably a salesman or a religious fanatic. I will get rid of him quickly.

"I heard noise. I knew you were in there. Where have you been?"

"What are you doing here?"

"You weren't answering either of your phones—the land line just rang and rang and I left several messages on your mobile. I came up a few days ago but couldn't hear anyone inside. I was about to phone the police. I'm running out of excuses with the twins. They keep asking what's happened to you."

The door is still open just a crack, just my head peeping out.

"Can I come in?" he finally asks.

I open the door wide, let him walk past me. "Please sit down," I say, pointing to the droopy fake leather black sofa. I sit across from him. This is his first visit to the Pigalle flat. His eye wanders wryly around the room, from the tasteless furniture, to the silly posters, and stops at the table next to the window with the thick pile of paper, now neatly stacked.

"Is that what you've been doing up here? Secretly working away on some manuscript? Is that why you disappeared?"

"No. Sort of."

"You're very thin. And what happened to your hair?"

"As you can see, I tried cutting it myself."

He stares at my head, his blue vein bulging on his white forehead. "I'm so sorry Elizabeth." He looks devastated, as if this whole mess were his fault, and I am too surprised to reply. "While we were in Brittany..." he continues, with obvious difficulty. "While we were in Brittany, Tristan...I don't know why I couldn't..."

"What are you talking about?"

Lucas pulls a handkerchief from his pocket and takes off his glasses, wipes his eyes. "Tristan told me that you confessed. About the fire."

"Yes. I did."

"You said I was a very moral man." Lucas' voice cracked and the tears welled up in his eyes again.

"Did I?" That café confession seems a lifetime ago.

"Yes you did. And how can I let him think that?" He looks at me—desperately, hopefully—I have absolutely no idea what he's talking about. "I thought you might know already."

"What? You mean about Lisa?"

"What do you mean, Lise?"

"I saw the ring she gave Ariane."

"Lise," he laughs, putting his glasses back on, his

handkerchief back in his pocket, "is a young Danish architect who did some work for me this summer. Her *husband* is Danish too. He was posted in Paris for the summer at the embassy. He is a diplomat. She liked the twins and even did some babysitting while Manuela was on holiday. They came to Brittany for a long weekend."

"Oh. Then what?"

"About Troy." All light has drained from his face.

So he does know about that, I think, but:

"About Troy and me," he says.

"About Troy and you?" Suddenly I feel as if I've just been given the answer to a ridiculously easy riddle. "You and Troy. Of course. I see."

"I didn't see it myself. Until it happened." For a moment he doesn't speak, just sits looking at his hands. Emerging from his reverie with a deep breath, he leans back in the chair. "That first night after you left for Nantucket, I got all my preparations for the meeting the next day done and I was feeling quite elated when Troy arrived early evening. I asked if he wanted to have supper with me. We ordered pizza, opened a bottle of wine. We talked and talked, opened another bottle. I was so enjoying myself that I asked him if he wanted to come to Rouen with me the next day. It might be interesting for you, I said, to see a small, provincial French city. With the apartment the city is letting me use, I said, there's plenty of room. Sure, he said. I would like to see another city in France. So off we went on my motorcycle early the next morning. I dropped him at the apartment, giving him the keys and telling him I expected the meetings to last well into the night, not to wait up for me, take the bedroom, just leave the front door open.

"But the meeting went better than I expected. They were finally seeing things my way and we were all done by eleven.

"When I walked into the flat, it was dark. Without thinking, I switched on the light. He'd been standing at the window, looking out at the Seine. Shirtless. We froze, both of us. I turned the light back off, as if maybe I could re-enter, un-see what I had just seen. After a minute, I walked over to the window where he was still standing. We both stood there, looking at the Seine. And then it just happened."

Has happened already. Between Troy and Hoyt Thorpe the sculptor, all those years ago.

"My work was all done and we had the whole next day. It wasn't until we got back to Paris, that I made him tell me how his back got scarred. Of course I already suspected it had to do with you and his reasons for coming here in the first place. For your strangeness in his presence." He pauses, then quietly: "Besides being shocked and angry and shaken—undone, really— I also felt jealous." When I don't answer, he continues: "I was sure something had gone on between the two of you."

"I told you. We slept together a few times."

"I mean in Paris," he says, looking down at Troy's sculpture on the table, then up at me questioningly: "I couldn't stop wondering. I always sensed something—some kind of current passing between the two of you. Then the night before you left for Nantucket, I came out of my office and though I couldn't see into the entry hall, it was too long and too quiet until you said good-bye."

I do not answer immediately, wondering if I should let all the skeletons out of the closet. "I don't remember. Maybe he was getting something out of his bag."

"And I wondered again, when I realized he'd covered up for you. That he hadn't told me you lit the fire." He harrumphs. "At first I was jealous because I thought you were in love with him. Then it was the other way around. It was crazy." He shakes his head. "But mostly I was in complete turmoil. God, those first days on Nantucket—it was if a bomb had gone off. And it didn't get much better in the months following."

"And I thought it was all about your anger and inability to forgive me," I say, shaking my own head now. "I kept telling myself that I deserved all that was happening. That I was bad and you were good."

"Did you really think it was that simple?"

"Most of the time, yes."

"There were times when I hoped you'd guess what was wrong, what I'd done. A few times I tried to tell you—like that last time you came to pack your bags—but you were so fixated on your own guilt, so angry. And I guess I didn't try all that hard."

"Maybe it was easier for both of us. Not to focus on the more complicated things going on underneath."

"Obviously it was more convenient for me," he says, voice full of self-reproach. "Though I can't say it was comfortable, living with my wife and four children, obsessed with another man, wondering day after day if maybe I weren't gay."

"And?"

"I've come to think it was just him. That mixture of grace and strength, of physical beauty and natural curiosity, his sense of fun and spontaneity—I was intoxicated by him." A little smile emerges on his unhappy face. "You know, I've never known anyone like him. I could talk to him about anything and everything." He pauses, the smile vanishing. "The trouble was that afterwards, nothing seemed the same. Not myself. Not us. In the months after he left, all feeling for you shrivelled up and died and I was helpless to stop the process." He looks at me, as if still completely bewildered by forces beyond his control.

"Did you tell Tristan?"

"No," he says bitterly, rolling his eyes, running both hands over his thinning hair. "I told myself it would be too much for him. That it would be more hurtful than helpful."

"You were right," I say, knowing that at least I have done the right thing by holding back myself. Those revelations too would be more hurtful than helpful and enough irreparable damage has already been done. "There is absolutely no reason for him to know."

"What? So he should go on thinking I'm a saint and you're the devil incarnate?"

"He'll forgive me. He'll see that what I did was human. Nothing more, nothing less."

"Maybe," he says. "I hope so."

***

Troy and Lucas. Of course. I hadn't forgotten about Troy and Hoyt, even if it was yet another element of the story I chose to leave in the shadows. Troy told me the whole story of that earlier seduction—detail by detail—after Hoyt had tired of him and he came running into my virgin arms for comfort. If I hadn't been so blinded by my own unresolved guilt, I might have seen.

But partly Troy and Lucas did not occur to me because of Lucas. Upright, always in the right, Lucas. Lucas with his narrow back and stiff bow. But now I can see the excited smile that would come across his face when Troy was around. A certain avidity in his eyes when they were talking. And while Lucas is not quite effeminate, he is not particularly masculine either. It is easy to imagine him attracted to another man, particularly a graceful, exotic one like Troy.

If indeed he acted with intent, I have to hand it to Troy. Understanding the power of sex, he went straight for the weak link and seduced us both, thus exacting an exquisite revenge: he let us self-destruct.

For the moment, Lucas' confession provides more relief than shock or anger. Things finally make some sense. It wasn't Lisa or Lise but the idea of his happiness and his seemingly more perfect self that I couldn't bear. Our shared unhappiness and turpitude now provide an impetus to move beyond.

In the post that has piled up these last weeks, there is something from Jean. Jean, who has nothing to do with this three-ring circus: "I thought this might help you to reconnect," he said in a note attached to a series of articles on new, small publishing houses. Places where I formerly would have felt embarrassed to work but that now seem infinitely preferable to secretarial work, even if the pay is likely to be inferior.

Another envelope contains confirmation of a transfer into my account from Lucas' for my share of the rue Laromiguière. It should be enough for me to buy a small place in a modest neighbourhood. Something big enough to house at least the twins. Before Lucas left Pigalle we also agreed that, as soon as it was possible, they would move in with me.

And from my father, there is a ticket, via London on his British Airway miles, to Majorca, with a programme for the conference. But what really attracts my attention is the hotel brochure, showing the beach and the water. The idea of sitting in the sun and swimming in the sea for a few days is irresistible. As is a strong urge to connect with my father, and the rest of my family in London on the way back.

I turn on my computer and write short e-mails to my father, my mother and my sister, then to Jean and to Tristan. They are a pleasant change from the stack of maudlin meanderings next to me on the table. My tone with Tristan is assertive; I insist that he see me. "I have checked the date on the internet and will be in London when the university term begins. I will meet your train and get you set up. We'll have lunch if you like but no obligations. You do not have to forgive me but I am your mother still." I am not at all sure he will comply but it is about time re-asserted some parental authority. It occurs to me that when I was his age, I would have liked someone to confront me in my anger.

After that I call Olivier's mobile and leave a message. Then I gingerly call the rue Laromiguière, my old home phone, and try to reassure the twins' shy voices. "I can't come see you this weekend," I say, thinking of my hair, thinking that I still need some time to pull myself together more generally. "But I'll come next Saturday. With a surprise, I hope."

***

By the end of the following week, the plans for my trip are

set. I have also been to a bewildered hairdresser who has cut my hair evenly; my small head accommodates the shortness well. And I have had back-to-back appointments to visit flats.

Saturday is cool. The sky is a sharp blue and the light is beginning to take on an autumnal obliqueness. At the rue Laromiguière, I am waiting on the pavement for the twins to come down, thinking what a pleasure it is not to be trudging up those stairs, ringing the doorbell and standing at the entrance, getting a glimpse and a whiff of my old home.

The front door clicks and the twins come out, looking taller and thinner than six weeks ago. I crouch down and take one in each arm and they allow this with something between reticence and relief. "Where have you been, Maman?" asks Gabby.

"You cut your hair," says Ariane, brushing her hand over the top of my head.

"I needed a change. I—" the door clicks open again. "Olivier —"

He wears such a look of spent pain and unhappiness on his face that I am rendered speechless. Underneath his expression I detect a look of forgiveness. Its source may be an inability to live in such conflict, but it is a look of forgiveness nevertheless. His very presence is an act of pardon. I stand up and embrace him, the invisible stubble of his cheek prickling my skin. "Are you coming too?" He nods sheepishly. "Well, my surprise is that I think I've found a new apartment. I'm afraid it's not as nice as the rue Laromiguière but it's closer, and a bit nicer, than Pigalle. And it will be mine—ours."

The apartment I hope to sign for Monday is in the thirteenth arrondissement and, like the Pigalle flat, is in a post-war building. Rundown concrete is the best I can do this close to the city centre and actually I have grown to like the short history of such places. The new flat is similar to but bigger than Pigalle, with two bedrooms.

"Tell me about your summers," I say.

Olivier's arrival has reassured the twins and they bubble over with information as we walk down the street, get on the bus. When we get off at the avenue des Gobelins I point to the right: "It's just down this street." But I'm looking to the left. "Do you see that building? That's where my first apartment in Paris was."

"The one with the falling plaster?" asks Olivier.

"The one with the falling plaster." When Tristan and Olivier were small, they used to beg for stories about that flat and its owner, Monsieur Cros, with his hairpiece and shiny suits, his Asian mafia friends. I began making things up to keep them satisfied.

"Was he a real person?" Olivier asks, as if everything I have ever told him must now be questioned for veracity.

"Yes. But I doubt he's still there."

"Can we check?"

"Who's Monsieur Cros?" asks Ariane.

"Some weirdo guy who owned the apartment Maman lived in when she was young."

"Why was he weird?"

"Is he mean?" asks Gabby.

"He couldn't possibly still be there," I say.

"I want to see," says Olivier, setting off towards the building, the twins in his wake. I trudge along behind them.

"The code's on," I say, when we arrive at the neglected door. "We can't get in."

Olivier pushes the door and it opens. "No it's not."

"We shouldn't really go in here," I say. "It's trespassing."

"We're not going to bother anyone," says Olivier. "We're just going to look in the courtyard. That's where you said he had his office. Where he did all his dirty deals."

"I'm scared," says Gabby.

"It's just a building," says Olivier.

"I want to see the bad man," says Ariane.

"He wasn't really that bad," I say.

"That's not what you told us," says Olivier.

"You knew perfectly well that I was making up most of those

stories."

Inside the place has fallen into complete abandon. Not one of the letter boxes has a functioning lock. The tiled floor underneath our feet is sticky and littered with stacks of dumped flyers.

"This place is spooky," whispers Gabby.

"It was never very nice," I say.

"I bet that man is still there. I bet he made it like this," says Ariane in a conspiratorial whisper.

The hair stands up at the back of my neck. I do not want to revisit this place where black children are now playing in the courtyard. Behind them, the door to Monsieur Cros' office is open and I can just make out the forms of several women, the children's mothers. One is standing over a burner and cooking something that smells exotic, pungent; the others are sitting in the shadows, talking, laughing. All I can really see is white teeth through the dark. Instinctively I look up at the windows that were mine. A crooked washing rack dangles wet clothes. The paint is peeling badly.

"Is it one of those squats?" whispers Olivier.

"I don't know," I whisper back, "but we are intruders and we must leave." The women in Monsieur Cros' former office have stopped talking and are looking at our gawping faces suspiciously.

"I lived here once," I say. "My children wanted to see."

Smiles appear again out of the dark. They go back to their cooking and chattering. "Now you've seen," I say firmly to the children. "Let's go."

Out on the street, Olivier repeats: "Do you think it's like one of those buildings with the illegal immigrant squatters, where there were those fires? The one I saw on television wasn't very far from here."

"I have no idea," I say. "I haven't been paying much attention to the news the last few weeks."

"That's really where you lived?" asks Ariane, partly in horror, partly in something close to respect.

"Yes, but it was different then." I start walking towards the rue de Croulebarbe. "Let's cross the street and go to the new place."

When I open the front door, my children expectantly behind me, I know this is the right choice. From the outside, the building is ugly but the inside space is light and comfortably proportioned. A narrow terrace runs along the sitting room and kitchen; the walls are white and there is an off-white wall-to-wall carpet. There is even a fake fireplace in white concrete in the living room, with pale wood bookshelves built in along either side. The two bedrooms are small but there is also an alcove that can serve as additional sleeping space. Olivier, Ariane and Gabby wander from empty room to empty room. When they all come together in the front hall, I say: "I thought that you two, Ariane and Gabby, could share a bedroom with bunk beds for a year. Until you, Olivier, get your Bac and go to university or move into your dad's *chambre de bonne*. By then you twins will be getting too old to share anyway. So what do you think?"

"Better than the other place," Gabby says, relieved.

"We can make it nice," I say. "Bit by bit."

"Bit by bit," nods Ariane.

"I'm hungry," says Gabby.

After a café lunch at the bottom of the rue Mouffetard, I walk the three of them back to the rue Laromiguière and say as I kiss them good-bye: "I'm going on a trip near the end of the week."

"Again?" asks Ariane, her nose pinched unhappily.

"Yes. This is a different kind of trip. I'm going with Grandpa to a conference, then to see Granny and your Aunt Molly. And I'll help Tristan get set up in London. But then I'll be back. For good."

That evening, sipping a glass of white wine, I am exhausted. But it is not a happy tired, as my mother used to call well-earned fatigue. Though it was good to see three of my children, there's still the missing fourth, who has not answered my e-mail. Though none of the three screamed or yelled at me, recriminations could well come later, in one form or another. Because you never know how long it takes for trouble to crawl out of its hole.

And that visit to the avenue des Gobelins was painful. It was where I lived when I first knew Lucas, when I could have told him. There were several occasions when I almost did. But each time I was afraid of his reaction, afraid of him. Just as he must have been, on some level, uncomfortable with me. Isn't that what he meant, when he told me last week he could talk to Troy about anything and everything? That he couldn't with me?

It wasn't just the sex; it was a basic inability to connect. Which makes me think that if it hadn't been Troy, it might well have been someone else.

***

I get off the train at Roissy Charles de Gaulle, but this time at Aérogare 1, the one where I didn't work. It is a doughnut-shaped structure built in heavy grey concrete with ascending escalator tubes rising through a circular central courtyard. Despite the hole in the middle, there is little natural light and the place looks seedy. Yesterday's vision of the future has not held up to time. Business has moved to the new terminals; the building has a left-behind feel to it, quite different from the bustle I remember from the last time I was here.

There are no signs; I turn the wrong way and end up walking almost all the way around the building before locating the British Airways counter. Without the badge around my neck, I'm just another traveller taking my place in the queue that snakes around the corner. The first of several—an almost endless stream of lines—one to present valid travel documents. Another to check in. And another to get through security, where I will also have to empty pockets and remove various pieces of clothing, before shuffling through the metal detector, redressing, and then waiting once again to board the plane. It's a laugh, really, to think that travel, particularly flying, was once upon a time equated with escape, a new start. It has become tedious and trying, almost humiliating.

A young couple is in front of me while I wait to check in. They are both small and dark and look the way I had imagined French people to look when I was a girl, when my only knowledge of the place derived from *The Red Balloon* and the French girl in my class when I was ten. The girl—Pascale was her name—had body odour and that made me think all French people must smell bad from a particularly early age. It took me some time to get over this prejudice, to understand that most French children do not smell any more than English or American boys and girls and that generally the adults I was likely to encounter used deodorant, just like everyone else I knew.

In fact the couple in front of me are not French but British, as I see from their passports. They must be returning to London after a holiday. Maybe even a honeymoon because they can't keep their hands off one another. They grope and kiss; the man's tongue wanders out of his mouth into hers.

They're still at it, several people ahead of me in the security queue, and I think of Jean, who is just a shuttle ride away, in Aérogare 2. In his e-mail back to me, he said: "I'll be really happy to see you when you get back from your trip," and I can almost see his infectious smile, the smile that makes me smile.

While I unload my phone and my keys from my pockets, take off my shoes and my belt, my thoughts are moving forward, to our first meeting when I come home. Because straight away I will tell him, tell him everything, from start to finish, no details left out, not a single one, and I'll just have to see his reaction. I'll just have to see—

"*Madame*," the man on the other side of the metal detector calls impatiently. "Move along, please."